# PRAISE FOR THE HARRIET GORDON MYSTERIES

"Skillfully and seamlessly weaves actual people and events of the time with rich, multidimensional fictional characters... By the end of this sharp, satisfying novel, you'll be anxious to find our what happens in the next adventure." *Kirkus Reviews (Starred review) on Singapore Sapphire.*

"Filled with all the hot, decadent splendor and sultry danger of colonial-era Singapore. Rich, atmospheric and fascinating!" *C.S. Harris, USA Today bestselling author of the Sebastian St Cyr series*

"Singapore Sapphire is a remarkably sensitive look at life in Singapore in 1910, with a wealth of historical detail as well as rich characterization." *Criminal Element*

A HARRIET GORDON MYSTERY

# A.M. STUART

# AGONY IN AMETHYST

Agony in Amethyst: A Harriet Gordon Mystery

1st edition Oportet Publishing

ISBN (print) 20249780645237931

Spelling throughout is US English

# DEDICATION

*This story is dedicated to the memory of my faithful companion of many years*
*TOBY KAT 2005-2024*
*#writerscat*

*"When the cat you love becomes a memory, the memory becomes a treasure." – Unknown*

# ONE

## SINGAPORE 1911

### WEDNESDAY, 28 JUNE

Harriet Gordon stood on the edge of what passed for the garden of St. Thomas House, watching the troop of resident Macaques in the undeveloped bushland beyond their boundary. Her fingers tightened on the paper she held scrunched in her hand and she smiled.

"He's coming home," she said to the monkeys.

They stopped their cavorting to glance at her with their dark, incurious eyes before turning their attention back to the youngsters, who gamboled in the leaves and branches as the young of any species will do, pushing and shoving, accompanied by squeals of delight. Occasionally one would overreach and tumble, brought up short by a lower branch, and with an indignant chatter he would bound back to join his cousins.

While they provided endless delight to Harriet, they were the bane of her cook's existence. Not a day went by uninterrupted by Lokman banging a metal spoon on a pot, indicating one of the bolder apes had attempted to broach the bounds of the kitchen. They were notorious thieves. Their marauding ways made even the house unsafe, so grills had been installed on the windows and the residents had learned to keep the front and back doors shut.

The gate that led from the headmaster's house through the hedge to the school squeaked, and Harriet turned to see her ward, Will Lawson, in muddy sports clothes, a streak of drying mud across his nose. Her heart lifted to see him, and she gestured for him to join her.

Harriet wrinkled her nose. "Look at you! A good rugby match, I take it?"

"We beat them," Will said. "I scored a try."

Will had recently turned eleven and was growing faster than his wardrobe. His sports top strained across his shoulders. He would never be tall, but he was sturdy and athletic, and she observed with pride that he was growing into a delightful young man. Like all the boys in the senior class, he would be leaving for school abroad by September. In Will's case, to the Royal College in Colombo. Not quite as far as England, but far enough for Harriet.

"What are you doing?" Will asked.

"Watching the monkeys," Harriet said.

Will lifted a shoulder. "I don't like monkeys."

She looked at him in surprise. It was so unusual for Will to express his feelings on any subject. "Why is that?"

He toed the hardy grass with his mud-caked boot.

"They stole my mother's locket. She cried for days. It had the pictures of my brother and sister. Papa was so angry with her for leaving it out where they would find it."

Harriet put her arm around his shoulders and drew the dear, damp and muddy boy into her. He never spoke of his parents or his life before the traumatic events that had left him an orphan. Will's mother had died of Blackwater fever, following his brother and sister into early graves. His father, John Lawson, had been a less than satisfactory parent and had been killed just over a year previously. Harriet and her brother, Julian, had become the boy's legal guardians.

As if reading her thoughts, Will leaned into her.

"Aunt Harriet? What did Papa do that was so bad?"

Not once, in the twelve months he had lived with them, had he asked about his father.

She hugged him harder. "Oh, Will ... what makes you ask that?"

"Something one of the boys at school said. He said that Papa was a criminal who got what he deserved."

"Who said that?" Harriet fought the rising anger.

"Hardcastle."

"Hardcastle doesn't know what he is talking about," Harriet said, but her heart missed a beat. How had such rumors of John Lawson's death got around?

Will turned his face up to her. "But is it true, Aunt Harriet?"

She sighed. She and Julian had agreed that Will should be told the truth about his father, but only when he was old enough to understand what his father had done. Had that time come?

"Will, this is a conversation to have with both of us. Julian is better at explaining things than I."

"But you were there, Aunt Harriet. Uncle Julian wasn't."

That was not a memory Harriet wished to revive. Yes, she had been present when John Lawson had been shot and she had been by his bedside in his last hours. She knew the whole story but now was not the time or place.

"I promise that before you leave for school in Colombo, we will talk to you."

Will stiffened and would have shaken her arm free, but she tightened her grip.

"I want you to know one thing, Will. You are as dear to Julian and me as my son, Thomas, and you remind me so much of him. I don't want you to forget that you are very dearly loved."

To emphasize her point, she dropped a motherly kiss on the top of his head.

Will colored. "And I... um... you know..."

*Love you too?* She smiled and gave his shoulders one final squeeze.

"I know," she said.

She released her grip on him and he gave a small shake, as if to dispel the stigma of physical gestures of affection.

"What are you two up to?"

Harriet turned to see Julian striding toward them.

"Just watching the monkeys and thinking how like us they are. They all have their own personalities and their place in the hierarchy," Harriet said.

Julian put his hands behind his back, and they stood in companionable silence for a few minutes, watching the antics of the monkeys.

"Well played this afternoon," Julian said to Will.

"Thank you, sir. I better go and wash up before supper."

For Will, Julian was 'sir' at school and 'Uncle Julian' at home, but sometimes the boundaries blurred.

Julian and Harriet watched the boy lope toward the house, his gait no longer that of a child.

"Back door!" Harriet shouted after him.

Their housekeeper, Huo Jin, would not thank her for the mud of a rugby field trekked through the house.

When she was certain the boy was out of earshot, she said, "He's growing up, Julian. He asked me about his father. One of the boys at school told him his father was a criminal who got what he deserved."

Julian's mouth tightened and he sighed. "Which boy?"

"Hardcastle."

Julian rolled his eyes. "Of course it was Hardcastle. I had to put him on detention today. Frankly, I can't wait for him to move on to school in England at the end of this term."

"What are we going to do about Will?" Harriet asked.

Julian took a deep breath. "We will have to tell him the truth before he goes to Colombo," he said. "Lies beget lies. We always agreed that when he asked, we would be honest with him."

"I just wanted him to be older..."

"As you said, he is growing up, Harriet. Once he goes to Colombo, we will lose him."

Tears pricked the back of Harriet's eyes. "Don't say that."

Julian patted her shoulder. "Come on, old thing. Time we got ready for supper."

As they strolled back to the house, Harriet pulled the crumpled telegram from her pocket.

In typical Curran fashion, it was short and to the point.

*Arriving back on overnight train from KL tomorrow.*

"Curran will be back in Singapore tomorrow."

"Permanently?"

"I think so."

*I hope so.*

Inspector Robert Curran of the Straits Settlements Police Force had been away from Singapore for months. His last case involved the uncovering of widespread corruption within the British administration in Kuala Lumpur. The case had ended in the Batu Caves, an incident during which Harriet had been wounded in the leg and the perpetrators caught. However, the ripples had spread through the colonial service and Curran had been summoned to London to give evidence in an internal investigation, which, he had told Harriet, would achieve nothing.

Julian took the telegram, read the few words, and handed her back the crumpled paper.

"Will you go to meet him?"

"Of course."

Harriet looked down at the unsatisfactory words on the telegram. They had been apart too long for such a fledgling relationship. She had written weekly letters, half afraid to betray too much of herself and her aching heart, but somewhat to her surprise, the letters that had come back from Curran written in his firm, illegible handwriting had given her hope. She had read and reread them, lingering on every loving word, stowing the envelopes in her drawer, only to take them out again, tucking them beneath her pillow like a lovelorn schoolgirl.

Julian, who probably knew her better than she did herself, laid a hand on her shoulder. "You both need to start again. The last few months have been difficult."

"I hope he still feels the same way as I do."

Julian smiled. "I'm sure he does."

Harriet punched her brother lightly on the arm. "And on that subject, what about Esme? You and Esme have been stepping out for months now, Julian..."

She cast him a sisterly, wide-eyed look of expectation.

A high color rose to her brother's cheeks. "Harri ... I'm terrified she will say no. There's been no one since Jane and I'm not sure how to even broach the subject."

Harriet tucked her hand into her brother's arm. "Oh Julian, we are a hopeless pair."

# TWO

When Harriet left home, she had given every appearance of being cool and collected. Now, standing in the heat on the platform at the Tank Road Railway Station, stray wisps of hair clung to her damp face, and perspiration ran down her back beneath her corset and camisole. She had purchased the beige linen suit with matching, ridiculously overlarge hat just for this occasion, and now she felt hot, uncomfortable, and foolish.

The train rounded the bend, belching steam and cinders as it drew to a clanking, grinding, screeching halt. Harriet took a deep, steadying breath, scanning the carriages, her heart skipping at the sight of every tall male, stooping to jump down onto the platform. At last, there was Curran, dressed in civilian clothes, a Panama hat pulled down low over his eyes, his linen jacket flung over his shoulder, and a leather suitcase in hand.

They walked toward each other. The walk became a run. He dropped his suitcase and jacket onto the dusty platform, and she was in his arms. She breathed in the familiar scent of sandalwood and shaving soap and the taste of his lips on hers.

From somewhere behind her, a disapproving matron *tsked*, but she didn't care. Curran was home in Singapore. Her Curran. To hell with propriety. They had months of enforced separation to make up for, and she didn't give a damn what people thought.

"Harriet, I have missed you," he said at last as they drew apart.

She smiled. "Liar. You have been far too busy to spare me more than a passing thought."

"You are completely wrong," he said.

He traced a finger down the bridge of her nose.

"I have missed those freckles, the way your mouth lifts slightly higher on the right side when you smile, the lines in the corners of your eyes—"

"I do not have lines in the corners of my eyes!"

He chuckled, and his arms tightened around her again. "That is a moot point we can discuss later. You look wonderful."

She took a moment to study his face, every loved and remembered detail. He definitely had lines in the corners of his eyes.

"You look tired," she concluded.

"Thank you," he chuckled, but the humor went from his face. "It has all been a massive waste of time. Nothing will change." He put an arm around her shoulders. "Let's go and find somewhere quiet where we can talk and catch up."

"Your motor vehicle awaits," Harriet said with a flourish, as they stepped out of the station.

Curran looked from the blue Sheffield Simplex to Harriet. "How...?"

She smiled. "I drove it. Julian has given me lessons."

"That's the last time I loan my possessions to your brother," he said. "I thought a clergyman could be trusted."

"He says I am very good, and it is a useful skill for an independent woman to acquire," Harriet said. "Would you like me to demonstrate?"

"Another time." Curran opened the passenger door and Harriet climbed in, tying on her hat with a scarf as Curran settled into the driver's seat.

"Breakfast at Raffles," he declared.

———

"Didn't you get breakfast on the train?" Harriet asked as Curran pushed aside the empty plate, having cleaned every skerrick of eggs, bacon, and toast.

"I am going to be living in the barracks in the police lines," Curran said. "The food is notoriously bad, even for the officers."

"What happens now?" Harriet asked.

He raised an eyebrow. "Meaning?"

"The promised promotion to Chief Inspector?"

He nodded. "I will meet with Cuscaden this afternoon and hopefully the news will be good."

"You mean it hasn't been confirmed?"

He shook his head. "All I was told was that I would be advised when the Kuala Lumpur case had been finalized and I return to duties in Singapore."

"And is the Kuala Lumpur case done?"

"Yes. All nicely filed and tucked away in the filing cabinets of Whitehall, never to be spoken of again. An unfortunate side note to history."

"And London?"

He shuddered. "Cold, wet, and dreary. However, I did have a chance to see Eloise."

Curran's cousin, Lady Eloise Warby, a hard-line supporter of the Women's Social and Political Union, had suffered for her loyalty to the suffragette cause, as Harriet had. The two women had been arrested at the same protest in London and sentenced to time in HM Prison Holloway. The force-feeding nearly killed Harriet, and she had been released, but Eloise continued her protests and had now served several harrowing stretches in Holloway.

"How is she?"

He frowned. "Frail," he said. "A strong wind would blow her away, but she is determined to continue the fight. I admire her courage, but her husband is desperately worried."

Harriet looked down at the half-drunk cup of tea in front of her. Unlike Eloise Warby, she lacked the courage to continue the fight. She had run away, escaping to Singapore. She still felt her desertion as a failure.

As if reading her thoughts, Curran put his hand over hers. "Harriet, she has not forgotten you. She sent her warmest regards and wishes you well."

Harriet nodded, but his reassurance only deepened her sense of guilt and failure.

Curran straightened and turned to buttering toast. "And your family," he said. "I had a most enjoyable evening at your parent's home. I have presents for you all, including Will. Your mother particularly wanted to know all about Esme Prynne." He looked up and narrowed his eyes. "She didn't seem to know anything about you and me."

"I haven't said anything, even to my sister Mary, and I swore Julian to silence. I didn't want to pre-empt..." She swallowed. "You and me."

Curran studied her for a long moment. "It did make things a little awkward," he said, "but fortunately, we could speculate on Julian and Esme's future without your mother becoming suspicious."

"I told you Esme is here in Singapore," Harriet said. "She is doing well as the acting Principal of the Singapore Ladies Academy."

"And she has you working for her?"

"I couldn't go back to the Detective Branch, and I needed employment," Harriet said. "Even with a scholarship, Will's schooling will take every spare penny Julian and I can manage. The work is no different from what I was doing for Julian. The only difference is I get paid a proper salary, and Esme even has me teaching shorthand and typing to the older girls."

"And where do things stand with Esme and Julian?"

Harriet rolled her eyes. "He has been writing her poetry. Thank heavens you don't write poetry, Curran."

His lips twitched. "I did write letters, though."

She smiled. "You did. They were lovely letters."

He searched her face. "Do you...?"

Harriet widened her eyes in mock naivety. "Do I what?"

"Do you still want to make this work? Has anything changed?"

She held his gaze. "No, nothing has changed, Curran. All we need is a bit of time."

He nodded. "Hopefully, we have that now life is back to normal."

"Will you come for dinner tonight?"

He shook his head. "No. Samrita and Lavinia are expecting me." He frowned. "How is Samrita? It was hard to tell from her two letters. She seemed happy enough."

Curran had only recently discovered his two half-siblings, Jayant, and his sister, Samrita. It had been a shock to discover the father he had thought of as long dead had survived the massacre at Kandahar and lived for many years in India with his second family.

When Samrita had been kidnapped, Jayant had sought him out to assist in finding her, and Curran had liberated his sister from the clutches of the notorious Topaz Club, which had been associated with the corruption scandal that had seen him sent to Kuala Lumpur late the previous year. His hope of getting to know his sister better was cut short when he received orders to go to London.

"Samrita is fine," Harriet said. "Ridley is employing her at the

Botanic Gardens to do botanical drawings, and her artwork is getting her noticed. You will hardly recognize her now."

"That's good to hear," Curran said. "Lavinia organized a proper art teacher for her, so that should be a help."

Curran took Harriet's hand, twisting her fingers in his.

"There is something you need to know. It will be in the paper tomorrow morning, but I wanted to tell you first. Edith Robertson was sentenced yesterday."

Harriet held her breath, knowing the answer even before she asked the question. "And?"

"She has been sentenced to hang."

She sighed. "That is not unexpected."

The previous December, Harriet and Julian had been guests of the principal of the Prince Alfred School in Kuala Lumpur, Henry Robertson, and his wife, Edith. Their visit had been cut short when Edith Robertson shot her lover, Walter Stewart, on the steps of her house. She had maintained that she shot him while defending her honor, but her story had always been shaky, and the judge and his two advisors had arrived at a guilty verdict without difficulty.

Now she would hang.

"Poor Edith... poor Henry and poor little Dottie. I had hoped that maybe the judge would be inclined to mercy," Harriet said.

"There is an uproar in KL," Curran said. "Whatever the English community may have thought of Mrs. Robertson, they won't see an Englishwoman hanged. There is talk of petitioning the Sultan of Selangor for clemency."

"Hypocrites," Harriet said with feeling. "The English community despised poor Edith, and now she is their heroine that they have to save? If she had been a woman of any other race, she would go to the gallows unremarked. Thank you for telling me."

Curran brushed the crumbs from his jacket. "Harriet, dearly as I would love to spend more time with you today, I am expected at South Bridge Road, and I need to find my rooms in the police lines and organize a uniform. I am afraid the next few days are going to be busy."

"Come for dinner on Saturday night," Harriet said. "Esme will be there too. I will catch a ricksha home if you need to keep moving."

Curran stood up and bent his head to kiss her.

"It is good to be home, Harriet."

She caught his hand. "And it's good to have you home."

He squeezed her fingers. "Until Saturday."

She watched as he strode out of the room, the eyes of the other diners covertly following him before swiveling back to her. She raised her chin as she passed the tables. The gossip's tongues would be sharpened and she didn't give a tinker's curse.

# THREE

At Curran's last meeting with Inspector General Cuscaden before leaving for London, Cuscaden had told him that plans were afoot to expand the Detective Branch with the appointment of a Chief Inspector. Stuck in London, Curran had heard nothing more, and he had an uncomfortable feeling that if Cuscaden and his superiors were not talking to him, they were talking about him.

Promotion at this point in his life would be timely... and well deserved. That last assignment in KL had nearly killed him, but he had brought the Topaz Club down and exposed the heart of a ring of corruption. Surely, he had earned some recognition for a job well done?

He tucked his regulation pith helmet underneath his arm and knocked on the solid door to Cuscaden's office. At a muffled "enter" he turned the handle and found the room empty.

The Inspector General stood on the broad veranda outside his office, looking down at the activity on South Bridge Road. He looked around as Curran entered but didn't move, compelling Curran to join him.

Cuscaden leaned his hands on the heavy stone balustrade.

"All done, Curran?"

"All done, sir. I'm not required anymore."

Cuscaden nodded. "You did a good job."

"I'm not sure everyone agrees," Curran said. "The Federated Malay Police didn't hide the fact they resented interference from outside."

Cuscaden snorted. "If they'd been doing their job in the first place, there would have been no need for your involvement." He straightened and cleared his throat. "One thing your absence has brought home is that we are seriously short-staffed in the Detective Branch. As I may have intimated when we last spoke, we are looking at expanding the branch under the command of a Chief Inspector with some additional staff from London."

Curran stiffened, holding his breath. Would this be the promotion? With the extra pay, he could afford to take on the responsibility of another person in his life and everything that went with that commitment.

Cuscaden coughed and an ominous sense of foreboding settled on Curran's shoulders.

"You've made an appointment, sir?"

"Yes. I'm sorry, Curran, but it's not you."

Curran could not contain the disappointment that washed over him. He schooled his face to neutrality.

"Who has been appointed?" he asked between stiff lips.

"I want you to know that this was not my decision. You were my strong recommendation. It would have been you... should have been you, but the Colonial Office felt your record has been a little," Cuscaden coughed again, "spotty. Assaulting prisoners, however provoked, does not read well and I gather you had a similar altercation in KL that resulted in a serious injury to a suspect."

Curran shifted uncomfortably. If it had not been for the intervention of Sergeant Singh, he may have killed Khoo Zi Qiang, the man behind the corruption in Selangor State and Curran's nemesis. Leaving the man with a scarred face was an act of hubris that he had regretted in the cold light of day.

"Who?" he asked again, hoping that Inspector Hughes from Johor, who had been keeping his chair warm while he had been seconded to London, might have been the appointment. Hughes was someone he could work with.

"We are bringing in a chap from the Yard," Cuscaden said. "He's expected in Singapore next week. Wallace. I believe you may already be acquainted—"

Curran stared at his superior officer, the red mist of fury clouding his eyes and his judgment.

"Wallace," he sputtered. "Wallace is a dolt."

*Worse than a dolt... a sycophant and a toady.*

"Curran!"

"I'm sorry, sir, but I worked with him at Scotland Yard."

"Is there no one you have worked with that you haven't managed to put offside?"

"He—"

It took all Curran's self-control to keep the anger and resentment bubbling inside him from spilling out. If Cuscaden had any inkling of what lay between himself and Wallace... but it was too late. Wallace was on a ship bound for Singapore.

Cuscaden fixed him with an icy glare.

"I don't give a damn what went on between the two of you at Scotland Yard," he said. "Chief Inspector Wallace will arrive next Tuesday, aboard the *Prometheus* with his wife and children. You are to be at the dock to greet them. We have secured a house on Mt. Sophia suitable for his rank and family, and you are responsible for escorting them and ensuring they are settled."

"Where does that leave me?" Curran said, trying hard to keep the sulky tone from his voice.

"Chief Inspector Wallace will be taking command of the Detective Branch, and two new inspectors will be appointed in the next few months. You will remain the senior officer and Wallace's second in command."

Curran swallowed down his anger and his hurt at the injustice of being overlooked for a position he had earned.

"Will that be all, sir?" he asked stiffly.

"For now." Cuscaden laid a hand on Curran's shoulder. "I know you're disappointed. Just keep out of trouble, Curran, and the next promotion will be yours."

"Nice of you to say that, sir, but it's no guarantee, is it? The Colonial Office makes the decision, not you."

"On the subject of the Colonial Office. The newly appointed Secretary of State for the Colonies, Sir Henry Cunningham, is doing the rounds. He is also expected in Singapore on the *Prometheus*. There'll be the usual round of social events and extra work for us. We'll have a full briefing when Wallace is behind his desk."

Curran had been in London when the appointment of the new Colonial Secretary had been announced and a cold feeling of dread washed over him.

Cuscaden was studying his face. "Do you know him?"

Curran stared at his superior. "Yes," he said, between gritted teeth. "I know him."

*And he knows me.*

Did Cunningham's imminent arrival explain the appointment of Wallace over Cuscaden's recommendation?

"Curran—" Cuscaden's voice held a warning purr.

"You have no reason for concern, sir," Curran said.

"Good. I don't need trouble during the official visit."

"Is that all? I should see that everything is in order for Wallace's arrival," Curran said, taking a step back.

"One last thing," Cuscaden said.

Curran bit his tongue before asking if the Inspector General had more bad news for him.

"I thought you should know that Khoo Zi Qiang is dead.

Knifed on the street in Canton. The person responsible has not been caught. It's thought he trod on someone's territory."

Curran stared out into the street without seeing anything as he assimilated that piece of information.

*Khoo Zi Qiang was dead.*

Khoo Zi Qiang should have been hanged for murder and any other number of serious crimes he had committed in Selangor State and Kuala Lumpur, but the Colonial Office didn't like to see its dirty washing hanging out in the public court system and Khoo Zi Qiang had been quietly banished from the Crown Colonies to Canton.

Curran bore scars from his encounters with Khoo, but he had survived and so had Khoo's sister, Curran's former lover, Li An. No more would either of them have to watch over their shoulders for Khoo or his murderous accomplices. They were both free of the man's lurking shadow.

He took a breath. He wouldn't ask if Khoo's death was, in fact, the result of internal conflict on the streets of Canton or a quiet operation by the British government. He didn't want to know.

"Thank you for telling me," he said. "Now, if you'll excuse me, I should see to my responsibilities."

As Curran closed the office door behind him, he reflected that his return to Singapore had not got off to a good start.

He strode into the Detective Branch, determined not to let his despondency show as he greeted the men, with whom he had worked so closely for the last few years: Sergeant Singh, Constable Tan, Constable Musa, and the newly promoted Senior Constable Greaves, the department's photographer and general scientist.

"Welcome back." Sergeant Singh drew himself up to his full height. Singh was not so much a subordinate as a close friend, and a slight frown demonstrated he sensed Curran's news was not good.

"Thank you. It's good to be back," Curran said. "Listen in, men."

He perched against the corner of a desk and crossed his arms. "You have probably heard the rumors about the appointment of a Chief Inspector."

From the expectant faces around him, he knew they had been speculating on his appointment to the role.

"It's not me."

"What?" the normally phlegmatic Greaves expostulated.

"Chief Inspector Wallace arrives next week. I have worked with him before." Curran left it at that. "Singh, I want a briefing on all current cases, and I want this office cleaned and tidied."

Curran closed the door to his office behind his sergeant. He could rely on Singh not to say anything out of turn, but despite his friend's impassive face, the anger oozed from his sergeant.

He laid a hand on his shoulder. "It's done, Singh. Let's make the most of the situation."

"This Wallace... when you say you worked with him...?"

"Ancient history, Singh. Tell me about the current cases."

Singh laid a file on the table. "This is our most pressing case. Two men, faces obscured, carrying a handgun have been robbing the gold shops around Serangoon Road. No one has been hurt, but shots have been fired and they have got away with a good haul from each."

"Descriptions?"

"Vague. Possibly Indian, but they cover their faces."

Curran picked up the file and began leafing through the statements. "No fingerprints?"

Singh shook his head. "No. Inspector Hughes did not think it necessary."

Curran sighed. Old-school policing was not going to solve cases like this. The next shop to be hit by the thieves, and there would be others, would be fingerprinted from the ceiling to the floor.

# FOUR

"Robert!"

Curran dismounted from his motor vehicle in time to catch his half-sister, Samrita, as she hurled herself into his arms. He put an arm around her shoulder and they walked up to the house where Lavinia Pemberthey-Smythe waited.

Lavinia was the eccentric widow of the commanding officer of his father's former regiment and the only person he knew who had met his father. He had come across her in the conduct of a case in the previous year and she had taken an almost maternal interest in him. She had an uncanny knack of appearing to know him better than he knew himself.

"You're late," Lavinia said.

He greeted her with a kiss on her cheek.

"Sorry. Too much to catch up on at South Bridge Road."

Lavinia waved a hand toward the table.

"Sit. Dinner is getting cold."

"What have you been working on?" Curran asked his sister, as he poured himself a beer provided by Lavinia's servant.

"She's doing wonderful illustrations of my orchids. She

persuaded me it's time I put my idea for a book together," Lavinia said.

A fetching color rose in Samrita's cheeks. "It is a small thing I can do to thank you for all your kindness, Lavinia."

"And the work you are doing for Ridley at the Botanic Gardens?"

"He pays me a small amount for each drawing," Samrita said, without meeting Lavinia's steely glare.

"Not nearly enough," Lavinia put in.

"I need the experience," Samrita said. "Tom says it is about building a portfolio."

At first, Curran could not place the name.

He frowned. "Tom? Is he the man Lavinia found to give you lessons?"

This time, the color in Samrita's cheeks turned a brighter shade of red.

"Thomas Barker, my drawing teacher. He's been finishing a big commission for the governor. It's been so exciting."

"He is. Tom is a brilliant artist," Lavinia said.

Before Curran had a chance to enquire how Mr. Barker, the artist, had become 'Tom', the servant appeared with their meal.

Curran presented the small presents he had purchased for both women while he had been away. A garden trowel and fork for Lavinia and a set of expensive camel hair paint brushes and watercolor paints for Samrita.

As they ate and chatted about London, Curran studied his sister. In the months since her rescue from the clutches of the Topaz Club, she had grown in confidence and, to Curran's biased eye, beauty—with her oval face and large, dark eyes and dark hair she wore coiled in the nape of her neck, western style.

Only when the conversation lagged did Samrita set down her table napkin and look up at him, her eyes sober and her lips pressed in a tight line.

"And Kuala Lumpur?" she asked.

He told them about the outcome of the Ethel Robertson trial, but he knew what she wanted to hear and with a deep steadying breath she asked, "And Kamini?"

Kamini was the daughter of Samrita's friend Lakshmi, murdered by the men behind the Topaz Club. After Lakshmi's death, the baby had been left with Samrita, and Kamini had ended up in the care of her nursemaid until someone could be found to look after the child.

"Kamini is now with her grandparents," Curran said. "Jayant kept his word and informed Lakshmi's parents of her death. They turned up in KL a few months ago to take the baby back to India with them."

Samrita nodded. Her eyes were at once haunted by the memory of those dark days.

"They were kind people. I hope Kamini brings them the happiness so cruelly taken from them by Lakshmi's death." Her mouth tightened. "And Jayant?"

Samrita's brother and Curran's half-brother, Jayant, had returned to India to pick up the threads of a life there. Jayant had betrayed his sister in the worst possible way and, although he had tried to make amends for his actions, brother and sister would probably always remain estranged.

"I believe he has found work with the railways in Calcutta," Curran said.

Samrita nodded. "I am glad. I hope he finds happiness."

"And Khoo Zi Qiang is dead. Murdered in Canton," Curran said.

Samrita's eyes blazed. "Good. I hope he died in excruciating agony."

Lavinia coughed. "I'm so sorry you missed the Coronation festivities last week," she said, adroitly changing the subject.

"Oh, trust me there were plenty of festivities aboard the ship," Curran said. "I hoped I had escaped the worst of it when I left London."

The coronation of King George V had taken place in London the previous week and the excitement had consumed every corner of the Empire. The newspapers had been full of nothing else. Each tiny detail had been noted, recorded, and reported on.

"There is to be a Coronation Ball at Government House next week," Lavinia said. "Not that I will be going. I received an invitation, but it would be my personal definition of hell."

"A little late, given the Coronation was last week," Curran said.

"Oh, there was a reception at Government House on the day, but apparently there is to be some visiting dignitary from the colonial office, so the governor decided to delay the ball until his arrival."

"The whole world stops for Sir Henry Cunningham," Curran said, making no effort to keep the bitterness from his voice.

Lavinia frowned. "Do you know him, Robert?"

Curran shrugged. "I've crossed his path in the past. It's not an acquaintance I wish to renew."

Lavinia drilled him with a hard, appraising look and changed the subject again.

"Have you seen Harriet yet? We hardly see her since she started working for Miss Prynne at the school."

"I saw her this morning. She met me at the station."

"And?" Samrita put in, fluttering her eyelashes.

He moved his gaze from one woman to the other.

"Don't look at me like that. I'm not saying anything else. That is entirely between Harriet and me. Samrita, I would like to see your artwork. You know I love orchids."

Lavinia snorted.

While Samrita went to her room to collect her portfolio, Curran turned to Lavinia. "What is going on between this Thomas Barker and my sister?"

Lavinia frowned. "Don't be like that, Robert. It ill behooves you to play the big brother. Tom Barker is a talented artist, and he has been a breath of fresh air in Samrita's life. Surely you must see the change in her?" Lavinia laid a hand on his arm. "Remember, you are not her father."

"I am responsible for her."

"Are you? Yours is an unconventional relationship, Curran. She hardly knows you and Samrita, more than anyone I've ever known, has earned the right to make her own way in life without interference, however well intended. Trust me. She is doing very well. You can be proud of her. It takes great strength of character to put these last years behind her."

Samrita reappeared, clutching a large cardboard folder.

"Talking about me?" she inquired, with an arched eyebrow.

"Of course we were," Lavinia said. 'Now let's clear some space on the table."

The botanical drawings, mostly of orchids and palm trees, were lovely, but Curran's eye was drawn to some of the other work she said she was doing with Barker: Still lifes and a collection of delicate drawings of an older Chinese woman. Curran asked how she knew the woman.

"That's Min. She's Thomas's housekeeper. Tom is known for his portraiture. His portrait of the governor will be unveiled at the ball at Government House." A faint flush rose to Samrita's cheek. "Thomas has asked me to accompany him, but I don't think I will go. I... I'm not the sort of person they want at such an event."

Curran stiffened. "Why ever not? You are to go to Raffles Place and pick out a new dress."

"Robert... I can't..."

"You can and you will."

"I will need help," Samrita said. "I am still learning about the correct fashion for the sister of the esteemed police inspector."

Curran shot her a narrowed-eyed glance and saw she was grinning.

Samrita glanced at Lavinia, who held up her hands in mock horror. "Don't look at me. I would be of no assistance."

Lavinia eschewed Western dress except when propriety demanded it.

"Perhaps Harriet can help?" Lavinia suggested.

"She is busy with her work. I shall ask Louisa Mackenzie," Samrita said.

Curran glanced at his watch. "It's getting late, and it's been a long day."

"Where are you going to be living?" Lavinia asked.

Curran pulled a face. "Police lines," he said. "There are officers' quarters, and I will have a batman to look after me, so it will do."

"And Leopold?" Lavinia asked.

Curran's horse, Leopold, was stabled with a man who looked after racehorses out near Bukit Timah.

"I haven't checked on him yet, but by all reports, he's doing well. However, I have treacherously become accustomed to the motor vehicle, so Leo will have to stay where he is for the time being." Curran pushed his chair back. "Now, if you will excuse me, ladies, I will leave you. Goodnight."

As he drove back to the police lines, his mind turned over the events of the day... Harriet, Cuscaden, the promotion that never was, Wallace, Cunningham, the death of Khoo Zi Qiang... Samrita and her artist. The next few weeks would be fraught and somewhere he had to make the time and the space for Harriet.

He desperately wanted to do the right thing by her, to court her properly, to spend time learning about each other, not as friends and colleagues, but as lovers, and he wished he had gone to visit her tonight. For a man who only twelve months ago had no real connections or ties, navigating this new world of family obligations and the woman he loved was proving challenging.

# FIVE

Harriet, Julian, and Esme sat on the wide veranda of St. Tom's House, chatting about the affairs of the week as they waited for Curran, who was late. Above the hum of insects and the rattle of the passing traffic on River Valley Road, the local troop of Macaque monkeys cavorted in the trees nearby. Huo Jin had to chase one out of the kitchen only that morning. They were getting bolder and cheekier by the day.

The sweep of headlights announced Curran's arrival.

Harriet pushed back her chair and jumped to her feet, straightening her skirt and pushing a stray lock of hair behind her ear as her heart leaped.

Skirt in hand, she bounded down the stairs. From behind her, Julian said, "Harri, you are not a giggling schoolgirl. A bit of decorum, please—"

Curran vaulted out of the car, and Harriet stopped, suddenly unsure of herself. Julian was correct. She wasn't a young girl, and the audience on the veranda reminded her that respectable widows did not throw themselves at men.

"You came," she said.

"Sorry if I'm a little late," he said. "Still catching up with work."

He reached into the back seat of the car for a variety of packages wrapped in brown paper.

"They look exciting," Harriet said.

"I could hardly return from London empty-handed," Curran said. "I have presents from your family and some trifles from me. Is Will around?"

Will had taken himself inside when Esme arrived. Adult conversations bored him, and he had a newly arrived copy of the *Scout* magazine to read. He came out onto the veranda, and Curran handed him two large packages.

"For you," he said. "The long one is from me. Belated birthday present."

There could be no mistaking the contents of the brown wrapping, and Will tore off the paper to reveal a gleaming new Gray & Sons cricket bat. A proper cricket bat, not Julian's battered spare with no proper grip.

The boy stared at the bat, his eyes as round as saucers.

"Will?" Harriet prodded.

Will looked up at Curran.

"Thank you," he said in a small, tight voice.

Curran cleared his throat. "You need something for this fancy new school you are going to."

Harriet wanted to kiss him. If there was something Will had longed for more than anything in the world, it was a proper cricket bat. The other parcel from Harriet's parents contained a copy of John Wisden's Cricketers Almanack for 1910.

"I told your parents that they had another budding cricketer in the family," Curran said with a glance at Julian.

Will stared at the heavy, hard-bound book, the title embossed in gold lettering, and with a noticeable crack in his voice, excused himself.

Harriet's mother had sent practical presents—jars of marmalade and preserves. Julian and Harriet's sister, Mary, had sent both Harriet and Julian handkerchiefs. Curran had several books that Julian had asked him to procure from Hatchards of Piccadilly. And he hadn't forgotten Esme, giving her a book of myths and legends.

"It's like Christmas," Esme said. "But what about Harriet?"

Curran caught Harriet's eye. "Later," he said, and Harriet could have sworn he was blushing.

They sat down for an excellent meal of chicken curry. There were questions about London, and looking at her brother and her friend, Harriet could see the light of homesickness in their faces. Even she began to wish for the damp, gray days.

"Did you get the promotion?" Esme asked Curran the question they had all been sitting on.

Curran set down his knife and fork and gave a quick shake of his head.

"I didn't. That's gone to a Yard man."

Harriet felt the disappointment ooze from him. He had put his life at risk for that promotion, and to see it go to someone else must have been a bitter blow.

"I'm so sorry, Curran," she said.

He nodded. "To be frank, so am I. Cuscaden as good as promised it to me when I took on the Topaz Club case, but I suspect he was overruled. I was counting on that promotion." He shrugged. "So am I, but I've only myself to blame. I've not always been judicious in the way I have handled certain matters."

They exchanged a glance, and Harriet understood what he was saying. He had been suspended for assaulting a suspect and, more recently, had deliberately wounded Khoo Zi Qiang in the course of arresting him. In both instances, he had been provoked, but she imagined, on the face of it, neither would look good on his record.

"But that's not fair," Esme protested. "You risked your life on an assignment no one else could be trusted with, and you've spent months on the Topaz Club case."

"Fairness doesn't have much to do with it," Curran responded.

"Do you know the man who got the job?" Harriet asked, indignation on Curran's behalf rising in her throat.

He grimaced. "Inspector Sidney Wallace of Scotland Yard. He will be arriving in Singapore on Tuesday to take on the role of Chief Inspector, followed, I am told, by two other detective inspectors who are yet to be appointed."

"And do you know this man, Wallace?" Julian asked.

"Yes." Curran paused. "We have different ideas on policing."

Harriet sensed that something darker lay between the two men, but that was a question for later.

Curran straightened. "Enough grumbling from me. How is the school going, Esme?"

"I am loving it. The girls are wonderful, and there is such satisfaction in being with children who want to learn."

"Is that meant as an indictment of the boys of St. Toms?" Julian said with a quirk of his eyebrow.

Esme laughed. "I am sure the boys of St Toms are equally delightful, but most of them are handed the right to education on a plate. The girls at the Academy come from families that know the value of education and will do whatever it takes to give their daughters that privilege. This is what I believe in, Curran. It was not just about the right to vote. It is about equality and opportunity." Esme smiled at Harriet. "I am most ably assisted by Harriet and the other wonderful teachers."

"A far cry from police work, Harriet," Curran remarked.

"I miss working in the Detective Branch," Harriet said with a smile.

"And you are missed," Curran said. "Nabeel's typing skills are not at your standard. Fortunately, there has been no major crime since I've been away, apart from a gang committing armed robberies on the jewelry stores around Serangoon Road that I need to get on to." He blew out a breath. "Monday's job will be clearing out my office for the new Chief Inspector."

"Do you want to tell us about this Wallace? Is he another Keogh?" Harriet asked, trying to get a measure of the man who had quite obviously crossed swords with Curran in the past.

The now disgraced Inspector Keogh of the Federated Malay Police had been brought in to replace Curran when he was suspended. Keogh had seen her dismissed from her role in the Detective Branch and had reported her criminal past as a convicted suffragette to the trustees of Julian's school. It had caused no end of trouble and sleepless nights.

Curran shook his head. "No. Keogh was an idiot, a venal idiot. Wallace is not a bad policeman, but he lacks imagination and independence. He will do what is asked of him. Maybe the years have mellowed him... mellowed both of us." He cleared his throat. "He is arriving with his family on the *Prometheus* on Tuesday, and I have been tasked with meeting him. Harriet, could I prevail on you to accompany me to the dock? It will be easier to deal with him and his family if I have an ally."

"You mean, can I be kind to Mrs. Wallace?"

"Something like that. It would make my life easier if we start on a positive acquaintance."

"Isn't the new Secretary of State for the Colonies arriving on that ship?" Julian asked.

"He is," Curran said. "When you think you leave the past behind, it has a nasty habit of coming back to find you. Wallace and Cunningham together are probably the last two people I ever wanted to see again, and yet here they are arriving on the same ship."

"Do you know Sir Henry Cunningham?" Esme asked.

In the soft light of the kerosene lamp, Curran's eyes glittered.

"I do," he said.

"His arrival is the talk everywhere," Esme said. "You'd think he was royalty. My girls have been asked to sing at the ball next Friday night. The governor's daughter, Mrs Farrant, is one of our trustees. The organization for such a huge event is phenomenal."

"The coronation has been the biggest social occasion I've ever seen since I arrived in Singapore," Julian replied. "Celebrations just seem to go on and on."

"The chap who gives Samrita art lessons is unveiling a portrait of the governor and has invited Samrita as his guest." Curran scanned the faces. "Are you all invited?"

"I suspect I've only been invited because I am helping with the choir," Harriet said. "But Julian and Esme are going, and Louisa and Euan Mackenzie. I suppose Griff Maddocks will be there for the paper." She smiled at Curran. "Will you be there? My dance card is empty."

He nodded. "A gilt-edged invitation was waiting for me."

Under the table, his fingers meshed with Harriet's, and they smiled at each other. They had danced together before, a night Harriet cherished. Curran, tall and impossibly handsome in his tropical evening dress... his arms around her.

Esme coughed and pushed back her chair. "Julian, you were going to show me your latest thoughts on Virgil's Ecologues."

"Now?" Julian frowned.

Esme prodded him. "Now," she said.

Realization dawned on Julian's face.

"Oh yes, do you mind stepping into my study? I have my work on the desk."

Harriet bit her lip to stop from laughing. She rose from the table and sat on the rattan daybed. Her cat, Shashti, jumped on her lap, but as soon as Curran sat down beside her, the traitorous cat promptly moved onto his knee, purring loudly.

Curran fumbled in the pocket of his trousers and pulled out a small box, a jeweler's box, leather with gilt decoration. Harriet's heart skipped, and she tempered her expectations. It did not look like a box containing a ring.

"I hope you like it," he said as he pressed the box into her hand. "Ellie helped pick it out for me."

Harriet held her breath and pressed the catch. The lid sprang open to reveal a plain, rectangular gold locket. It had no ornamentation on the surface, and when she opened the locket, the two panes were blank.

"I..." Curran cleared his throat. "I hope you like it. I thought maybe you have an image of Thomas you can put in it."

She smiled at him. "It's lovely, and yes, I do have a picture of Thomas and a lock of his hair..."

She trailed off, the memory of her dead child suddenly bright and clear. A lump rose to her throat, and she dashed a hand across her eyes.

"Everyone tells you to put the death of a child behind you, but you can never do that. He's always there, a little shadow I see out of the corner of my eye. A part of myself I will never find again."

She'd never said the words out loud, and Curran slipped an arm around her shoulder, drawing her closer, his lips brushing her hair.

"Harriet, I want you to know that I have thought about you every day I was away."

She wriggled herself closer into his embrace. "I love the locket, Curran. Thank you."

She turned her face up to his. A smile curved his lips, and his eyes creased at the corners.

"I have said this to only one other woman, Harriet, and that is no secret from you. She is in the past." He paused, and his forehead rested against hers. "I love you, Harriet Gordon."

She breathed in the scent of the man and closed her eyes. "And I you, Robert Curran."

His lips brushed hers, and she reached for him, hungrily letting herself meld into his embrace with the sense of coming home to somewhere safe and familiar.

# Six

The Serangoon Road bandits had targeted another jeweler that morning, causing Curran to abandon his plans for the day and head for 'Little India' to meet up with Sergeant Singh.

The area around Serangoon Road had been largely settled by the Indian population, with the area known in Malay as *Kandang Kerbau,* meaning Buffalo Enclosure, as the area to the west had become the center of the local cattle industry. The population included herdsmen from across India, attracted by reliable jobs in the slaughterhouses and tanneries and the provision of milk to the city's inhabitants.

In turn, a wide variety of other industries and food purveyors, tailors, sellers of saris and spices, and jewelers had established themselves in the shophouses. The resulting population—Tamils and Sikhs, for the most part—made for a noisy, bustling, and colorful corner of Singapore.

Even on a Sunday, the lower part of Serangoon Road, near the market and Stamford Road, was crowded with stalls of produce and wares, and busy with pedestrians who parted as the two policemen approached. Most knew Singh and greeted him respectfully. He was one of them, a local, who lived with his family, above his brother's tailor shop near the *Sri Veeramakaliamman* Temple.

A crowd had gathered outside the targeted shop. Most of the glass cabinets displaying the jeweler's wares were smashed and empty. The disconsolate shopkeeper waved his hands over the damaged property.

"All gone," he said. "Hundreds of dollars lost. You must catch these bad men, Inspector."

"Can you describe them?" Curran asked.

The man shook his head. "No. They had wound a cloth around the lower part of their faces."

"Indian?"

The man shrugged. "They made their demands in English, but yes, I think they were Indian."

"What was taken?"

The man shook his head. "Gold bracelets, necklaces, earrings. The best of my stock."

"Provide a list to the sergeant," Curran said.

He glanced over the undamaged cabinets with their displays of bright gold, inlaid with semi-precious jewels and enamel. Too heavy and gaudy for his Western taste, but for many the items were a visible representation of a family's wealth.

"Did they have a weapon?"

The man pointed at the Webley on Curran's belt. "One carried a gun like that. It was very frightening. My wife was with me in the shop when they came in. She is still prostrate with shock."

Curran assured the man that every effort was being made to catch the thieves, and he and Singh stepped back out onto the hot, dusty, busy street. Curran removed his pith helmet and wiped his brow.

"How many shops have they hit now?"

"This is the third."

Inspector Hughes from Johor, who had filled in during Curran's absence, may have deemed it unnecessary to deploy Greaves to look for fingerprints at the scenes of the earlier robberies, reasoning, no doubt that in such a busy place there would be hundreds of prints.

Curran gave orders to the shopkeeper to touch nothing, leaving the man with the assurance that one of his men would be coming to dust for fingerprints. The concept took some explaining, but the man's eyes brightened at the thought that the culprits could be traced. Curran didn't like to disillusion him. The records at South Bridge Road, like the science itself, were still in a fledgling state.

They interviewed the other two shopkeepers but gleaned no new information from them. There seemed no discernible pattern to the robberies. One had been carried out in the late afternoon and the second as the shop closed. This one had been carried out in the morning just as the shop opened.

Curran stood in the middle of Serangoon Road and looked up and down at the milling tide of people. Where did he even begin to start looking? He reasoned the perpetrators would probably melt the gold into a more easily disposed of commodity. One of his constables patrolled the area out of uniform and he would set him to asking questions.

His nose twitched in appreciation at the scent of spices mingled with the peppery scent of the chrysanthemums used by the garland makers, overlaying the smell of drains and other more unsavory smells. He and Singh walked past street vendors and little cafes serving spicy curries on banana leaves and stopped to purchase a couple of the more easily consumed pastries called *samosas,* crammed with a spicy vegetable mixture.

"We missed you," Singh said, brushing pastry crumbs from his mustache.

"It's good to be back to some honest crime," Curran said with a laugh.

Singh nodded. "That was a bad business in KL."

He paused and coughed.

Curran knew what his friend wanted to say, but he was too loyal a policeman to display any disrespect to a senior officer.

"I admit I am disappointed about the Chief Inspector's job," Curran said. "But I only have myself to blame. We must make the most of the hand we are dealt, Singh."

"You have served with this man before?"

"Yes. At the Yard. He was junior to me in rank, but his promotion came rapidly."

"Hmm," Singh responded.

"And as for new inspectors being brought in from London, that makes me angry, Singh. You are as good as any of them."

"But my skin is brown," Singh replied. "It will take many years before they appoint a native to an officer rank."

He spoke without obvious bitterness, but Curran sensed it in the man's tone.

# SEVEN

## MONDAY, 3 JULY

The Singapore Academy for Young Ladies, or Singapore Ladies Academy as it was more commonly known, occupied a grand old mansion, not unlike Julian's school, St. Thomas. It boasted an enrollment of one hundred and fifty girls drawn from all corners of Singapore—English, Chinese, Indian, Malay, and a smattering from the other ethnicities that comprised the *entrepôt* that was Singapore. They took girls from the age of eleven and saw them through to matriculation with the hope they would go on to further education, but outside of England and Australia, there were still few universities opening their doors to young women.

The teaching staff were mostly English, but since assuming the position of headmistress, Esme had set out to recruit a teaching staff more representative of the student population. For Harriet, Esme's teaching philosophy represented everything she had believed in when she had joined the suffrage movement. Equal opportunity. Why was that too much to ask? It still rankled that her father had denied her request to study law.

The school enjoyed the patronage of the oldest of the governor's two daughters, Mrs. Georgina Farrant. The governor, being a widower, relied on his daughters to play the first lady of the colony, and both young women, although only newly married, worked hard for their father. From Esme's perspective, Mrs. Farrant's interest in the school provided considerable kudos.

When she arrived at the school on Monday morning, Harriet found Mrs. Farrant taking tea in Esme's study. When Harriet excused herself for the interruption, Esme gestured for her to join them.

"We are just discussing arrangements for the ball this Friday," Esme said.

"I swear it will be the death of me. Kate and I are run off our feet with the organization," Georgina Farrant declared as she set a typewritten sheet of paper on Esme's desk. "I have a draft running sheet here. The girls will sing the National Anthem as the official party enters the ballroom at eight and then a short bracket of songs at the break for supper at nine fifteen. They will not be required again and, of course, you will be free to enjoy the rest of the evening. There will be fireworks at ten and we have an eight-piece orchestra booked until midnight. The only other small matter of business is the unveiling of Papa's portrait by Sir Henry Cunningham, and we will attend to that immediately on the arrival of the official party." She stood up. "Thank you for the tea. The Cunninghams arrive tomorrow, and I had better see everything is in order for their stay at Government House. I look forward to seeing you on Friday. I hope the girls will be in good voice. I would like them to make a good impression."

Esme walked Mrs. Farrant to her motor vehicle and returned to her office, where Harriet had started going through the urgent paperwork.

"I am very much looking forward to the ball," Esme said.

Harriet looked up and smiled. "So am I."

She fingered the locket around her neck, that now contained

an image of Thomas Gordon and a lock of his hair. As far as she was concerned, she would dance every dance with Curran.

Esme glanced at her watch. "It's time for choir practice."

As part of her duties at the school, Harriet had become the assistant to the music teacher when it came to the choir. It had been years since she had played the piano seriously, but none of the other teachers owned up to any skills on the pianoforte, so it had fallen to Harriet.

The choir practiced during lunch hour, and they were still assembling. Seeing Esme, they stood and chorused, "Good morning, Miss Prynne."

Esme waved them back to their seats. "Relax. We have just come to hear you practice. Mrs. Farrant visited this morning with the arrangements for the ball on Friday." One girl caught her eye, and she frowned. "Amelia Hardcastle. That is not how a lady sits."

The star of the choir, Amelia Hardcastle, sat on the edge of a table, swinging her feet as she talked to her best friend, Louisa Mackenzie's eldest daughter, Heather.

Amelia, the older sister of Bertie Hardcastle, who had caused Will so much recent distress, slid off the table, her hands behind her back. At fifteen, she was a bright but rather precocious girl.

"Sorry, Miss Prynne." The glint in her eye belied her contrition. "Mama and Papa are going to the ball, and it will be so exciting to see everyone all dressed up." Amelia executed a twirl, holding out the dark blue skirt of her school uniform.

The uniform for the school comprised a cotton skirt and white blouse with a sailor collar and a dark blue tie. Like all the girls, Amelia wore her thick fair hair in a long plait secured with a grosgrain ribbon to match the tie. It flew out behind her as she turned.

"Miss Hardcastle, the choir is only there to sing," Miss Prynne said. "It is not an invitation to attend the ball, and you will all be sent home as soon as the last bracket is finished. As for dressing up, you will all be wearing your school uniform. Now I shall leave you with Miss Brown. I shall expect *God Save the King* to be note-perfect!"

Esme left the room and Harriet sat down at the piano and ran her fingers along some warm-up scales as Miss Brown, the music teacher, handed out the music. Esme's school would be on full display and they all wanted to be at their very best.

Miss Brown raised her baton and Amelia took the solo, her crystal-clear voice hitting every note of *English Country Garden*.

Mrs. Farrant would not be disappointed.

# EIGHT

TUESDAY, 4 JULY

With the *Prometheus* set to dock on the morning tide, Harriet spent some time in consideration of what to wear to greet the new Detective Chief Inspector. She settled on a new dress of sprigged Indian cotton made by Singh's brother on Serangoon Road.

Curran called for her promptly at the appointed hour.

"You look very nice," he said, holding the passenger door open for her. "Is that a new dress?"

Harriet smiled, pleased he had noticed.

Curran's uniform was impeccable, but tension oozed from him, his fingers tapping the steering wheel as they drove to the dock at Tanjong Pagar.

Harriet touched his arm. "Curran? What's bothering you?"

He glanced at her and gave her a lopsided smile. "Am I that transparent?"

"Yes," she said.

"Wallace and I have a history. He's the main reason I left Scotland Yard for this posting. I am not looking forward to working with him again."

"It's been a long time. Perhaps you have both mellowed?" Harriet suggested.

"Perhaps," Curran said, with no conviction in his voice.

He parked the motor vehicle and after he had secured the services of a *gharry* for the newly arrived family and their luggage, they wandered down to the dock, where the steamer was drawing alongside. Harriet raised her parasol, and they stood waiting in the tropical sun as the dock hands ran the ropes out and secured the ship to the bollards.

"Is that a band?" Harriet waved a hand at the uniformed musicians assembling beneath a marquee, decorated in bunting bearing the *Union Jack*.

"It is. The governor will probably attend in person to greet Sir Henry Cunningham and his wife," Curran replied.

The gangway was lowered and uniformed servants in government house livery ran out a red carpet to the marquee. The governor, Sir John Anderson, resplendent in ceremonial dress had arrived in the official vehicle and now waited, his cockaded hat almost hitting the roof of the tent, with Georgina Farrant beside him, a smile fixed on her face.

Above them, the passengers gathered at the rails of the ship as a lady and gentleman appeared at the head of the gangway. The band struck up the national anthem, and the pair descended. Harriet was too far away to make out the man's features, but she had the impression of a man of slight build with a narrow, mustachioed face, beneath a pith helmet. His wife, slightly taller than her husband, carried a lace parasol and wore a blue and cream ensemble with matching ribbons in her enormous hat.

Sir John came forward to greet the couple, gesturing them toward the marquee and, beyond that, the Government House motor vehicle, a gleaming new Rolls Royce. Only after the official party had departed and the red carpet rolled up could the ordinary passengers begin to disembark.

"That's him."

Curran indicated a stocky man in an incongruous tweed suit and bowler hat who paused at the head of the gangway, surveying the crowd. His gaze fell on Curran, and he raised his hand. He clumped down the gangway followed by a woman with two children in tow, a boy of about seven and a girl a couple of years younger.

"Curran," the man said as he approached.

"Wallace," Curran responded and held out his hand.

It took a fraction too long for Wallace to clasp it briefly in greeting. Sidney Wallace was considerably shorter than Curran, broad-shouldered and solid with receding ginger hair and a raggedy ginger mustache. His nose seemed too large for his face and his eyes too small.

"Welcome to Singapore, Mr. Wallace," Harriet said brightly.

Wallace seemed to notice her for the first time, fixing his rather too-small eyes on her.

"Your wife, Curran?"

"No, a friend of mine, Mrs. Gordon," Curran said.

Harriet held out her hand. "Pleased to meet you, Chief Inspector. Curran thought a friendly female face might be more welcoming for Mrs. Wallace."

Wallace shook Harriet's hand, his flesh warm and damp in the unaccustomed humidity. He turned to the woman, who held both children tightly by the hand, her face flushed with the heat. The girl was fretful, tugging on her mother. The boy wore a sullen look.

"My wife, Sadie, and our two brats, Gerald and June."

Harriet turned her smile on the man's wife. "Lovely to meet you, Mrs. Wallace."

"Pleased, I'm sure," Mrs. Wallace said.

"I'm hot," whined June. "I want to go home."

"This is home," Mrs. Wallace said. She looked at her husband. "They did say there'd be a house for us."

"I'm here to take you there," Curran said. "I have arranged transport for you, and I'll make the arrangements to have your luggage sent up as soon as it is unloaded. Harriet, can you keep the Wallaces company, while I see to the luggage?"

He strode off, leaving Harriet alone with the Wallaces.

Mrs. Wallace fanned herself. "Is it always so hot?" she said.

"Always," Harriet said. "But you get used to it."

Sadie Wallace cast her husband a reproachful look. "I'll never get used to it."

"I'm bored," Gerald said.

This is going well, Harriet thought.

She indicated the now deserted marquee. "Was that Sir Henry Cunningham that disembarked first?"

Mrs. Wallace brightened. "It was. Fancy traveling with such an important person. I met them both a couple of times and they were so kind. He always had sweets in his pocket for the children, but of course, we weren't traveling first class, so we didn't mix. The poor man was not in the best of health. I heard the doctor was called to attend to him several times."

Harriet tutted appropriately.

Curran returned with a porter to collect the luggage the Wallaces had been travelling with and the party left the dock.

Mrs. Wallace took one look at the *gharry* and declared she was not traveling in 'that filthy contraption'.

"I'm afraid I can only take a couple of passengers in my vehicle," Curran said.

"Then the children and I will travel with you. Sid, you can go in the carriage with Mrs. Gordon."

Harriet shot Curran a mutinous glance, and he gave a barely perceptible shrug. At least the journey would not take long.

In the *gharry*, Wallace removed his bowler hat and wiped his brow.

"Have you lived here long, Mrs. Gordon?"

"Just over a year," Harriet said, "but I have lived in India for some years, so Singapore felt less strange to me."

"And you're a friend of Curran's?" Wallace asked, his eyes slightly narrowing.

"I did some secretarial work with the Detective Branch when they needed some extra help," Harriet said.

Wallace's lip curled back. "A woman?"

"Typing and paperwork," Harriet said.

"But you don't work there anymore?"

"No. I have a job with a girls' school."

"That's good. I don't hold with women working in the police force."

There was no answer to that, and they lapsed into an uncomfortable silence.

"I need to find a good school for the boy," Wallace said at last.

"I can recommend St. Thomas. My brother is the headmaster, and you should be able to employ the services of an *amah* for your daughter as she is so young. I'm sure your wife would find that a great help."

Wallace gave a snort of laughter. "I'm sure she will," he said.

"The house comes with a cook and a house servant, I believe," Harriet said.

"Does it now? Mrs. Wallace won't know herself."

The police house was a standard bungalow with a wide veranda, green awnings, and a view out over the old town to the Keppel Harbour. Curran had already arrived and was standing on the veranda talking to Mrs. Wallace.

She had a face like thunder, her lips drawn together in a rictus of fury. She turned to her husband the moment he set foot on the veranda.

"We can't be expected to live here."

Even Wallace looked surprised.

"Why ever not? Looks fine to me," he said.

"It's... it's..." she shuddered. "Not English," was the best she could come up with.

"Mrs. Wallace," Harriet said. "The English style of house is not suitable for this climate. You will find in a few days you will be living out here on this lovely veranda, which gets the sea breeze, and wondering how on earth you ever survived an English summer."

"I hate it. It smells," Gerald said.

Harriet cast a sympathetic glance at the two house servants who stood in the doorway watching the new English *mem* with apprehensive eyes.

Curran introduced the staff, and Mrs. Wallace seemed to relax a little.

"Servants?" she said.

"A cook and a houseboy. They come with the house but you can employ additional servants, such as an *amah* to help with the children," Curran said.

The anger faded from Sadie Wallace's face and she sniffed.

"I'm sure we'll get used to it, in time," she said.

Curran spun his hat between his hands. "We'll leave you to settle in," he said. "I'll see you in the morning, sir."

Harriet did not miss the barely perceptible pause between the words 'morning' and 'sir'.

As they drove away, Curran's hands tightened on the steering wheel, the knuckles showing white.

"I don't think I can do this, Harriet."

"What?"

"Work with Wallace again."

"You have to, Curran."

He glanced at her. "Perhaps for the moment, but it may be time to explore other postings... like East Africa. They are crying out for police in Nairobi."

Harriet stared at him. "You would leave Singapore?" *Without me?*

His eyes met hers.

"Not alone," he said.

She met his gaze. "What do you mean?"

He stopped the motor vehicle, pulling into the shade of a large rain tree. Harriet's heart skipped a beat, but he wasn't looking at her. He was staring out into the undergrowth.

"I don't know what I mean, Harriet." He reached for her hand. "I'm just restless. It's the story of my life."

He looked down at the hand he held—her left hand.

"You're not wearing your wedding ring."

"No. I thought it was time to start letting go. Have you let go of your past, Curran?"

"What do you mean?"

She swallowed. "I need to know if Li An—" She took a breath. "What you had with Li An was something I know we will never have, but it doesn't mean we can't build something stronger."

He sat back, a smile curving his lips.

"Harriet. Li An is married. Her trading companies in Penang are doing well. I said my farewells to her months ago with no regrets on either side. She is now my past, not my present, and certainly not my future." He turned to look at her, all the humor gone from his face. "You are my future, Harriet."

A wave of relief swept over her. "Thank you, Curran. I needed to hear that."

He glanced at his watch. "Right now, I need to return you home and I have work to do. Thank you for coming with me this morning. I think it made things much easier. I tell you what, shall we go to the moving pictures at the Alhambra? We can make a party of it with Julian and Esme and Maddocks and Doreen."

Harriet smiled. "That sounds like a good idea. Maybe next week, after the ball is over and life has settled down."

# NINE

**WEDNESDAY, 5 JULY**

Curran slept badly in the narrow, lumpy bed in his new quarters. In his nightmares, he was once again in the pitiless dark of the cavern beneath the Topaz Club with no hope of rescue and a long, lingering death ahead. He woke, lathered in sweat, in the dark hours of the morning, gasping for breath. When his heartbeat and breathing had returned to normal, he lay awake, staring up at the ceiling, his mind racing through this new world under Chief Inspector Wallace.

It would be so easy to leave and seek his fortune in another corner of the Empire, but for the first time in his life, he realized he had ties to a place he had never had before—Harriet and Samrita and true friends. Leaving would be hard. He would have to learn humility and go along with whatever Wallace had in mind for him.

He arrived early at the Detective Branch of the Straits Settlements Police. The Branch occupied the upper floor of a building at the rear of the main headquarters that fronted South Bridge Road. It consisted of a large, open area dominated by a long table used to display evidence. Several desks were arranged around the walls, and near the entrance was the glass-paneled office that had, until yesterday, been his office.

Someone had painted out his name and stenciled CHIEF INSPECTOR WALLACE onto the door in gold lettering. Curran found himself consigned to a desk in a corner of the outer office. He had always hated the paperwork that went with the command, but now, as he sat looking at the glass panels of his old office, he felt bereft.

His staff circled him, not meeting his eyes. Constable Greaves, being adept at crime scene photography and modern policing techniques such as fingerprinting, filled the role of the evidence officer. He occupied the far corner, where he'd set up a small dark room and a bench covered in scientific equipment of varying sorts. Nabeel, the administrative clerk, had the desk Harriet had used. He hunched over the heavy typewriter, ponderously hitting one key at a time. Constables Musa bin Osman and Tan Jian Ju, were pretending to write notes but kept looking up, casting him deeply concerned looks. Sergeant Gursharan Singh stood beside the table in the center of the room, where they had laid out the sparse evidence from the jewelry store robberies, apparently deep in thought.

But the truth was they were all tense, listening to the footsteps on the wooden staircase.

The door opened and Inspector General Cuscaden stood back to allow Sidney Wallace, in a stiff new uniform, to precede him. Singh called the men to attention, Constable Greaves's chair falling over with a clatter in his haste.

Curran rose more slowly and, with some reluctance, saluted.

"At ease, gentlemen," Cuscaden said. "I'd like to introduce you to your new Chief Inspector. Wallace comes highly commended from Scotland Yard and his arrival is the beginning of a major expansion to this department. We have two new inspectors arriving within the next few months, but in case there is any doubt, Inspector Curran will remain as second in command." His gaze scanned the men in the room. "I will leave you to get acquainted, Wallace."

As the door closed behind Cuscaden, Wallace straightened.

"Introduce me to the men, Curran."

Curran took him around the room, introducing each man and explaining their role in the detective branch, concluding, "And we have two men, currently in the field, working undercover. Constable Goh keeps an eye on the opium dens in Chinatown and Constable Gajendra is on site in Little India."

"Very good. Get on with your work, men. Curran, my office," Wallace said.

*My* office, Curran thought with a stab of resentment as he closed the door behind him.

Wallace took the seat behind the desk and leaned back, swiveling to look out over the courtyard as Curran laid the current files on the desk.

"Family settled in?" Curran enquired, sitting, although he hadn't requested permission to do so.

Wallace swiveled back. "Did I say you could sit?"

Curran returned the hostile gaze.

"This is not Scotland Yard, Wallace. I'm not prepared to play any little power games with you. I have to work with you, and I would rather we approach our working relationship with professional courtesy."

Wallace's lip drew back. "No, it's not Scotland Yard, but I'm not prepared to let standards slip just because we're in the tropics. In future, you do not sit until I say you can."

Curran took a breath, barely containing the rising explosion of anger and frustration. He remained sitting and leaned forward.

"Do you want a brief on our current workload or not?" he said.

Wallace narrowed his eyes. "Go on."

"Top of the list is a current spate of jewelry robberies around Serangoon Road—"

Curran took his time going through each file. To his credit, Wallace asked good questions.

"Now, which of these men is the interpreter?" Wallace asked, laying the last file on the pile.

"What do you mean?"

"I don't speak the bloody lingo, Curran, I need someone who can interpret for me. How about Singh?"

"He's a sergeant and a damn good policeman, not an interpreter," Curran said. "None of them are interpreters. I understand the language difficulty, but you'll need to learn at least Malay if you are going to get on. Most of the Chinese speak it. In the meantime, ask Cuscaden to provide you with a proper interpreter, all my men have policing to do."

Wallace's mustache twitched.

"On another subject—Sir Henry Cunningham," Wallace leaned forward, his elbows on the blotter. "He is here for the next week. I have his schedule. You are to go nowhere near him. Do I make myself clear, Curran?"

"I have no intention of going anywhere near him," Curran replied, stiffly. "No one in the Detective Branch should have any need of contact with him."

Wallace squared his shoulders. "As it happens, my wife and I have been invited to attend a ball at Government House on Friday night in honor of Sir Henry and to mark the recent coronation."

"I am sure your wife will have a most enjoyable evening," Curran said. "I, too, will be in attendance."

Wallace glared. "You? How did you get an invitation?"

Curran mentally counted to five. "I have recently been involved in an important and potentially damaging case that has saved the colonial administration a great deal of embarrassment." He paused. "And Sir John Anderson is rather fond of cricket."

Wallace sniffed, and he looked at a point beyond Curran's

shoulder as he said, "That's all very well, Curran, but I am instituting a proper roster, and you, I am afraid, will be the duty officer on Friday night."

A hundred retorts, none of them judicious, rushed into Curran's mind, but he kept his mouth closed.

"Very well," he said, rising to his feet. "If that is all, sir. I would like to return to Serangoon Road and I will take Sergeant Singh with me. I have only recently returned to Singapore myself and I have some catching up of my own to do."

Wallace waved him back into the chair and leaned forward.

"Curran, I'm not being vindictive. It's for your own good. You don't need to be anywhere near Sir Henry Cunningham."

It wasn't Sir Henry on Curran's mind, it was Harriet... He would have to tell her he would not be attending. He felt a little like Cinderella in a khaki uniform.

"Is there anything else?" he said between stiff lips.

Wallace waved a hand at the door. "Go."

With pleasure, Curran thought and restrained himself from slamming the door behind him.

# TEN

## THURSDAY, 6 JULY

Harriet did not work at the Ladies Academy on Thursdays, reserving the day to play a little tennis and catch up with some of the work that St. Tom's required of her. She sat at breakfast making a list of things she needed to do. The arrival of a chauffeur-driven motor vehicle interrupted her thoughts. A servant in the government house livery dismounted from the vehicle.

"I am ordered to await your reply," the man said and handed her an envelope.

She scanned the contents of the brief note, her surprise barely contained.

*My dear Mrs. Gordon. I hate to inconvenience you, but I can think of no one else who can assist. Sir Henry Cunningham has urgent correspondence to deal with and has requested the exclusive services of someone proficient in shorthand and typing. If you can spare the time, please attend at Government House at your earliest*

*convenience. I can assure you that your services will be remuner-
ated appropriately. Yours most sincerely, Mrs. G. Farrant.*

Harriet penned a hurried note for Julian and within fifteen minutes she was seated in the back seat of the motor vehicle, being driven through the magnificent wrought-iron gates of Government House. She had never been to Government House in the eighteen months she had lived in Singapore and her first sight of it as she rounded a bend in the carriageway took her breath away.

The British did like to stamp their authority on their colonies, she thought as she stepped out onto the graveled forecourt. The white wedding cake-like building soared above her, with arches on the upper-story veranda fitted with white plantation blinds. These blinds could be rearranged to catch the prevailing breeze and keep out the worst of the heat.

The governor's private secretary, an amiable Australian, Claud Severn, met her in the black and white marble-tiled hall. Claud, a bachelor, played tennis when his official duties allowed, and they were on a nodding acquaintance.

"So glad you were available, Mrs. Gordon. Of all the days for our typist to be off sick. Something is going around, I fear. Wait here and I will let Mrs. Farrant know you have arrived."

The sound of hurried footsteps coming down the stairs echoed around the enormous hallway. Always impeccable, Georgina Farrant's face was flushed, wisps of hair clinging to a damp forehead. She seized Harriet's hands between hers.

"Oh, I am so glad you could spare the time," she said. "Sir Henry is quite agitated and there is no one on the Government House staff to assist him. Our typist is indisposed, and no one takes shorthand."

Harriet smiled. "I am happy to help," she said.

"Come with me. The Cunninghams are taking tea with Papa in the drawing room. We have had the typewriter carried up to a room that can be used as an office."

Harriet held up the case containing her precious Corona Folding Typewriter, that she had collected at the last minute. "I brought my own, just in case."

Georgina shot her a grateful smile. "I knew you were just the ticket," she said. "This way."

Harriet followed the governor's daughter up the magnificent staircase to another airy hallway with high doors to the right and left. The door to the right was open and without hesitation, Georgina entered, gesturing for Harriet to follow. Two men and a woman were taking tea, served on a table between stiffly upholstered furniture in the style of Louis XIV.

Sir John Anderson, the Governor of the Straits Settlements, rose to his feet as the women entered. A tall, white-haired Scotsman with a neatly trimmed beard and mustache, he was a popular and hard-working man. He held out his hand.

"Mrs. Gordon, a pleasure to meet you," he said with his soft highland lilt. "Allow me to introduce Sir Henry Cunningham."

Up close, Sir Henry Cunningham was an unprepossessing man of slight build. He had combed long strands of hair over his receding hairline, and biscuit crumbs clung to his overlong mustache. A gray tinge to his complexion hinted at a man not in the best of health.

Harriet took his proffered hand. It felt like grasping sweaty dough. The touch was brief and unpleasant and she had to resist wiping her hand on her skirt.

"You are a lifesaver, Mrs. Gordon," he said. "Allow me to introduce my wife, Lady Evangeline Cunningham."

He turned to the woman who had remained seated, and Lady Cunningham inclined her immaculately coiffed head. In contrast to her husband, she looked calm and collected in a loose tea gown of pale muslin, exquisitely embroidered in a matching silk. She was not a classic beauty nor in the first flush of youth. Her hair was a rich golden blonde, tinged with silver threads. Her chin was a little too long and her nose slightly crooked, but she was possessed of excellent bone structure and clear hazel eyes that surveyed Harriet with a cool, appraising look. A woman of her class who knew her station in life.

A man in his late thirties stood behind the sofa, his hands behind his back, also waiting for an introduction. He had a trim figure in a well-cut linen suit, his dark hair combed back and his mustache neatly trimmed.

"Charles Gilmore," he said with a smile, extending his hand. "As Sir Henry said, you are a lifesaver."

"Charles is my private secretary," Sir Henry said. "He can walk you through our requirements. You'll be working with him today. I have to get this report done and on the ship tomorrow."

A private secretary who did not type or take shorthand, Harriet thought uncharitably as she followed Gilmore out of the room to the anteroom that had been set aside for her. It contained a table and chair and a comfortable lounge chair. They had set up a large typewriter, similar to the one she had used in the Detective Branch, on the table with a stack of fresh paper to one side.

"I am sure I do not need to tell you, Mrs. Gordon, that the work is highly confidential. Nothing you see or hear or produce is to leave this room," Gilmore said.

Harriet shot him a look with narrowed eyes. "Mr. Gilmore, you can trust me implicitly. I understand about government confidentiality. If you require me to swear an oath on the bible, I will do so willingly."

Gilmore smiled, revealing a row of neat white teeth. "I trust you, Mrs. Gordon. No need for swearing oaths. Now, how shall we proceed? I have Sir Henry's notes. Shall I dictate for you to take in shorthand? Then you can type the report up for Sir Henry to correct this evening."

The morning passed quickly. Gilmore sat in the one comfortable chair in the room and dictated a long and tedious report on the state of the economy in Ceylon. At one o'clock, a gong sounded, announcing lunch.

Coming from a comfortable middle-class family in Wimbledon, life in grand houses was not one with which Harriet was familiar, but she understood the hierarchy that existed below stairs and Government House was no exception. The English *majordomo*, Mr. McMullen, ran the household with clockwork efficiency, and at lunchtime, he directed Harriet to the senior staff quarters on the lower floor.

Charles Gilmore, she noted, retired to eat with his employer and host.

Everyone greeted her cordially. Sir John's Indian valet and the visitors' staff joined the senior staff in the small private dining room off the servant's hall. Sir Henry's valet introduced himself as Mr. Ellis and Lady Cunningham's maid, Miss Brown, a young woman in her late twenties greeted her with a smile. Ellis would have been well into his forties, a small, round man with very little hair and a soft face. Both visitors were wilting in the heat, dressed in inappropriate clothing, more suited for London than Singapore.

Lunch was a soup followed by a chicken stew with fresh fruit to finish. As they ate, Harriet asked the visitors if they had the opportunity to see anything of Singapore.

"I'm going to die," Miss Brown declared, fanning herself with a napkin. "The last thing I want to do is go outside into that heat. Her ladyship has had me ironing all morning. Everything has to be perfect for her. Not a crease. I don't know how you lot can live here."

"You get used to it," Harriet said.

"We've still got months of travel," Mr. Ellis joined in the complaints. "Hong Kong and then Australia next. Sir Henry's not well and this climate is not doing him any good."

They chatted about the Cunninghams' itinerary for a little while and somewhere in the house, a clock struck two. After a morning of taking dictation, Harriet now had the report to type, so she excused herself and returned to the little room.

Charles Gilmore rejoined her and resumed his seat, checking each page as it came off the typewriter. He was an exacting taskmaster and if she made a mistake, she had to retype the entire page.

By the end of the day, the report was done, and Harriet returned home exhausted, with the expectation that she would return the following morning to finalize the document. Harriet had no choice but to send a short apologetic note to Esme, requesting leave for the day on Friday, with the expectation of the evening to look forward to.

# ELEVEN

Harriet returned to Government House the following morning. The door to the room she had been using as an office stood open, and, lost in her own thoughts, she started at the sight of Sir Henry Cunningham seated in the chair Gilmore had used the day before, reading through the report. The pile of paper at his feet covered in red pencil annotations indicated Harriet had a long day ahead of her.

He looked up. "Good morning, Mrs. Gordon."

"Sir Henry."

Her gaze went to the corrected papers on the floor.

"Do you have a problem with the quality of my work?" Harriet asked.

"Your work is quite satisfactory," Sir Henry said. "The amendments are mine, not your errors." He dropped the last paper on the floor and stood up. "I will require the finished report by lunchtime no later. It has to be on a ship to London this evening."

As he passed her at the door, he turned to look at her. "I have asked about your background, Mrs. Gordon. Had I known I was employing a woman with a criminal record, I would have declined your services."

She returned his gaze without blinking. "And I would defy you to find anyone else in Singapore who could have met your exacting standards, Sir Henry."

His mustache twitched. "This suffragette nonsense is a distraction to good government, Mrs. Gordon."

"Then give women the vote and be done with it, Sir Henry."

To her surprise, he laughed. "That would be the simple answer, wouldn't it, Mrs. Gordon, but it will not happen in my lifetime."

Memories of the meetings of the WSPU, the endless petitions, the marches on Parliament, and the violence perpetrated in the name of this man's government, rose like gorge in Harriet's throat.

With a supreme effort, she choked back the emotional response. "Other countries have given women the vote," she said, her throat tightening on the words.

"True, but Britain did not get to be Great by pandering to the whims of hysterical females. My own office was vandalized by a group of harpies incited by that Pankhurst female. What did that achieve? Nothing. It just confirmed my views that women are not stable or sensible enough to have the responsibility of a vote."

So many things she could have said, but before Harriet could respond, Sir Henry raised a hand, indicating the discussion was over.

"I require the finished report by lunchtime. I will leave you to your work, Mrs. Gordon."

The conversation had been overheard by Charles Gilmore who had been waiting outside the room. He greeted Sir Henry as they passed.

"I am afraid Sir Henry has no sympathy with the suffrage movement," Gilmore said, shutting the door behind him.

"Evidently," Harriet agreed. "What about you, Mr. Gilmore?"

He shrugged. "It will come."

"But not in Sir Henry's lifetime?"

He studied her for a long moment. "Governments change, Mrs. Gordon. Don't give up hope."

She managed a tight smile. "Never."

Gilmore stooped and picked up the fallen papers, grimacing as he scanned them, putting them back in order.

"Sir Henry did not approve of either of our efforts," he said as he handed them to Harriet. "Shall we...?"

Harriet sat at the typewriter and drew a fresh sheet of paper from the pile beside her, rolling it into the machine.

"How long have you worked for him?" she asked as she straightened the paper.

"Two years," Gilmore said. "He may well be the next Prime Minister." He laid the amended papers on the table beside her. "Let's get on with it. If you have trouble with Sir Henry's writing, I shall interpret."

Harriet looked down at the first page with its multiple crossings out and scribbled addendums and began to replicate the previous day's work, pausing every so often to clarify something with Gilmore. They worked through luncheon, reliant on a plate of sandwiches and tea provided by the housekeeper to sustain them and the clock struck three before Harriet pulled the last paper from the typewriter and eased her aching back.

"Please tell me that is done," she said.

Gilmore nodded. "It is. I will take it to Sir Henry for his final approval, and then we can get it into the private mail bag. You have been a godsend, Mrs. Gordon, but I can't release you just yet. Do you mind waiting a little longer in case we need further amendments?"

"I need fresh air," Harriet said. "I'll take a stroll in the garden."

The magnificent gardens of Government House provided a

relief from the stuffy little room in which she had been closeted, and she breathed deeply as she strolled the graveled pathways. Her perambulations took her to a large, new building—more a pavilion— constructed behind and slightly to one side of Government House and linked by a covered walkway.

Harriet peeked inside an open door.

"Our new ballroom," said a voice behind her and she turned to see Catherine Perkins, Sir John's youngest daughter, her arms full of red, white, and blue bunting.

"It was only finished last year, and we've hardly used it," Catherine continued. "You're Harriet Gordon, aren't you? Georgie has mentioned you. We are looking forward to the Ladies Academy singing tonight. I do like to encourage girls, and Georgie and I nixed the idea of getting one of the boys' schools." She grinned. "We ladies must stick together."

"Indeed," Harriet agreed.

Georgina Farrant had never expressed an opinion on women's suffrage, and it was refreshing to hear that the sisters might harbor private support for the cause.

Catherine set the bunting on a table and looked around the large, empty space.

It's quite lovely, isn't it?"

It was a room designed for entertaining, with double doors opening onto wide paved terraces on two sides. At one end was a stage presided over by a bust of Queen Victoria and, at the other, the main doors and portico through which the guests would enter. A gallery, accessed by external stairs off the terraces at the front and back, ran around the upper floor with high arches at regular intervals which would afford a bird's-eye view of the main floor. When open, the shutters on the external arches would admit plenty of air.

The final touch was the life-sized marble statues of Greek goddesses in each corner of the room. Probably copies of famous originals and intended more for the garden than a ballroom, but they seemed to fit.

"It even has electric lighting." Catherine looked around the room. "I shall miss it,"

Harriet looked at her. "You're leaving?"

The governor's daughter smiled, a little sadly.

"The news will be public knowledge soon enough. Papa is being posted back to London."

"I am sorry to hear that. Your father is greatly loved and respected. Will you go too?"

Catherine shook her head. "No. Both Georgie and I are married now. We will stay with our husbands, of course. Since Mama died, we have been at Papa's side. I'm not sure what he will do without us, should he get another diplomatic posting." Laying a hand on the bunting, she smiled. "In the meantime, we have a ball tonight and a long list of things to do."

"And I have a report to finish."

Catherine leaned forward. "Is Sir Henry being beastly? Georgie let slip that you had been a suffragette, and I thought the man was going to have apoplexy. Fortunately, Papa reassured him you were trusted and valued by the police, and he calmed down."

"Thank you. It doesn't pay to get a future Prime Minister of England offside," Harriet said.

Catherine's tightened lips said everything.

# TWELVE

The new electric lighting illuminated Government House, spilling onto the carriageway as the residents of Singapore from all corners of society, dressed in their very finest, presented for the rare occasion of a Government House ball. The new ballroom stood with all the doors open, the light and the gentle refrain of the orchestra from within welcoming the guests.

Harriet and Julian had traveled with Euan and Louisa Mackenzie and their daughter, Heather, who was to sing in the choir. As she alighted from the Mackenzie family motor vehicle, Harriet fidgeted with her headdress, a single, gray ostrich feather to match her gray evening gown. The wretched thing drooped over her eyes and tickled her nose and her feet already hurt in the gray, leather kid leather evening shoes she had only worn on a few occasions since her arrival in Singapore. It would have been nice to treat herself to a new dress for the occasion, but money was tight, and after her recent acquisitions, she could hardly justify another new dress when the one she wore was not even eighteen months old and had, her sister Mary assured her, been the height of fashion in Belgravia.

"Let me fix that for you."

Louisa Mackenzie, cool and beautiful in pale green silk, artfully tweaked the errant feather so it no longer tormented the wearer.

"You look lovely, Harriet," Louisa said, and arm in arm they walked into the magnificent ballroom.

Georgina and Catherine had done a marvelous job with the decorations, placing enormous vases of greenery and orchids beside the goddesses, who were similarly draped in greenery. They had left Queen Victoria unadorned. She would not have been amused. However, an enormous easel covered in a red cloth had been placed on one side of the late Queen Emperor.

The two women greeted friends among them, the superintendent of the fire service, Monty Pett, was present in full dress uniform with his wife, Edie. The lawyer, Clive Strong, and his wife had brought along a young man Alice Strong introduced as her son, Oliver, who had just returned from schooling in England.

"He's going up to Oxford in September," the proud mother announced. "He intends to be a lawyer like his father."

Clive patted his son on the shoulder. "Strong & Strong," he said. "Great name for a law firm, don't you think?"

Harriet made all the proper responses, wishing the young man well, but she was happy to find a position with Louisa beside one of the open doors leading onto the front terrace. Euan and Julian abandoned them, one to fetch drinks and the other to find Esme Prynne.

Louisa flicked open her fan. "It's going to be hot with all these people," she said. "Is Curran coming tonight?"

"No," Harriet replied, unable to disguise the irritation in her tone. "He's on duty. Wallace's idea, no doubt."

She had received a brief note and an apology advising that he would not be in attendance. No explanation except to say he was 'on duty'. She forced herself to swallow her disappointment and was determined to have a wonderful night, with or without him.

Louisa cast her a knowing look. "I suppose he now has a Chief Inspector to answer to. What a bore. Is that the new man at the Detective Branch?"

Louisa jerked her fan toward Chief Inspector Wallace, looking hot and uncomfortable in full ceremonial uniform with his wife, wearing a bright pink ball gown, on his arm. She was looking around with large, bright eyes and seeing Harriet, smiled and waved.

Harriet gestured to her.

"Oh, thank heavens, a friendly face," Sadie Wallace said as she joined them, sending her husband on a mission to find a drink.

Harriet introduced Louisa.

"You must be the doctor's wife," Sadie said. "I was told Dr. Mackenzie was the man to see. Our eldest is not coping with the heat. He's come out in a heat rash all over. Is your husband here tonight?"

"Oh dear," Louisa murmured in faux sympathy. "Then you should definitely see my husband. His clinic will be open on Monday morning. In the meantime, I suggest frequent cold baths and a liberal use of calamine lotion."

"Apart from the heat rash, how are you settling in?" Harriet asked.

Sadie huffed out a breath. "I can't get the cook to understand that we want English food, not the muck he serves up. Too much spice for me. Disagrees something terrible." She frowned as her husband caught her eye, jerking his head to indicate that Sadie should rejoin him. "There's Sid. I better get back to him. So many new people to meet." She brightened. "Oh, and there's Sir Henry and Lady Cunningham. Doesn't she look a picture?"

Sadie Wallace hurried off to join her husband, who had wheedled his way to the front of the crowd that greeted the official party's entry from the house to the ballroom by way of the covered walkway, which was now illuminated with red, Chinese lanterns.

Sir John Anderson headed the party, with Lady Cunningham on his arm. Lady Cunningham wore the very latest London fashion, a rich pale blue satin gown, high-waisted with a lace over-gown and train and matching feathered headdress, the color perfectly enhancing her fair hair. Catherine Perkins followed on Sir Henry Cunningham's arm. Even from where she stood, Harriet could see perspiration glistening on the back of his neck and sliding down behind his high starched collar. His face looked puffy and gray.

And behind the official party came the rest of the Government House staff and guests, including the governor's private secretary, Claud Severn, who surveyed the room from behind his round tortoiseshell glasses, an anxious frown creasing his brow. Bringing up the rear, Charles Gilmore cut a fine figure in his evening dress. He ambled behind the others, his hands behind his back, his gaze scanning the crowd with a lazy smile on his face.

"Good evening, ladies."

Both women turned with a warm smile to welcome their friend, Griff Maddocks, a journalist on the *Straits Times*. He was accompanied by a young woman in an old-fashioned evening dress of green silk with large-puffed sleeves and a neckline that was too large for her slender frame, so she had to keep hoisting it up. Her red-gold hair had been inexpertly put up and already fell in locks around a pretty, freckled face. The girl wore wire-rimmed glasses that kept sliding down her nose.

"May I introduce Miss Sarah Bowman," Griff said, with little enthusiasm. "She's taking on the social columns."

"A female journalist?" Louise arched an eyebrow.

"I'm there on sufferance," Sarah said. "I haunted the editor until he agreed to give me a trial for three months covering the social rounds."

"No more lady's hats for you, Griff," Harriet said.

Maddocks had thoroughly disliked the social rounds, but now he looked more than a bit put out.

"We'll see. I'm here to show her the ropes," Maddocks muttered.

"Who's that good-looking chap talking to Mr. Severn," Louisa said, leaning into Harriet.

"That is Sir Henry's private secretary, Mr. Charles Gilmore," Harriet said.

"How do you know?" Maddocks said.

"I've been doing some work for Sir Henry over the last couple of days."

Griff brightened. "Have you indeed? Perhaps you could introduce us. I have some questions about the timing of Cunningham's visit and rumors that the governor is to be shipped back to London."

"It's a social occasion, Griff," Harriet said, rolling her eyes.

But Maddocks had turned back to his companion. "Now, Sarah, our readers will be anxious to know every detail of Lady Cunningham's dress and I somehow think 'pleasant shade of blue' may not be sufficient for the purposes."

Sarah shot him a sharp glance. "Blue moiré silk overlaid with cream Belgian lace."

She produced a small notebook from her reticule and started scribbling.

"She is a very handsome woman," Louisa said.

Lady Cunningham had taken her place on the official dais in front of the bust of Queen Victoria. Beside her, her husband seemed almost dwarfed by her presence.

"I hear Curran's back. Haven't had a chance for a beer with him yet. Is he coming tonight?" Maddocks enquired.

"No. He's on duty," Harriet said. "Oh, it looks like formalities are about to commence. The girls are just about to sing."

The girls from the school, immaculate in their school uniforms, shuffled into position to one side of the dais. Amelia Hardcastle took her place front and center. She was rather tall for her age and could easily be taken for a much older girl. She took a solo leading off with *God Save our Gracious King, Long Live our Noble King*, before the rest of the choir joined in the second line, in a very pretty harmony.

The music teacher conducted, and Esme stood with Mrs. Farrant to one side of the choir. Both were smiling with pride at the girls' performance. Julian, Harriet noted with a smile, hovered close at hand, his eyes only for Esme.

Everyone present stood rigidly to attention.

Once the choir finished, Sir Henry, his wife, and Gilmore made their way towards Esme and Mrs. Farrant. Harriet deduced from their animated gestures and smiles that Esme was introducing the choir to the guest of honor. Amelia stepped forward with a small posy of flowers for Lady Cunningham and from the fetching color that rose to the girl's cheeks, it seemed her performance had been noted and appreciated.

Griff leaned into Harriet. "So what is the gossip about the governor?"

Harriet hesitated. It would be public knowledge soon enough.

"He's been ordered back to London," Harriet said.

"Who will be the new governor?" Louisa asked.

"Probably Sir Henry Young. He's currently with the administration in KL so it makes sense," Maddocks said.

"If it means another ball..." Louisa said, swiping a glass of champagne from the tray of a passing waiter.

They joined Sarah Bowman, who stood at the back of the crowd, nursing a glass of flat, warm champagne

"How long have you been in Singapore, Miss Bowman?" Louisa asked.

"A month." The girl smiled. "I didn't know I would attend a ball. I had to borrow this dress from one of the girls at the hostel."

"It looks very nice," Harriet lied.

Sarah shrugged, but her concentration was elsewhere. "So that is Sir Henry Cunningham."

She made it sound like a statement, not a question, and Harriet looked at the girl curiously.

"It is. You've not come across him before?"

"Not in the flesh," Sarah said. "But I know all about him."

Before Harriet could probe any further, Samrita joined them. Harriet introduced the two women.

"That dress is lovely," Sarah Bowman said, her gaze fixed on Samrita's simple, unadorned evening dress of artfully draped, deep burgundy silk.

"Thank you. Louisa helped me choose it," Samrita said.

"And I have excellent taste," Louisa said. "You look lovely, my dear."

Oblivious to the envious glances of the women and the admiring glances of the men, Samrita's gaze swept the room.

"Looking for someone?" Louisa asked.

A flush rose to the young woman's cheeks.

"I am the guest of Thomas Barker," she said.

"Oh, the artist," Louisa said. "Isn't his portrait of Sir John going to be unveiled tonight?"

Samrita gestured at the easel on the dais.

"That's it. Oh, there he is... talking to Sir John."

Sir John Anderson stood beside the dais in conversation with a young man with thick, dark, shaggy hair and disheveled evening dress. Thomas Barker could only have been in his early to mid-thirties, his careless dress giving the impression of a young man with little regard or time for his appearance. Sir John was interrupted by Claud Severn. As they talked, Barker looked around with a frown, scanning the faces in the ballroom. Harriet had no doubt who he was searching for. When his gaze fell on Samrita, he smiled before returning his attention back to Sir John.

"Is he the one you've been taking art lessons from?" Harriet asked.

Samrita smiled. "It is. He is a wonderful teacher."

Harriet gave the younger woman an appraising glance. From

the sparkle in her eyes and the color on her cheekbones, it was possible that Mr. Barker meant more to her than just a teacher of art.

Sir John stepped onto the dais and a tinkling of glasses called the guests to silence. The moment had come for the unveiling of the portrait. Sir John spoke about how it had taken six months to paint the portrait and the countless sittings, ending with his delight in the final outcome, which he would donate to the custodians of Government House.

Lady Cunningham did the honors, tugging on a golden cord. The curtain fell away, and the audience gasped and then politely applauded. Sir John, in full ceremonial uniform, his high plumed hat on a table beside him, stood with one hand on a straight-backed chair and the other on his sword hilt. The work was skillful and accurate, bringing out the geniality and humanity of Sir John where others would have seen only the pompous formality of the position, not the man.

"Your Mr. Barker is very talented," Harriet said to Samrita, who nodded.

"Very. I shall introduce you."

The crowd began to disperse, drifting away to the cool of the garden and Barker pushed through the stragglers until he reached Samrita.

"You came," he said with eyes for no one else. "You look smashing, Samrita."

The color returned to Samrita's cheekbones.

"Let me introduce you to my friends, Mrs. Gordon, Mrs. Mackenzie, and Miss Bowman and Mr. Maddocks from the paper," she said.

Barker shook Maddocks' hand. "I hope you'll say nice things in the newspaper."

A muscle twitched in Maddock's temple.

"I only ever say nice things," he said.

Sarah Bowman brandished her notebook and pencil and

scribbled as Louisa asked how long the artist had been in Singapore.

"Just under a year. I wanted to explore a different environment for my painting and had decided on Australia. I found Singapore fascinating, so I decided to stay for a while and someone recommended me for this job. I was not going to say no to such a prestigious commission." He glanced back at the portrait. "An artist has to eat."

Now the formalities were done, the small orchestra struck up and couples moved onto the floor.

"May I have the pleasure of a dance, Mrs. Gordon?"

Harriet turned to see the Inspector General of the Straits Settlements Police standing behind her, one hand outstretched, the other behind his back.

"Of course," she stammered, allowing Cuscaden to lead her onto the floor.

"To what do I owe this honor?" Harriet asked as he whirled her away in a waltz.

"I am aware that Inspector Curran is on duty tonight." He paused. "I am also very well aware that something of an attachment has formed between you."

"Not much escapes you," Harriet remarked drily.

Cuscaden's mustache twitched in a rare smile. "I am a policeman, Mrs. Gordon."

He turned her so fast that her feet left the floor.

"Then I am sure you will understand when I say that your treatment of Curran has been shabby," Harriet said.

Cuscaden didn't reply for a long moment.

"Unfortunately, my hands were tied and for all the good work Curran has done, he is seen as being... unpredictable."

"That is exactly why he is so good at what he does."

"I agree, but not everyone does."

The spirited waltz drew to a close, and the Inspector General inclined his head. "Thank you for the dance, Mrs. Gordon. Enjoy the rest of your evening."

Maddocks claimed her for the next dance.

"How is Doreen?" Harriet asked, referring to Maddocks's usual social partner, Doreen Wilson, a nurse at the hospital.

Maddocks's mouth tightened. "She's taken a post in Hong Kong," he said. "Leaving in a couple of weeks."

"I'm sorry."

He gave a slight shrug of his shoulder. "It was nothing serious, but she was fun, and I'll miss her. I don't seem to have much luck in love."

The hairs on the back of Harriet's neck prickled, uncomfortably aware that Maddocks may have entertained feelings for herself at one time. She liked him and he was one of her dearest friends, but there was Curran, always had been Curran.

"Why don't you ask your Miss Bowman for a dance?" Harriet asked.

"Would that be appropriate? She is supposed to be working."

"Griff! She is a pretty young woman at a ball. Of course she wants to dance. Look at her."

Sarah Bowman stood against a wall, watching the dancers, her fingers tapping her empty glass and swaying slightly in time to the music.

Hot from the dance, Harriet and her friends took glasses of champagne and found some spare chairs against the wall. Harriet waved at the girls from the choir, who peered through the gaps in the balustrade surrounding the gallery above them, broad smiles on their faces as they whispered together and pointed. They were no doubt discussing in intricate detail which of the lovely evening dresses they favored.

Julian danced with Esme and Harriet felt a pang that was at once both joy that her brother had found love again and disappointment that she was alone tonight of all nights. They made a lovely couple, completely at ease with each other and she hoped

Julian would not wait too much longer before asking the question she knew Esme was waiting on.

Maddocks had taken Harriet's advice and asked Sarah Bowman for a dance. The lively polka had the desired effect, reducing the frosty atmosphere between the two journalists. Both were laughing and red-faced from exertion.

Esme and Julian left the floor and joined the two women. Esme collapsed onto a spare chair, fanned herself, and checked her watch.

"Ten minutes to round up the girls for their moment," she said.

She stood up, smoothing down her skirt, a dusty pink silk that looked, to Harriet's eye, new. Before she could move, a couple approached her.

"Miss Prynne?" The woman asked, her voice a little tight. "I'm Ellen Hardcastle and this is my husband, George. We just wanted to thank you for your work with Amelia. We know she's not exactly an easy child."

Esme smiled. "Amelia is a delight," she said. "Particularly when she is doing something she loves doing. Like singing."

"I know now's not the time, but we've decided that when young Bertram goes to England this summer to start at his new school, we're sending Melly along too. My sister has recommended a good finishing school and hopefully that will knock a little sense into her starry eyes," Mr. Hardcastle said.

"We will miss her," Esme said. "The school will be very quiet without her singing. Now, if you'll excuse me, it's almost time for our showcase. I really must get the choir together."

"We've told Melly she can stay on a little longer. There's going to be fireworks at ten and she'll love to see them. We'll send her home after that," Mrs. Hardcastle said.

The Hardcastles drifted away, and Harriet retrieved the music from the ladies' cloakroom where she had left it. Fighting back performance nerves, she took a seat at the grand piano and arranged the music in front of her. She had played it so often, but now the notes seemed to blur before her eyes.

The choir shuffled into place. Amelia took center stage again, looking calm and cool as she surveyed her audience. Beside her, Louisa's daughter, Heather, looked rumpled and hot. Rather oddly, Amelia had pinned a pretty lace edged handkerchief with what looked to have an embroidered initial in one corner, to her plain school blouse. A small act of rebellion against the severity of the school uniform?

Miss Brown picked up her baton and nodded to Harriet, who took a breath and started to play. Amelia took the solos, and the girls performed a delightful medley of old English folk tunes to much applause from the audience. Sir John Anderson took to the dais to thank the girls and Esme, and the choir dispersed. Out of the corner of her eye, Harriet noticed Sir Henry leaving the ballroom accompanied by Charles Gilmore.

Louisa had gone in search of her daughter, and it was some time before she rejoined Harriet.

"She's in the motor vehicle on her way home. I found her lurking around the back of the building. Wouldn't tell me what she was doing there," she said. "I got an argument from Heather about staying to watch the fireworks because Amelia's parents have given their daughter permission to stay. Between us, Harriet, I will not be sorry to see Amelia leave for England. Heather worships that girl and darling Melly is not always a good influence."

"Where is Amelia?" Harriet asked.

"Who knows? That girl is like dealing with mercury. Let's get some supper. I'm famished."

The orchestra had changed to a soft accompaniment as the crowd milled around the two long tables groaning with food, that had been set up at the far end of the room.

"The girls did so well," Louisa said as Esme joined them.

"Now I can relax," Esme said as Julian appeared at her elbow with a plate of food and a fresh glass of champagne.

They sat together eating and chatting and had just set down their empty plates when a sudden sharp bang made Harriet start, nearly spilling the contents of her glass onto the floor.

"The fireworks!" Louisa said.

The assembled guests hurried out onto the wide front terrace overlooking the gardens, where a truly impressive fireworks display entertained them for the next ten minutes. Even the servants appeared in the shadows, watching the display with rapt faces. It concluded with spontaneous applause.

Within the ballroom, the orchestra had commenced dancing music again, and couples drifted onto the floor for another waltz.

Charles Gilmore appeared at Harriet's elbow.

"My apologies, Mrs. Gordon, I have just been seeing Sir Henry back to his quarters. I hope I might have the pleasure of this dance?" he said with a slight bow.

Harriet allowed herself to be led onto the floor and, as she might have predicted, Gilmore was an elegant and proficient dance partner. He led her with skill and precision.

"Is Sir Henry unwell?" Harriet ventured.

Gilmore frowned. "He's not in the best of health at the moment and thought an early night might set him up for a busy couple of days."

"What ails him?" Harriet asked.

A slow smile spread across Gilmore's face. "That is a somewhat impertinent question, Mrs. Gordon."

Harriet bit her lip. "It was, and it is none of my business," she said. "My brother says curiosity is my greatest fault."

"Your brother?"

Harriet indicated Julian and Esme, who were dancing nearby.

"I take it from the dog collar that your brother is a priest?"

"Church of England," Harriet said. "Headmaster of St. Thomas."

"And you are connected with the school that sang tonight?"

"Yes. I do some administration and a little teaching," Harriet said.

"And play the piano."

"Not well!" Harriet laughed.

As the dance ended, Gilmore said, a frown creasing his forehead. "To answer your question. We don't know what ails Sir Henry. Even the best doctors in Harley Street can't find an answer."

"Lady Cunningham doesn't look too concerned," Harriet said with a glance at Lady Cunningham, who held court in a corner of the ballroom.

"Lady Cunningham hides her worry well. Sir Henry was insistent she stayed on to enjoy the evening." Gilmore brought his heels together and inclined his head. "Thank you for the dance, Mrs. Gordon."

Harriet rejoined Esme, and they stood watching the next dance. Samrita was dancing with Barker. Surprisingly, the young artist proved a proficient dancer, and they made a lovely couple.

"Miss Prynne!"

Both women looked around to see Ellen Hardcastle hurrying toward them.

"So sorry to bother you, Miss Prynne, but we can't find Amelia," she said. "She's not where I told her to wait. Have you seen her?"

Both Harriet and Esme shook their heads.

"Have you checked the restrooms?" Harriet suggested.

"Yes. I've even had a discreet look around the main house. George is out in the garden now. No sign of her." She frowned and bit her lip. "She'll be in such trouble when we catch up with her."

"I'll help you look. She can't have gone far," Esme said, gathering her skirts.

Ellen gave a small dismissive gesture with her hand. "No, I

don't want to bother you. I'll go and find George. I saw him in the front garden."

The woman left them, and Harriet was considering a second helping of cake from the remnants on the supper table when a high-pitched shriek followed by the tinkle of shattered glass cut through the room, silencing the happy chatter in an instant.

The scream broke across the music, the dancing couples pausing to look around for the source of the disturbance. The band stopped playing, a solitary violin trailing away in the silent room as time stood still.

# THIRTEEN

Almost as one, the crowd surged to the doors on the far side of the room.

Esme grasped Harriet's hand and the two women exchanged glances, the feeling of foreboding rising between them as they pushed their way through the murmuring crowd. The scream had come from one of the household servants who stood beside the door, a tray of broken glasses at his feet. A supervisor came forward and hustled the shaken man away.

At first, Harriet could make no sense of the crumpled form that lay on the terrace, just beyond the lights streaming out from the ballroom. A woman, wearing an evening dress of amethyst color, lay face down on the paving stones. A thick dark stain pooled around her head, through which the tresses of long, unbound hair trailed.

Chief Inspector Wallace pushed his way forward. "Straits Settlements Police. Everyone stay back."

Inspector General Cuscaden followed Wallace and the two men knelt by the figure on the ground and exchanged glances.

Cuscaden moved first. "It appears to be an unfortunate accident. Please return to the ballroom, ladies and gentlemen. However, I would ask if Doctor Mackenzie could join us."

No one moved. Wallace stood up and straightened, puffing out his chest.

"Please return to the ballroom," he repeated in a tone that carried long-practised authority. "Sir John," he addressed the governor, who stood with an arm around his youngest daughter. "Please, can you assist by having these doors shut?"

The crowd turned back to the ballroom, murmuring among themselves. Sir John issued curt orders to the servants as he followed the crowd back inside and the doors shut behind them.

Esme, Harriet and Julian did not move, and they were joined by Charles Gilmore. Behind them, servants closed the shutters, leaving barely enough light to illuminate the grim scene. Harriet could hear Sir John addressing his guests, offering his apology for having to cut the evening short, but he would have to ask everyone to leave.

Wallace scowled at the knot of people who remained.

"Please return to the ballroom."

"I am the Reverend Edwards," Julian said.

"And I am Miss Prynne. I am the headmistress of the Singapore Ladies Academy. I... I think this girl might be one of my pupils."

"What makes you think that?"

Esme gave a choked sob and pointed at the body.

"Her shoe—"

Harriet put an arm around her friend and forced herself to look again. Beneath the ripples of amethyst-colored fabric, one small foot could be seen. The sensible laced shoe was not an evening slipper but regulation school footwear.

Cuscaden looked up to the open windows of the gallery above them.

"Could I be right in thinking she fell from up there?"

Wallace cleared his throat but whatever he might have been

about to remark, he was interrupted by the arrival of Claud Severn.

"Sir John has called an end to the evening and told everyone to go home. What's happened, Cuscaden?" Severn demanded.

Harriet held her breath, expecting the two policemen to prevent the rapid exit of possible witnesses, which is what Curran would have done, but neither of them said anything.

"An accident," Cuscaden replied.

Severn's lips tightened, and he cast a glance at the crumpled body. His face remained a professional mask, but he reached into a pocket and pulled out a snowy white handkerchief which he dabbed to his mouth.

"Is she dead?" he asked.

Cuscaden nodded. "I fear so. Ah, Doctor Mackenzie."

Mac had followed Severn and now knelt by the crumpled figure. He felt for a pulse and shook his head before gently turning her over. Everyone present held their breath, fearing what they would see. Esme buried her face in Julian's shoulder, and he put an arm around her.

Mac huffed out an audible breath as he sat back on his heels.

"I know this girl," he said.

Her voice muffled by Julian's jacket, Esme asked, "Is it Amelia?"

"Aye, I believe it is." Mac looked up at the windows above them. "Did she fall from there?"

"We think so," Cuscaden replied.

Esme clutched Harriet's hand. "Her parents. They're looking for her."

"I'll find them," Gilmore said. "Something useful I could be doing."

Esme straightened and took a step toward Wallace. "Let me see her?"

"Please Miss Prynne, stay back. It's no sight for a lady," Wallace said.

"I am made of sterner stuff than you think, Chief Inspector."

"Let them through," Mac said.

Sandwiched between Harriet and Julian, Esme stepped forward, stopping just short of the body. Her fingers tightened on Harriet's arm. It was not a sight for the faint-hearted. The girl's face and head had suffered severe damage, with blood congealing around her nose and ears. Despite that, there could be no doubt as to the girl's identity.

"That is my missing schoolgirl, Amelia Hardcastle." Esme's voice had fallen to a whisper.

They all looked around as a shriek cut through the silence and Ellen Hardcastle came running around the corner from the front of the building, her skirts bunched in her hand. Her husband and Gilmore came running after her. Gilmore caught her before she reached the body and she fought against him.

"Is it... is it, Amelia?" Hardcastle asked, his low, controlled voice a contrast to his wife's tears. "We were searching the front gardens when someone said..." He trailed off.

Ellen stopped fighting, her knees sagging as she dissolved in grief. Gilmore relinquished her to her husband as Esme, her head held high, walked over to the distressed couple.

"It is Amelia. It looks like she fell from the window above us. I suggest you come with me, Mrs Hardcastle," Esme said. "There is nothing you can do for her."

"But I want to see her."

Esme exchanged a glance with George Hardcastle and gave a shake of her head.

"Later, dearest." He looked around the assembled group. "An accident?"

Cuscaden answered. "Too early to tell, Mr. Hardcastle. We will have to do a thorough investigation—"

"What on earth is she wearing?" Ellen Hardcastle strained against her husband's restraining arm, peering into the gloom at the body of her daughter. "Where's her school uniform? What's happened to her—"

"Come away, dearest," her husband said. "As Miss Prynne said, there's nothing we can do."

Julian joined the couple. "I'll take you home."

"I'll come with you," Esme said.

"Harriet?" Julian asked.

Harriet addressed Cuscaden. "I would like to stay with her, please. She needs a friend."

Wallace gave her a skeptical glance. "She's dead, Mrs. Gordon."

"She is a child," Harriet responded. "She should not be alone."

"As you wish," Cuscaden said. "Just don't get in the way."

As the Hardcastles left, Cuscaden, Wallace, Mac, and Claud Severn stood in a circle around the broken body. A servant passed a tablecloth through the door and scuttled away. Mac gently laid it over the girl, giving Amelia the anonymity and dignity she deserved.

Harriet remained in the shadows beside Charles Gilmore, grateful for his silent company. For all her precociousness, Amelia Hardcastle had been a child and she prayed that her death had been swift.

"Cause of death?" Wallace asked Mac.

"She has a broken neck and severe head injuries. It's my opinion that she fell headfirst but I will need to confirm that with an autopsy," Mac said.

Every gaze moved to the open window above them.

"Inspector—" Harriet ventured.

"Chief Inspector," Wallace corrected.

"This does not look like an accident—"

"Mrs. Gordon, are you a police officer?"

"No, but—"

"Please keep your own counsel."

"Why is she dressed like that?" Harriet persisted.

"What do you mean?" Wallace responded.

"She was wearing her school uniform when the girls performed earlier this evening."

"Mrs. Gordon is correct," Mac said. "This is not what the girl was wearing an hour ago, and I can see no reason a young girl would fall from a window such as this. Also, to fall headfirst is unusual. I suggest you—"

"Doctor. Please confine yourself to your role," Wallace snapped. He turned to Claud Severn. "Sir. This unfortunate accident does seem to warrant further investigation. May I have the use of a telephone and I shall summon my officers?"

"And I need the mortuary cart," Mac said. He looked up at the dark sky. "I think it might rain and I want her under cover before that happens."

"You can use the telephone in my office," Severn said.

"I better speak with Sir John," Cuscaden said. "The Cunninghams will need to be informed of this unfortunate... accident." He fixed Harriet with a hard glare. "We shall deem it an accident until such time as we have evidence to the contrary."

One by one, they dispersed, leaving Mac and Harriet alone with the dead girl. Mac stood with his hands in his pockets, looking up at the window. Harriet followed his gaze.

"What makes you think she fell headfirst?" Harriet asked.

Mac grunted. "That window is what, twenty feet from the ground? Most people who jump do so feet first. I would expect broken legs and pelvis and, in some cases, the possibility of survival." He frowned. "That's not how her injuries are presenting. She has serious head wounds, indicating she fell headfirst."

They lapsed into silence. Mac lit a cigarette and Harriet subsided onto a bench, her head in her hands. How did a fifteen-year-old girl come to fall headfirst from a window?

"Harriet?"

Harriet looked up to see Maddocks coming toward her across the garden. He stopped short of the shrouded body.

"Good God, it's true." Maddocks gestured at the shrouded body. "Who...?"

"Amelia Hardcastle, one of the girls from Esme's school. You shouldn't be here," Harriet said.

"Harriet, this is a story," Maddocks said. "A real story. And what are you doing here?"

That was a good question and not one Harriet could answer. She had less right to be there than Griff Maddocks.

Maddocks met her gaze. "How did it happen?"

"She fell from that window," Harriet said, pointing up at the windows above them. "Or was thrown."

"Harriet," growled Mac. "Don't speculate."

"But it's true, and while we're standing out here, evidence is disappearing. It could be an hour before Curran gets here and I have no faith in Wallace, or even Cuscaden, to secure the scene of the crime," Harriet said.

"If there was a crime," Mac put in.

"Even so... where is her school uniform? Why is she wearing a party dress?" Harriet stood up and straightened the feather that had drooped in her eyes again. "Euan, someone has to check the window she fell from. Can you stay here with Amelia? I'm going up to that gallery."

"Not without me," Maddocks said.

# FOURTEEN

"Harriet—"

Maddocks broke into a trot to catch up with Harriet as she hurried toward the staircase leading up to the gallery.

The walls of the building enclosed the gallery itself, but it had two identical external staircases for access. One staircase was on the main house side of the terrace, and the other was at the back near where Amelia's body had been found. Anyone could access the gallery without being seen from within the ballroom.

No light shone in the stairwell and hampered by her evening dress and shoes, Harriet had to take them carefully. The door at the top stood open, and she paused on the gallery to see what was happening beneath them.

The governor stood at the far end of the room, with his daughters and their husbands, farewelling the last departing guests. The band was packing up their instruments and Government House staff were already busy clearing away the discarded glasses and supper plates. Cuscaden and Wallace were deep in conversation at one of the doorways leading out onto the main terrace. Of Severn and Gilmore, there was no sight.

Any light on the gallery came from the chandeliers that hung along the ballroom's center ridge, which meant that the gallery with its heavy arches and balustrades was well-shadowed. Harriet glanced up and down the length of the gallery and across to the other side. Nothing or no one moved. They were alone.

"Why are we here?" Maddocks whispered.

"Because any evidence will likely be cleared up before Curran gets here."

"What are we looking for?"

"Her school uniform and... I don't know... anything that strikes you as being out of place. You take that side of the gallery. I'll take this."

She began at the window through which Amelia had fallen. Like all the windows in a building of this importance, it was sizeable and contained no glass, just a pair of white-painted adjustable shutters, which fastened in the middle. All the shutters had been thrown wide open, presumably to facilitate as much air circulation as possible.

Without touching anything, Harriet leaned out of the window. The sill came to her waist. Amelia would have been a little shorter, making it hard to accidentally tumble out of the window. She would have had to be leaning right out, and why would she have been doing that?

A far more disturbing image came to mind of a shadowy figure upending the helpless girl headfirst onto the paving below.

Why assume she was helpless? Surely, she would have had to be immobilized to have fallen without a struggle or crying out, but if she had died during the fireworks display, there would have been no one to hear and no one to see Amelia's last moments. If it had happened later, after the dancing had recommenced, someone would have heard something, even the thud of a body hitting the ground.

Harriet shivered, straightened, and turned her attention to the window surrounds. In the gloom, it was impossible to see if there were any marks or anything that could tell the story of Amelia's last fight for her life, so she pulled back from the window and made her way along the gallery. For symmetry, the architect had included two rooms off the gallery that exactly matched the two staircases. Downstairs, these spaces served as the restrooms - one for ladies and one for gentlemen.

She stood outside the closed door to the room on her side and waited for Maddocks to join her.

"Nothing," he whispered and gestured at the door. "This space on the other side is open and has some chairs and low tables. The area over the portico is bare. What's in here?"

"I haven't looked."

Catching the material of her dress in her hand, Harriet opened the door. The exact purpose of the room they entered was a little uncertain. To begin with, it was in total darkness with the shutters across the window pulled shut.

"Do you have a light?" she asked Maddocks.

"I rarely carry torches in my evening wear." Maddocks sounded terse. "If we close the door, we should be able to switch on the light without it being seen from downstairs."

They did this and found the cord for the light switch. Blinking in the sudden glare of electric light, they looked around. The room appeared to be arranged as a private dining room with a round table with four chairs in the center. There was a side table on one side of the room and a velvet upholstered daybed on the other. A full-size white marble statue of Diana and her hunting hound, similar to the statues downstairs, stood to one side of the door, and Leda and her swan to the other. An empty bottle of champagne lay on its side on the table beside a single champagne glass. One chair lay on the floor as if it had been tipped backward.

Harriet took a step and her foot crunched on broken glass. Maddocks crouched down for a closer inspection.

"Looks like a champagne glass," he said.

"Don't touch anything," Harriet warned. "There may be fingerprints."

Maddocks straightened. "Either someone left in a hurry or there was a struggle in here," he said.

"I agree," Harriet said. "This feels wrong. I wish Curran was here."

"What's behind those curtains?" Maddocks gestured at the heavy red velvet drapes pulled across the full width of the far end of the room.

Harriet skirted the fallen chair and slipped behind the curtains. It appeared to be a serving area with a sideboard and, set into the wall, what looked to be a cupboard. Harriet recognized it as a 'dumb waiter' of the sort used to lift dishes from the kitchen to the dining room in her parents' home.

"Do you have a handkerchief?" she asked Maddocks.

"It's clean," Maddocks said, handing over a neatly folded red-spotted kerchief.

Using it to cover her fingers, Harriet opened the door of the dumb waiter. The space only contained the ropes used for lifting the cabinet. The cabinet itself was below them. No doubt ready to be loaded with whatever was required for a private dinner.

Harriet hauled on the rope, and the cabinet moved easily, gliding into position with a gentle shudder. It revealed a dark, empty space divided by a single shelf. Harriet reached into the maw and carefully felt around. Quite what she expected to find, she had no idea. Her fingers touched cloth, and she caught her breath. Ignoring her own directive about touching evidence she leaned in and pulled out a navy-blue *grosgrain* ribbon.

She turned it over in her hands, and an overwhelming sadness swept over her. She turned to Maddocks.

"Amelia's hair ribbon," she said.

Maddocks frowned. "She was in the dumb waiter?"

Harriet shrugged. "I doubt it. No person, even a child, could fit in there, but maybe her clothes were."

"Hadn't you better put it back? Chain of evidence and all that?"

Harriet shook her head. "No. I think we'll hold on to this. Put it in your pocket, Maddocks. This dratted dress doesn't have pockets."

They started at the sound of the door opening and came out from behind the curtains.

One of the uniformed household staff stood in the doorway. His eyes widened at the sight of the two guests apparently consorting behind the curtain.

"Beg pardon, mem, tuan, I have come to clean the room."

"Touch nothing," Harriet said. "The police will want to see this room exactly as it is."

"The police?" The man's eyes widened even further.

"Yes. A girl has died tonight, and this room is important. No one is to touch it. Do you have a key?"

"No, mem. I will be in trouble if this room is not cleaned."

The servant shuffled his feet and glanced back into the gallery.

"No, you won't," Harriet said. She refrained from adding that he would be in more trouble if the room was cleaned.

"What's going on in here?"

Both Harriet and Maddocks stiffened and looked at each other. The servant scuttled away from the doorway to be replaced by Sidney Wallace. He stood with his hands on his hips, his face scarlet with mounting anger, looking from one to the other.

"Who are you?" he demanded of Maddocks.

"Maddocks of the *Straits Times*," Maddocks replied.

"I might have known we would have bloody reporters snooping around. Out of here, both of you."

"But..." Harriet protested.

"Out!"

Harriet suspected he would have thrown them both out bodily, so like a pair of scolded school children they trooped past him onto the gallery. The servant had disappeared.

Wallace slammed the door shut behind him.

Harriet turned to face the policeman. "I suggest you order the room to be locked, Chief Inspector. One of the staff has already tried to clean it and there is evidence—"

"I won't be told my job by a jumped-up clerk and a newspaper reporter. I have told you to leave. Kindly do so before I throw you both in the cells for the night for obstructing an investigation."

Harriet opened her mouth, intending to do exactly what Wallace didn't want... teach him his job.

Maddocks touched Harriet's arm, diffusing her indignation. "I have my motor vehicle, Mrs. Gordon. I will give you a ride to your home."

Harriet sniffed and, with her head held high, stalked off.

In the motor vehicle, Maddocks pulled the ribbon from his pocket and handed it to Harriet.

"Here, you better take custody of this," he said.

Harriet looked at the pathetic piece of fabric in her hand and tears pricked the back of her eyes.

"Poor child," she said. "Who did this, Maddocks?"

He turned to look at her. "That is Curran's job, not yours, Harriet."

# FIFTEEN

Curran had occupied his evening of being 'on duty' by taking a patrol out to Serangoon Road. A visible police presence on the streets, he hoped, would deter the jewelry store bandits. Being in Little India had the added advantage of a good meal with Sergeant Singh and his family.

Singh's wife, Sumeet Kaur, was an excellent cook. Being in the company of Singh's family was always a pleasant diversion. Singh had a son and two daughters. Hardit, at seventeen, stood on the cusp of manhood and a certain tension was playing out between father and son, as Hardit had expressed a desire to go to India and join the army. Of the girls, the studious and intelligent Jasmeen was now fifteen, and the precocious Sarna, aged eleven, was the apple of her parents' eye.

Back on the street, Singh stomped along in brooding silence.

"I do not understand the boy," he said at last. "I... his grandfather and even his great grandfather, have served loyally in the police force. We have put food on the table and enabled our children to go to school. Maybe it is a surfeit of education that has turned my son into a revolutionary. He talks of freeing India from the British."

"Joining the army hardly makes him a revolutionary," Curran said. "He is a man now, and he is seeing the world through different eyes from you. Forcing him to do something he has no appetite for will only breed more resentment."

"Bah!" Singh responded.

"Inspector Curran!"

A young constable from the local police post came running down the street toward them. "Inspector Curran, the Chief Inspector is looking for you."

"You found me. What is it?"

The constable handed over a folded paper. Curran read the short order.

> Unfortunate accident at Government House. Please report with full Detective Branch immediately. Wallace.

"What sort of accident requires the attendance of the whole branch?" Singh wondered aloud as he scanned the note.

"I don't know. I'll go now. You need to rustle up Greaves, Tan and Musa and meet me up there."

Singh nodded. "You better go with the wings at your heels, Curran. The Chief Inspector will not be pleased you have been so hard to reach."

Curran grimaced. "I expect the Chief Inspector will not be pleased, whatever the circumstances."

---

Curran was correct in that assumption.

"Where have you been?" Wallace demanded the moment Curran appeared at the main door to the Government House ballroom. "Drinking beer with your feet up, no doubt?"

Stung into a response, Curran straightened. "I have been on

duty, leading a patrol in Little India... sir. What do you need me for?"

The color in Wallace's face dissipated. "A young girl fell from a window. She's dead—broken neck."

"Accident?"

Wallace frowned. "Not sure. An autopsy will tell us. Tread carefully, Curran. There are high-ranking sensibilities involved."

"You mean Cunningham?"

Wallace's eyes flashed. "Of course I mean Cunningham. He is a guest at Government House and I do not want him bothered. I have no reason to suspect he had any involvement with this girl beyond a few polite remarks about her singing. Do I make myself clear? This is nothing to do with him."

We'll see about that, Curran thought as he followed his superior through the magnificent ballroom and out onto the terrace at the back of the building.

Mac stood in the shelter of the stairwell, smoking a cigarette.

"Hurry up, Curran. I need to get her out of here before it rains."

As if in response to his statement, a distant flash of light and rumble of thunder presaged a storm.

The once pristine white tablecloth that covered the body was now stained in places where it had come in contact with the injuries. Curran asked for extra light, and a couple of lanterns were produced. They were not much help, but better than the thin light coming from the ballroom.

He hunched down and lifted the tablecloth away from the body.

The girl wore an evening dress of some sort of purply color, low cut with big puffy sleeves and beads and lace around the bodice, and a lacy overskirt of the same color. Curran was not an expert in women's clothing, but even he could see that the bodice had been cut for a lady with a much larger bust. A plain cotton chemise with lace edging was visible above the bodice line.

"Who is she?" he asked.

"Amelia Hardcastle. One of the girls from the Ladies Academy who sang here tonight," Wallace said.

Amelia Hardcastle stared up at him from a face that was a mask of blood, and he drew a deep breath. He leaned over and closed her eyes. Mac moved to stand behind him.

"Thank you for doing that, Curran," Mac said. "I didn't want to interfere."

"How old was she?"

"Turns sixteen next month," Mac said.

Curran turned to look up at Mac. "Is she George Hardcastle's daughter?"

Mac gave a quick nod of affirmation. "You know him?"

"He plays the occasional game of cricket for the Singapore Cricket Club when he's in town." He forced his gaze back to the dead girl. "Wallace said she broke her neck. Is that your conclusion, Mac?"

Mac shrugged. "She has a broken neck, and at this stage, we can safely assume she plunged headfirst from that window." Mac turned to point out the particular window. "Someone's closed it now but second from that wall. I can tell you more tomorrow. Now, can I move her?"

Curran stood up, nodding to Singh and Constable Greaves, who had appeared in the doorway.

"She can be moved after Greaves has taken some photographic images," Curran said.

Mac grunted and subsided onto the lower steps of the gallery stairs and lit a cigarette as Constable Greaves set up his camera, moving the lanterns to get better light. A flash of lightning and a roll of thunder presaged the approaching storm.

"What time did she die?" Curran addressed Wallace and Mac.

"Of that, we can be fairly sure," Wallace said. "She was discovered by one of the servants, about ten twenty. She was last seen by her parents at nine-thirty. So somewhere in that hour."

"Who discovered the body?"

"One of the staff. There were fireworks at ten. Everyone was at the front of the building," Wallace said. "The dancing had just recommenced, and he stepped out here to see if any dirty glasses or plates had been left out and saw the body."

Curran put his hands on his hips and surveyed the area. The working areas of Government House were only a hundred yards away. Surely there would have been a trail of servants moving between the house and the ballroom. Someone must have seen something.

He left Greaves and Mac to their work and re-entered the empty ballroom. It looked as if the room had been cleaned and tidied in the time it had taken for him to reach Government House. He bit back his annoyance.

"Where are the witnesses?" he asked Wallace.

"Witnesses?"

"The couple of hundred people who attended the ball."

"Sir John sent them home and he and his guests have retired to bed."

"And you permitted the premises to be cleaned?"

Wallace scowled. "This is Government House, Curran, not a sordid little dive in the West End."

Before Curran could respond, Cuscaden, resplendent in his evening dress, strode over to join them, accompanied by Claud Severn. Severn was another man Curran knew from the cricket club. The cheerful Australian was a solid middle-order batsman.

"Curran, as you are here, I will leave you to it," Cuscaden said. "If you need anything, Severn here is your man."

Curran thanked the Inspector General, and Cuscaden strode off, tugging at his slightly tight jacket as he went.

"What do you need, Curran?" Severn said.

He needed witnesses and an undisturbed crime scene, but he had neither.

He looked at Wallace.

"If Greaves has finished with the girl, she can go with the mortuary attendants," Curran said.

"Are you ordering me?" Wallace said.

Curran drew a breath. "No, sir. I am asking. Please, could you deal with Greaves and the mortuary attendants while I inspect the place from where she fell?"

Wallace scowled. "I caught that friend of yours, Mrs. Gordon, and a journalist chap snooping around up there. They've probably mucked up any useful evidence."

"Where were they?"

Wallace pointed up to the darkened gallery. "There's a private dining room just to the left of the window from which she fell. They were in there."

Harriet and Maddocks had probably done exactly the opposite of what they were accused of, and as Curran turned away, Wallace said, "And Curran, I do not want that Gordon woman anywhere near this case. It is none of her business. Do I make myself clear?"

"Yes, sir," Curran said between gritted teeth. He turned to Severn. "Do you mind accompanying me, Claud? You know this building."

"Not very well," Severn said. "It's comparatively new and only been used a couple of times since I've been with Sir John." As they walked toward the stairs, Severn continued. "I saw your name on the invite list."

"I had to be on duty tonight," Curran said.

Severn's lips tightened. "When did that man Wallace arrive?" he asked in a low voice as they took the external stairs to the gallery.

"On Tuesday. Same ship as Sir Henry Cunningham."

"I'm surprised they brought someone in over you," Severn said.

Curran cast the other man a glance. "You know how these things work, Claud."

Severn nodded. "I do indeed. The powers that be in Westminster control our lives."

They passed through a doorway onto the gloomy gallery, and Severn waved a hand. "The gallery runs around the ballroom. The girl was a part of the choir from the Singapore Ladies Academy. I saw them all up here earlier in the evening. Can't believe that child died so horribly." He paused. "Her poor parents. They were in attendance... they saw her... Terrible thing. Not married myself, but I can imagine."

Curran grunted a non-committal response.

He leaned on the balustrade, looking down over the ballroom. "Why were the girls here?"

"They sang the National Anthem and then, just before supper, they entertained the guests with a bracket of songs. Quite charming."

"And supper was served at what time?"

"Nine-thirty and then we all went out to the front to watch the fireworks at ten."

"How long did they last?"

Severn shrugged. "Ten or so minutes. Cost a fortune."

"All to impress Sir Henry Cunningham?"

Severn shrugged. "We don't have coronations every day. It seemed like a good excuse. As it was, Cunningham didn't stay to watch. He retired as soon as supper was announced."

Curran stiffened. "So, he wasn't present when the girl died?"

"No. He's not in the best of health and complained of being tired. Lady Cunningham stayed on," Severn said.

"And after the fireworks?"

"The orchestra resumed, and the dancing was underway when we heard the scream from the man who found her."

"What time was this?"

"Ten twenty. I remember because I looked at my watch."

They walked around the gallery to the window from which the girl had fallen. The shutters had been closed and bolted. Any useful fingerprints were now obscured. Curran threw the shutters open and peered out. The sill was high... too high for Amelia Hardcastle to have accidentally fallen.

She had either jumped, or someone else was involved.

He had noted when he had been downstairs that on either side of the ballroom were short wings providing, he assumed, service facilities such as cloakrooms. The wings extended upwards to this level, and he indicated the doorway to their right.

"What's in there?"

"It's a private dining room or withdrawing room. I'm not sure what it was ever intended to be, but Mrs. Perkins thought it might be useful for Sir Henry and Lady Cunningham if they wished for a little privacy during the evening."

The door was unlocked, and Curran threw it open. Inside it was dark and stuffy, the heavy shutters pulled tight.

Severn pulled the electric light cord, and bright light illuminated the room, which was immaculate. Every chair was in place, and there was no trace that anyone had been there all evening.

Curran circled the room, pushing through the velvet curtains to find a serving area beyond. A quick inspection of what appeared to be a cupboard revealed it to be a dumb waiter. The lift was operated by means of a rope pulley and the cabinet was at their level. Curran considered the lift for a long time.

"Where does this open on to?" he asked Severn.

"There's a room downstairs accessible from the outside. It was put in to provide ease of access to the kitchens in the event anyone wished to dine up here. Don't ask me why. To be honest, it's not something I've ever concerned myself with."

"Was this room locked tonight?"

Severn shook his head. "I doubt it."

"So, anyone could have accessed it, including the dead girl?"

"I suppose so."

"I'll need to come back in daylight and search it properly," Curran said. "Please give orders that no one, and I mean no one except my officers, is to enter this room, and it is to be kept locked."

Severn locked the door behind them, and the two men made their way back down to the terrace where the mortuary attendants were lifting the body of Amelia Hardcastle onto a stretcher. It had begun to rain, great heavy drops accompanied by a show of thunder and lightning. Not the weather anyone wanted to be outside in.

One small, pale hand slipped from beneath the canvas covering. Curran gently lifted the covering and replaced it, folding it across the beaded bodice.

"Do you have children, Curran?" Severn asked as they circled the back of the small wing to check out the external access to the dumb waiter.

"No," Curran replied. "I always find cases involving children the hardest to deal with."

"Then you are human," Severn said. "Ah, here's the servery you were asking about."

Directly below the private dining room was the gentlemen's cloakroom, only accessible from within the building. However, a door behind the wing opened up onto a path. It stood ajar, and they pushed it open.

"Shouldn't this be locked?" Curran asked.

"Not tonight," Severn said. "It would have been left unlocked in case the staff needed to send up food and refreshment."

The small room that occupied space in what would be a corner of the gentlemen's cloakroom had no electric light and no window, but enough light trickled in from outside for Curran to see that it contained nothing more than a few empty shelves and the dumb waiter. There was no access from the room beyond.

Curran opened the door to the dumb waiter, revealing the ropes and pulleys. He pulled on the rope and the cabinet slid smoothly down the shaft, settling with a gentle thump. The empty cabinet yawned in front of him.

"Would it be possible for a person to go up in this?" he asked aloud.

"Only if you took out the shelf," Severn said, "And they'd need someone to pull the rope. It's not motorized."

Curran closed the door.

He returned to the main ballroom, where Wallace was in conversation with Greaves.

"Any luck with photographs?" Curran asked his constable.

"Too dark to get anything of quality but good enough for our purposes," Greaves said.

"We'll come back in the morning." Curran turned to Severn. "See that every door in the ballroom is locked. No one is to enter until I have cleared the scene."

Severn nodded and took his leave. As the three policemen stepped onto the front porch, lightning split the sky, followed by the deep bass roll of thunder.

"That's close," Greaves said, flinching as another shaft of lightning skittered across the roiling sky.

Behind them, the massive entrance door shut with a bang, and the lights were extinguished, plunging them into a damp, depressing darkness.

"Stow your gear in my motor vehicle, Greaves. I'll give you a lift back to the lines."

"And I would appreciate a ride home too," Wallace said.

No one spoke until after the motor vehicle turned out onto Somerset Road.

Wallace cleared his throat. "You have to understand, Curran, this is a delicate matter. We can't have a full-scale police investigation at Government House. We'll work on the assumption it was an accident."

"I disagree. How do you know it was an accident? Did anyone see her fall? Hear anything?"

Wallace shifted his weight, his chin coming out defensively. "She fell from the window."

Curran held his peace. Leopards don't change their spots and Wallace would be looking for the easy answers, the first opportunity to close a file.

Curran dredged the recesses of his schoolboy history knowledge and came across an incident in Prague sometime in the 1600s when loyal Catholics had been assisted out of windows by irate Protestants ... or something like that. There was a word for people who involuntarily fell from windows. Defenestration. That was the word.

# SIXTEEN

## SATURDAY, 8 JULY

It was past midnight when Julian returned from the Hardcastle's home. Harriet had changed into an old and comfortable house dress and sat waiting for him on the veranda with Shashti curled up on her lap and a glass of whisky beside her. Julian walked up the steps as if he carried the weight of the evening's event on his shoulders.

Julian shrugged off his jacket and undid his collar and cuff-links as Harriet poured him a drink. He took the glass she held out to him but didn't drink, swirling the amber liquid in the light thrown by the single kerosene lamp.

"How do you get over the death of a child?" he said at last.

He looked up at Harriet, his gaze searching her face, looking for an answer he didn't want to hear.

"You don't. I didn't," Harriet said at last. "I don't think any parent ever recovers from that loss. You just learn to get on with life."

He nodded and took a swig of his drink.

"They want me to conduct the funeral." His voice cracked.

Harriet leaned across and placed her hand over his. "There must be days when you feel the collar around your neck is a noose."

Julian huffed out a laugh and cleared his throat. "So observant."

The rain had passed, and the sounds of the night resumed as they sat in silence. Over the buzz of crickets and crash of monkeys, the gravel on their driveway crunched, and a shadow loomed out of the dark. Harriet's heart jumped to her mouth and Julian was on his feet.

"Who's there?" he demanded.

The shadow materialized as he stepped into the pale circle of light. Curran, hatless, his hands in his pockets.

"Do you know what the time is?" Julian sputtered.

"Just past one and I am guessing that you, like me, cannot sleep," Curran said.

Harriet rested a hand on the veranda post. "Julian has been with Amelia's parents. He's just got back. Come and sit down."

Julian waved at a crystal decanter and an empty glass. "Help yourself..."

Curran shook his head. "Whisky at this time of night will just make me maudlin and I'm depressed enough as it is." He sank into one of the chairs and ran a hand over his eyes. "It's always worse when it's children," he said. "I can only imagine how the parents are handling it. To lose a child—"

He glanced at Harriet and held her gaze in complete understanding. At that moment, she ached for him to take her in his arms and kiss that pain away. She rarely talked about Thomas, and no one mentioned his name in her hearing. Sometimes, she thought, it was as if he'd never existed. But without her words, Curran had understood. He had given her the locket so she could hold Thomas close to her again.

"We didn't hear you drive up," Julian said, resuming his seat.

"I left my vehicle on River Valley Road. I didn't want to wake you if you were asleep." He paused. "Harriet, do you mind if I ask you a question?"

"You may as well," Harriet said.

"Wallace said he caught you and Maddocks snooping in the gallery. What did you find?"

Harriet's eyes widened. "Snooping?"

Curran smiled. "Of course you were."

Julian sighed. "Harriet!"

"There is a small private dining room off the gallery," Harriet said. "There were two champagne glasses and an empty bottle. One champagne glass was broken on the floor, a chair over-turned... what?"

Curran stared at her in obvious incredulity.

He drew a deep, steadying breath. "It was clean and orderly by the time I got to it."

"We turned one of the staff away," Harriet said. "They were hell-bent on restoring order so someone must have gone in after us."

Curran swore.

"We found something."

Harriet rose and hurried back into the house, re-emerging with the hair ribbon in her hand. She handed it to Curran.

"We found this in the back of the dumb waiter."

"You removed evidence from the scene of the crime?" Curran said, but the twitch of his lips gave lie to the stern tone. "What am I looking at?"

"It was the ribbon Amelia had in her hair. We found it tucked into a dark corner of the dumb waiter at the back of the room, so we thought that maybe Amelia, or her murderer, had stuffed her clothes into the dumb waiter and sent it down to the ground. Then all he had to do was extricate it and nobody would be any wiser."

Curran smoothed the wide grosgrain ribbon across his knee

and shook his head. "Your theory sounds quite plausible." He looked up. "You said murderer... you think it was murder?"

Harriet met his gaze. "Someone dressed her in a fancy dress and removed her school uniform. She didn't accidentally fall out of that window, Curran."

Curran took out his notebook and asked for a detailed description of what Amelia had been wearing that evening, which Harriet supplied, adding, "When she sang the last bracket of songs, she had an embroidered handkerchief pinned to her blouse."

"Is that odd?" Curran asked.

"Very odd," Harriet said.

He snapped the book shut. "I will need statements from both you and Maddocks in the morning, and thank you for your snooping. This might have been lost." He folded the ribbon and put it in his pocket as he stood up. "You two need to get some sleep. Once again, my apologies for disturbing you so late at night."

Julian rose to his feet with an audible groan. "No. Your visit came at a good time. It is helpful to talk through these matters while they are still fresh. Excuse me but my bed is calling."

Harriet and Curran sat in silence, listening for the sound of Julian's bedroom door shutting.

"Well, I..."

"Harriet..."

They both spoke together and smiled sheepishly.

"You don't have to go right this minute," Harriet said. "I don't think I can sleep yet."

Curran pulled out his cigarette case. His hand shook as he lit a cigarette, a testament to his exhaustion. He stuffed his right hand in his pocket and stood looking out into the dark garden.

"A room full of nearly two hundred people and staff. I just hope someone saw something." He grimaced. "The frustrating thing is there is one person I have to interview, and I know I am going to be barred from talking to him."

Harriet came to stand beside him. "Who is that?"

"Sir Henry Cunningham," he said, after a long pause.

She stared at him. "Sir Henry? But why him, Curran? He had nothing to do with Amelia's death. He left the ballroom before supper was served. I saw him go."

"He could have come back," Curran said.

"Why would he do that?"

Curran stubbed out the cigarette and leaned his weight on the veranda rail again, his shoulders hunched. He leached frustration tinged with despair.

Harriet gathered her courage and touched his arm.

"What is it, Curran? Whatever it is, you can tell me," Harriet said. "It will go no further."

He turned to look at her.

"I know I can trust you, but the thing is, Harriet, it's about an old case, about my own failure."

Failure, Harriet had learned over the time she had known Curran, cut him deeply.

"Is it related to Amelia's death?"

He drew in a breath. "It could be."

"Then talk to me, Curran."

He searched her face, and she held his gaze, willing him to unburden himself of whatever it was that troubled him about this man.

"You once told me that the worst thing you can do is hold something to yourself," she said.

He gave a huff of laughter. "Did I? How hypocritical of me. Very well, what I am about to tell you is in the absolute strictest confidence, Harriet. Not a word to anyone."

She smiled. "As if you need to ask."

She had been with him through several difficult cases, and she hoped she had demonstrated that he had no reason to doubt her.

He took a breath. "Six years ago, I was a newly promoted Inspector at Scotland Yard. A woman came to the Yard, and I happened to be the one who spoke to her. That's where it all began."

"Go on."

"Her name was Alice Venning. She was a widow of modest means supporting two children. James, the eldest, was fifteen and a talented musician. His sister, Mary about three years older. James came to the notice of a wealthy member of parliament, who gave him patronage. This man paid for the boy's school fees and music tuition and in return, James was invited to entertain the man's guests at private functions."

He paused to light another cigarette before continuing, "His mother noticed her son becoming more withdrawn and moody, to the extent of refusing to attend his patron's soirees, but they needed the money and so she insisted. Two weeks before she came to the Yard, James took his own life. He threw himself off Waterloo Bridge. He was only sixteen... not much older than Amelia Hardcastle."

"How sad."

Harriet tried to imagine that mother's shock and grief and failed. Were there degrees of a mother's grief? Was losing a child to murder or suicide so much worse than losing a child to disease?

"That in itself is tragic, but James had left his mother a letter. They had lost their only source of income and needed to take in lodgers, and she found this letter tucked in the back of a book when they cleared his room. In it, James outlined in detail exactly what occurred at those soirees."

Harriet's breath hissed. She was a woman of the world, and she suspected she knew what was coming.

"Go on."

"These evenings were only attended by men of rank with a taste for..." Curran's lips twisted. "Young flesh... boys and girls. They were quite indiscriminate and completely ruthless. Some children came from the streets but others, like James, were from good families, shamed or bought into silence."

Harriet's hands flew to her mouth. "Oh, Curran, how horrible. And this man? His patron?"

"Sir Henry Cunningham."

The name hit Harriet like a blow and Curran's strange demeanor of the past few days suddenly made sense.

"And you think...?"

He held up a hand. "It gets worse. I showed the letter to my superior. He took the letter from me and assured me it would be dealt with at a higher level, but I was not to approach Cunningham and to stay away from Alice Venning. Another inspector would take over the case."

She studied his face, seeing the bitterness written in the lines. "Wallace?"

He gave a curt nod. "He'd only just been promoted and they knew he wouldn't ask too many awkward questions, upset the powers at Whitehall or the establishment."

He flicked the butt of the cigarette into the bougainvillea, the tip still glowing red as it circled in the darkness.

"Filthy habit. I must give it up." He huffed out a breath. "Alice Venning still kept coming to me for answers and I had none to give her. You know me, Harriet. I couldn't let it go. Despite the risk to my career, I confronted Sir Henry with the accusation. He denied it, of course, and challenged me to produce the evidence. I had nothing, only Alice Venning's second-hand testimony. When I went looking for it, I found James Venning's letter had disappeared. I was formally reprimanded and threatened with demotion and it was suggested if I wanted to avoid total disgrace, I should seek greener pastures. That's how I came out East."

He took a breath and closed his eyes. "I will never forget the look on Alice Venning's face when I told her that it was all being swept under the rug. The betrayal, the hurt, and the grief, Harriet, but there was nothing I could do."

"And now?"

"Now, Sir Henry Cunningham is here in Singapore and a young girl of the age he has a preference for has died."

She was watching him. "There's something else, isn't there?"

He nodded. "Cunningham liked to dress his victims up in pretty dresses... boys as well as girls."

"Just like the one we found on Amelia?"

Harriet looked away, her hand held against her mouth to stem the revulsion and rage. Her father, a Crown Prosecutor, had dealt with such men, and Harriet, in her capacity as his unofficial assistant, had read the files. She knew what depths of depravity men could sink to, but now the presence of Sir Henry Cunningham had brought that horror to her doorstep... maybe.

"I shouldn't have burdened you," Curran said, mistaking her silence for disgust.

She turned back to look at him. "Thank you for confiding in me. I am not a vapid female. I've seen, or at least I thought I had seen, some of the worst things one human can do to another in the slums of Bombay, but this ... it is beyond comprehension."

"And the worst of it is, I can't prove any of it," Curran said. "In London, the powers that be closed around Cunningham. They made Venning's accusation disappear. God knows how many of them may even have been involved in Cunningham's circle, and now I have Wallace, who knows exactly what I know, standing between me and Cunningham. If I were a cynical man, I would believe that this promotion is his reward for services rendered."

He leaned back against a veranda post, his feet crossed and looked out into the night.

"You didn't fail Alice Venning," Harriet said. "She was fortunate to have a champion in you. If it had been Wallace she had stumbled on first, she would have got nowhere. At least you listened to her and believed her... and her son."

He turned back to face her, smiling without humor. "Thank you, Harriet."

"Is there anything I can do?" she said.

He shook his head. "You know there isn't."

A thought occurred to Harriet. "Does Lady Cunningham know about her husband's other life?"

"Oh, yes. She knows because I told her six years ago. What she chose to do with the information..." Curran shrugged. "I suspect it was her influence, more than his, that shut down the case."

Harriet took a tentative step toward him. This time he did what she had longed for him to do, pulled her into his arms, and kissed her.

"Thank you for being you," he whispered into her hair. "It helps to talk it through with someone with fresh eyes."

"I don't think I was any help."

"You were, but I trust you not to say a word to anyone. Not Julian and particularly not Esme."

She leaned her head against his shoulder.

"Curran! I am offended you should think so poorly of me. When have I ever betrayed a confidence?"

# SEVENTEEN

Mac preferred to get autopsies done as early as possible, and Curran attended the morgue at seven the following morning after only a few hours' sleep. He had called in at Chief Inspector Wallace's home to see if Wallace would care to accompany him, but Wallace was still in his dressing gown and declared that Curran could see to it and brief him back at South Bridge Road later in the morning.

"I hate this," Mac said, in a rare display of partiality as the two men stood outside the mortuary smoking in the early morning freshness. "She was Heather's best friend. I had to break the news to her this morning and then leave her devastated. She's too young. I should not be autopsying a girl who was at my house only last week."

Curran nodded. "I have yet to speak to the parents."

Mac shook his head. "You have a devil of a job, Curran."

"I thought I would wait until after..." Curran grimaced and waved a hand at the door to the mortuary. "Until I had something to tell them. I've no doubt they would like her returned to them as soon as possible."

Mac nodded. "Understandable. Let's get on with it."

The mortuary room, with its two heavy stone tables, stank of carbolic and death. Curran hated every moment he spent in the room. He tried not to look at the slight figure on one of the tables, concealed beneath a stained cloth.

So small, so frail... so young.

He turned instead to Amelia's clothes, that had been neatly folded on a table against a wall, the purple evening dress at the top of the pile.

"Was this everything?" he asked.

"Yes. It looks like she had put the evening dress on top of her usual undergarments. Like a little girl playing dress-ups," Mac said. "Sort of thing my daughter would do. Any sign of her school uniform?"

Curran shook his head. "I have men up at Government House searching the grounds. There's a lot of area to cover." He flicked his notebook open. "We're looking for a navy skirt and a white cotton blouse with a sailor collar with a blue tie, according to Harriet."

Mac blew out a breath. "I better make a start." He flicked back the stained sheet and frowned. "Interesting. Curran, look at the bruising on her arms. I didn't notice that last night."

Purpling bruises marred the pale skin of Amelia's upper arms. Curran held his left hand to her right arm and looked up at Mac.

"Someone held her—hard."

Mac nodded. He reached for a magnifying glass and peered down at the ruined face. "I wouldn't mind betting that this mark..." he indicated a bruise on her left cheek, "also occurred before death."

"Someone hit her?"

"That would be my opinion."

The door opened to admit Constable Ernest Greaves and his photographic equipment. Greaves looked at the body on the slab and blinked behind his wire-rimmed glasses.

"Same age as my sister," he said.

"Got to put that thought away, young man," Mac said. "You have a job to do."

Greaves nodded and set his jaw as he took images of the external damage. Curran studied the rigid line of the surgeon's jaw. He too, had to put his own connection with the victim away and get on with his job.

Silence descended on the room, accentuating every move Mac made. He issued instructions to his assistant in a low, modulated voice and the two men worked together in long practiced amity. Curran stood with his back flat to the wall, Greaves, pale and sweating beside him. He longed for a cigarette or a whisky or both.

"Curran, look at this," Mac said.

He had turned the body over and pointed to the back of the girl's head.

"I didn't notice this in my cursory examination last night. She landed face-first. The position of the body does not account for this wound," Mac said.

Curran studied the injury Mac pointed out, trying to make sense of what he was seeing. A depression injury that had fractured the back of her skull.

He looked up. "Was she hit?"

Mac shook his head and, using a metal rod to indicate the angle of the wound, said, "Maybe. It's a piercing wound. She could have been hit with something hard and not large. Something like a hammer or an ice pick."

Curran frowned. "Not the sort of objects I would expect to find in the ballroom at Government House," he said. "Did it kill her?"

"Now that is the question. There is massive internal bleeding to the brain, so it occurred before death." He looked up. "Before she went out of the window."

Curran looked up at the doctor. "She was still alive when she fell?"

"Yes. This injury would have killed her within a short time, but it was the fall that finished her. She broke her neck. Now let me finish up and we'll talk."

The interminable hour came to an end and Mac straightened, turning to the sink to scrub his hands while his assistant restored some dignity and humanity to Amelia's body.

"Step outside. I need fresh air," Mac said.

Outside on the wide, cool veranda, Curran reached for his cigarette case. Greaves declined his offer of a cigarette, sinking to his haunches, his head in his hands. Mac produced his stinking Gauloise cigarettes, and the two men stood in silence for a long moment watching the smoke curl into the morning air.

"Had she been interfered with?" Curran asked the question he had been dreading.

Mac shook his head. "No."

"That's something."

"But she was held forcibly by the arms and there is the injury to the back of her head. It's hard to tell because of the damage to her head and face, but I am fairly certain she was hit hard across the face before death."

Curran took a deep drag on his cigarette as he tried to imagine the scene. The bruises on her face and arms and the strange injury to the back of her head...

"Was he... or she... trying to cover up a crime by making it look like a suicide or an accident?"

Mac scoffed. "Then they didn't know much about how these things work. In my experience, someone jumping or even falling accidentally would be unlikely to land headfirst in that position from that height."

"It's not unknown though."

Mac shrugged.

Curran exhaled the last of his cigarette and ground the butt out under his heel.

"You are telling me that in your medical opinion, she was murdered."

Mac nodded. "You know me, Curran. I only tell you what I see. It's up to you to draw the conclusions. All I can tell you is that she has injuries inconsistent with a fall from a window."

Curran huffed a humorless laugh, opened his notebook, and made some quick notes. He remembered Harriet's observation about the two champagne glasses in the private dining room. Had Amelia's murderer pressed alcohol on her, no doubt to make her compliant? To force her into doing... what? He didn't like to think about what someone would want with a young girl like Amelia, but the suspicion was not something he could dismiss.

"Any indication that she had consumed any champagne?"

Mac shook his head.

Greaves hauled himself upright. "She was a fifteen-year-old girl. Who could do such a thing?"

Curran laid a hand on the young man's shoulder. "If you are ever going to make a career out of policing, you are going to have to overcome your belief in the goodness of humanity, Greaves. Let's get back to South Bridge Road. You can develop your images and I need to speak to the parents."

———

Back at headquarters, Curran found Wallace in his office, reading through files. The man looked up as he entered.

"Knock first," Wallace growled.

"I've just been at the autopsy," Curran said. "Forgive my lack of manners."

"Well?"

Curran summarized Mac's findings.

Wallace sat back and nodded. "Poor girl. So, it is looking like it was not an accident?"

"If it wasn't an accident and someone threw her from the

window. I would call it murder. I want to interview Sir Henry Cunningham," Curran said.

"Why?"

A flash of anger misted Curran's eyes. "Why? The girl met with someone who dressed her up in a woman's evening dress and had champagne laid out... Is none of this sounding familiar, Wallace?"

Comprehension dawned, and Wallace stared back at him. "You're not suggesting...?"

"Of course I am," Curran snapped at last. "Sir Henry Cunningham has a known penchant for young girls and boys for that matter. He dresses them in evening dresses and—"

"None of that was ever proved."

"Because the one boy willing to give evidence killed himself, Wallace."

"We are not going through this again, Curran. Blackening the name of a good man and distinguished member of parliament, the colonial secretary no less, will not help your career."

"I am not making any accusations, Wallace, not without a witness and proper evidence, but you have to admit that the circumstances around Amelia Hardcastle's death have strong similarities to that case in London."

"The case you were taken off, Curran."

"Because I got too close to the truth."

The two men glared at each other across the desk.

"There is nothing to suggest Sir Henry is in any way involved. I was there. He retired from the ball when supper was served." Wallace drove his forefinger into the blotter to emphasize his point.

"Did you see him leave?"

Wallace paused for a heartbeat. "No, but it can be easily ascertained that he retired to his bed. Start with his valet."

Wallace huffed out a breath and sat forward, his elbows on the desk. He picked up a pencil and circled it in his fingers.

"Very well, I agree Sir Henry may need to be questioned, but if anyone is going to speak to either Sir Henry or Lady Cunningham, it will be me, and I want something more compelling to necessitate that conversation. Do I make myself clear, Curran?"

"Perfectly clear... sir," Curran replied between stiff lips. "Now, with your permission, I would like to speak with the girl's parents and take Greaves up to Government House to see the scene of the crime in daylight."

"Very well, but heed my warning, Curran. Stay away from the Cunninghams."

# EIGHTEEN

Harriet slept badly in the few hours before daybreak. She woke heavy-eyed and with a nagging headache. Julian did not look much better. At the breakfast table, they picked at their food without much enthusiasm. Their ward, Will, looked from one to the other.

"Is it something I did?" he asked.

Julian blinked behind his glasses. "You? Good heavens, no, Will." He took a breath. "Bertie Hardcastle's sister died last night."

Will replaced his half-eaten toast on the plate and looked down. "I'm sorry."

"He probably won't be at school for a while," Julian said.

Will looked up. "How did she die?"

"A terrible accident," Harriet said. "Now finish your breakfast. You have school this morning and a rugby match this afternoon. Life goes on, Will."

Will departed for the school, the hours for which extended to Saturday mornings, with an obvious show of reluctance and a message for the senior master that Julian would not be in until much later.

The now familiar chug of a motor vehicle engine made Harriet and Julian look up as Curran's motor vehicle turned into the drive.

"The harbinger of doom is here again," Julian said glumly.

Harriet shot her brother a sharp look. "That's harsh, Ju."

"It's true. Wherever Curran goes, he brings death."

"It's his job."

"I know."

With his familiar leather satchel slung over his shoulder, Curran joined them on the veranda. He looked as grim as Harriet felt.

"Did you sleep?" she asked, pouring him a cup of tea.

He took the cup and shook his head. "Not much. I've just come from the girl's autopsy."

Julian spoke first. "And?"

"She sustained a mysterious head injury before she fell from the window."

Harriet gasped, her hands going to her mouth. "Please, no. Someone murdered that child?"

Julian's lips tightened. "There are times I wonder where God is when you need him."

Curran shook his head. "He was not with Amelia Hardcastle last night."

"No," Julian said. "Why are you here again, Curran?"

"I would appreciate Harriet's opinion of the dress the girl was wearing."

He produced a paper bag from his satchel, took out the roughly folded dress, and laid it out on the table. The once lovely object was stained with dark blotches that could only be dried blood. Julian hissed an inward breath and Harriet had to stop herself recoiling.

Curran looked up at her. "Well? What do you think?"

Harriet was not a great authority on women's fashion, but she recognized quality. The underskirt was of amethyst silk, and it had an embroidered and beaded overskirt of silk organza. The bodice was heavy with more beadwork—amethyst glass beads, seed pearls, and silk embroidery. The work was exquisite with every tiny bead hand stitched. However, the left shoulder of the organza sleeve had been torn at the seam, dislodging a line of beads that hung loosely from a thread. She could not recall seeing fallen beads on the floor of the private dining room, but it had been dark.

"I suspect it's a few years old," she concluded. "The sleeves are no longer worn that full and waists are higher. I remember thinking when I saw her lying there that it was far too big for her." She paused and ran a hand over the overskirt. "A fifteen-year-old girl would have thought it was wonderful."

She regarded the sad garment and thought of Amelia, so full of life and promise.

"Mac said it reminded him of a child playing dress-ups," Curran said.

Harriet sighed, and they exchanged glances, the poignancy of that picture almost too much to bear.

She turned to the inside of the bodice.

"The maker's label has been cut out and there are no laundry marks to help you identify the original owner," she said, "but I would wager that it is English, maybe even a Worth gown. This level of fine hand stitching sets it apart as something special. Where would she have got it?"

Curran folded the garment, his mouth a grim line. "Perhaps she was given it by her murderer?" he said. "The question is where did he get it?"

"There are plenty of places in London specializing in the rag trade that would sell such garments," Harriet said.

He looked up at her as he stowed the garment back in his bag.

"Harriet, can I borrow you for the morning?"

"To do what?" Harriet asked.

Curran cleared his throat. "I need your help. I'm on my way

to visit the parents and they will want to know how she died. It may help to have you with me."

Harriet nodded. "Of course. I'll fetch my hat."

As she left the two men, she heard Julian say, "Curran, tread carefully with Harri. You know she lost her own child. Things like this bring it all back."

"I know," Curran said. "That's why I need her. She understands."

# NINETEEN

Curran and Harriet sat with Amelia Hardcastle's parents. Curran twisted his hat in his hand, wishing himself anywhere except for the comfortable villa on Emerald Hill. They were seated on a pair of beautiful but hard, inlaid rosewood chairs probably procured in China where the Hardcastles had been posted before Singapore. Amelia's parents sat huddled together on a similar piece of furniture designed for at least three people. They looked small and lost within the confines of the imposing piece.

Mrs. Hardcastle's eyes were puffy and swollen, her face blotchy. If she had slept at all last night, Curran would have been surprised. Her husband's face was gray with exhaustion. There was no sign of the two younger children, but he thought he heard a child crying in the back of the house.

Harriet must have heard it too. She straightened and looked at the door.

"How are the children?" Harriet asked.

"They've taken it hard," George Hardcastle said. "Their amah is with them."

"Do you have any news?" Ellen Hardcastle ventured, at last, her voice thick with grief.

Curran took a steadying breath. "Dr. Mackenzie conducted the autopsy this morning—"

This provoked a sob from Mrs. Hardcastle, barely contained by the sodden handkerchief she pressed against her mouth with one hand, while the other groped for her husband's. They were willing him to say it was all a terrible mistake or, at worst, an unfortunate accident.

"I'm sorry," he said. "Every indication is that someone was involved in your daughter's death."

George Hardcastle blinked. "Someone killed her?"

Curran gave a reluctant nod. "She has a wound to the back of her head that is not accounted for in the injuries she sustained in the fall."

Hardcastle stared at him. "You're saying that someone hit her over the head and threw her from the window... threw her away?"

Curran forced himself to meet the man's red-rimmed eyes. He wouldn't have put it that way, but Hardcastle was right. Whoever had killed Amelia had tossed her from that window like a piece of rubbish. He had no answer to Hardcastle's question. All he could do was spread his hands in defeat.

Ellen Hardcastle moaned and buried her face in her husband's shoulder.

"Did she suffer?" George asked.

The question any loving parent would ask and not one Curran could readily answer truthfully.

"The blow to her head would probably have rendered her unconscious," he said. "So no, she would never have known what happened to her."

His answer seemed to satisfy George. He nodded and looked away, momentarily composing himself before asking the other question, the question no father should have to ask of his beautiful daughter.

"Was she...?" Hardcastle shot a look at his wife. His voice cracked. "Did he... touch her?"

Curran lowered his voice. "We do not believe anyone interfered with her."

The man's relief was palpable. He slumped back and his wife fell weeping into his arms.

Beside Curran, Harriet stiffened as if she were about to leap to the woman's comfort, but she remained where she was.

"I am sorry, but I do have to ask you both questions," Curran said.

"We understand," Hardcastle said.

"When did you last see Amelia alive?"

Ellen Hardcastle pushed away from her husband and straightened.

Taking a deep breath, she said, "The choir finished singing at nine-thirty. Supper was served, and we had agreed with Amelia she could stay to watch the fireworks." Her lip trembled, and she pressed the handkerchief hard to her mouth again. "We said, as long as she wasn't a nuisance to anyone and didn't get in the way she could watch from the gallery."

"Did you see her go up to the gallery?"

Ellen shook her head. "No. I... we... trusted her to do as we asked."

"When did you notice she was missing?"

"I went looking for her just before ten, but she wasn't in the gallery."

"You went up to the gallery?" Curran interrupted.

She nodded. "Just before the fireworks started."

"Did you see anyone up there?"

She shook her head. "I walked around it, but I didn't see anyone. Everyone was downstairs." She paused. "Strange, because the view from the gallery was magnificent. I... I paused to watch for a moment."

"Did you look in the private dining room?"

"The room to the side? I opened the door and called her name, but it was dark."

"Did you notice anything unusual in the room?"

She shook her head. "It was too dark to make anything out."

Curran turned this piece of information over in his mind. Amelia, dead or alive, had to be concealed somewhere in that room at the time her mother came looking for her. What if Ellen had switched the light on? Could she have saved her daughter, or was she already too late?

The thin line between life and death was a series of 'what ifs'.

"What did you do then?"

"The fireworks had started, and George and I were looking everywhere we could think of. I even went into the main house. We were just going around to the back of the ballroom when Mr. Gilmore found us, and she was lying there... dead."

She hiccuped, and the tears began again.

Curran pulled out the large paper bag containing the ball dress and a second bag with the rest of Amelia's clothing.

"I'm sorry to do this, but I need you to identify the clothing Amelia was wearing when she was found and tell me if anything is not hers or anything is missing."

Ellen Hardcastle nodded and grasped her husband's hand as Curran set the items out on the table between them. She picked up the chemise with a shuddering sob and, oblivious to the bloodstains that speckled it, she pressed it to her face.

"It's all here, except her skirt and blouse," she said, her voice muffled by the cotton fabric. She lowered her hands and pointed at the evening dress. "And that...That's not hers. I've never seen it before. Put it away, Inspector. It's obscene."

Curran held out his hand. "I need the garment you are holding, Mrs. Hardcastle."

"It's needed for evidence, Ellen," Harriet said.

"But it's all I have of her—" Ellen sobbed.

Harriet stood and crossed to the woman, gently wresting the garment from Ellen's grip and handing it to Curran, who packed the clothing back in the two paper bags and returned them to the satchel. Their gaze met, and he saw the pain in Harriet's eyes. Maybe it had been a mistake to bring her.

Ellen gave a choked sob and buried her head in her husband's shoulder. "She's gone. She's really gone, George."

Hardcastle cleared his throat. "When can we get her back, Inspector?"

"You can instruct the funeral directors to collect her this afternoon."

Hardcastle nodded. "We'll bury her on Monday. We've asked the Reverend Edwards to conduct the service."

The last of Ellen Hardcastle's composure deserted her, and she howled, burying her face in her hands.

Harriet stood up and held out her hand to the woman. "Come with me, Ellen. We'll leave the men to talk."

Ellen collapsed into Harriet's arms and let Harriet lead her from the room.

Hardcastle heaved a sigh as the door shut behind his wife and Harriet. "I'm sorry about that," Hardcastle said. "Ellen is—we both are—"

"Don't make apologies, George," Curran said. "This is an unforgivable, horrible crime and I will find the perpetrator."

Hardcastle nodded. "It's reassuring to know you are in charge of the case, Curran."

Curran hesitated. "I... In the normal course of events I would be," he said, "but the Chief Inspector may wish to take it on, seeing as it involves Government House."

"That is disappointing."

"If you have any concerns or questions, George, I am a friend."

George Hardcastle managed a small, humorless smile.

"Just find who did this, Curran."

———

Harriet caught the look of relief that crossed George Hardcastle's face as she led his wife away. He was shouldering everyone's grief while not leaving any room for his own. She hoped Curran might help ease that burden in Ellen's absence.

"Where are the other children?" Harriet asked.

"I can't face them," Ellen said. "I hate them seeing me like this, and how can I explain what happened to their sister?"

Ellen stopped by a closed door and turned the handle.

"This was Melly's room," she said. "I think I would just like to sit in here for a while. I can't face Curran again."

"Would you like me to sit with you?" Harriet said.

Ellen nodded.

The room was small but beautifully furnished with a narrow bed, with a well-polished brass bedhead, covered in a lace cloth, the mosquito net coiled neatly above. A much-loved doll with a porcelain face and hands, her hair scraggly and her dress faded, smiled benignly from the pillow.

Ellen sank onto the bed and picked up the doll, pressing it to her heart.

"This is Bessie," she said. "We gave it to Melly for her second birthday. George had to send away to England—"

Harriet felt her own eyes prickle. The doll served as a stark reminder that a child had died. Amelia Hardcastle may have thought herself grown up and sophisticated, but the small girl who had loved that doll was still a child who had died at the hands of a monster.

She swallowed back the tears and looked away.

A button-back velvet chair with a lace cushion, practical rag rugs, and a dainty dressing table covered with a pretty, embroidered cloth on which sat a mirror comprised the rest of Amelia's world. A tortoiseshell hairbrush and comb and a silver-edged tortoiseshell hand mirror were laid out on the dressing table, and Harriet could imagine Amelia perched on the stool in front of that mirror, brushing her hair for the big performance at Government House—barely twelve hours ago.

She picked up a porcelain statue of a shepherdess of some age that also sat on the dressing table.

"Melly loved that piece," Ellen said. "It belonged to my mother."

Harriet set it back and turned back to Ellen Hardcastle.

"I lost my son, Thomas," Harriet said. "He was only seven. He died of typhus in India."

Ellen Hardcastle looked up at her. "I had a son, between Amelia and Bertram. Measles went through Canton. He was eighteen months old." She closed her eyes. "But somehow that doesn't seem as soul-destroying as this. I don't know how I will ever recover, Harriet."

The two women looked at each other in a long silence as the shared grief of two bereaved mothers wound around them with rivers of tears, shed and still unshed.

Harriet broke the silence. "Did Amelia keep a diary?"

Ellen blinked. "A diary? She was always scribbling. My brother sent her a notebook for her last birthday..." Her voice cracked, "Her last ever birthday."

"Can I have a look around her room?" Harriet asked.

When Ellen didn't answer, she took that as tacit agreement and discreetly searched the room, looking for the diary. She found it tucked into a corner of a drawer, under neatly pressed and starched school uniform blouses.

"May I borrow this?" she asked.

"Why?"

"It might give the police an idea of what she was doing last night."

Ellen Hardcastle gave a small shrug. "If it will help, but I would like it back."

Like a small child, Amelia's mother curled up on the bed, with Bessie held in her arms, tears now trickling unchecked onto the lace counterpane. Harriet sat down on the bed and laid a hand on Ellen's shoulder. She had no words. Not even a prayer would bring comfort to this poor woman.

# TWENTY

As Curran turned the motor vehicle onto Orchard Road, Harriet cleared her throat.

"I have Amelia's diary," she said.

"How did you get that?"

"I asked. Ellen would like it back."

Curran nodded. "Of course, but there are no secrets when it comes to murder, Harriet." He glanced at her. "Do you mind going through it to check if there is anything relevant? I trust you to spot it."

"Your new superior won't be happy about you asking me to help," she said.

He cast her a glance that told her exactly what he thought of his new superior.

"Curran," she chided, "you are your own worst enemy."

"If you have some time now, I have another favor to ask," Curran said.

"Yes?"

"Come with me to Government House? Singh and Greaves and several men are up there now searching the grounds, but I need you to show me exactly what you saw in that private dining room last night. By the time I got there, the efficient household staff had cleared it out."

Harriet nodded, and they drove on in silence, weighed down by the Hardcastle's grief.

The guard stopped them at the gates to Government House but admitted without argument. Claud Severn met them in the front hall.

Harriet held out her hand to the genial Australian. "A pleasure to see you again, Mr. Severn," she said.

Claud Severn returned the greeting with, "And you, dear lady." He glanced at Curran. "Mrs. Gordon was only here yesterday doing some work for us and, of course, I saw you at the ball." The good humor faded from his face. "Seems like a lifetime ago."

They followed Severn into the peace of the private secretary's comfortable office.

Severn stood by the window, his hands behind his back. "Your men have been searching the grounds all morning. Have they found anything?"

"I don't believe so," Curran said.

Severn turned back to face them. "What news about the girl? A tragic accident?"

"No, we believe she was murdered," Curran said.

"Dear God." Severn pushed his tortoiseshell glasses back up his nose. "How could such a thing happen in so public a place? It's simply dreadful. What can I do for you?"

"I need to see the scene of the crime."

"Of course. Anything else?"

Curran considered his next question. He had already disobeyed one order this morning by involving Harriet. He would not let an opportunity pass him by. Far better to sin and ask forgiveness, he thought.

"And I will need to speak with Sir John and his guests."

"You're too late. They're not here. They've taken the government yacht up to Malacca and Penang on an official tour and will be gone a good few days."

Curran stared at him. "They've left Singapore?"

"This morning. Caught the morning tide. Official visits stop for no man, Curran."

"This is a murder investigation," Curran said.

"As of last night, it was an unfortunate accident," Severn reminded him. "Why do you need to speak to them? Surely, they have nothing to do with this?"

"Who's gone with them?"

"The Cunninghams have taken their staff. Sir John has taken his youngest daughter, his valet, and his ADC."

"Have you had much dealing with Sir Henry Cunningham since his arrival?"

Severn blinked a few times. "Sir Henry, no, apart from the social niceties. My dealings are with his secretary, Charles Gilmore." The man's lips tightened. "He's a smooth young man, don't you agree, Mrs. Gordon?"

Harriet smiled. "Quite charming."

A flash of something Curran vaguely acknowledged might have been jealousy, caught him unawares. Why did this man's name keep coming up in relation to Harriet?

Severn sighed. "I'm not speaking out of turn, and it will be public knowledge soon enough. Sir John has been recalled to London and Sir Arthur Young will be replacing him as the governor." He blinked. "I don't, of course, mean to imply Sir John has been recalled for any failure. It is just the way the colonial service works."

"And you?" Curran asked.

Severn shrugged. "I will stay to settle in the new governor. After that—" he shrugged. "I go where my masters tell me."

"Is the recall the reason for Sir Henry's visit?"

"Partly, but the man is doing a general tour of the colonies. He's going on to Hong Kong and Australia after the Straits Settlements."

"How long will the governor and his guests be gone?"

"They'll be in Penang tomorrow for twenty-four hours and then sailing overnight to Malacca for meetings on Monday. I expect them back on Wednesday. There are some official functions here and a chance for a bit of a rest. They are scheduled to sail on to Hong Kong on the 17th."

"Something of a flying visit," Curran remarked.

Severn shrugged and said with a perfectly straight face. "It is a great honor to host Sir Henry. Now, is there anything else I can help you with? I have a mountain of paperwork to deal with."

"And I am about to add to it. I need to interview everyone present last night."

Severn rolled his eyes. "Good God. We had nearly two hundred guests and then there is the band... staff—"

"A guest list would be a start and perhaps you could direct Sergeant Singh to the staff quarters, and he can start interviewing the staff on duty last night. In the meantime, I would like to inspect the ballroom in the daylight."

Severn pulled a key ring from his desk drawer. "This way. All locked up like you ordered."

As they walked down the covered walkway to the ballroom, Curran asked, "What about you, Severn? Did you see anything out of the ordinary?"

The Australian stopped, pushing his glasses back up his nose again. "The girls sang... very prettily too." He glanced at Harriet. "You were an excellent accompanist, Mrs. Gordon."

"Thank you. It has been a long time since I have had the opportunity to play, and it is a particularly fine piano."

Severn grimaced. "We'll see how long it lasts. This climate is not kind to fine instruments."

"After the girls had finished...?" Curran prompted.

"Oh yes. Supper was served, and I'd just helped myself to a plate when I was called to the kitchen where there had been a disaster with one of the dishes." He rolled his eyes. "The tasks of a private secretary are many and varied. I missed the fireworks and had just returned to the ballroom when I heard one of the staff scream. The poor lad is quite prostrate with shock today."

Severn unlocked one of the side doors to the ballroom, stood back, and handed Curran the keys.

"If you don't need me, I have work to get on with."

"Just before you go, what entrance were the staff using to access the supper tables and serve drinks?"

Severn indicated a door to the left of the dais. "That one. They have a covered walkway directly to the kitchens."

"So, it's unlikely that any staff were in the area where the girl was found. What about the private dining room? I saw there is a dumb waiter to service it."

"Oh yes. Mrs. Perkins thought that our honored guests might appreciate a quiet space for supper, but there were no requests for food to be sent up to that room and Sir Henry retired early. Is that all?

Curran nodded. "For now."

Severn left them standing alone in the vast, empty ballroom. It was hard to visualize that less than twenty-four hours earlier it had been bright with lights, beautifully dressed people, and alive with music, while only yards away a young girl had died.

"I wish you'd been here," Harriet said. "It was a wonderful evening... up until—"

"I would have liked to have attended, but Wallace is determined to keep me away from the Cunninghams."

"Then why did you ask to see them?"

"Because I am not very good at taking orders."

"Then it is probably just as well they were not here," she observed.

"You're right. Where were you when you heard the man scream?"

"I had just finished dancing with Charles Gilmore," she said and smiled with a mischievous glint in her eye. "He is a very good dancer."

Curran ignored her gentle baiting and that nagging twinge of jealousy. He should have been present last night to partner Harriet and to deal with the immediate moments after Amelia's body had been found. No witnesses would have been sent home, and the scene would not have been cleared.

He looked up at the gallery. The balustrade consisted of arches and columns interspersed with solid, bulbous balusters between.

He sent Harriet up to the gallery and the two of them experimented with different angles. He concluded it was almost impossible to see the door to the private dining room or the window from which Amelia had fallen anywhere within the ballroom.

In life, Amelia Hardcastle had been a little shorter than Harriet and unless she had been standing behind the balustrade, looking down at the ballroom, she would not be seen. Even had she been with an adult, no one casually looking up would have seen anything amiss. Assuming no one else was in the gallery, a strong adult could have carried her to the window and dropped out without being observed.

The thought of the child being casually thrown from the window sickened him. Just as George Hardcastle had said... thrown away like a piece of unwanted rubbish.

He joined Harriet on the gallery and found her looking at the window through which Amelia had fallen.

"Maddocks checked the far side of the gallery, and I came down this way. This window was wide open," she said. "All the windows were open to let the breeze in."

Curran removed his pith helmet and wiped his brow. The

room was hot and stuffy enough without two hundred bodies in it.

"Where did you go next?"

She turned and pointed along the gallery. "I went to that room—the one Severn calls the private dining room."

Curran unlocked and opened the double white painted doors that led into the private dining room. Enough light filtered in through the shutters to illuminate the room.

Harriet gasped.

"You're right, it has been cleaned. It did not look like this last night."

Curran threw open one of the shutters, admitting full daylight.

"Can you describe what you saw?"

Harriet closed her eyes. "There was a single champagne glass on the table and a half-empty bottle of champagne. The other glass was on the floor, smashed." She looked down at her foot. "Here. I put my shoe on it. One of the chairs had been tipped—"

"Which one?"

Harriet moved the chairs into the positions they had been in when she first saw the room and indicated the position of the intact glass and champagne bottle. Curran sketched the scene she described in his notebook.

They inspected the servery, hauling up the dumb waiter.

"Where was the hair ribbon?" Curran asked.

"Right at the back. I only found it with my fingers."

Harriet demonstrated, reaching into the far corner of the bottom shelf. Curran stood behind her with his pencil poised and a frown creasing his brow.

"What are you thinking, Curran?" Harriet asked.

Curran sighed. "I don't know what to think yet. One thing I probably can say is that her school uniform went into the dumb waiter at some point in the evening."

"To be taken away by her killer?"

He nodded. "Do you mind helping me search the room?"

"What are we looking for?"

"Anything that might indicate Amelia was here."

They both got down on hands and knees, searching under the furniture and any crevice without even really knowing what they were looking for.

"Curran!" Harriet held up something small between her thumb and forefinger.

She dropped it into the palm of Curran's hand and stood up, brushing her knees.

"Where was it?" Curran asked.

Harriet indicated the daybed. "It was wedged under the foot."

Curran held the small, amethyst-colored bead up to the light.

He took the dress from his satchel and spread it out on the table. The bead Harriet had found matched the other beads on the bodice and looked to have come from the torn area near the sleeve. Had the damage happened during a struggle?

Harriet smoothed the fabric. "It's beautiful, but I can't imagine it is something Ellen Hardcastle would wear. It was made for a much taller and more statuesque woman." She looked up at Curran. "Do you think the killer brought it with him? To dress Amelia in adult clothing and—" she stopped herself. "It's too awful to contemplate."

"Then don't," Curran said and folded the dress, stowing it away again. He placed the glass bead Harriet had found in an envelope, noting the details of its find on the outside. "At least this proves she was here."

That left the murder weapon. He had found nothing in his search that would account for the wound to the back of her head. Of course, it was possible the killer had taken it with him, just as he had taken the school uniform. Unless there was another explanation...

"Harriet, do you mind standing here?"

He placed her on the spot where the upturned chair had been and grasped her by her upper arms.

"If I was holding you like this and you were a young, hysterical girl..."

"I would want her to stop making a noise," Harriet said.

"So I hit her across the face." Curran released his grip and mimed the blow.

Harriet took a step back and Curran released his breath. "She wasn't hit. She fell."

Just behind Harriet was a life-sized statue of a goddess in a state of undress, carrying a small bow and a quiver of arrows. The goddess had her hand on a deer or a dog. It was hard to tell.

Harriet followed his gaze.

"Diana and the other one is Leda," Harriet supplied.

"Useful having a brother into classics," Curran observed as he kneeled to do a close inspection of the hefty chunk of marble.

"What are you looking for?" Harriet asked.

"Something pointy and sharp. Like the horns on this deer," Curran said.

"You mean the ears on the dog," Harriet corrected.

"Artistic license," Curran grumbled as he began a close inspection of the statues.

It took little effort to find what he was looking for. Embedded in the animal's carved eye socket was something dark and too red to be dust or dirt.

"That looks like blood," he said, rising to his feet with a grunt. "I'll get Greaves up here to confirm, but I would think that when he hit Amelia, she fell back and hit the back of her head on the point of that deer's horn, sorry, dog's ear. If she fell with enough force, it would be hard enough to penetrate her skull—Are you all right?"

Harriet sat down heavily on one of the chairs and fanned herself. All the color had drained from her face and he thought for a moment she looked like she might faint.

"It's too awful to imagine," Harriet said. "If there had been more blood, I'm sure I would have seen it last night."

Curran shook his head. "The perpetrator probably cleaned it and there probably wasn't that much blood."

He stood up and gave the room another sweep. If he closed his eyes, he could imagine a confrontation. The girl, in her pretty evening dress, being held by the arms... a heavy blow across the face, sending her sprawling backward, her head hitting the statue?

Harriet was correct. It was too awful to imagine.

"I doubt I'm going to get anything more from here. I should take you home."

"Please," she said in a small voice, and for the first time, he noticed she was crying. Silent tears ran down her face.

"Oh, Harriet. I'm sorry. I should never have... Julian warned me..."

He took her in his arms and held her, letting her weep.

"I never talk about Thomas," she said, her voice muffled by his khaki tunic. "Everyone said it was best not to mention him. It was as if they wanted me to pretend he never existed, but he did, Curran. He was my son, he was a part of me, and when he died..." The tears came unchecked now. "I want to talk about him. I want to remember him, but he is fading away. I can't recall his voice anymore or the way he used to frown when he was trying to learn his words. And I can't even visit his grave... spend time with him."

Curran was lost for any words of comfort. He hadn't thought about children in his own life until recently. Would it help to say that he very much hoped that they... the two of them... might have a child? He or she would be no replacement for that lost child, lying in a lonely graveyard in Bombay, but would it ease the pain...? No. The agony that this woman in his arms was enduring in her steadfast way may have lessened over time, but she would always carry Thomas with her.

"Harriet," he whispered and kissed her hair. "Harriet, I want you to tell me everything about Thomas... everything."

She coughed and shuddered and looked up at him, her eyes swollen and her face blotchy.

"But maybe not right now?" she suggested with a ghost of a smile.

"Maybe not right now," he agreed. "But when you are ready."

She drew a last, long, shuddering breath and accepted his proffered handkerchief.

"Take me home, Curran."

# TWENTY-ONE

Curran spent a tedious Saturday afternoon working his way through the paperwork and statements Singh and his men had gathered in the morning. None of the staff working at Government House that evening had seen anything unusual, but by their own admissions, they were very busy.

Singh shook his head as he looked at his notes. "Even the staff were distracted by the fireworks. No one is admitting to seeing anything—they were all busy, but one piece of gossip might interest you. Sir Henry is far from well. He has hardly eaten since he arrived and is suffering..." Singh paused, "... intestinal issues. He left the ball early after the girls had finished singing and retired to his bedchamber."

"But was there anybody to see if he left his bedchamber after he was supposed to be in bed?" Curran asked.

Singh shrugged. "There are enough entries and exits from the main house to make your way around to the back of the ballroom and up the stairs to the gallery without being seen."

Curran slapped the palm of his hand on the table in frustration. "We need to speak with his man, but he's gone with him to Penang."

He directed Singh to send Greaves up to the private dining room to inspect the statue and take whatever samples and despatched his constables to take preliminary statements from the guests.

The men returned by five with nothing useful to report, and with the governor and his party *en route* for Penang, there wasn't much more Curran could do. The hour between Amelia finishing with the choir and the discovery of her body remained blank.

Disheartened by the lack of progress, he made his way to Lavinia Pemberthey-Smythe's house on Scott's Road.

There was one guest at the ball who did not appear on the official list—his own sister, Samrita, and yet he knew she had been at the ball as the guest of the artist, Barker.

He found Lavinia sitting alone on her veranda, a gin and tonic in her hand.

"Where's Samrita?" he asked after he had greeted his friend.

Lavinia smiled and waved the glass in the direction of her orchid house. "Showing my orchids to Mr. Barker."

"Barker is here? That's useful."

Another witness he had yet to catch up with.

"Mr. Barker is staying for dinner. Are you?"

"If there's room for me."

"There's always room for you, Robert."

Lavinia, and occasionally Samrita, were the only people of his acquaintance who addressed him by his given name. Even Harriet still called him Curran.

"Too kind. I'll go and find them. I need to speak with Barker as well."

Lavinia rolled her eyes. "Always work with you. Very well. Go and find the youngsters, but I suggest you whistle loudly."

"Why?"

Lavinia rolled her eyes, and he caught her meaning.

"There's something between my sister and Barker?"

"You don't approve?"

Curran didn't approve on several levels. He hadn't met Thomas Barker, but not only was he his sister's tutor, but he imagined the artist to be some years older than her. The thought that Samrita had become romantically involved with her art teacher provoked a strange reaction in him. He had never been a parent or, indeed, a brother, but he had risked his life to find his sister and an older brother's right to be protective came instinctively.

Then there was the matter of everything Samrita had endured over the past few years. She had survived a kidnapping and forced slavery at the Topaz Club. When he found her, she had been living with the man who had taken her away from the Topaz club. Ashton Blake had been a decent, hardworking man, but he had died trying to protect Samrita when the men of the Topaz Club had come for her. So much trauma in such a short life.

"She's not ready to throw herself into an exclusive relationship," he said.

Lavinia studied him with a frown. "You are not her father, Robert, and neither do you have the right to be the overprotective big brother. Yours is a slender link of blood and shared experience. Samrita is more than capable of making her own decisions."

"But—"

"But you are you. Do what you must, and tell them that supper will be served shortly."

Hands thrust into his pockets, Curran took the steps down into Lavinia's jungle of a garden. He considered disregarding her advice and surprising the couple, but, as he rounded the corner, he heard voices and Samrita laughed.

He stopped. He hadn't heard her laugh, not really, and this was a sound of such happiness, he realized Lavinia was correct, he had no right to control the direction of his sister's life. He may have rescued her and destroyed the Topaz Club. He may have provided her with the means to make her way in the world, but it was her path to make, not his.

He backtracked and dredged in the corner of his memory for something to whistle, only coming up with *I am the Very Model of a Modern Major General* from Pirates of Penzance.

As he entered the orchid house, he found Samrita and Thomas Barker seated at opposite ends of the bench in the middle of Lavinia's pavilion surrounded by the colorful array of precious and rare blooms. He was not fooled for an instant. Samrita had a fetching color to her cheeks and a lock of her hair had become unpinned.

Barker was younger than he expected, probably only in his early thirties. He had the air of a man who looked perpetually disheveled and there were paint spots on the frayed cuffs of his shirt. Barker's skills as an art teacher had come on the recommendation of a friend of Lavinia's and as long as Curran was prepared to pay for Samrita's tutelage, Barker had been happy to take her on. Now he wondered what exactly he had been paying for.

"Robert!" Samrita stood up, smoothing down her plain, dark blue skirt and tucking a lock of hair that had come loose back behind her ear. "I don't believe you have met Mr. Barker?"

"No, we haven't had the pleasure."

Curran held out his hand to the younger man, fixing him with the sort of cold-eyed glare he reserved for hardened criminals, but Barker just smiled and returned the handshake with a firm grip.

"Supper is about to be served." Curran waved a hand toward the house.

"Discussing the finer points of botanical drawing?" he enquired of his sister as they walked back to the veranda.

She shot him a narrow-eyed glance. It was unnerving that even on such a short acquaintance as theirs, she seemed to be able to read him like a book.

"None of your business, Robert," she said.

He smiled. "I'm teasing you, Samrita."

"I know."

As they settled to supper, Curran turned to the artist. "How long have you been in Singapore, Barker?"

"About eight months. I was heading for Australia, but there seemed to be a few opportunities here, so I decided to stay on for a little while."

"How would you classify yourself, Mr. Barker?" Lavinia asked. "A portrait painter?"

He smiled. "I love landscapes, but portraits pay the bills, Mrs. Pemberthey-Smythe, and I am told I am quite good. Would you like me to paint you?"

She waved a hand. "Oh, call me Lavinia," she said, "and no, you can save your talents for the more deserving. I have no one who would be interested in putting my aging visage up on their wall."

She spoke with a smile, but there was no humor in her eyes. Her only son had died tragically and, as far as Curran knew, she had no family to speak of back in England. But she had friends, he chief among them. If it fell to him to see she had care and love in her old age, he would shoulder the responsibility gladly.

"Thomas is a very good teacher," Samrita put in.

Barker smiled at the young woman. "Only when I have talented pupils."

Spare me, Curran thought and changed the subject.

"You were both at the ball last night?" he ventured.

The light went from Samrita's eyes. "It was a terrible thing that happened," she said. "Poor girl. Who was she, Curran?"

"Amelia Hardcastle. One of the Academy girls."

Samrita's eyes widened, and her hands went to her mouth. "One of the girls from the choir? But she was only a child. Was it an accident?"

"No. Murder."

Samrita's mouth tightened. "Was she...?"

Her hand sought Barker's, and he wondered how much she had confided in him. Samrita had experienced the worst of mankind, and she could have no illusions about Amelia's death or what men could do to women and girls.

"No."

The color had drained from Barker's face.

"Amelia? I don't believe it."

"Were you acquainted with her?" Curran asked, curious about the evident distress in the young man's reaction.

"Yes. I've been doing some portrait work for the Hardcastles, and I have done some preliminary sittings with Amelia and her sister. The poor family."

"What was your impression of the girl?" Curran asked.

Barker didn't answer for a long moment. "Amelia was one of those girls who is too eager to grow up. School bored her, but she liked the music and singing. She told me she wanted to get to London and go on the stage."

Lavinia scoffed. "As if her parents would permit that."

"Did you speak to her on the night of the ball?" Curran asked.

Barker shook his head. "Me? No. I was busy being feted around the room." He glanced at Samrita and smiled. "I did manage a couple of dances."

A significant look passed between them.

Curran cleared his throat. He'd speak to his sister privately later.

"When did either of you last see her alive?"

"When the choir sang," Samrita frowned. "Of course, then it was supper and the fireworks. So many people milling around. I can't say I saw her again."

"What about you, Barker?"

"I was cornered by a couple of people, keen to talk to me about getting their portraits done, but I'm off to Australia shortly, so I'm not taking any new commissions. I watched the fireworks, and Samrita and I were on the dance floor when someone screamed."

"Did either of you see anyone in the gallery during supper?"

Both Samrita and Barker shook their heads.

"I'm sorry, Robert, I saw nothing unusual," Samrita said.

"Oh dear, oh dear," Lavinia said. "How awful for the family. Who could have done such a thing?"

The three people at the table were staring at him, willing him to provide an answer, but he had nothing. His only suspect was on his way to Penang and he had to acknowledge that the worst thing he could do, as a policeman, was to assume that there was only one obvious suspect. He would have to cast his net wider. Somewhere among the two hundred people present at the ball on Friday night, a murderer hid in plain sight.

# TWENTY-TWO

## SUNDAY, 9 JULY

The morning service at St. Andrews Cathedral was a somber occasion. The Hardcastle family, normally seated toward the front of the church, were notable by their absence. The death of one of their own, particularly a girl as young as Amelia, fell heavily on the English community, and all the talk at the church door was of the Governor's Ball and the 'poor Hardcastles'.

After the conclusion of the service, Harriet stood to one side waiting for Julian, who always took forever to round up the boarders from the school and share godly talk and church gossip with the clergy.

"Mrs. Gordon?"

Harriet started at the sound of her name. She looked around to see she had been joined by Griff Maddock's new colleague, Sarah Bowman.

"Oh, Miss Bowman, you made me jump."

Sarah Bowman smiled. "Sarah," she said.

"How are you enjoying your stint at the *Straits Times*?" Harriet asked.

Sarah shrugged. "Reporting on galas and weddings and fashionable ladies' attire is not what I enjoy, Mrs. Gordon." She paused. "I know who you are."

A cold wave washed over Harriet. "What do you mean?"

"In London, I worked for the WSPU... undercover, you might say. It was my job to research the politicians and where they stood on the suffrage question and to give fair warning, anonymously of course, to my newspaper colleagues of demonstrations that Mrs. Pankhurst wished to ensure press coverage."

Harriet stared at the young woman. "I never heard of you."

"You wouldn't. I had to maintain my position at the Daily Telegraph. It is tough for a woman to be taken seriously in the world of newspapers."

"I imagine it is," Harriet said. "As it is in any profession."

Sarah's lips compressed in a thin line. "Quite," she said. "I believe you are a friend of Inspector Curran who is investigating the death of the girl on Friday night?"

"I am."

"I need him to verify something for me."

Sarah unclasped her plain, black leather handbag and handed Harriet an envelope. It contained two pages of closely typewritten script and as Harriet began to read, her heart raced. She stopped and looked at Sarah.

"Do you know what this is?"

"Yes. It is known as the Venning letter," Sarah said. "Not the original of course. That was destroyed."

"How did you come by it?"

Sarah smiled. "Humble police constables are not well paid, and one in particular used to earn a few extra shillings by passing on interesting tidbits to my predecessor at the Telegraph. I found it tucked into a folder he had no doubt forgotten." She paused.

"Inspector Curran was given the original letter by Venning's mother, so he is ideally placed to verify that this is a true copy."

"Why do you need him to do that?"

"I intend to write a piece exposing Sir Henry Cunningham for the monster he is. Curran did the original investigation into the claims by James Venning that Sir Henry had... how do I put this delicately... used him and other young people in a most shameful and degrading way. This is his opportunity to see Cunningham destroyed. "

Harriet swallowed. "Miss Bowman—"

The woman's eyes glittered. "I need to establish myself as a serious journalist and something of this magnitude could make me."

"Or break you," Harriet said.

"I need the world to see that the men upholding the virtues of our society are scum... worse than scum and I have the perfect opportunity with Sir Henry present in Singapore at the moment."

"The *Straits Times* won't publish something like this," Harriet said.

"Maybe not, but I know other papers that will. Curran couldn't get him, but I can. But this is worthless if it is not a true copy and, as Curran is one of the few who saw the original letter, I need his verification."

Harriet turned back to the document in her hand, forcing herself to read the excruciating detail of the crimes committed against the young man who had been so desperate he took his own life. Small wonder his poor mother had come to Curran for help, only to see the powerful men in Whitehall make the whole unfortunate incident disappear.

Small wonder that mention of the case brought a black mood on Curran, but whatever his personal feelings, he was still a policeman, a servant of the Crown.

"I can't guarantee he will cooperate with you," she said, folding the papers to return to the journalist.

"Maybe not, but from what I know of the man, he would have felt the political interference in the case and taken it badly."

That was true. She had seen the bitterness in his face when he told her James Venning's story. He had nearly lost his career over it.

Harriet held the papers out for Sarah, who held up her hand with a shake of her head.

"Please keep that copy and give it to Curran. I have others."

"Harri? Are you ready to go?"

Julian came striding across the grass toward the two women. He tipped his hat to Sarah Bowman.

"How lovely to see you, Miss Bowman."

"And you, Reverend," Sarah said with a winning smile. "Thank you for your time, Mrs. Gordon. We must take tea at John Little sooner rather than later."

Harriet placed the papers in her handbag.

It felt like she now carried a dead weight of expectation that she was doubtful she could fulfill.

———

After lunch, Harriet sat at the table on the veranda of St. Tom's House, reading Amelia Hardcastle's diary. She could see why Curran had offloaded the task of reading it himself. The giddy ramblings of a young girl made for exhausting reading. She would not wish to be fifteen again for all the tea in China. It made her think of her niece, Fleur, back in London. Fleur, the eldest of her sister Mary's children, would now be seventeen, and her school days were behind her.

She conducted a sporadic correspondence with Fleur. She had been in India for much of Fleur's life, but in the two years she had lived in London after her husband's death, she had made an effort to get to know the girl and saw much of herself in her headstrong niece. Fleur had recently expressed a desire to go on to further education. Harriet hoped that the girl's parents might be more liberal-minded than her father had been, but she suspected Mary's conservative husband shared his father-in-law's views on education being wasted on women.

Forcing herself to the task at hand, she scribbled notes... starting with the friends Amelia mentioned most frequently. Heather Mackenzie topped the list and Harriet thought she might have a quiet word with Heather when she went to school the following day.

Her interest perked up when someone called only 'OS' began to be mentioned in entries dating a good month before the ball.

> *OS has returned to Singapore. I saw him today at church and hardly recognized him. He will be going up to Oxford in the autumn. He is so grown up and handsome that I nearly swooned when he brought me a cup of tea. We sat and talked for ages.*

It didn't take much deduction to work that 'OS' was probably Oliver Strong. Like all the sons and most of the daughters of the English community, he had returned to England for his schooling, returning only for the long holidays. He had been at the ball and Harriet had seen him with his parents at church the previous day.

She started scanning the entries for more mentions of OS and found he appeared in nearly every entry after that first meeting. Amelia had fallen hard for the young man, a few years her senior. She wondered if Oliver Strong had the slightest inkling of Amelia's infatuation, a question answered when she reached the last entry written on the Sunday before the ball.

> *After church today, I contrived to slip OS a note. I said I hoped to see him at the governor's ball. If I could find some time to be alone*

*in a private place I know of, I would pin a hankie to my shirt, and
he would see it. I can hardly breathe. Will he meet me? Kiss me? I
so long to be kissed.*

Harriet sat back and studied her notes. Oliver Strong had
struck her on their brief meeting as a solid, respectable young
man, not given to secret trysts with young girls but Amelia was
very attractive and to have a pretty, young lady all but throwing
herself at you, was an offer too good to refuse. It would have
ended in tears, of course, and once again she thanked God, she
would never be fifteen again.

Had they met up at the ball? Was it possible that the
rendezvous had gone wrong?

She shut the book and sat looking at it. Curran needed to
know about Oliver Strong.

She scrawled a hasty note and summoned Aziz.

———

In the drowsy late afternoon, the residents of St. Tom's house sat
in companionable silence on the veranda. Harriet was forcing
herself to darn Will's stockings, a job she hated. Julian sat at the
table, engaged in writing the homily for Amelia's funeral. He had
run his hand through his hair so often, it now stood on end.

Will lay on the daybed reading Rudyard Kipling's *Jungle Book*,
which he had borrowed from the library, Shashti perched on his
stomach. He set down the book and pushed Shashti off.

"I think that's Curran's motor vehicle," he said, moments
before the familiar vehicle turned in through the gates.

"You have the hearing of a cat," Julian said, closing his notebook, smoothing down his hair, and rolling down his sleeves,
before rising to greet Curran, who bounded up the steps to the
veranda two at a time.

"What brings you here?" Julian said.

Curran cast Harriet a glance. "Harriet sent for me."

"Did she indeed?" Julian said. "Will, I think that is our cue to practice a little slow bowling at the back of the house before supper. Go and fetch your bat." As Will scampered inside, Jullian asked in a low voice, "Caught the murderer yet, Curran?"

"No."

Julian huffed out a breath. "Amelia's funeral is tomorrow at the Bidadari Cemetery, at eleven in the morning. The family has requested it be private." He paused. "Will you be there?"

Curran nodded. "Yes. Duty dictates."

Julian nodded. "Leave you to whatever secret business brings you here."

Left alone, Curran slumped onto the seat beside Harriet with a heavy sigh.

"What is so urgent?" he asked.

"Two things. I went through Amelia's diary as you requested. The poor girl was hopelessly infatuated with Oliver Strong."

"Clive's boy?"

"That's the one. She had contrived to organize a rendezvous with Oliver at the ball. I don't know whether they met up or not... I certainly didn't see them together at any point. Wait there, I will fetch my notes."

She hurried into the house and collected the diary and her handwritten notes, together with an envelope containing the papers given to her by Sarah Bowman.

She handed the diary and her notes to Curran, and he read through them, checking them against the diary entries.

"Thank you. This is the closest thing I have to a sound lead in this case. I am going to need a chat with young Oliver Strong."

As he started to rise, Harriet put a hand on his arm. "There's something else. I fear I am about to add to your troubles. You need to see this."

She handed him the envelope containing the copy of the Venning letter. Curran unfolded the papers and began to read.

He took a sharp inward breath and looked up at Harriet. The color had drained from his face, his mouth a grim line.

"Where did you get this?"

Harriet swallowed. "I was given it by a journalist. A woman by the name of Sarah Bowman."

Curran shook his head. "Is she the new girl at the *Straits Times*?"

Harriet nodded.

"Did you read it?" he asked.

"Yes. It's horrific, Curran. No wonder the poor boy took his life. Is it the Venning letter?"

He nodded. "Word for word. What does this woman want?"

"She wants you to verify its authenticity."

"To what end?"

"She intends to use it to destroy Sir Henry Cunningham. Sarah Bowman is a member of the WSPU and Cunningham is one of the most vehement voices in the Asquith government against the suffrage cause. I don't think her motives have anything to do with justice for James Venning. Sarah is prepared to be a martyr to the suffragette cause, I fear. I have met her like before."

Curran looked up at her. "Harriet, if this comes out—"

"I know," she said. "It will destroy everyone in its radius, including you."

He swallowed. "And she wants me to confirm that it is an authentic copy? I can't do that, Harriet." He set the papers down and paced the veranda. "Ironically, only two people can verify its authenticity. Alice Venning is dead, and her daughter is... who knows where? The other person is Sidney Wallace and he won't do it. You're right, if this letter becomes public at this stage, it will destroy me completely. It will be me who will take the blame for covering up the investigation. I'm not a coward, Harriet, but I can't go through the hell they put me through in London six years ago. I was lucky to escape with my rank and a job."

"All either of us can do is avoid her," Harriet said. "Unless she can verify that is the Venning letter, she won't be able to publish."

He replaced the papers in the envelope and stuffed it into his pocket.

"Hopefully, I can avoid the woman," he said, leaving unspoken 'but it is a small island."

"I'm sorry, Curran."

"What for? It's nothing to do with you, Harriet. The Bowman woman is correct, Cunningham should be exposed for what he is, but he is not my concern at the moment. Right now, I need to find the man who killed a fifteen-year-old girl. And much as I would like it to be, I don't think it is Cunningham." He glanced at his watch. "I need to speak with Oliver Strong."

Harriet walked with him to the motor vehicle, where he turned and pulled her into his arms. He bent his head and kissed her, her arms going around his neck drawing her into him.

When they broke apart, she took a step back, restoring her disordered hair.

He stroked her cheekbone with his thumb. "I'm sorry I have so little time."

She smiled. "We can wait."

# TWENTY-THREE

It was a testament to Clive Strong's success in his legal practice that the family lived in an elegant home on Kent Hill, looking out over the harbor to the islands beyond. Curran found the family and several guests taking their leisure on the pristine lawns beside a well-tended tennis court. From the abandoned racquets and the tennis whites they all sported, he was interrupting a tennis party.

Clive rose to his feet and came ambling across the lawn to greet Curran with an outstretched hand. Curran had always liked the affable little lawyer who was now the senior partner of the firm of Lovett, Strong & Dickens. Charles Lovett had returned to England, a broken man after the terrible events surrounding the Singapore Amateur Dramatic and Music Society, leaving only his name behind him.

"Curran, good to see you, old chap! I hear you've been in London. How is the old country?"

"Cold and depressing," Curran said.

"Come and join us. The young people have been enjoying a spot of tennis, but we are done for the day and enjoying a sundowner."

A beer would be tempting, but Curran shook his head. "I'm here on business, Strong. I need to talk to your son."

Clive's eyes widened. "Oliver? What about?"

"The death of Amelia Hardcastle."

"But we've given our statements about that matter. One of your chaps came around yesterday afternoon."

After leaving Harriet, Curran had returned to South Bridge Road. He had read Oliver Strong's statement and decided it was missing a few key details, such as any mention of knowing Amelia Hardcastle, let alone arranging a tryst with her.

"Just need to clarify a couple of things with Oliver."

"He's not in trouble, is he?"

"No. Stop being the lawyer and just let me talk to him."

Strong gestured for his son to join him. "Curran here has a few questions for you, Oli. Do you want me to stay?"

Oliver rolled his eyes. "Father, I am quite capable of answering Mr. Curran's questions. You get back to our guests."

Clive shot Curran a suspicious glance, but did as his son asked and returned to the party.

"Is there somewhere we can talk privately?" Curran asked.

"The veranda?" Oliver suggested.

Curran had met many Oliver Strongs in his life: amiable young men from the public school system, with receding chins and foppish hair, which would probably desert them by the time they were thirty. Oliver was no exception. He clearly thought highly of himself, flicking back his overlong fair hair and talking about his time at Harrow and his plans for Oxford, as he and Curran walked toward the house.

In the shade of the wide, tiled veranda, furnished with white-painted rattan furniture and brightly colored cushions, Oliver sat down, carelessly crossing one leg over the other, a picture of wealth, confidence, and ease.

"What do you wish to talk to me about, Inspector?" he enquired.

"I won't keep you long," Curran said. "I am just clearing up a couple of matters from the incident at the ball on Friday night."

A small frown creased the young man's smooth forehead. "Oh yes, terrible business. Poor Melly Hardcastle. Word is that she was murdered. Have you caught the bastard who did it yet?"

"Not yet. I am still in the early stages of making inquiries."

Oliver hastily uncrossed his legs and sat up. "Oh God, I hope I'm not one of your inquiries?"

"What makes you say that?"

"It's rather embarrassing, but the silly thing had a bit of a crush on me. She just kept hanging around with great big puppy dog eyes."

"Did you give her any encouragement?"

A muscle twitched in the lad's cheek. "She was a pretty little thing. Hard not to feel a bit flattered by the adoration."

"Did she give you a note requesting a rendezvous at the Governor's Ball?"

Strong cleared his throat. "Yes. She passed it to me after church the previous Sunday."

"Do you still have it?"

"God, no. I tore it up the moment I got home. I had no intention of keeping the rendezvous. It had stopped being a game and I could see she was getting serious. I knew the only way to get rid of her was to cut her dead at the ball. Which is exactly what I did."

"Very gentlemanly," Curran said. "What did the note say?"

"Something about meeting me in the gallery during supper. If she could get away, she would wear a handkerchief pinned to her school blouse. All rather silly, childish stuff."

"When did you last see her?"

"The choir finished singing, and she saw me. She pointed to the gallery but as I just told you, I didn't go. I got into a chat with one of Pa's colleagues and he has contacts at Lincoln's Inn, and that was infinitely more interesting than a quick dalliance with a fifteen-year-old girl." He looked up. "You think I'm a cad?"

"I think you are a young man with your future ahead of you. Something, sadly, Amelia no longer has." Curran stood up. "Did you see her after that?"

Strong shook his head. "No. I thought she must have gone home, but then the unthinkable happened."

"Why didn't you put any of this in your statement, Mr. Strong?"

Oliver Strong stiffened. "I didn't think it was important."

Curran regarded him for a long moment. "A word of advice, Mr. Strong. If you are to make a future in the law, you need to learn that what you may or may not think is important is for others to judge."

"Point taken." Oliver looked down at his hands. "I'm not proud of myself, particularly in light of what happened. I keep thinking that if I had gone up to the gallery, she'd still be alive."

*That was probably true.*

"That is a matter for you and your conscience." Curran stood up and held out his hand. "Thank you for your time, Mr. Strong. My regards to your parents, I shall see myself out."

He stood beside his motor vehicle for a while looking out across the view of Singapore harbor and going through what Oliver had just told him. He would have to verify Strong's alibi, but he tended to believe that the young man was telling the truth.

Amelia Hardcastle, who had dreamed of nothing more than being kissed, had gone unwittingly to her death.

# TWENTY-FOUR

## MONDAY, 10 JULY

The late morning sun blazed down on the new British cemetery at Bidadari. In the absence of any shade, Harriet was thankful for her parasol as she walked slowly down the graveled paths between the graves with their bright new headstones. There were far too many for a cemetery that had only been opened three years previously. The pitiless climate spared no one.

A small knot of people stood around the gaping hole in the ground: Julian in his black cassock and white surplice with a black tippet hung around his neck, stood at the head of the grave, his prayer book in hand. Ellen and George Hardcastle stood beside the casket. The woman Ellen Hardcastle had been was lost in the severity of her mourning clothes, a heavy, dark veil covering her face. She clung to her husband on one side and on the other, Esme Prynne stood ready to provide an extra hand.

Harriet's fingers tightened on Curran's arm. They were the last to arrive. Julian caught her eye and nodded. He opened his prayer book and began...

"I am the resurrection and the life, saith the Lord: he that believeth in me, though he were dead, yet shall he live: and whosoever liveth and believeth in me shall never die—"

Ellen Hardcastle gave a choked sob and sank to her knees, throwing her arms across the coffin. Her husband and Esme gently lifted her away, and George Hardcastle put his arm around her shoulders as Julian continued, the old familiar words of the Book of Common Prayer some comfort for such a tragic occasion.

Harriet took a deep, steadying breath. The scar that never quite healed ripped open, and it took all her willpower to stifle tears that refused to be stilled. Beside her, Curran caught her hand. With the gentle pressure on her fingers, she knew he understood.

After the funeral, Curran drove Harriet and Julian back to St. Tom's House. It was a silent journey. No one had words to express the tragedy of a promising life cut so brutally short. Despite an offer of lunch, Curran didn't linger and Harriet watched him drive away and tried to imagine the weight of expectation he carried to find the girl's killer.

Both schools were closed for the day as a mark of respect. After lunch, Julian still went up to his office at the school. He had held the whole grueling process of laying a fifteen-year-old child to rest and he, probably even more than she, needed the time alone.

Will had gone across to Louisa Mackenzie's, leaving Harriet alone in the house. She distracted herself by catching up with some overdue correspondence for Julian's school—her unpaid job —that she was growing to resent more and more each day. Now she sat staring at the typewriter, drained and barely able to summon the energy to drink the cooling cup of tea beside her.

"Harriet!"

She looked up to see Lavinia Pemberthey-Smythe striding up

the driveway. Much as she liked Lavinia, she was in no mood for company.

"So glad I caught you in," Lavinia said.

She smoothed down her skirt and sat down across from Harriet, her face pinched and her eyes sparkling. It was unusual for Lavinia to pay visits. Even more so to find her dressed in her old-fashioned but still stylish 'best'.

"It has been a trying day, Lavinia—" Harriet began.

Lavinia blinked. "Oh, of course, the girl's funeral. I forgot. I won't keep you long."

Manners dictated politeness and Harriet asked, "What brings you here, Lavinia?"

"I've done it, Harriet."

"Done what?"

"I have an appointment to meet with Lady Evangeline Cunningham tomorrow afternoon."

"I thought the Cunninghams were in Penang?"

"They've returned early, so I decided to take the bull by the horns, so as to speak."

"Why do you want to speak to Lady Cunningham?"

Lavinia smiled. "I intend to ask her to be the patroness of my book on orchids, but Harriet... this is it... our chance to have the ear of the wife of an important member of the government."

It took a moment for Harriet to comprehend exactly what Lavinia was saying.

She frowned. "You mean to put to her the suffrage manifesto?"

"Of course."

Harriet pinched the bridge of her nose. "Lavinia, apart from getting this interview under false pretenses, I have already had words with Sir Henry on the subject, and he was quite clear that he abhors the suffrage cause. He called it a 'distraction to good government' and 'pandering to the whims of females'."

Lavinia sat back. "You didn't tell me this, Harriet?" She sounded hurt.

"I haven't had much of a chance to speak to you in recent days," Harriet pointed out. "What do you hope to achieve by speaking with Lady Cunningham?"

"A wife's opinion can hold great sway," Lavinia said.

"I think you overestimate Lady Cunningham's influence on her husband," Harriet said, "but I wish you well."

Lavinia took a deep breath, the lace on her bosom rising and falling.

"I would like you to come with me."

An icy chill ran down Harriet's spine. "Me? Why?"

"Because I am a realist. You and I do not have husbands whose careers can be ruined, and you can speak personally about the atrocities being committed by Asquith's government."

"Lavinia, I can't. Please don't ask me to do this."

The thought of baring her soul, the pain and humiliation of those days in Holloway to a woman like Evangeline Cunningham, filled her with horror. She knew Lady Cunningham's sort. Whatever her private views, she would uphold the views of her husband, and Harriet was all too well aware of where Sir Henry's sympathies lay.

"Yes, you can. Please Harriet, for the sake of our sisters in Holloway. You need to speak up, tell them what is happening."

Harriet turned and looked out across the garden, not seeing the bright bougainvillea or the lush green of the tropical foliage. Instead, she saw the damp, gray walls of Holloway, heard the footsteps on the flagstones outside her cell, and felt again the dread and mind-numbing fear of what was to come.

The force-feeding of hunger-striking suffragettes had not let up since her experience. If anything, as more women were incarcerated, it was becoming more and more prevalent. The British Government was torturing its own citizens. Perhaps Lavinia was right. She needed to speak up and educate people about what was happening behind those tall, gray walls. Maybe Lady Cunningham held some influence with her husband. Certainly, nothing would be gained by standing by and letting it continue.

"Harriet, please!" Lavinia sounded desperate.

Harriet swallowed. "What time tomorrow?"

Lavinia smiled. "Ten in the morning." Lavinia clasped Harriet's hands between her own. "Dear Harriet, there is so little we can do to help our sisters from so far away, but maybe this is something that might help."

"Maybe," Harriet said, but in her heart, she doubted it.

# TWENTY-FIVE

After the funeral, Curran arrived at South Bridge Road to find Chief Inspector Wallace in his office. The man looked far from well. He had a gray, pasty complexion and his face was sheened with sweat.

"Where have you been?" Wallace snarled.

"At the Hardcastle girl's funeral," Curran said.

Wallace grunted a grudging acceptance of the explanation. "How are the parents?"

"Destroyed," Curran said.

Wallace nodded. "And how are your investigations progressing?"

Curran updated Wallace on the investigation, adding his frustration at finding the governor and his guests had been allowed to leave the island.

"And how do you propose I could have stopped them?" Wallace responded. He wiped his forehead. "As it is, they're back. Not that you will be going anywhere near them."

Curran stared at him. "Why are they back so soon?"

Wallace shrugged. "Sir Henry is unwell."

"Someone will need to speak to them at some point," Curran said.

Wallace nodded, pressing the handkerchief to his lips.

"Speaking of unwell. You need to go home, Wallace," Curran said.

"Nonsense, I'm fine. Just got a touch of Delhi Belly. The whole family's down with it. Something in the filth that the cook is producing."

"Any illness in this climate can turn nasty very quickly," Curran said. "Go home."

"You just want to be rid of me." Wallace's tone was petulant.

That might have been true. Curran did want to be rid of the Chief Inspector, but at this moment, his concern for the man was genuine. He knew exactly how quickly the smallest illness could turn nasty in this climate.

He counted to five and said, "You are no good to anyone in this state."

"But I'm needed. I have to interview the governor and the Cunninghams."

"They won't thank you for seeing them in your current condition, Wallace."

"No. I suppose not. Damn it. There's no one else. Cuscaden's at a meeting in Johor for the next few days."

"At least let me speak to the governor," Curran said. "He knows me."

Wallace grunted and rose to his feet with an obvious effort.

"Very well. You can speak to Anderson and any of the government house staff we have missed. I'll go and see a doctor and get out of your hair for the rest of the day. I'll be back tomorrow, Curran. Keep your nose clean."

He clapped his helmet on his head and stumped out of the room.

Curran scowled at the man's departing back. What did Wallace think he was going to do?

Probably exactly what he intended to do... conduct the investigation as he saw fit, and if that meant disobeying orders and speaking to the Cunninghams, then so be it.

———

As Curran turned the motor vehicle into the gates of Government House, he confided his intentions to his sergeant.

Singh turned to look at him.

"This is a very bad idea, Curran. Wallace could take your commission for this."

Curran's hands tightened on the steering wheel. "I have to find the girl's killer, Singh, and I'm not going to do that until I have spoken to Sir Henry Cunningham."

"But the Chief Inspector—"

"Wallace can take my commission when I have solved this case, Singh, and this case cannot be solved unless I speak to everyone involved, including Sir Henry Cunningham."

"Are the Cunninghams and their staff in residence?" he asked Claud Severn on entering Government House.

"They are."

"Why was the official visit to the other Straits Settlements cut short?"

"Sir Henry has not been well since his arrival and Lady Cunningham was of the opinion that his health did not permit the journey to continue. The decision was made to return to Singapore. A doctor has just been, and Sir Henry has been ordered to rest."

"Mackenzie?"

"No. Doctor Garland I think his name is. He has ordered complete rest."

"He can rest after I have spoken with him," Curran said and turned for the staircase.

Severn all but jumped in front of him.

"Curran! No. Why is it so important that you see him?"

"Because he was there... at the ball... I need statements from both Sir Henry and Lady Cunningham and their staff. Anyone present that night has to be spoken with. It doesn't matter whether it's Sir Henry Cunningham or the lowliest kitchen hand."

"They are guests of Sir John. You can't just go barging up there."

"Then let me speak to Sir John."

Severn pointed at the black and white tiles on the floor. "Stay here. Do not move. I'll see what I can do."

Severn left Curran and Singh to kick their heels in the vast tiled hall of Government House. Curran felt the growing resentment prickling his neck and hoped it didn't show.

The vast double doors to the reception room on their right opened and Sir John Anderson himself strode out.

"What's this about, Curran?" he demanded. "Sir Henry is unwell, and I don't want him bothered. Doctor's orders."

"My apologies, Sir John, but I am just trying to do my job. I need to speak with you, too."

Sir John narrowed his eyes. "Where's your Chief Inspector? He gave me to understand he would be the one to interview me and that Sir Henry would not be troubled."

"Like Sir Henry, Chief Inspector Wallace is indisposed, so it is me. The quicker I can speak with you all, the quicker I can leave you in peace."

Sir John's lips tightened. "Very well." He turned to Claud Severn who had followed him out of the reception room. "Show Inspector Curran upstairs to the Cunninghams."

Curran turned to Singh, but Sir John held up a hand. "Just you, Curran."

Leaving Singh standing silent sentinel in the vast space of the entrance hall, Curran followed Claud Severn up the wide, marble staircase. The stairs were set at an uncomfortably low rise, no doubt to deliberately humble anyone ascending them. The staircase divided halfway up bringing the visitor up through the vast cavernous space into an area that echoed the space below, a wide hallway with formal rooms to the right and left.

Severn turned and led Curran in the opposite direction, toward the living quarters, past doors that he assumed were bedrooms. Another corridor cut across at right angles and they turned left, stopping before a solid, white-painted door.

"Wait here," Severn said.

He knocked, and the door opened a little way. He glimpsed a man behind the door and a whispered conversation.

The door shut and Curran and Severn waited in silence before the door opened again.

"Sir Henry and Lady Cunningham will receive you now."

A small man, absurdly attired in a heavy English woolen suit complete with a high starched collar and tie, opened the door wide to admit them. Curran recognized him at once as Ellis, Sir Henry's valet. The intervening years had not been kind to Ellis who had grown portly, his hair receding to a monkish fringe around the side of his head.

"Mr. Curran," Ellis said in a low, cold voice. "Never thought to see you again."

"It's a small world, Ellis," Curran said, equally as chilly. He hadn't liked or trusted Ellis six years ago. "Don't go too far. I have to speak with you as well."

Ellis inclined his head. "Very good, sir. This way."

A wide, airy veranda surrounded the vast guest chamber on three sides. Maneuvrable wooden louvers served in the place of window glass, admitting light and air. In this pleasant space, Sir Henry reclined on a white-painted, rattan daybed decorated with Indian silk coverings and cushions. He wore a silk dressing gown over a shirt and trousers. His wife sat on a rattan chair beside him, reading a small leather-bound book.

Neither of them rose to meet the policeman.

Sir Henry looked unwell. His cheeks had an unnatural hollowness and his clothes hung on him, indicating he had lost a great deal of weight. Curran thought of the man he had met six years previously. The intervening years and his illness had diminished him almost beyond recognition. By contrast, his wife, a stunning beauty in her youth, had mellowed into a strikingly handsome woman. Impeccably turned out in a sprigged muslin dress, she looked cool and collected—and not at all pleased to see him.

"Inspector Curran, Sir Henry," Claud Severn said.

The introduction was unnecessary. Both the Cunninghams had their gaze fixed on Curran with recognition, their loathing ill-disguised.

"We are acquainted with Mr. Curran. You may leave us, Mr. Severn." Lady Cunningham said. "And you, Ellis."

"If you are sure, my lady." Ellis cast Curran a doubtful look.

"Quite sure," she replied.

Curran waited until he heard the door shut.

"Well, Curran?" Lady Cunningham's tone dripped ice.

Brought up, as he had been, among the aristocracy, the patrician airs and graces of Lady Evangeline Cunningham did not intimidate Curran. She may have been the daughter of an earl, but he was the grandson of an earl. They stood on the same rung on the social ladder, in a manner of speaking. Whereas Henry Cunningham had been nothing more than an ambitious civil servant when he had married Evangeline for her considerable dowry and influence.

"Well indeed, Lady Cunningham. I had not expected we would meet again and in such sad circumstances."

Her nose twitched as if he had brought something unpleasant into the room. "I hoped we never would. Have you come to make more nasty little insinuations about my husband?"

"Not at all, m'lady. My only concern is with the murder of an innocent child. I have questions that need to be asked of every guest who was present at the ball on Friday night."

Lady Cunningham's eyes widened. "Murder? No one said it was murder. Just a tragic accident."

"Our investigations have progressed, and we have been forced to the conclusion that her death was not accidental."

Sir Henry spoke for the first time. "That is terrible news, Curran. How are the parents?"

"Devastated, as you can imagine. I would like this case resolved quickly for their sake."

"Then ask your questions and be quick about it. My husband is unwell, and the doctor has ordered him to rest," Lady Cunningham said.

As if in response, Sir Henry coughed into his handkerchief.

"I won't keep you long. I just need to know your movements on that night."

"Why? We had nothing to do with the unfortunate girl's death," Lady Cunningham said.

Curran took a breath. "Please, Lady Cunningham, the quicker we can get through my questions, the quicker I will be gone."

Lady Cunningham rolled her eyes. "Oh, very well. We arrived at about eight. A girls' choir sang the national anthem, rather badly I thought. A portrait was unveiled. There was dancing and more tedious singing before supper."

"Do you recall the girl who died?"

"Someone mentioned it was the girl who sang the solos," Lady Cunningham said. "She was rather a pretty, young thing. Nice manners too. She gave me a nosegay of flowers."

"Her name was Amelia Hardcastle," Curran said.

"Was that her name? It was all very dreary and hot and the company quite boring. Lawyers and shopkeepers and the like." As if to demonstrate her disdain for the local populace, Lady Cunningham fanned herself with a pretty, painted fan. "I was on the point of making my excuses when the accident occurred, and the evening came to an abrupt end."

Curran turned his attention to Sir Henry. "Did you notice Amelia Hardcastle, Sir Henry?"

Henry Cunningham scrutinized Curran with narrowed eyes as if he were waiting for Curran to accuse him of impropriety there and then.

"I had no reason to speak with any of them, beyond politely thanking them," he said. "I was quite fatigued so I retired to my bed as soon as I could politely withdraw."

"What time was that?"

"About nine-thirty," Lady Cunningham said. "Sir Henry is finding the travel and this infernal climate very hard." She leaned over and patted her husband's hand.

"It wasn't my choice to come on this tour," Cunningham mumbled, mopping his brow again.

"So, if you retired to this room around nine-thirty, can anyone vouch for you, Sir Henry?"

There it was. The stick that poked the wasp's nest.

"What are you implying, Curran?" the man growled.

"Nothing," Curran said. "I just need to reassure myself that you are accounted for in the time that the girl went missing to her body being found."

"My valet and my private secretary can certainly attest to my movements," Cunningham almost spat the words at Curran. "Other staff members saw us."

A knock on the door interrupted Curran's next question and he turned to see who entered.

A slight young woman, in a navy dress, buttoned up to her neck and relieved only by pristine white collar and cuffs stood in the doorway holding a tray on which a pretty, blue and white flowered teapot and cups had been placed.

Her gaze met Curran's, and he had to stop himself from saying her name aloud. She would be in her late twenties now.

Her face had lost the glow of her youth and carried instead the tragedies she had to bear. But he would have known her anywhere, and from the frightened look he gave her, she knew him, and she was willing him to say nothing.

Mary Venning, James Venning's older sister.

"So sorry, ma'am," the woman said, forestalling anything he had to say. "I bought Sir Henry's tisane."

"Just set it on the table," Lady Cunningham pointed with her fan.

"And you are?" Curran found his voice.

"My maid, Mary Brown," Lady Cunningham said.

"Don't go too far, Miss Brown, I will need to speak with you as well," Curran said.

"I can't see that she would have anything to say that would be remotely of interest," Lady Cunningham shrugged, "But if you must. That will be all, Brown."

Mary Brown effected a small, bobbed curtsey and left the room without looking at Curran.

Curran recovered his composure and thoughts and unbuckled his satchel, pulling out the paper evidence bag containing the purple dress.

"Have either of you ever seen this before?"

Lady Cunningham's lip curled. "Is that blood?"

"Yes," Curran replied. "Have you seen this dress before?"

"Put that disgusting object away," Lady Cunningham turned her head, fanning herself. "It's not one of mine. Why are you showing it to us?"

"The girl was wearing this dress. Sir Henry, have you ever seen it before?"

"No, I have not, and I don't like your implication, Curran," Sir Henry responded.

"I'm not implying anything. I merely asked if you had seen this dress before?"

"I told you I haven't. Now put it away. You are upsetting my wife."

Curran complied, tucking the evidence back in his satchel.

Lady Cunningham rose to her feet, a signal that, as far as she was concerned, the interview was over. She moved across to the table and poured a pale liquid from the teapot that her maid had brought into the room.

"My husband needs to rest. Good day, Inspector Curran."

He had pushed them as far as he dared.

Curran turned on his heel and left the room.

He found Mary Venning waiting for him in the shadows of the corridor, her arms wrapped tightly around her slight frame.

"I think I am owed an explanation," he said.

Her lips twitched. "Not here. This bedroom's empty."

She flung open a door, and he followed her into an unused bedroom, the furniture covered in dust sheets and a faint musty odor in the stale air.

"Mary Venning," Curran said. "How in God's name did you end up calling yourself Mary Brown and working as lady's maid to Lady Cunningham of all people?"

"Keep your voice down," she said. "These walls don't just have ears, they have a telegraph service."

"You haven't lost your sense of humor," Curran said.

The woman he knew as Mary Venning responded. "Oh, I have, Curran. I find myself with precious little to smile about these days." She met his gaze. "I was not left with much choice but to look for work below my station in life. After James died, Mother went into a decline. I nursed her to the end, but the cost of medical treatments took the last pence my father had left. The house was heavily mortgaged, and we had long since been evicted. All the light went from my life after our beautiful boy left us."

"I'm sorry, but Lady Cunningham of all people ... does she know who you are?"

Mary shook her head. "No. I'm just plain Mary Brown to her and that bastard of a husband."

"What's wrong with him?"

She shrugged. "No one knows. He's been poorly on and off for nearly a year now. He didn't want to come on this trip, but the Prime Minister insisted."

"How long have you been with Lady Cunningham?"

"Almost two years now." Her lips twisted in a humorless smile. "I forged my references."

Curran ran a hand over his eyes. "You still haven't told me why you are working for them. I don't for a minute believe it was a coincidence and you needed a job."

Her chin came up. "I thought I could succeed where you failed, Curran."

He flinched, and she touched his arm. "That's unfair. I know you didn't fail us. It was taken out of your hands. I saw an opportunity to be on the inside of the house and find the evidence we needed to bring Cunningham to justice for what he did to James."

"And have you?"

Mary's lips twisted. "It's not been easy. If that sort of activity occurs, it's when Lady Cunningham adjourns to the country estate. Me with her."

"He uses the London house?"

Mary's eyes slid sideways. "What does it matter? None of this brings James back and men like Henry Cunningham never see justice."

Curran looked away.

"It matters, Mary. A young girl died here on Friday night and there are aspects of her death that are very reminiscent of the conduct described by James."

Mary looked up at him, her eyes wide. She bit her lip. "I heard about the girl's death, of course. The servants can talk about nothing else, but do you think Sir Henry could be involved?"

"He says he left the ball and retired to bed early. Did you see him?"

"I was busy packing for Lady Cunningham. We had an early

start on Saturday morning, but I can confirm Sir Henry came back early. Mr. Ellis came looking for me to make up the tisane for him, like the one I just took in for him."

"Do you always do that for Sir Henry?"

Mary shrugged. "He likes the way I do it. A herbalist in London prescribed it when he first started getting sick and he says it helps his sleep and settles his digestion."

"What time was that?"

Mary shrugged. "The fireworks had started, so it was just after ten and you have my word, Sir Henry was tucked up in bed."

"Have you seen this dress before?"

He pulled the purple dress out of his satchel and spread it out on the bed. Mary ran her hand over the fabric, her fingers lingering on the bodice and the torn sleeve.

She shook her head. "No. It's old... five or six years at least. Not in very good condition either. See the scuffing at the hemline? Was she wearing it?"

Curran nodded.

Mary withdrew her hand from the object as if she had been scalded. "I'm sorry. I can't help you, Curran. Now, unless you have any further questions, I will return to my duties. And as far as you are concerned, my name is Mary Brown and we have only met today."

"Mary, before I go, you said you were packing, but tell me exactly what you were doing on the night of the ball?"

She gave a snort of bitter laughter. "I told you I was here— pressing and packing Lady Cunningham's vast wardrobe for the trip to Penang. I got her ladyship dressed and saw her off just before eight. She returned around ten thirty, which surprised me. I'd not expected her back so soon, but she told me that the festivities had concluded following an unfortunate accident. She didn't elaborate. I only found out later the girl had died."

"How did she seem to you?"

"Like she always is."

"Not the easiest of mistresses?"

Mary's mouth twisted. "What do you think, Curran?"

"And did you see anyone else that evening?"

"Just Ellis. Now, if there's nothing else, I have things to be getting on with."

"For now. Where will I find Ellis?"

"If he's not with Sir Henry, try his room."

She turned for the door and as she laid her hand on the door-knob, he said, "Mary, I'm sorry. I never got a chance to tell you and your mother how truly sorry I was."

"We knew what had happened," Mary said. "You did your best, Mr. Curran but the Cunninghams are too powerful."

Even the powerful were not invincible and he thought of the letter he carried in his pocket, not trusting to leave it anywhere it could be found. All it would take was a single word to a journalist and the Cunninghams would be destroyed. James Venning deserved justice, but that was not why he was here. Another young person also cried out for justice, and Amelia Hardcastle was his priority.

He tracked the valet down to a small, stuffy cupboard of a bedroom, where he found the man polishing shoes.

"Mr. Curran," Ellis said with a curl of his lip. "What can I do for you?"

"Can you tell me your movements on Friday night?"

Ellis laid down his brush and set down the shoe he was work-ing on.

"Friday night. Sir Henry didn't want to go to the ball. He was tired from the day's activities, but he felt he had to make a show, so he got dressed up, and off he went. I wasn't surprised to see him back about nine-thirty, ready for his bed. I saw to his needs and put him to bed. He was firmly tucked up by ten. The fire-works had just commenced when Brown came in with his tisane."

"And you were with him the whole time?"

Ellis did not blink as he said, "I was with him the whole time.

I know what you're thinking, Mr. Curran, and I can tell you that he had nothing to do with that unfortunate girl's death." He paused. "All of that's in the past. He's not well."

"So, everyone keeps telling me. What ails him, Ellis?"

Ellis gave a half shrug. "Gastric disorder, the doctors call it. Her ladyship has been a saint, nursing him through his bad days. Never thought a lady like her would have it in her, but she's always there to hold his hand and wipe his brow. I won't hear a bad word against them. Either of them."

Curran turned for the door and thanked the valet for his time. He had one more person to interview and halfway down the grand staircase, Curran encountered Sir Henry's private secretary and asked for a moment of his time.

Gilmore shrugged. "I am at a bit of a loose end at the moment. You've probably heard that Sir Henry is unwell?"

"I have spoken to him."

Gilmore quirked an eyebrow. "Have you indeed? I thought—"

"You thought I had been told not to bother him? Unfortunately, Chief Inspector Wallace is himself indisposed and someone had to talk to him."

Gilmore flushed. "Very well. What do you want to ask me?"

"Your movements on Friday night?"

"I was on duty, Inspector. Made sure the right people met Sir Henry and at nine-thirty, I escorted him back to the main house as he wished to retire."

"Did you stay with him?"

"I returned to the ballroom just before the fireworks and the delightful Mrs. Gordon and I had just taken a turn on the dance floor when the girl's body was discovered."

"Did you see Sir Henry again?"

"No. Sir John shut proceedings down and I retired to my bed. I knew we had an early start in the morning so I was in bed by eleven-thirty at the latest. I did not see Sir Henry from the time I left him with Ellis to the following morning when we embarked on the Government yacht."

"Tell me, Gilmore, how long have you been with Sir Henry?"

Gilmore smiled. "Nearly three years, Inspector." He paused. "Lady Cunningham has informed me of your history with the Cunninghams and if your next question touches on past events, I can assure you I have seen nothing in my time with the man to give me any pause. I have the highest regard for him."

Curran summoned a smile. "Pleased to hear it, Mr. Gilmore. Back to the present. Did you happen to see the girl or anyone talking to her during the evening?"

"I saw nothing untoward, Inspector, and you have my word if I do recall anything, I shall be sure to tell you."

Curran bid the man good day and let him continue on his way.

Dispirited, he joined Singh in the front hall before going in search of Claud Severn. They found him in his office. He stood up as Curran entered and removed his glasses, polishing them on a handkerchief.

"Are you done, Inspector?"

Curran nodded. "Thank you for your co-operation and pass on my regards to Sir John."

Severn blinked as he returned the glasses to his nose. "I hope that is the end of it, Curran."

"It will not be at an end until we find who killed the girl, Severn."

"Of course," Severn blustered, "but it was not one of us, Curran."

That remains to be seen, Curran thought as he drove away from Government House.

# TWENTY-SIX

## TUESDAY, 11 JULY

Harriet tossed and turned during the night, struggling for a reason... or an excuse... anything to evade Lavinia's meeting with Lady Cunningham, but in the end, dressed in her Sunday dress and matching hat, she joined her friend, and the two women arrived at Government House in a hackney.

They were met in the front hall by a uniformed servant and told to wait. It was ten long minutes before the servant reappeared and advised that Lady Cunningham would receive them in the upstairs drawing room.

Despite having recently traversed these hallowed halls, Harriet struggled to control her nerves as they followed the man up the broad stairs to the upstairs landing. It was a building designed to intimidate, and it succeeded. She just wanted to turn and run.

The man paused before the massive doors to their right, and opened both intoning, "Mrs. Pemberthey-Smythe and Mrs. Gordon."

Lady Cunningham was arranged, Harriet thought, on a Louis

XIV sofa covered in a cream and gold striped fabric. She wore a simple dress of a green sprigged muslin and sat with a back so straight she could have been used as carpenter's level.

She indicated two chairs, identical in style, similar in covering and discomfort, to the sofa. To add credence to her story, Lavinia carried a large portfolio containing, she told Harriet, Samrita's recent botanical drawings of her orchid collection and she set this down on the table between them.

"Ladies, please sit. What can I do for you?"

Lavinia undid the tapes that secured the portfolio. "Lady Cunningham, I am something of an acknowledged expert in Orchidaceae—orchids—and I have been working on a definitive study of the orchids of this region." She glanced at Harriet. "Mrs. Gordon has been assisting me with typing up my notes, and this is a selection of some of the paintings I intend to use as illustrations."

Lady Cunningham picked up the first one.

"This is exquisite," she said. "Who is your illustrator?"

"A young woman who has been studying under the artist Thomas Barker, who painted the portrait of Sir John. She is very gifted," Lavinia said.

Lady Cunningham picked up the next painting. "I would hang these on my wall." She laid them down and fixed Lavinia with an enquiring eye. "Why are you showing them to me?"

"Because I would like to ask you to be the patron of my book," Lavinia said. "Someone of your status in life will be greatly helpful in seeing my dream of this book come to fruition."

Lady Cunningham raised a perfectly arched eyebrow. "I am very flattered, of course, but what does that entail?"

Lavinia held up a hand. "I have a publisher. I just require a foreword to the book and some assistance in promoting the book among your friends and acquaintances."

"I think I can do that," Lady Cunningham said. "In return,

could I ask for six of these paintings to hang in my home in London?"

"Of course," Lavinia said.

An awkward silence followed. Lady Cunningham looked from one to the other. "Is there something else I can assist you with?"

The butterflies in Harriet's stomach beat a warning tattoo as Lavinia found her voice.

"Your ladyship. I am secretary of the Women's Social and Political Union here in Singapore."

Lady Cunningham's eyes widened. "You are here to discuss orchids, Mrs. Pemberthey-Smythe," she said. "If you wish to discuss the disgusting behaviour of the WSPU then I am afraid our interview is over."

She made to rise.

"Disgusting behavior?" Harriet said, her reaction coming from her exhaustion, not from any sensible part of her mind.

Lady Cunningham turned her hard gaze on Harriet. "Vandalism and rioting. Sir Henry's own office had all the windows broken. His staff were terrified."

"I do not condone the Deeds Not Words policy by some of the more extreme elements of the organization," Lavinia said. "It is about suffrage. Allowing you... and your daughter an equal right to a say in government. You have a daughter, I believe?"

Lady Cunningham's long, patrician nose twitched.

"I have two daughters and I am being careful to shield them from such nonsense as the WSPU and the like are espousing. They know their duty lies in the hearth and home in support of their husbands, just as I have done."

"Lady Cunningham," Lavinia continued. "I have brought some literature for you to read." She laid the pamphlets on the table between them. "You are in a unique position to bring some influence to bear on your husband. For example, the current government policy of force-feeding the women imprisoned for doing nothing more than highlighting the inequity of a system that denies women the right to vote is cruel and degrading."

Lady Cunningham's lip curled. "Those women get everything they deserve."

A red mist of growing anger rose in Harriet's breast, and she uttered a sound that came out as a squeak. Lavinia laid a hand on Harriet's arm, but it was too late.

"Those women, as you refer to them, are political prisoners. They have committed no offense except to bring the injustice of our system of government to the attention of the public and yet they are tortured... in the name of your husband's government."

"Nonsense," Lady Cunningham interposed. "They bring it on themselves. If they are foolish enough to go on hunger strikes, they should be grateful that their lives are preserved by the administration of nourishment."

"Do you know anything about how the nourishment is administered?" Harriet's right hand began to shake, and she clutched it hard with her left and continued before Lady Cunningham could interrupt. "The women are held down in a chair by four wardresses and tipped back in such a way as to be rendered helpless. A metal gag is forced into their mouths and a filthy tube is inserted down their throat or their nose. The nourishment, as you call it, is then tipped into a funnel and down the tube. They are subjected to what amounts to an act of utmost cruelty and degradation for what? Trying to make their voices heard?"

Lady Cunningham had gone completely still. "And how do you know this?"

"Because it happened to me," Harriet said. "When the tube was wrongly inserted, I nearly died."

The woman's cold, gray-green eyes did not leave Harriet's face.

186 A.M. STUART

"And why, pray, were you in Holloway? I can only assume that a court of law sent you there?"

"A group of us marched peacefully on the Houses of Parliament. We were set upon by the police. We only defended ourselves."

Lady Cunningham did not speak for a very long moment, but two bright spots of color had appeared on her high cheekbones.

"And what do you think I can do?" she asked, her tone frigid, inviting no response.

"You can inform yourself, Lady Cunningham. Talk to your husband. I am sure he will listen to you," Lavinia said.

This time Lady Cunningham did stand, a signal that the interview was over. Lavinia and Harriet followed suit.

Lady Cunningham turned to Harriet. "My husband is a loyal member of Mr. Asquith's government. There is nothing I can do or say that would dissuade him of those views," she said. "I am sorry for your experience Mrs. Gordon and while I might have some personal sympathy for your story, my husband abhors the unseemly behaviour and tactics of these so-called suffragettes. As a pillar of society, he cannot be seen to condone such aberrant and unladylike behavior."

This time, the red mist turned into an unstoppable flood.

"A pillar of society who seeks out sexual congress with underage boys and girls?" Harriet burst out and immediately wished the ground would open up and swallow her.

Both Lavinia and Lady Cunningham were staring at her, with their mouths agape.

"How dare you make such a defamatory claim without evidence or basis. Where did you hear such a scurrilous tale?" The words dripped like ice from Lady Cunningham.

"You might have thought the evidence destroyed," Harriet could no longer contain herself, "but it still exists. A letter left by one of your husband's victims who took his own life. I have read it and if I was not a woman of the world, I would not in my wildest imagination have thought such depravity existed, let alone committed by your so-called pillar of society. A journalist has that letter and any day a story could come out with the truth about your husband's unpleasant private life."

Lady Cunningham's eyes widened, and the color drained from her face. "The letter exists? Who has it? Tell me their name?" The woman's shoulders shook as if she were trying to suppress an urge to lunge at Harriet, but she drew back, her eyes narrowing. "I know exactly who has been spreading these stories. Curran. I can destroy him, Mrs. Gordon. If one word of what has passed here today becomes public knowledge, I will know exactly where it came from."

Harriet glanced at Lavinia and the full implications of what she had just said was written in Lavinia's shocked expression. Harriet's heart swooped to her guts and she thought she might be sick.

"Get out." Lady Cunningham's voice was low, and her words slow and calculated. She was more terrifying in that moment than she would have been if she had screamed and thrown cushions.

Harriet turned for the stairs, tears blinding her as she ran out onto the graveled driveway with Lavinia behind her.

Lavinia grabbed her by the arms and whirled her around to face her. "Harriet, what on earth got into you? What were you saying? What is this letter?"

"A letter written by a young man detailing Sir Henry's proclivities. Sarah Bowman has a copy of the letter. It was vile, Lavinia. The man is a pervert of the worst kind."

"But how do you know it is true? Was she right? Did Curran tell you about Sir Henry and this letter?"

Harriet nodded. "Yes. He worked on the case back in London before it was all made to disappear. I promised him, Lavinia... promised him I would say nothing about it. He'll never forgive me."

She needed Lavinia to reassure her and tell her she was being foolish and, of course, Curran would forgive her. He loved her.

But Lavinia remained silent.

"Oh, Harriet, what have you done?" was all Lavinia could say.

# TWENTY-SEVEN

C urran stood at the evidence table, deep in thought, nursing the vain hope that inspiration or some previously overlooked detail would reveal itself. He had arrived that morning braced for a confrontation with Wallace about his flagrant ignoring of orders and his interviewing the Cunninghams.

To his profound relief, Wallace was, according to Nabeel, quite unwell and unable to attend the office. The doctor had ordered him to keep to his bed for the next few days. That suited Curran down to the ground. If he could solve the case in that time, he would mitigate the risk of further disciplinary action being taken against him.

"Inspector," Nabeel hovered at his elbow. "There is a lady at the front desk who wishes to speak to you."

Curran looked up. "Name?"

"She didn't say."

Curran's instincts prickled, and he hurried down to the front desk, in the hope that this anonymous woman might have the critical piece of the puzzle that would lead to the crime being solved.

A neatly dressed English woman, wearing a straw boater and wire-rimmed glasses, sat waiting on the hard bench, her hands crossed over a sturdy leather handbag.

"Inspector Curran?"

"Yes, and you are?"

The woman smiled and rose to her feet, holding out her hand to him.

He took it as she said, "Sarah Bowman. I work for the Straits Times."

The hairs on the back of his neck prickled. This was the woman Harriet had mentioned, the one in possession of the Venning letter and he suspected she came in search of information rather than to provide it.

"How can I help you, Miss Bowman?"

"I won't keep you long, Inspector. Is there somewhere we can talk in private?"

He showed her into an adjacent interview room, and she took a seat at the table. He remained standing.

She wasted no time. "Has Mrs. Gordon spoken to you?"

"She speaks to me often."

"Let's not play games. Did she show you the letter?"

The very letter that burned a hole in his pocket as she spoke.

"Yes," he said.

"Well?"

"You want to know if I can confirm if it is a copy of the original letter?"

"That is correct."

"I'm not going to do that, Miss Bowman, and my advice to you is to desist in your pursuit of the matter."

"Inspector, this is your opportunity to get justice for James Venning. All I need is for you to confirm the letter's authenticity."

"I want nothing to do with it."

Her mouth quirked. "A girl has died. Did Sir Henry have anything to do with it?"

"Miss Bowman, you will get nothing from me. Now please excuse me, I have matters that need attending to."

Sarah Bowman compressed her lips and stood up. "Whatever you say, I will not rest until Sir Henry Cunningham is brought to justice,"

"I appreciate the sentiment, Miss Bowman, but I do not understand your interest in this case."

Her eyes glinted. "Cunningham is a member of the Asquith government," she said. "The government that is imprisoning and torturing honest women for merely asking for a right to vote. Bring him down and the rest will fall."

"So, your interest is not in justice for James Venning or his family?"

She bridled. "Of course it is. What happened to him is monstrous and is probably still going on. It has to be stopped. Don't tell me that you haven't considered the possibility that Cunningham is involved in the death of the girl?"

"Her name was Amelia Hardcastle, and no, I do not believe he was involved. Now, please excuse me, Miss Bowman."

He opened the door and ushered her out, waiting until she was back on the street before he turned back to his office. Whatever his private feelings about Sarah Bowman's crusade, he had to concentrate on the present, not the past.

Amelia Hardcastle's death had, he was sure, nothing to do with Sir Henry Cunningham, however much it suited his sensibilities to bring the man to justice. But he could not afford to underestimate Miss Bowman. He recognized a zealot when he met one.

# TWENTY-EIGHT

There had been a time, not so long ago, when the stairs up to the Detective Branch had seemed as familiar to Harriet as the steps to her own front door. Now her boot heels echoed dully in an unfamiliar atmosphere.

She played the forthcoming scene between herself and Curran over in her head, and it never ended well. He had been angry with her on other occasions when she had overstepped the bounds of her authority, but this time she had crossed not just a line, but an ocean. She had done the one thing Curran could never forgive. She had betrayed his trust and there would be consequences not just to their still fragile relationship but to his work, his life—and their future.

Having braced herself to confront Curran, she found the office empty except for Nabeel, who now sat behind the typewriter at what had been her desk, pecking at the keys with two fingers and a frown of concentration.

She coughed, and the clerk jumped up with a broad smile.

"Mrs. Gordon, it is good to see you," Nabeel said. Always softly spoken, his voice barely raised above a whisper.

"And you. Do I need to give you some typing lessons, Nabeel?"

Relief flooded his face. "You can do that? The Chief Inspector wants everything typed, and I..." He spread his hands in a gesture of defeat.

"I will see what can be arranged," Harriet said. "Is Inspector Curran around?"

Nabeel shook his head. "He is, ma'am, but he is interviewing someone." Nabeel gestured at the visitor's bench. "Will you wait?"

Overwhelmed by the desire to turn and run, Harriet glanced at the hard bench outside the office that had once been Curran's but now had CHIEF INSPECTOR WALLACE painted on the door. Wallace was the last person she needed to see today.

She must have grimaced because Nabeel smiled. "The Chief Inspector is indisposed. You are quite safe."

Relieved that she didn't have to face Wallace, Harriet walked across to the evidence table, where the items relating to the crime were displayed. She found herself drawn to the amethyst silk and lace evening dress Amelia had been wearing and, without touching anything, she bent over to study the bead-encrusted bodice, once again impressed by the fine needlework.

The door crashed open, and Curran entered the room.

"Bloody woman," he said.

He tossed his hat onto a desk and pushed back his damp hair. Only then did he appear to notice Harriet, standing motionless beside the evidence table.

"Who is the bloody woman you refer to?" she asked.

"Sarah Bowman. Harriet, what are you doing here?" He jerked his head at Wallace's office. "I think in future you are best to ask for me at the front desk."

She flushed. Of course, this was no longer Curran's domain and there were new rules in force. She took a breath and forced a smile. "I need to talk with you. It's important."

"If it's about that Bowman woman, I've just seen her."

She shook her head. "No." Harriet looked around. "Not here. Can we go outside?"

He shrugged. "Of course. I could do with some lunch. Shall we pick up a samosa from the wallah on South Bridge Road?"

Harriet wasn't hungry, but she readily agreed. They purchased the fragrant pastries from the street vendor and wandered around to the back of the police complex where there was a courtyard dominated by an old rain tree, under which someone had obligingly placed a bench. Curran waved her onto the bench, and they sat together in companionable silence, dropping flaky golden pastry crumbs for the raucous Myna birds to pick up from the ground at their feet.

Curran brushed the last of the crumbs from his uniform and wiped his fingers on a handkerchief which he offered to Harriet, saying, "It's clean."

"Sarah Bowman wasted no time," Harriet said. "What did you tell her?"

"That I wouldn't help her. She can fight her own battles. However, I doubt she'll give up easily." He paused. "She can always try asking Wallace. He knows as much about the Venning case as I do."

"Do you think she would?"

"I think he'd run a mile." He shrugged. "She's one of your lot, isn't she?"

"My lot?"

"The WSPU?"

Harriet nodded and the reason for her visit settled like a dead weight on her heart. Her stomach lurched and for a horrible moment, she thought she might be sick.

She looked up at him.

"Curran, I did something foolish."

He frowned. "Go on."

"Lavinia and I went to meet with Lady Cunningham. Lavinia

had implied it was to discuss her book on orchids, which it was, but she was determined to raise the issue of the suffragettes."

Curran frowned. "And she took you along for moral support?"

Harriet looked at the ground where one persistent Myna still poked around, looking for crumbs.

"I should never have agreed to go. It was a mistake. I told her Sir Henry's views on the suffrage movement, but she hoped that his wife may be more amenable."

"And was she?"

"No. She was beastly. She told us that the women in jail deserved to be there and they should be grateful that they were being kept alive with force-feeding." Harriet took a breath. "It got worse. She... she riled me with her talk about how her husband is a pillar of society and... and... I blurted out what I knew... what you told me in confidence about Sir Henry and about the letter —"

Curran flinched. "Ah."

She turned to him, fighting back the tears. "I'm so, so sorry, Curran. I broke my promise to you. You know it's not like me to be so careless, but she made me so angry."

He stood up and took a few steps, running his hand through his hair and for a moment, she feared the worst and braced for him to deliver the coup de gras, ending their relationship. But when he turned back, she saw no anger in his face. He sat down beside her and took her hand in his.

"Harriet, what you endured in Holloway is the scar that will never quite heal. What Evangeline Cunningham did was to tear it open again."

"But she said she is going to destroy you."

He huffed out a humorless laugh. "I hear the weather is very pleasant in the mosquito-ridden swamps of West Africa," he said.

Harriet stared at him, and he smiled, his fingers tightening on hers.

"I can fight my own battles, Harriet. She's scared... terrified may be a better word."

"But it gets worse. I told her about the Venning letter."

Curran's mouth tightened. "Did you say who had it?"

She shook her letter. "I just said a journalist had a copy."

Curran said nothing for a long moment and Harriet blurted out. "Curran, I'm so sorry."

"Stop apologizing. I'm not angry, Harriet. I don't think she'll come after me again. This time I hold the cards. I know copies of the Venning letter exist and all I have to do is tell Miss Bowman what she wants to hear, and it becomes public. Too many people know the truth and she won't want to risk the public exposure."

Harriet stared at him. "Are you sure?"

He smiled. "I'm never sure about anything, Harriet, except you. I am sure about you, and I am not going to let Lady Cunningham come between us." He stood up and held out his hand to help her rise. "Now I need to get back to work, and I am sure you have better things to be doing."

# TWENTY-NINE

Curran returned to his desk in a daze, Harriet's words ringing in his ears.

Poor Harriet... He could only imagine what it had taken for Lady Cunningham to provoke such a response from her. He blamed Lavinia, who should never have put Harriet in such a position.

He had told her the truth when he said he held the upper hand with regard to Lady Cunningham, but that didn't mean she couldn't make life very unpleasant, particularly if she involved Wallace or Cuscaden. He had only been half joking about the mosquito-ridden swamps of West Africa. There were worse outposts of the British Empire than Singapore to which he could be posted.

He could not settle to the notes that needed writing up. He needed to clear his head, so he took his motor vehicle out to Bukit Timah where his horse, Leopold, was stabled, and took Leo for a long ride down the laneways and deep into the jungle surrounding the hills.

Dusk was closing in when he returned to the stables, hot and tired and still without any clear answers. He saw to Leopold and remembered he was expected at Lavinia's for dinner.

It was too late to change, and he turned up at Lavinia's home hot, sweaty, and disheveled. Lavinia greeted him without the usual humor on her face and he apologized for his appearance.

"You could at least have washed," she said. "You smell of horse."

Chastened, he took himself off to the bathroom to do his best. When he returned, he found her seated at the table, a bottle of beer beading moisture onto the table in front of his place.

"That's better," she said. "Have you seen Harriet today?"

Curran took a swig of the beer. "Yes, I have, and I blame you, Lavinia."

"Me?"

"You put her in an invidious position. What happened to Harriet in Holloway it's... it's like a soldier on the battlefield. It never goes away, and it can take the smallest thing to bring all that horror back."

Lavinia had the grace to look away. "I hadn't anticipated Lady Cunningham's reaction," she said. "It was brutal. The woman goaded her. Do you think she will make a formal complaint to Cuscaden?"

Curran shrugged. "As far as I know, Cuscaden is unaware of the Venning case. As I told Harriet, it seems to me that she can hardly make a complaint without the subject of which she is complaining, becoming more widespread knowledge than it already is."

Lavinia ran a finger around the cut decoration on her glass of gin and tonic.

"Is it true? Sir Henry Cunningham is involved in..." she paused, seeking for a word, "perversions?"

Curran sighed. "I don't know what was said in your conversation with Lady Cunningham, but it is probably best you don't know the details. Leave it at that, Lavinia."

Lavinia frowned. "Do you think Sir Henry had anything to do with the girl's death?"

"Much as there is a part of me that would like to think he did, it is looking doubtful." Curran looked out into the darkening garden. "Where is Samrita tonight?"

Lavinia shrugged. "Probably with Tom."

Curran frowned. "How often is she 'with Tom'?"

"Is it any of your business?"

"Well... yes. I pay her bills... and his too."

"Are you afraid you are losing her?"

He shrugged. "She was never mine to lose."

"Then you have answered your own question. We are rarely blessed to meet our soul mates and for Samrita to have found someone like Tom Barker, particularly after everything she has suffered, is something to be rejoiced."

Curran took the second beer Lavinia's servant held out to him. They ate their dinner, restricting conversation to the mundane, before Curran took his leave and returned to the police lines where he consumed most of a bottle of Scotch. It would have been a whole bottle, but after a couple of glasses, he had sat staring at his glass with the realization that turning to whisky every time life dealt him a blow had become something of a bad habit.

He pushed it aside and fell into his bed and another nightmare of darkness and death.

# THIRTY

A pounding on Curran's door woke him at first light.
Bleary-eyed and nursing a splitting headache, he opened
the door to a bright young constable.

"Sorry to disturb you, Inspector, but there is an emergency.
You are wanted on the telephone."

Curran pulled on trousers and his dressing gown and stumbled down to the duty room where a telephone had been recently
installed.

"Curran," he mumbled into the speaker.

"Claud Severn, Curran. There's been a..." Severn swallowed
audibly. "A death. You are needed at Government House."

"Wallace—"

"Rang him. Can't raise his head off his bed, according to his
wife. She said to ring you."

"Right. I'll be there in half an hour, Severn."

He issued instructions to the duty Constable to rouse
Greaves, who also lived in the police lines, and send a message to

Sergeant Singh. He washed and shaved, nicking himself in his haste, and pulled out a fresh uniform.

Still dabbing at the cut on his chin, he collected Greaves and drove, as fast as his limited motor vehicle would permit, to Government House. The guards on the gate admitted him without preamble and, leaving Greaves to unload his camera and equipment, he met Claud Severn in the front hall.

The normally unflappable private secretary looked as if he had dressed hurriedly. His tie was not properly knotted, his glasses were slightly askew, and he was unshaven.

"Take a breath, Severn. Tell me what's happened."

Severn glanced up the stairs to the private quarters. "It's Sir Henry. His valet went to wake him with a cup of tea at six, as was the man's habit, and found him dead."

Curran ran through the possible scenarios. Sir Henry had not been well. Had he passed away in his sleep? If that was the case, why the urgency? Why the police?

As if reading his mind, Severn went on. "It's a horrible scene, Curran. Don't mind saying it turned my stomach. I don't know much about these things, but it was not what you might call a peaceful passing in his sleep."

"Has the doctor been sent for?"

"Dr. Mackenzie is on his way."

"Sir John, Lady Cunningham... have they been informed?"

"They have. Sir John said to bring you upstairs as soon as you arrived."

Curran turned to Greaves, who had staggered in through the front door laden with his equipment.

"Follow us, Greaves."

Leaving Greaves to wait at the top of the stairs, Severn showed Curran into what appeared to be a private drawing room adjoining Sir John's bedroom. Through a half-open door, he glimpsed a large bed in a state of disarray. Sir John, in a tartan silk dressing gown, stood on the veranda beyond the wide-flung doors, his hands behind his back.

Severn announced their presence and Sir John turned and came into the room.

"Good to see you, Curran," he said. "I gather your man, Wallace, is still out of commission?"

"He is. It's me, I am afraid."

Something like a smile twitched the corners of Sir John's mustache. "I have every confidence in you, Curran."

"Lady Cunningham?"

"She is in her bedroom, being attended to by her maid. I wouldn't let her view the scene. It is most distressing."

"Ellis found the body?"

"He did. He is in a state of shock, as you can imagine. Quite hysterical. I told him to return to his room and compose himself. I suppose you want to see the body?"

What a peculiar turn of phrase, Curran thought as he and Greaves followed Sir John Anderson down the corridor to the room where Curran had interviewed Sir Henry the day before. He certainly didn't WANT to see the body, but his job demanded that he must.

Sir John stopped before the heavy white-painted door and took out a key.

"A precaution," he said. "When I saw the body, I knew it was unlikely to be natural causes."

The stench hit before Curran even crossed the threshold—the unmistakable odor of stale vomit and worse. Telling Sir John and Claud Severn not to enter, he steeled himself and stepped into the grand room.

Sir Henry lay tangled in sheets on the floor beside the bed.

From the contorted position of the body, it was clear he had died in agony. His eyes were open, and his face smeared with dried vomit. Even Curran, who had no love for the man, flinched. Sir Henry Cunningham had died an undignified and horrible death and Curran did not need Mac to tell him that it had not been a natural one.

Greaves swallowed. "Nasty," he commented and gulped, his hand going to his mouth.

"Just do your job and try not to think about it," Curran said. "If you're going to be sick, find a bathroom outside this room. I don't need you contaminating the evidence."

Greaves overcame his natural aversion and got to work, setting up his camera to take images of the body and the state of the room while Curran walked around the room, which was the size of the detective branch, looking for anything out of place.

He noted a jug, half full of water, and a crystal glass were on the nightstand beside the bed, along with an empty medicine bottle. Curran peered at the bottle without touching it. It had Bromidia written on a label in a dispensing chemist's clear copper-plate handwriting. Bromidia was a common enough sedative. His aunt used it.

He glanced at Greaves. "Know anything about Bromidia?"

Greaves joined him. "A mix of chloral hydrate and potassium bromide with a few other substances such as cannabis. Taken in too large a dose, it can be a poison."

The label POISON on the side of the bottle would seem to confirm Greaves' opinion. The fact it was empty also seemed to tell its own story.

"It might have fingerprints. Take it with us, Greaves, and the glass and jug. Find something for the rest of the water in that jug. It will also need testing."

The other object he singled out for further examination was the teapot and cup he had seen Mary Venning with the previous day. The cup had been used, with a faint staining on the bottom indicating the greenish color of the liquid.

The tall French doors that led onto the veranda where he had spoken with the Cunninghams only yesterday stood open and

Curran stepped out onto the veranda. The louvers were open, and he was grateful for the breeze.

"Curran?"

He returned to the room to find Dr Euan Mackenzie had arrived and stood looking down at the body.

"This is awkward," Mackenzie said. "A minister of the Crown."

"Don't feel sorry for him," Curran said and promptly regretted his words when Mac looked up at him with a puzzled glance. "I meant don't stand there feeling sorry for him. How and when did he die?"

Mac cocked his head to one side. "I would bet my medical qualification that the how is fairly obvious. Poison, Curran. As to when," Mackenzie shrugged. "Sometime during the night."

"Very helpful," Curran said, his tone vaguely sarcastic.

Mackenzie shot him a smile.

Even the phlegmatic Mac flinched as he crouched down beside the body.

"Nasty way to die," he said. "Probably took a few minutes to finish him off in excruciating agony. Can someone help me to lift him onto the bed and we'll try to give the poor sod some dignity?"

Curran looked at Greaves who still looked a bit green. It was one thing to take images but another to handle corpses. With a sigh, Curran took the man's feet and he and Mackenzie hoisted the stiff, contorted body onto the bed.

"So, when did he die?" Curran asked again as they stood on either side of the bed, looking down at Sir Henry Cunningham.

"Rigor mortis is well advanced, even in this climate. I would say he's been dead six to eight hours."

"And you can confirm he was poisoned?"

"I'd need the autopsy to be sure, but yes." Mackenzie straightened. "My colleague Garland told me yesterday that he attended Sir Henry on Monday. I was busy with a childbirth and he deputized for me. I'll need to check his notes but I gather Sir Henry had not been well for quite a while."

Curran pointed at the bottle on the nightstand. "What does Bromidia do? It has poison stamped on the bottle so I could make an assumption..."

Mac peered at the bottle. "That's interesting. I see the bottle is empty. Ask his valet how much was left when he left Sir Henry last night. As to what it does, Bromidia is primarily prescribed as a sleeping draught but if taken in excess, it can cause a range of symptoms up to and including death."

"And those symptoms?"

"Restlessness, weakness, confusion, vomiting and nausea and often a rash." Mac picked up Cunningham's left hand and frowned. "See here. He has a skin discoloration, but I can't say for certain if it's Bromism, the effect of long-term consumption of Bromidia."

"If it was an overdose, could that be self-administered?" Curran ventured.

"You know me better than that. I am not going to speculate, Curran. We have tests for poisons. Once I get him to the mortuary, I'll have a better idea."

Curran cast another glance around the room. Apart from the tisane and the Bromidia, there were no obvious signs the man had consumed any other food or drink in his room before turning in for the night.

Mac and Greaves were busy, and he was now superfluous. It was time to talk to Lady Cunningham, an interview he was not prepared to do without Sir John Anderson being present. It was a conversation that might well require a witness.

# THIRTY-ONE

**M**ary Venning answered Curran's knock on Lady Cunningham's door.

"Her ladyship is resting." Mary looked from Curran to Sir John and made to close the door.

"I realize this is most distressing for her, but the police must speak to her," Sir John said.

"Admit them, Brown," Lady Cunningham's voice came from behind the maid.

The room occupied by Lady Cunningham lay on the opposite side of the residential wing and was identical in every respect to that occupied by Sir Henry. Lady Cunningham, wearing a loose robe amply covered in lace and ribbons, reclined on a velvet-covered daybed, a damp flannel on her forehead and her hair, tied with a satin ribbon cascading over one shoulder.

"What news, Sir John?" she murmured without opening her eyes.

"I have a few questions for you," Curran interposed before the governor could answer.

Lady Cunningham's eyes snapped open. "You! Where is that

nice Chief Inspector Wallace? I only wish to speak with him or Cuscaden, not this man."

"Chief Inspector Wallace is unwell, and the Inspector General is up country," Curran said. "So, I'm afraid it is me."

Evangeline Cunningham swung her feet, clad in pale, embroidered calfskin slippers, to the floor and sat up.

"Ask your questions and be gone."

"Firstly, please accept my condolences on your loss," Curran said, but maybe the lack of conviction in his voice caused Lady Cunningham's eyes to narrow.

"Inspector Curran, let us be clear. That unfortunate matter in London broke my husband's heart. He has not been a well man since you brought those heinous allegations to our door."

Curran felt Sir John Anderson's eyes boring into his back.

"That has nothing to do with his death today, Lady Cunningham." Curran paused. "Or does it?"

"far be it from me to hazard what was on his mind last night, but owing to his poor sleep, he is in the habit of taking Bromidia. Did you find the bottle?"

"We did?"

"And was it full or empty?"

"Why do you ask?"

"Because when I saw it beside his bed last night. It was a fresh bottle. You can ask Ellis. He can confirm. Well, I am waiting. Was it full or empty?"

"Nearly empty," Curran conceded. "Are you implying he took his own life?"

"I am implying nothing of the sort. That would be scandalous. I am saying he may have taken too much in an effort to ease his sleep."

"The autopsy will—"

"There will be no autopsy!" Lady Cunningham shot to her feet. "My husband was a Minister of the Crown. I will not have him butchered in death." Her gaze shot to Sir John. "Sir John, am I quite clear in my instructions?"

"No autopsy? But do you not want to know the cause of his death... or his illness?" Sir John asked.

"No. Poor Henry accidentally consumed an overdose of Bromidia, and his weak heart gave way. That will be what is recorded on the death certificate. What do you call it... death by misadventure?"

"Lady Cunningham, I must protest. Your husband died an unpleasant and agonizing death. There are procedures to be followed," Curran said. "You can't just dictate what will appear on his death certificate... The coroner—"

"I have said no, Curran, and I expect my instructions to be followed. His body is to be conveyed to the best undertakers in this benighted town and prepared for transport back to England at the earliest opportunity." She turned to Sir John. "As governor, I expect you to have the authority to override these petty, bureaucratic requirements, Sir John."

Curran turned to the governor. Sir John was too good a politician to allow his frustration to show, but a vein pulsed in his temple. He gave a curt nod of his head in acquiescence to her wishes.

Lady Cunningham subsided onto the daybed and reclined against the cushions, a hand covering her eyes.

"Now leave me. I am quite overcome."

"I have more questions—" Curran said.

"No more questions." She dropped her hand and fixed him with an icy stare. "I hold you wholly responsible, Curran. When I told Henry that the interfering suffragette woman knew about the affair in London and had tackled me with it, and a journalist was spreading scurrilous stories about that letter, he was mortified. Poor, poor Henry." She jabbed a finger in his direction. "Your indiscretion cost Henry his life."

"Really—" Curran's anger rose at the unjust accusation against both himself and Harriet, but Sir John touched his arm.

"I think we should leave Lady Cunningham to rest, Curran. You can ask your questions later when she is more composed."

Outside in the corridor, both men exchanged glances. Out of earshot of the room, the pent-up anger exploded.

"I will get nowhere with her—" Curran caught himself and apologized to the governor.

Sir John shook his head. "I'm rather inclined to agree with you, Curran. The arrogance in thinking I can ride roughshod over proper process..." He heaved a sigh. "But I have my career to consider and for now, I will have to concede to her demands."

"No autopsy? No coroner? Don't you find that suspicious? She's very quick to blame his death on an accidental overdose of Bromidia!"

"What are you implying, Curran? And what did she mean about the affair in London and a letter?"

Curran bit down on the words that rose to his lips. "It would be wrong of me to imply anything, Sir John. As to the other issues, I am afraid that is old history between myself and the Cunninghams. It has no bearing on what occurred here today. If anything, I find Lady Cunningham's cavalier attitude to her husband's death... unusual."

Sir John stroked his beard. "Aye, you might be right," he said and frowned. "But she's not a lady easily crossed, and she can pull enough strings in Whitehall to make both our lives very unpleasant. I'm too old to spend out my days as Governor of the Falkland Islands, so if Lady Cunningham has ordered no autopsy, then no autopsy will be done. Am I clear, Curran?" He paused. "What next?"

"We have to search the whole building, Sir John, including the private apartments."

"Are you prepared for another confrontation with her ladyship when you go to search her room?"

Curran nodded... the first confrontation with Lady Cunningham had left him drained and now he had to break the news to Mac that there would be no autopsy.

# THIRTY-TWO

The atmosphere at the Singapore Academy for Young Ladies could only be described as gloomy. Amelia had been popular, and her death had hit all the pupils hard - from the youngest to the oldest. The girls Harriet passed in the corridor walked in silence, black bands around their arms. They greeted her with subdued 'good mornings'.

Harriet found Esme in her office, seated at her desk, her head in her hands. Normally a resilient and cheerful person, Esme particularly seemed to have taken Amelia's murder as a personal failing on her part.

She looked up as Harriet entered, and Harriet was shocked by her friend's haggard appearance. There were dark circles under her eyes, her hair dull and lifeless and pulled into a disheveled bun, rather than Esme's normal careful coiffure.

"Esme! Have you slept at all?"

Esme shook her head. "Hardly. I keep going over and over in my mind what I could have done differently..."

"Nothing. You are not to blame for Amelia's death. The only person responsible is the one who took her life."

Esme looked away, pressing the knuckles of her right hand to her mouth. "I know all this, Harriet, but—"

"You are human, Esme, and you care deeply about your students, but you have one hundred and thirty-three other girls outside this room who need you and need your strength."

Esme nodded. "You are right." She glanced at her watch. "It is nearly time for assembly." She stood up and donned her black academic robe. "Would you—"

A timid knock at the door caused both women to glance at each other.

"Come in."

"Can I speak to you, Miss Prynne?"

Louisa and Euan Mackenzie's daughter, Heather, materialized slowly from behind the door. A quiet, shy girl, Heather had not inherited her mother's fair good looks. Like her father, she had red, curly hair and freckles that stood out on her pale skin. Today she looked even paler, the freckles more pronounced.

"Of course, but make it quick, Heather. It's nearly time for assembly," Esme said.

Heather glanced from Esme to Harriet. "It's about Amelia," she said.

"I'm sorry, Heather. I know she was your friend," Esme responded.

Heather sniffed. "I promised her I wouldn't tell but now she's... she's not here, it's all right to tell, isn't it?"

"Anything that will help the police find who killed her is absolutely fine," Harriet said.

Heather bit her lip. "She had a bit of a thing about Oliver Strong."

Esme frowned and glanced at Harriet. "Who's Oliver Strong?"

"Son of one of the local lawyers," Harriet provided. "He's back in Singapore for a few months before going up to Oxford."

She looked at Heather. "We know Amelia was quite enamored of him."

Heather's lip trembled. "She was. If he so much as glanced her way in church, she imagined he was sending her secret messages."

Esme sighed. "Young girls," she said. "What has this Oliver Strong got to do with her death?"

"She said she was going to meet him at the ball and tell him what she thought about him."

Esme raised an eyebrow. "She always was a forward young lady."

"After we finished singing, she told me she was going up to the gallery to meet him in secret. I saw her go out of one of the side doors to the back stairs and that was the last time I saw her." Tears welled in Heather's eyes.

Harriet patted the girl's hand. "The police know all this, Heather."

"The thing is, she asked me to keep watch in case her parents saw her go, so I was watching the back stairs. Oliver was talking to some men, and I could see he had no intention of meeting up with her, and I was thinking of going up to tell her when I saw someone else."

"Who?" both women chorused.

"Lady Cunningham," Heather said. "She went up the same stairs as Amelia."

Harriet had to temper the excitement. "How long after Amelia had gone up?"

Heather shrugged. "Just a few minutes. I don't think anyone else saw her. They were all busy getting food from the tables at the back of the room."

"Did you see her come back down?" Harriet asked.

Heather shook her head. "No. Mama came to fetch me because the motor vehicle was ready to take me home." Tears welled in her eyes. "I said nothing because I didn't want to get Amelia into trouble for meeting a boy."

Esme smiled. "You have nothing to reproach yourself for, Heather. You were a good friend and Amelia's death was nothing to do with her meeting Oliver Strong."

"However, you need to tell Inspector Curran exactly what you have just told us," Harriet said.

Heather's eyes widened. "Oh, won't he be cross with me?"

"Of course he won't," Harriet said. "It's very important information."

Heather's eyes widened. "Is it? But Lady Cunningham couldn't have hurt Amelia?"

"It is not for any of us to speculate, Heather," Esme said. "There's the bell for assembly. Off you go."

The door closed behind the girl. Esme leaned her hands on her desk, her head bowed.

"I love your brother very much, Harriet," she said, "but sometimes I wonder where God is in all of this. A young girl with her life before her is murdered, her family left devastated... and for what?"

"I wish I had an answer for you," Harriet said. "Now get to assembly. You will be late, and I have work to be getting on with."

Esme looked at the papers on Harriet's desk. "Nothing that can't wait, Harriet, if you need to speak with Curran."

"I will look for him at lunchtime," she said. "A few hours won't make any difference."

Harriet shut the door behind Esme, sat down at the typewriter, and ran the first sheet of paper through the roller. Her mind kept turning back to Heather's words, and she tried to remember if she had seen Lady Cunningham at the supper table. She had been at the fireworks, but in that critical half hour between Sir Henry leaving the ballroom and the fireworks, where had she been?

# THIRTY-THREE

An unnatural stillness hung over Government House as the morning wore on. Singh had ordered all the staff into the staff dining room and he would be questioning them while Curran dealt with the residents and guests.

As he had predicted, Mac had not taken the order about the autopsy well.

"Who does she think she is? The bloody Queen of England?" Mac had raged. "This man died of poisoning. I have an obligation to justice to see what killed him."

"I'm no happier than you, but while she may not be the Queen, she is still the wife of a Minister of the Crown and Sir John has endorsed the order, so we are stuck with it."

Mac looked around the stinking room. Sir Henry had been covered with a sheet, but that had done little to dispel the evidence that the man had died badly, and the stench was getting worse as the heat of the day rose.

"There may be another way," Mac muttered darkly. "Leave it with me, Greaves, let's finish up and get out of here."

Leaving Mac and Greaves to secure the evidence from the room and see to the removal of the body, Curran had to face the other residents of Government House. He had set Constable Musa on the State rooms and unused spaces and he had personally conducted a search of Sir John's private rooms. That left Lady Cunningham and the Cunninghams' staff. For the first time, he found himself wishing Wallace was not languishing on his sickbed. He would happily leave the Chief Inspector to deal with Lady Cunningham. However, she had to be faced, and the sooner the better. Squaring his shoulders, he asked that the residents and guests gather in the main drawing room.

It had taken persuasion from Sir John himself to move Lady Cunningham from her room, and she now reclined on one of the brocade sofas in the living room with Mary Venning standing behind her. Lady Cunningham had dressed in a black dress with a high collar and long sleeves, her hair scraped back into a coil at the base of her neck rather than rolled to the top of her head, as seemed to be the current fashion. She looked pale but composed and the picture of widowhood.

Charles Gilmore stood with his hands behind his back, looking out of the windows. Claud Severn looked poised and ready to flee by the main door. Only Sir John, seated on one of the uncomfortable armchairs, maintained any sense of calm.

"Where's Ellis?" Curran asked.

Gilmore turned around. "Mr. Ellis discovered the body, and he's in shock. He fainted, so I told him he could remain in his room until you need him."

Lady Cunningham let out a sound that could have been a 'harrumph' of displeasure.

"I'm not going to gild the lily," Curran said. "The doctor is of the opinion that Sir Henry died from poison, but in the absence of an autopsy, we cannot be certain what sort of poison or how it was administered."

He directed his gaze at Lady Cunningham as he spoke. She merely waved a slender white hand, dismissing his objections.

"Inspector Curran, there is nothing for an autopsy to find.

My husband was in the habit of taking Bromidia. He was in very low spirits and not sleeping well, he could simply have misjudged the dosage, or—"

She left the implication hanging in the heavy air. Or he deliberately took an overdose?

"There is nothing sinister in my refusal to allow an autopsy. I will not have him butchered. It doesn't change the fact he is dead."

Curran took a breath before responding. "That is your request, Lady Cunningham, and it will be honored. However, we have to complete our search and that includes your rooms. No one is to leave or move from this room until I have cleared the house."

"Is that necessary, Curran?" Claud Severn said, "We're talking about the Governor of the Straits Settlements here. You can't just..."

Sir John held up his hand. "It's all right, Claud. Dinna concern yourself with my sensibilities. I've given my permission."

Severn sniffed. "I hope you have no objection to me working in my office. I have urgent matters to attend to. You know where to find me."

Curran acquiesced, and Severn slipped from the room.

Lady Cunningham's reaction was entirely predictable. She rose to her feet, the picture of outraged aristocracy. Curran did not budge. Outraged aristocrats did not intimidate him for a moment.

She glared at him. "I object! I will not have a policeman— particularly THIS policeman—pawing through my private possessions."

Sir John held up a hand. "I understand, but in the circumstances, Lady Cunningham, it has to be done."

She sat down with a huff of fury. "This is outrageous."

"I'm sorry for the inconvenience," Curran said. "Everyone's

room will be searched. I will do yours first to minimize the inconvenience to you."

"What on earth do you think you'll find?" Gilmore asked. "If it was poison, then you already have the Bromidia."

"I have to be sure," he said.

He turned back to Lady Cunningham

"Lady Cunningham, perhaps Miss Brown can accompany me to your room and ensure that any pawing is kept to a minimum."

Leaving Lady Cunningham to continue howling her outrage to Sir John Anderson, Curran collected Ernest Greaves and followed Mary to Lady Cunningham's bedroom.

At the doorway, he turned to the maid. "Before we begin, Mary. Tell me, when did you last see Sir Henry?"

"I didn't see him at all," she said. "I prepared another tisane at nine-thirty, but Ellis took it up to him."

"And was it in the same teapot and cup that I saw you use yesterday?"

"Yes, it is Sir Henry's traveling tea set. He is... was... very particular."

"And after that?"

"I came up here to wait for Lady Cunningham, who was dining with Sir John and his family."

"And how was her ladyship?"

Mary shrugged. "Her normal self," she replied enigmatically. "I helped her undress. She washed and retired to bed at about eleven."

"Did she visit her husband before coming in here?"

Mary frowned. "I don't know. I told you, I was waiting here in her bedroom from the time I handed Ellis the tisane until she returned about eleven. If she visited her husband, she certainly said nothing to me."

Not wishing to add offending Lady Cunningham's modesty to the many things the lady held against him, by rifling through her underthings, Curran asked Mary to do the dirty work. The girl methodically went through the wardrobe and chest of drawers, showing Curran every pot and potion. Curran checked every other possible hiding place but found nothing untoward, apart from a healthy respect for Mary Venning's job as lady's maid.

"Now your room," he said.

Her eyes widened. "Mine?"

"We are searching everyone's room, Mary."

Mary had been assigned a small but pleasant room not far from Lady Cunningham's. It contained a single bed, covered in an embroidered coverlet, a wardrobe, a chest of drawers, and a desk and chair with some pretty, but dull watercolors of English vistas on the walls.

Mary's belongings were sparse. Three plain, cotton dresses of dark blue or black, petticoats and drawers, stockings, collars and cuffs, a hairbrush and mirror, and a couple of books of the 'penny dreadful' variety. Nothing that he wouldn't expect a lady's maid to be carrying with her.

"The suitcase?" He pointed to a brown cardboard suitcase under the bed.

Mary pulled it out. "Just some warmer clothes," she said. "Lady Cunningham said it could be much cooler in Australia."

She humped the case onto the bed and threw open the lid and gasped.

On top of the pile of neatly folded dark blue woolen dresses and a black woolen coat was a small metal box with no distinguishing marks or features. Curran looked from the object to Mary.

"Have you seen this before?"

She shook her head. "As God is my witness, Curran. I've never seen that box before."

She stretched out her hand to grab it up, but Curran caught her wrist.

"Don't touch it. Step away," Curran ordered.

She complied, and he instructed her to sit on the chair. He

called Greaves into the room and asked him to secure the tin. Putting on a pair of white, cotton gloves, Greaves gently pried open the lid. It was empty except for a few grains of white powder caught in the corners.

"Any idea what it is?" Curran asked.

Greaves frowned and took a cautious sniff.

"I'll do some tests back at headquarters, but I think it might be arsenic. My mother used it for the rats."

"Curran, you must believe me. I've never seen that before," Mary said.

He turned to face her. "Did you keep your suitcase locked?"

She shook her head, her eyes wide and brimming with tears. Mary Venning looked up at him, her eyes huge in her pale face. Her shock and surprise seemed genuine, but whatever his private thoughts might be, he was a policeman first and she had been caught with the possible murder weapon in her possession. That made her his chief suspect.

"What is there to steal? Anyone could have put it in there," she said.

"Mary, you can see how this looks. I am going to have to take you down to police headquarters and formally interview you."

"I didn't kill him, Curran," she said, but her voice lacked conviction.

A shadow crossed the door.

"Mr. Curran?"

It was Finley Ellis. The valet looked terrible. His face had an unhealthy sheen and pallor, and he wore no jacket or tie, his shirt rolled up to his elbows.

"Mr. Gilmore said you wanted to see me, Mr. Curran."

Curran looked from Ellis to Mary Venning. He should have taken Mary straight to South Bridge Road, but some matters needed to be concluded at Government House while the incident was still fresh.

"Yes, I do, Ellis. Wait for me in your room. I will be with you shortly."

Mary would have to wait. He just had to find a secure place to leave her. There was no key in the door to her room, so he took her by the arm and led her down the nearest stairs to Claud Severn's office.

The Australian looked up from his paperwork as Curran entered without knocking.

"I say, Curran—"

"Just a small favor, Claud. Can you keep an eye on Miss Brown while I finish up here?"

"Why?"

"She's agreed to come back to South Bridge Road with me, haven't you, Miss Brown?"

Mary said nothing. Her face had assumed a sulky cast, and she glared at him from under her eyelashes.

"Is she under arrest, Curran?" Severn asked.

Curran considered the question for a long moment. "No, but it will be easier to interview her there." He guided Mary to an armchair and sat her down in it. "Your word, Miss Brown. You will be here when I return."

Mary glanced from Curran to Severn and lowered her gaze. "Of course, Mr. Curran," she replied.

# THIRTY-FOUR

Leaving Mary in Severn's custody, Curran went in search of Finley Ellis. He found the valet lying on his bed in the poky, stuffy room to which the valet had been assigned. The man's eyes were red-rimmed, and he clutched a sodden handkerchief in his hand. As Curran closed the door behind himself, Ellis sat up, swinging his feet over the edge of the bed, but he seemed to lack the energy to move any further. All the fight and belligerence had gone from him.

Curran pulled up the plain, straight-backed chair and sat down.

"You don't look well, Ellis. Do you wish to see the doctor?" he asked.

Ellis shook his head. "No. It's all got a little much... what with the heat and the shock. Mr. Gilmore thought it would be all right if I rested for a while."

"Are you up to answering a few questions?"

Ellis nodded.

"When did you last see Sir Henry alive?" Curran began without preamble.

"It would have been about ten. I took his tisane up to him and made him comfortable."

"Who prepared the tisane?"

"Miss Brown, like she always does."

"Did he drink the tisane in your presence?"

"No. He said he would wait for it to cool and read a bit. I left it with Sir Henry, as he liked to imbibe it slowly while he read. Poor Sir Henry. How did he die, Inspector?"

"We believe he was poisoned."

Ellis's lower lip trembled. "How?"

"I am open to suggestions," Curran said. "What did he eat for dinner last night?"

"A rather good chicken curry," Ellis said.

"Was that wise, given his uncertain stomach?"

"He could never resist a curry and it was only mild. I had some myself and it was jolly good."

"From Sir Henry's plate?"

Ellis stiffened. "I'm not his taster," he said. "No. The senior staff enjoyed it for dinner in our own dining room."

"Did Sir Henry eat all the curry?"

"I have no idea. He sent for me about nine thirty and the tray had gone from his room. I asked Miss Brown to make up his usual tisane, and she brought it up about ten."

"Ah yes, back to the tisane... do you know what was in it?"

"I've no idea. Miss Brown always prepared it. I think it was mostly a peppermint concoction. He said it settled his stomach before sleep. I never tried the stuff. Give me a good old-fashioned cup of tea any day."

"Who prescribed the tisane?"

Ellis frowned. "When Sir Henry started getting ill, Miss Brown suggested to Lady Cunningham that she thought a gentle herbal concoction might help ease his stomach. She said it had helped her mother."

Mary Venning, this is not looking good for you, Curran thought.

"And did you or Miss Brown take the tisane into Sir Henry?"

"I did. I met her in the corridor and took the tray from her."

"Miss Brown said Sir Henry used his own traveling crockery."

"That's correct. A small teapot and a cup of blue and white china. Isn't it in his room?"

"It is."

Curran pushed on, asking about Ellis's final interactions with Sir Henry.

"I left him propped up in bed reading. He said he didn't require me anymore, so I came back here, read for a bit, and went to sleep."

"Did anyone else visit Sir Henry last night?"

Ellis bridled. "How would I know? I told you I retired to my room just after ten. If anyone visited him after that, I wouldn't know."

"You didn't hear Sir Henry cry out during the night?"

Ellis shook his head. "There are too many solid walls between this room and his. I had no way of knowing if he needed me. If we'd been at home, my bedroom is next to his and I would have heard him." He shivered. "I took a cup of tea into him about six this morning. It was still dark, but I knew something was wrong the moment I opened the door. Oh, Mr. Curran, I have never seen anything like it. He must have been in agony when he died."

Curran had no answer for that.

"Tell me about the Bromidia beside his bed," Curran said.

"He had been prescribed it by his doctor in London to help him sleep at night."

"How much did he usually take?"

"A teaspoon in a glass of water every night."

"And who administered it? You or him?"

"He preferred to do it himself."

"And the bottle by his bed, was it full or empty?"

"It was a fairly fresh bottle. I had obtained it myself from an apothecary in Colombo."

"So, when you saw the bottle last night, how full was it?"

Ellis frowned and made a gesture with his thumb and forefinger, indicating a sizeable quantity of the liquid that had been in the bottle. Curran said nothing. He'd have to wait until Greaves and Mac had done what they could before he could be sure it was the Bromidia or something else that had killed Sir Henry.

He decided to explore the other possibility, the one Lady Cunningham seemed so keen on.

"I believe Sir Henry had been unwell for some time? How would you describe his state of mind?"

"He was unwell, but not..." Comprehension dawned on Ellis's face. "Oh no, Mr. Curran, he would never take his own life." Ellis ran a hand across his balding pate. "No. He would never do anything like that. Not Sir Henry. Why would he do such a thing? He was rising through the ranks. Some said he might be the next Prime Minister."

Curran paused, formulating his next question. "Ellis, you had been with Sir Henry a long time. We both know he had a dark secret that could have destroyed his political career had it been made public."

Ellis stiffened. "That has nothing to do with his death. I'm not saying anything or speaking ill of the dead. You caused enough trouble with your insinuations last time, Mr. Curran. That Venning boy wasn't in his right mind. He took his own life if I remember rightly. No blame was ever placed on Sir Henry."

No, because we couldn't prove it, Curran thought.

He took a breath. "Are you aware of Sir Henry pursuing his... his interests on this trip?"

Ellis shook his head. "Sir Henry has not been well enough to undertake anything beyond his official duties for some considerable time."

Curran took the man's meaning, but he held Ellis's gaze until the other man looked aside and made a show of dabbing his eyes.

"What happens now, Inspector?"

"Lady Cunningham has expressed the intention of returning his body to England."

Ellis nodded. "I suppose I will need to find a new job. Not easy at my age."

"I am sure Lady Cunningham will give you good references." Curra stood up. "One last thing. I need to search your room, Ellis."

"Why?"

"For the sake of completeness."

Like Mary Venning, the valet's belongings were sparse and those clothes he was not using remained packed in a well-polished, locked leather suitcase. Curran completed his search and stood looking down at the forlorn little man.

"I'm done, Ellis. I know this has been a terrible shock. Are you sure you don't want Dr. Mackenzie to look in on you?"

Ellis shook his head. "I'd prefer just to rest until I am needed to help Lady Cunningham with the arrangements." He looked up at Curran. "Where is he... Sir Henry?"

"On his way to the undertaker. Lady Cunningham has refused an autopsy, so he will be prepared for transportation back to England."

Ellis nodded. "Then I will see to his wardrobe. He should be properly dressed for his final journey."

Curran left Ellis and went in search of Gilmore. He found the private secretary in his room, his feet up, reading a book. He set it down and jumped to his feet.

"You took your time. Have you any idea how much work I have to do?"

Curran apologized for inconveniencing the man and undertook a search of Gilmore's room. Like the man himself, his belongings were well cared for and impeccably organized.

He asked when Gilmore had last seen his employer.

"Before supper. He was not in the mood for company and asked that his meal be taken in his room. I left him to look through some papers and spoke to Ellis. I dined with Sir John and Lady Cunningham. The party broke up at about ten-thirty and I retired to my room to finish some work. I knew nothing until this morning. Poor man. Are you sure it was poison? He had a weak heart."

"Did you see the body?" Curran asked. "Do you believe that is how someone with a weak heart dies?"

Gilmore shrugged. "I have no experience in these matters, Curran. I do know it was nasty."

"It wasn't his heart. We need to confirm whether it was poison, but it seems likely."

Curran glanced at his watch. He needed to get Mary Venning down to South Bridge Road.

He left Gilmore and met Singh in the servant's quarters. They exchanged their findings, which on Singh's part amounted to nothing of interest. One of the household staff had collected Sir Henry's dinner tray at about nine. The dishes and glasses had all been washed and put away. The search of the public and unused rooms had been fruitless. That left the tin found in Mary Venning's suitcase.

Leaving his sergeant to finalize the search, he returned to Claud Severn's office and found it empty.

He swore and turned on his heel, in time to see Claud coming down the corridor carrying two cups of tea.

"Where is she, Claud?"

"Who?"

"Mary Brown."

"In my office. She was looking peaky, so I said I'd fetch some tea for us both. She promised to stay put."

Curran flung open the door and gestured at the empty room. The window on the far side of the room stood open.

"I told you not to leave her alone."

"You told me she wasn't under arrest," Severn pointed out, setting the cups on his desk.

"She may not have been under arrest, but she had some important questions to answer," Curran said.

"Oh dear," Claud said.

Curran's career crashed around him. Not only had a Minister of the Crown died violently during the night, but he had now lost the chief suspect. If Cuscaden wasn't going to take his commission over the other missteps in his life, he would be sure to make sure Curran served out his contract in the farthest reaches of the Burmese jungle.

# THIRTY-FIVE

It had turned into a busy day at the school and the final school bell had rung before Harriet could go in search of Curran to give him the message about Heather Mackenzie.

Mindful of Curran's directive about staying away from the Detective Branch, she asked at the front desk and was told to wait. It seemed an age before Nabeel appeared.

"Mrs. Gordon. It is good to see you again. Inspector Curran is not here. No one is here."

Harriet cursed under her breath. "Can I leave a note for him? It's important, Nabeel."

The clerk nodded. "Come with me."

She followed him to the Detective Branch, which was, as he had said, deserted.

"Where is everyone?" she asked.

Nabeel looked to the right and left and lowered his voice as if he expected the walls to overhear. "There has been another death at Government House."

Harriet blinked. "Another death? Who?"

"Sir Henry Cunningham."

Dumfounded, Harriet stared at the clerk. "Sir Henry. Are you sure?"

"Of course, I am sure. I took the telephone call. Here is paper and a pencil, Mrs. Gordon. You may write your note and I will be certain the Inspector will get it."

Harriet bent over Nabeel's desk to write the note.

As she straightened, the door burst open. Both Harriet and Nabeel turned to face a florid and perspiring Chief Inspector Wallace.

"Where's Curran?" he roared.

Nabeel opened and shut his mouth a couple of times before he managed, "Still at Government House, Tuan."

Wallace worked his jaw and seemed to notice Harriet for the first time. He jabbed his finger at her.

"Mrs. Gordon, what are you doing here? This is no place for you. You are not authorized—"

"I had an important message for Inspector Curran," Harriet cut across his blustering.

A vein in Wallace's temple pulsed. "This is not the time to be leaving little love notes."

"How dare you imply that was the purpose of my visit," Harriet responded. "My message was to do with the murder of Amelia Hardcastle. I have discovered a potential new witness."

"You have, have you?" Wallace narrowed his eyes. "I thought I said you were not to interfere."

"I am not interfering. One of the girls at the school came to me."

Wallace harrumphed and waved a hand. "Then leave your message with umm..." He waved a hand in the direction of the clerk.

"Nabeel," Harriet said.

"Yes, this chappy, and in the future, Mrs. Gordon, I would thank you not to call in uninvited and unannounced. If you have messages, leave them at the front desk. This is an important place of work, not a lady's social activity."

The heat rose to Harriet's face, and she straightened, struggling to keep her anger under control. "Chief Inspector, I would thank you not to address me in that tone. I came here in good faith, as a member of the public, with important information. I will not be spoken to in such a way. Good afternoon and I hope that next time we speak, it will be an apology for your rudeness."

With that, she gathered her skirts in her hands and swept from the room, with her head held high. Her bravado lasted until she shut the door behind her. She leaned on the balustrade, looking down into the stairwell as she fought a sudden lightheadedness. Wallace's particular brand of bullish belligerence brought back memories of London and her encounter with mendacious and violent policemen.

The door downstairs opened, and Curran entered. He looked up and saw her, taking the stairs two at a time to reach her on the landing halfway up the stairs. She fell into his arms, burying her face in the reassuring solidity of heavy khaki cloth.

"Harriet? Are you all right?"

She pushed herself away and straightened a lock of hair that had fallen into her eyes. "I'm fine. I just had an encounter with Wallace. The man is insufferable."

Curran glanced up at the door above them. "Was he rude to you?"

"Yes."

A muscle twitched in Curran's cheek. "I will speak with him."

She shook her head. "Leave it, Curran. You have your own troubles with the man. Don't make it worse. I held my own with him, I think."

"Why are you here?"

She took a breath to compose herself. "One of the girls at the school saw something on the night of the ball."

"Who?"

"Heather Mackenzie."

"Mac's daughter?"

"Yes. She says she was watching out for Amelia and saw Lady Cunningham go up to the gallery."

Curran stared at her. "Lady Cunningham? Is she certain?"

"You will have to speak to her, but yes. I wrote it all down, but Wallace walked in on me and gave me a thorough dressing down."

The door opened, and Wallace's shadow appeared in the doorway. "I thought I heard voices. Curran! Up here now."

Curran glanced up, his jaw tightening. "I better go and face the music."

As he stood aside to let Harriet pass, she leaned into him and said in a low voice, "Is it true, Sir Henry Cunningham is dead?"

"It's true."

"How?"

He turned to look at her. "Poison. A nasty death. Go home, Harriet. We will talk when I have time."

She took a steadying breath and hurried downstairs and out into the bright day, leaving Curran to deal with the pugnacious and unpleasant Wallace.

# THIRTY-SIX

"This is intolerable, Curran," Wallace, still looking far from well, red-faced and furious, raged at Curran. "Why wasn't I summoned immediately? Instead, I have Sir John's secretary on the phone to me, wondering why it is you, not me, conducting the investigation. And what's this about your main suspect escaping?"

Curran took a breath. "You were contacted first thing this morning, sir," Curran said. "But your wife said you were unable to leave your bed."

"So, you just thought you'd go sailing off to Government House without checking back with me?" Wallace roared. "God damn it, man, Sir Henry Cunningham is dead."

"Yes, sir, and I was intending to come up to your home to brief you, but you are here now, so you have saved me the trouble."

"Brief me."

Curran gave a concise and accurate brief of the day's events.

Wallace sat back in his chair, tapping a pencil on the blotter on his desk. "The man had been unwell and had a weak heart. Is it possible he died in his sleep?"

Curran gave his superior a narrow-eyed look. "You wouldn't think that if you saw the body, sir. Greaves will be back shortly, and you can see the images for yourself when he has developed them. There is no doubt in my mind, or indeed anyone who had the misfortune to see the body. Cunningham was poisoned."

Wallace mopped his face. "Poisoned? Good God... with what?"

"It could have been the Bromidia he used as a sedative, but a box that once contained a white powder has been found in suspicious circumstances." He paused. "It's unlikely we will know exactly what killed him because Lady Cunningham has prohibited an autopsy."

"Can she do that?" Wallace frowned.

"Sir John overrode my objections. The lady has been less than cooperative."

"Have you been talking to her?"

"Yes. I—"

"After I expressly ordered you not to?"

Curran fought to keep his temper under control. "Who else was going to talk to her?"

Wallace ignored the question. "As for being uncooperative, her husband has just died. The shock alone should preclude your interference. A woman in grief—"

"She didn't seem too overcome by grief," Curran muttered, annoyed at his own defensiveness.

Wallace raised a finger. "Enough, Curran. Stay away from Lady Cunningham!"

Curran took a deep breath and said nothing.

Wallace sat back in his chair and grimaced. He should be in his bed, but Curran was not going to suggest the man return home. He would probably have done the same thing in Wallace's situation, and the man didn't need an insubordinate inspector to add to his misery.

"So you think it was murder?" Wallace's tone had dropped.

"He may have deliberately taken an overdose of Bromidia, and that is what Lady Cunningham would like us to believe, but the discovery of the powder in the maid's luggage indicates something else altogether."

"And this suspect you lost?"

"Lady Cunningham's maid, Mary Brown." He braced for a new explosion. "Another thing. She's not who she says she is. Her name is Mary Venning. She is James Venning's sister."

Wallace stared at him with red-rimmed eyes. "When did you discover that important fact, Curran?" His voice was low and, if possible, more intimidating than his roar.

Curran hesitated. "When I saw her on Monday. I recognized her at once."

The color had risen in Wallace's face again. The man would give himself a heart attack at this rate.

"And you said nothing?" he raged.

"To be fair, sir. You were not around."

"Curran, your incompetence is monumental. If anyone has a motive to wish Sir Henry Cunningham ill, it is that woman, and here she is masquerading under a false name in the Cunningham household."

"She's been with Lady Cunningham for some time. There was ample opportunity to do him ill in that time. Why choose here and now?"

"That's a question for her, except for one thing... you have lost her, Curran. Hardly the actions of an innocent woman. We have a suspect with motive, means, and opportunity, and now she's gone. I'd stake my life that she's our girl. You lost her, you find her. Now get out of my office."

"One last thing, sir," Curran said. "I would thank you to treat Mrs. Gordon with basic decency and respect."

"What do you mean?"

"She was upset by your treatment of her just now."

Wallace snorted. "Upset? I know her sort, Curran. I've asked a few questions about your precious Mrs. Gordon. I take it you know she's been in Holloway? One of those rabid suffragette women. They're hard as nails with no respect for the uniform."

Curran struggled to contain his flash of anger. "You know nothing about her, Wallace. She was entirely undeserving of your heavy hand. She had important information on the Hardcastle case."

Wallace's eye twitched. "What information?"

"A potential new witness."

"And who is this witness?"

"Heather Mackenzie. A school friend of Amelia's. If it is all right with you, I will leave the Cunningham matter with you and speak to the Mackenzie girl."

Wallace waved a hand. "You better get going, and Curran?"

Curran turned back. "Yes, sir?"

"I will apologize to Mrs. Gordon. I am not myself at the present."

Curran met his superior's hard gaze. "Thank you."

# THIRTY-SEVEN

It had gone dark by the time Curran reached the Mackenzie's comfortable home on the hospital grounds and he was pleased to find that Mac was, for once, at home early.

"What's this about, Curran?" Mac asked when Curran asked to speak with Heather.

"I've been told Heather wishes to tell me about something she saw the night of the ball," Curran said.

Mac's mustache twitched. "She's said nothing to her mother or me. Who sent you here?"

"Heather spoke to Harriet and Esme Prynne this morning. You can stay for the questions."

"Aye, I'll do that. I want to hear what she has to say. Meanwhile, Curran, I have some information for you. I told you there was more than one way to skin a cat."

"An unfortunate metaphor."

Mac frowned. "It's my conclusion that Sir Henry Cunningham died of arsenic poisoning."

"Not Bromidia?"

"No. I judiciously scraped up some of the man's emesis—"

"Emesis?"

"Vomit," Mac's lip curled. "There are tests I can run, and the man had consumed enough arsenic to slay an elephant."

"Dear God."

"Combined with what I assume would have been his usual dose of Bromidia, and he didn't stand a chance, but there's more."

"More?"

"A long-term exposure to arsenic poisoning leaves tell-tale signs on the body. Signs I don't need an autopsy for. I observed a white ridge on his fingernails and, more significantly, the dark pigmentation on his lower limbs. Put those together with the symptoms of exhaustion and gastrointestinal issues from which he had been suffering for some time and I would stake my medical reputation on long-term exposure to arsenic, enough to weaken him over time. It would have killed him eventually, but it's my opinion someone got in and finished him off with a massive overdose."

Curran stared at the doctor. "Someone has been administering arsenic for months?"

"Probably longer."

"But why finish him off like that? If he was being systematically poisoned, why accelerate his death?"

Mac shrugged. "That's for you to answer, Curran. I am just giving you the facts as I know them."

Systematic poisoning. That pointed to several suspects... those with close contact. Mary Venning, Finley Ellis and... he gritted his teeth... Lady Evangeline Cunningham. Of those three, Mary Venning had the obvious motive and, as Wallace had pointed out, the means and opportunity. He had every policeman in Singapore looking for her, but something in her reaction when they found the tin in her suitcase gave him pause. It would take a consummate actress to fake that genuine shock. He needed to find her, for her sake.

Louisa Mackenzie entered the room with one hand on

Heather's shoulder. The girl bit her lip and glanced from her father to Curran.

Curran smiled—or at least he hoped it was a smile intended to put the girl at ease, and not a grimace.

"It's all right, Heather. You're not in trouble," he said. "I just need you to tell me what you saw at the ball on Friday night."

Heather nodded. "I know I should have said something before, but I was so upset about Amelia that it went straight out of my head. It was only last night when I was thinking back... wondering how I could have stopped her going up to the gallery that I remembered."

Curran listened as Heather recounted Amelia's supposed tryst with Oliver Strong and how she had kept watch by one of the doors onto the rear terrace. Oliver Strong had not followed, but a woman had taken those stairs minutes after Amelia... a woman in a blue dress.

"Are you sure it was Lady Cunningham?"

Heather nodded. "I had been admiring that dress all night. It was so lovely."

"And you didn't see her come down again?"

Heather shook her head. "Mama came and told me the car was ready to take me home. I wish I'd gone up to tell her Oliver wasn't coming."

Tears pricked the girl's eyelashes and Louisa folded her daughter into her arms with comforting words.

Curran stood up. "Thank you, Heather. That is important information. You have been very helpful."

Heather sniffed. "It didn't help Amelia though."

No, it didn't.

"One last thing, Heather. Amelia was wearing an old ball dress when she died. Do you know anything about it?"

Heather shook her head. "She said she had a surprise for Oliver that would make him see her as a woman, not a little girl."

Curran thanked Heather for her information and was relieved when the girl gave him a watery smile.

"I'm glad I told you. Amelia made me promise not to, but I thought it could be important."

Curran smiled and assured the girl she had done the right thing.

Heather looked up at Curran with wide, frightened eyes. "Do you think he'll come for me? The man who killed Amelia?"

Curran shook his head. "You are quite safe, Heather, more so now you have shared your story."

Heather's lip quivered. "I keep imagining I see him at my window or under my bed."

"Oh, darling." Louisa folded the girl into her arms and kissed the top of her head. "Papa and I will never let anything terrible happen to you, and if it makes you feel safer, you can come and sleep with me tonight."

Mac walked Curran to his motor vehicle.

"Poor wee lass," he said. "When you're a parent, you just want to keep your children safe and happy. I wish I could have spared her the darkness of humanity. Now she knows that not everyone is her friend and people we love can die violent deaths."

"The real world is an unlovely place, as we both know, Mac."

Mac thrust his hands into his pockets. "Find the bastard who did this, Curran. My little girl needs to sleep at night."

---

It was never easy returning to the parents, especially when he had nothing to tell them, but Curran's conversation with Heather had raised some questions he needed answering. He collected Singh and drove up to the lovely house on Emerald Hill.

George and Ellen Hardcastle sat poised on the edge of their uncomfortable seat, with an air of expectancy.

"I'm sorry," Curran said. "I have nothing more to tell you about Amelia's death, but I do have a question for you?"

Ellen Hardcastle's shoulders slumped, and her mouth drooped.

"Anything to help," George said.

"Had Amelia ever been to Government House before?"

The Hardcastles looked at each other. "The school choir sang at a garden party about three months ago," Ellen said

"And did she visit the ballroom on that occasion?"

Ellen nodded. "Yes. They sang on the front terrace, but the ballroom was open, and people were going in and out because the teas were served in there."

"So, it is possible Amelia knew the layout of the gallery?"

Ellen looked at her husband. "I suppose so. She wasn't out of my sight for very long, but she was a curious child. She loved exploring."

"How did she arrive at the ball?"

Ellen frowned. "She came with us, of course. We have a horse and carriage, and our driver dropped us at the entrance and took the carriage around to the back."

"And did Amelia stay with you?"

Ellen straightened. "No. She said she had left something important in the carriage and went off to find our driver."

Curran paused. "Is it possible she had hidden the dress we found her wearing in the carriage?"

George frowned. "I suppose so. You would have to ask our driver."

Curran nodded to Singh, who slipped out of the room.

"Did you know Amelia had proposed a secret rendezvous with Oliver Strong?"

George Hardcastle's eyes widened. "Good God, no. Did he...? Is he a suspect?"

Curran held up a hand. "No. He did not follow up on the arrangement."

"Poor Ollie. He had no interest in her," Ellen said, fumbling for a handkerchief in her waistband. "I told Melly that he was too old for her, but you know how young girls are. She was convinced he felt the same way as she did. The poor boy only had to look twice in her direction, and she was planning a wedding."

Curran, who had very little idea how young girls thought, said nothing.

Singh returned to the room. He gave Curran a nod.

"Well?" George Hardcastle asked.

"Your driver confirms that shortly after arriving at the ball, Miss Hardcastle sought out the carriage. She had secreted a brown paper parcel under one of the seats," Singh said.

Ellen's mouth quivered as she fought to control herself. "Melly took the dress to the ball?"

"I think we can assume that was what was in the parcel," Curran said.

"Why?" George Hardcastle looked confused.

"Oh George, you idiot," his wife said. "She wanted to impress Oliver." She looked at Curran. "But where did she get the dress? I told you before, it wasn't one of mine. I'd never seen it before. Could she have borrowed it from one of the girls at school?"

Curran conceded that was a possibility and assured them he would make inquiries in that direction. He stood up and thanked them for their time.

"I hope next time I will have better news for you," he said.

# THIRTY-EIGHT

"You're very quiet," Julian remarked over dinner.

Harriet, who had been maundering over the conversation with Curran and the run-in with Wallace, pushed her plate away, the food hardly touched.

Will looked up from his plate.

"Do you want me to go?" he asked, with a look of dull resignation, and Harriet realized how often they conducted conversations out of his hearing.

Harriet shook her head and smiled. "No, Will. We always seem to be chasing you away." She looked at her brother. "I think now is the time, Julian?"

The boy would be leaving them in a short time and perhaps now was as good a time as any to tell his father's story.

Julian nodded.

"Do you still want to ask us about your father?" he said.

Will looked from one to the other. "Yes."

A muscle twitched in Julian's cheek and he looked away for a moment before swinging his gaze back to Will.

"I think," Julian began, "the one thing you need to remember more than anything else is that your father loved you. You were in his last thoughts. Everything that led up to his death, he thought, was to better your life."

Will met his guardian's eyes. "Uncle Julian, he was wrong. The men my father was involved with kidnapped me and Aunt Harriet. I know what Papa was doing for them... the statues and the rubies. What I want to know is if it is true that Papa killed someone?"

Julian and Harriet looked at each other, and Julian took a breath.

"Yes," he said. "I can't dress it up, pretend it was an accident. At best, your father was provoked beyond rational thought and acted without thinking. You are an intelligent boy and you deserve the truth and only those of us who were with him when he died heard his confession. It is inevitable in a small place like Singapore that gossip gets out. I'm sorry that the rumors have touched you."

Harriet did not dare take her eyes off the boy. He sat quite still, dry-eyed, his face betraying nothing.

In his short life, Will Lawson had faced more than any child should ever have to bear, and now this. He was already old beyond his years.

"Thank you for telling me," he said. His mouth quirked, and he looked away. "Does Inspector Curran know about Papa?"

"Yes," Julian said. "He was there when your father died."

Harriet took a breath. "Julian—"

Curran knew about John Lawson, knew what he had done, but had chosen to keep the information to himself. He was in enough trouble at the moment without it coming out that he had concealed a murderer.

Julian's gaze had not moved from the boy. "Do you want to speak to Curran?"

Will's lips tightened. Harriet, knowing him so well, judged him to be on the verge of tears. She longed to hold him in her arms, but the distance across the table could have been a mile.

Instead, it was the cat, Shashti, the little animal Will had rescued, who jumped onto the boy's lap, butting her soft head against his hand.

Will swallowed, and he looked down at the cat as he stroked her, provoking a loud, rumbly purr as two large tears dropped onto the cat's fur.

"Will?" Harriet found her voice.

He looked up, his eyes swimming with the unshed tears. "It's all right, Aunt Harriet. I know Papa loved me... loved all of us... but Mama said he was unreliable." He sniffed and stood up, still holding the cat. "Please excuse me."

Harriet made to rise as he walked away, but Julian laid a hand on her arm. "Let him go, Harri."

From within the house, a door slammed.

Harriet dashed at her own eyes. "It's too much, Julian."

Julian's hand tightened on her arm. "If I thought for a moment, it was too much for him to bear, I would never have told him," he said, "but Will is stronger than we give him credit for."

"Why does he want to speak to Curran?"

"Because whatever we are in Will's life, Curran is something more."

Huo Jin appeared at the door. She looked from Julian to Harriet, her gaze mutinous. "What you say to William? He is a good boy."

Julian held up a hand. "He's not in trouble. He just needs a little time by himself."

Huo Jin did not look convinced. Casting them both narrow-eyed glances, she cleared the table with her distinctive gruff efficiency, leaving Harriet in no doubt that as far as Huo Jin was concerned, the only ones in trouble were the two of them.

Casting a glance at the door to Will's room, Harriet fetched a book from her room and settled in her favorite seat on the veranda to read. Julian likewise sat with his beloved Virgil, and they let the noises of the night settle around them... the hiss of the kerosene lamp, the chirrup of the night insects, and the crash and chatter of the monkeys in the trees behind the house.

The peace did not last long. A ricksha trundled through the front gate and brother and sister stood to greet Samrita as she stepped from the ricksha, telling the ricksha wallah to wait.

"Samrita, this is a surprise," Julian said.

She smiled. "I wish to borrow Harriet for a little while."

"Is there trouble? Anything I can do?" Julian frowned.

"No trouble, I just need Harriet's advice on... a womanly matter."

That was enough to cause any man to retreat. Julian coughed and turned back into the house.

Harriet took the young woman by the arms. "What on earth is the matter? Is it Lavinia?"

"No. She's fine. There is someone who needs our help, Harriet. Can you come with me?"

"Of course. Where are we going?"

"To Tom Barker's studio," she said.

"I will fetch my hat," Harriet said and instructed Aziz to hail a second ricksha as she hurried inside.

# THIRTY-NINE

The rickshas trundled down the road toward the Singapore River and onto an island known as Pulau Saigon. They stopped outside an old shop house. The women paid off their rickshas and Samrita knocked on the rickety door, which was opened by an elderly Chinese woman.

Seeing Samrita, she broke into a toothless smile.

"This is a friend, Min," Samrita said, and the woman nodded.

Samrita turned to Harriet. "Do you trust me, Harriet?"

"Of course."

Her curiosity piqued, she followed Samrita up a creaking, ill-lit staircase to a large open room at the top of the stairs. It took her a moment to realize that the strange shapes lurking in the shadows were unframed canvases and easels stacked against the wall. The only furniture were some unmatched chairs, a daybed, swathed in embroidered cloths—saris and other exotic materials —and, beside a large easel, a table covered in paints, palettes, and brushes. The large painting on the easel had been covered with a stained canvas.

At the far end was a curtained-off area and as they reached the top of the stairs, the curtain parted, and Thomas Barker stepped out. He was in shirtsleeves, rolled up to the elbows, his crumpled linen shirt open at the neck, and worn untucked over loose Indian-style trousers and sandals.

"Mrs. Gordon, thank you for coming."

"It's all very mysterious," Harriet said, hoping she sounded calmer than she felt. "Is this your studio, Mr. Barker?"

"It is. During the day, it is very well lit and I can work undisturbed for hours on end."

Harriet looked from one to the other.

"What can I do for you, Mr. Barker?"

Barker and Samrita exchanged a glance, and he gave a curt nod. Samrita slipped behind the curtain and emerged with her arm around the shoulders of a young English woman. The woman wore a simple, dark blue dress relieved by a white collar and cuffs. One cuff was missing, and her hair was coming down around her face, which was blotched and streaked with dirt.

Harriet recognized her from lunch in the staff quarters at Government House.

"Miss Brown, what on earth are you doing here?"

"My name is Mary Venning," the woman said, "and I am afraid I am wanted by the police for the death of Sir Henry Cunningham."

"James Venning's sister?" Harriet said.

"You know his story?"

Harriet nodded. "I have read his letter," she said.

"The journalist showed it to you? I overheard Lady Cunningham telling Sir Henry that a journalist had his letter. What is his name?"

"A woman, Sarah Bowman."

Mary sank onto the daybed and buried her face in her hands, her shoulders shaking. Samrita sat beside her and put an arm around her.

"I don't understand how you come to be calling yourself

Mary Brown and working for the Cunninghams of all people?"
Harriet said.

Barker waved at the chairs. "Please sit down, Mrs. Gordon.
We have much to discuss."

A hundred questions raced through Harriet's mind as she
sank into a once grand armchair, the springs of which were
broken and squeaked in protest.

"What is it you think I can do?" she asked.

"You can trust Mrs. Gordon," Samrita said. "She is a friend of
my brother."

Mary nodded and looked up. "Inspector Curran was good to us,
my mother and I, but he couldn't bring Sir Henry Cunningham to
justice, so I decided to do it myself. Get the evidence the police
needed. Irrefutable evidence that they couldn't just sweep under a
carpet. So, I went to work for Lady Cunningham as her lady's maid."

She looked up at Thomas Barker, who sat down on the other
side of her and smiled at him fondly. "Tom had been at school
with our brother, and I met him again when Tom came to paint
Lady Cunningham's portrait. I told him about James' death and
Sir Henry's culpability."

"I tried to make a few discreet inquiries in a way Mary
couldn't," Tom Barker said. "But the Cunninghams gave nothing
away and their staff likewise and once the portrait was finished, I
set off on my travels, intending to go to Australia but as you can
see, this is as far as I have got."

Mary smiled at her friend. "I knew Tom was here and he
would be a safe hand into which I could pass my evidence. I had it
well hidden in the lining of my suitcase, but I was worried Lady
Cunningham or Gilmore or Ellis may discover my true identity."

"Lady Cunningham did not know who you were?"

"I don't believe so. Although now I am not so sure."

"This is all very well, but I still don't understand why I'm
here," Harriet said.

Mary Venning leaned forward. "I'm in terrible trouble, Mrs. Gordon. Sir Henry is dead."

"Yes," she said. "Curran told me he had been poisoned."

Mary Venning bit her lip. "Worst of it is, when Curran searched my room, he found a tin in my suitcase that might have contained arsenic. As God is my witness, Mrs. Gordon, it wasn't me. I wanted him dead, but more than anything, I wanted him in front of the courts. Dying was too good for him. Just last night, I came across one of the young girls from the household staff in tears on the back stairs. I asked her what had happened, and she told me she had gone to Sir Henry's room to turn down the bed. He was alone and as she bent over the bed he came up on her from behind, pinning her to the bed, and—" she swallowed.

Harriet, Samrita and Barker stared at her.

Mary's mouth twisted as she struggled to control her emotions. "She fought him off and made good her escape, but she was badly shaken."

"What did you do?" Samrita asked.

"I told her not to say anything, that he was not in his right mind." Her gaze went from one to the other. "But I was angry, so angry that I told Lady Cunningham."

"And her reaction?" Harriet asked.

"She told me the girl was making things up. Her precious Henry would never do anything like that, and I was not to mention it again, not to anyone."

"And next morning, he was dead," Barker said.

"After they found the tin in your possession, what happened?" Harriet asked.

"Curran didn't have any choice, did he? I knew he had to arrest me, so when an opportunity presented, I scarpered." Mary's lower lip trembled. "And now they've got every policeman on the island out looking for me. I've no money, no nothing and I'm afraid I will hang for something I did not do."

Harriet spread her hands. "What help do you want from me? I have no money—"

"No. I don't want money. I want my story told. I have to speak to that reporter. Can you arrange for me to meet her tomorrow morning?"

"I think you should speak to Curran—" Harriet said.

Mary shook her head. "Curran is a good man, but he is still a policeman, Mrs. Gordon, and all the evidence points to me. I'm not a complete fool. Someone planted that tin in my luggage - the possible means of Sir Henry's death. Whoever did it must know I am James Venning's sister, so that gives me motive. I was the one who prepared Sir Henry's evening tisane, the perfect opportunity to administer the poison. On the face of it, I have motive, means, and opportunity and no alibi. No jury on earth will acquit me. "

Harriet leaned forward. "Do you know who that someone is?"

The hesitation was infinitesimal, but it was there, and her tone was defensive. "No. Not for certain." She straightened. "I have proof of Sir Henry's infamy. Once I speak to the reporter, it is in her hands and I can disappear."

Harriet frowned. "Do you have these papers with you?"

Mary glanced at Tom. "I gave the envelope to Tom for safe-keeping when I first arrived in Singapore. I didn't want to risk keeping them with me any longer."

"I have kept the papers safe," Tom Barker said. "They're well hidden. This is an old building used to holding secrets."

Harriet looked from one to the other. Every instinct screamed at her to go straight to Curran.

She took a breath.

"Mary, please go to the police—to Curran," Harriet said. "I know the evidence against you is damning, but for what it is worth, I believe you, and I am sure Curran will too."

Mary sighed and ran a hand over her eyes. "Even he can't work miracles. If he could, James' tormentor would even now be rotting in jail." She stood up. "Mrs. Gordon, please promise me that you won't go to the police tonight?"

Harriet continued to hesitate, her conscience tempered by what she had read in the Venning letter and her own interaction with the Cunninghams. Sir Henry did not deserve to be lauded as a fine and upright member of society when he had been a sadistic pervert and a member of a government that condoned the torture of its own citizens.

She forced Mary to hold her gaze, as she said, "If I help you, it will be on the condition that you will give yourself up to Curran in the morning. The police will be watching the ports and the stations. This is an island, Mary, and there can be no escape. It will go better for you if you cooperate."

Mary screwed up her face and closed her eyes, tears leaking from beneath the lids. "Very well. Let me meet with Sarah Bowman and give her the information I have. After that, you have my word that I will hand myself into Inspector Curran." She nodded. "I promise."

Having extracted that assurance, Harriet relaxed.

"Where do you propose to meet Miss Bowman?" Harriet asked. "Here?"

"No. I don't want to get Tom into trouble. Somewhere out in the open."

"The bandstand at the Botanic Gardens early morning. There won't be many people around," Samrita suggested.

Mary nodded. "That will do. Mrs. Gordon, if you could be there, you can take me to Curran when I have done what needs to be done. Tom, can I have some paper? I'll write a note to this reporter. Mrs. Gordon, will you take it to her? She knows you."

Harriet nodded.

Mary scrawled a note, sealed it in the envelope, and handed it to Harriet before sinking back against the cushions on the daybed, her face gray with exhaustion.

"Thank you all for your help," she said with a sweeping gaze that took in everyone. "It's late and I am very tired."

"Take my bed," Barker said. "I can sleep on the daybed."

They waited until Mary had disappeared behind the curtains. While Thomas Barker poured whisky into mismatched glasses, Samrita checked on the young woman.

"She is asleep," she said in a low voice.

Barker handed around the glasses. "I am sorry to have to involve you, Mrs. Gordon. We didn't know who else to turn to."

"How did you know James Venning?"

"His brother was my contemporary at school. James was a lot younger than Marcus and I. Marcus joined the army and died in South Africa ... and then James took his life. Such a tragic loss. James was so talented. He didn't deserve to meet Sir Henry Cunningham. His mother was broken by his death. Both her sons are dead. She never recovered."

Harriet drained her glass and went to set it down on the table, already cluttered with tubes of paint and turpentine rags. She moved a sharp, paint-spattered knife to make room for it before looking around the room.

Her gaze was drawn to the painting on the easel, only partly covered with a cloth. She stood up and lifted the cloth to reveal an oil painting of an artist's model lying on the daybed in the studio: Her naked back to the artist, her head half turned, a rich fall of thick, dark hair falling down her back and across her arm. No mere artist model...

She gasped and turned to look at Samrita.

Samrita straightened. "I am not embarrassed, Harriet." Her hand sought Tom Barker's, and they exchanged a glance that told Harriet everything she needed to know.

"I intend to go to Australia with Tom," Samrita said. "I just don't know how to tell Robert."

Harriet tried to imagine that conversation and failed.

"Whatever you do, don't show him that painting," she said.

Samrita laughed. "I don't think my brother is so easily shocked." Her face sobered. "I wish there was more we could do for Mary. Do you believe her, Harriet?"

Harriet shrugged. "I don't know. If she is innocent but has been made to look like the guilty party, the evidence is over-whelming."

Samrita stood up. "It's getting late. Lavinia will be wondering where I am."

Harriet suspected Lavinia knew perfectly well where Samrita was.

"How will you get the note to Miss Bowman?" Samrita asked.

"I will go myself," Harriet said.

The three of them walked down into the quiet street. Barker fetched two rickshas from a nearby stand and they parted company.

Harriet looked at the note in her hand. She had no idea where Sarah Bowman lived, but she knew someone who would know.

To say Griff Maddocks was surprised when she turned up on his doorstep at ten in the evening would be an understatement, and as she expected, he had a flurry of questions that she refused to answer.

In the end, he drove her to the hostel where Sarah Bowman boarded. Leaving Maddocks in the vehicle, she knocked on the door. It took some persuasion for the doorman to fetch Sarah.

The young woman was still fully dressed, her ink-stained fingers a testament to the fact she was probably still working.

Harriet handed her the note.

"What is this about, Harriet?" Sarah asked, scanning the note with a puzzled frown.

"I think it is the story you are after," Harriet said.

Sarah looked up, a gleam in her eyes. "She really does have the evidence to bring down Sir Henry?"

"So she says," Harriet said. "Be at the bandstand at seven-thirty. Goodnight, Sarah."

Back at the motor vehicle, she climbed into the passenger seat beside Griff.

"Harriet," he said. "What are you getting yourself into?"

Harriet huffed out a breath. "I don't know, and common sense tells me I should not be getting involved."

"Since when have you listened to common sense?" Griff said as he turned the motor vehicle back out onto the road. He cast her a sideways glance. "I know you're not going to tell me what this is about, but is it something Curran should know about? Shouldn't you go to him?"

Harriet's conscience screamed at her to do just that, but she shook her head.

"I made a promise," she said. "The matter will be resolved in the morning. Can you take me home, Griff?"

They drove back to St. Tom's in silence. Harriet resisted Julian's attempts to pry information from her by retiring to her bedroom and shutting the door.

She had told Maddocks that it would be resolved in the morning, and she hoped, with all her heart, that would be the case. Mary would meet with Sarah Bowman and then they would both go straight to South Bridge Road. No argument, no pleading.

But even as she lay awake, staring up at the mosquito net, her instinct nagged at her, telling her nothing was ever that simple.

# FORTY

The soft light of early morning shadowed the paths of the Botanic Gardens as Harriet made her way to the rendezvous arranged by Samrita.

'Mad' Ridley's original vision for the Botanic Gardens had been purely practical—plantings of crops that could be of economic value to the area to see what survived and what didn't —but over the more recent years, it had devolved into an oasis for rest and recreation with the construction of a peaceful lake just inside the main gates on which swans cruised in the still, warm air.

An ornate bandstand dominated the highest point of the gardens. The pretty structure had been the scene of a murder the previous year in a case involving the officers of the South Sussex Regiment. Its gruesome history didn't seem to bother the usual crowd of Sunday visitors who came to listen to the music or stroll the paths lined with a variety of tropical plants, all of which were thriving under the care of Ridley and his army of gardeners.

However, there were no visitors at this early hour. It had been raining steadily through the night and even Harriet's umbrella did little to keep her dry as she hurried up the path toward the bandstand. Despite the rain, the workers, hessian sacks over their shoulders were already hard at work sweeping stray leaves from the immaculate paths with their hand-made whisk brushes. They stopped and nodded as Harriet bid them good morning.

As she approached the bandstand, her footsteps slowed. It had been over a year since an officer of the South Sussex Regiment had died in the lovely place. Alone in the silence and the rain, she could almost imagine she heard the gunshot ringing out over the lawns, and a shiver ran down her spine.

Sarah Bowman had arrived before her and sat on a bench in the shelter of the bandstand, tapping the finial of her furled umbrella on the tiles. She looked up as Harriet rushed breathlessly up the steps and stopped to shake out her umbrella.

"Mrs. Gordon. I didn't expect you. What are you doing here?"

"Mary Venning and I have business after she has met with you," Harriet said.

Sarah bit her lip. She could barely conceal her excitement. "You don't know what this means to me, Harriet. Mary Venning can validate the authenticity of the letter and—"

"Sir Henry Cunningham is dead, Sarah. I fail to see what possible purpose your story can serve."

"It serves to discredit the entire Asquith government." Sarah's eyes blazed with the zeal of her cause. "Surely you, more than anyone, want to see them brought down."

"Tell me, Sarah. What has Government House told the paper about Sir Henry's death?"

Sarah frowned. "The official release says he died peacefully in his sleep. Is that not so?"

"No. That's not how he died." Harriet threw caution to the wind. "It is most likely that he was poisoned, and the main suspect in his death is the woman you are meeting this morning. Hardly a credible witness."

Sarah stared at her. "Murdered? Did she do it?"

"You can draw your own conclusion after you have spoken with her."

"Mrs. Gordon, I get the feeling you don't—"

What Sarah had been about to say was interrupted by running feet.

A hatless and soaked Thomas Barker came belting up the path toward them.

"Is she here?" Barker pulled up at the foot of the steps, his hands on his knees, panting as he looked up into the bandstand.

"If you mean Mary Venning, no, she's not," Harriet said. "I thought she was coming with you."

Barker straightened. "She must have slipped out early before I was awake. I waited but she still hadn't returned—" His shoulders slumped. "I hoped she might have made her own way here."

"Where would she have gone?" Harriet asked.

Barker shook his head. "I have no idea."

Harriet subsided onto the bench and ran a hand over her eyes. What had she been thinking? She should have gone to Curran when she knew where Mary Venning was hiding. Now it looked like Mary had eluded her.

"She's probably on a train or a boat as we sit here like the fools we are," Harriet said bitterly

"But she has no money," Thomas said. "I didn't give her any."

Harriet stood up and straightened her skirt. "I knew I should have gone to the police last night."

"This information she said she had," Sarah Bowman said. "Do either of you have it?"

Barker shook his head. "No, it was gone from where we had hidden it."

Harriet's lips tightened. "If Mary Venning was innocent, she would be here now. Enough of these games, Barker. I am going to Curran."

God knows what he would say when she told him she had known where Mary Venning was hiding.

She had barely taken ten steps when a loud cry reverberated around the gardens, sending a troop of monkeys screaming into the trees. It came from the direction of the lake near the entrance.

The three of them looked at each other. Thomas and Sarah set off at a run, down the path toward the lake, in the direction the sound had come from. Harriet followed, reaching the lake in time to see Thomas Barker sprinting to the far side where one of the gardeners stood looking down into the reeds that fringed that side of the lake.

Before she reached the edge, Harriet knew what the man was looking at and she didn't want to see it. She grasped Sarah's arm and pulled her back.

Sarah tried to shake her off. "Let me go. I have to see—"

"No, you don't," Harriet said. "Reporter or not, it is not our place."

From where she stood, she could see a woman in a dark dress floating face down, caught in the reeds, her arms outstretched and her hair loose, streaming out like seaweed.

Even without seeing her face, Harriet knew they were looking at Mary Venning.

# FORTY-ONE

**M**ary Venning lay on the muddy path beside the lake, staring up at Curran with glassy, dead eyes. He crouched down beside her and touched her neck but there was no pulse. Despite the immersion in the water, the damp skin still held a vestige of warmth. She had not been dead long.

He wished he had something to cover her. It felt wrong to leave her sprawled in the mud for every curious eye.

As if reading his mind, one of the gardeners came forward with an old hessian sack.

"For the memsahib," he said.

Curran took it with thanks and waited until Greaves had taken his photographs before laying the cloth across Mary. It covered no more than her head and upper body, but it served to give her some dignity and protect her from the rain.

The mortuary men arrived with their cart and a message that Doctor Mackenzie was unavoidably detained in surgery. They were to convey the deceased directly to the mortuary and he would attend to an autopsy in the afternoon.

Curran flicked his wet hair out of his eyes and left the mortuary attendants to their work. He crossed to where Harriet and Sarah Bowman stood huddled under their umbrellas with Thomas Barker, apparently too wet to care about the rain.

"Who pulled her out of the water?" he asked.

Barker raised his hand. "I did... with the help of one of the gardeners. We pulled her out on the off chance there might still be a chance to save her, but she was dead." Barker paused. "It also felt wrong to just leave her there. Sorry, Curran."

"What was she doing here?" He narrowed his eyes, looking from one to the other. "What are any of you doing here?"

"She had arranged a meeting with me," Sarah Bowman said.

Curran fixed his gaze on Harriet. "And you?"

"I was a party to it," Harriet said in a small tight voice, adding, "against my better judgment."

Harriet had dark shadows beneath her eyes, and she looked exhausted, but he couldn't help the flash of irritation. What in God's name was she doing arranging clandestine meetings with his missing main suspect?

He rubbed his eyes, trying to organize his thoughts. "Harriet, when did you find out where Mary Venning was hiding?"

Her gaze slid away. "Last night," she mumbled.

The irritation burst into full-scale annoyance. Last night? She knew Mary's whereabouts last night? If she'd come to him, he could have saved Mary Venning. She would be safely locked up in a police cell, not dead by the side of a pretty lake.

"It's my doing," Barker said. "Mary came to me yesterday and I... well, I believed her story. I don't think she killed Sir Henry."

"That's good of you, Barker, but that is for me to decide, not you. How do you even know her?" Curran said, his tone dripping ice.

Barker cleared his throat and shuffled his feet. "Long story, Curran, but I've known her for years."

"If you know her so well, what makes you believe that she did not kill Sir Henry Cunningham? She certainly had a reason."

Barker swallowed. "All she wanted to do was tell the world

about Sir Henry. She had evidence of his activities that she believed were sufficient to reveal the monster he was."

"And where is this evidence?" Curran demanded.

Barker shook his head. "I don't know. She must have taken it with her when she left my rooms this morning. It wasn't where we hid it."

"Describe it."

"A beige envelope, quite a thick one. About this big..." Barker indicated the size with his hands. "Nothing written on the outside."

There had been nothing on Mary's body. He would have to set his men searching for it in the general vicinity.

"What did she intend to do with this evidence? Don't tell me —she intended to sell her story to the press?"

Curran swung his gaze to Sarah Bowman and fixed her with a glare that would have quelled the worst villain. Sarah Bowman returned his look without flinching.

"I told you, Curran, I want this story very much and if you couldn't or wouldn't confirm the veracity of the letter, then she could," Sarah Bowman said. "I just wish I had got to her sooner."

A thousand questions crowded Curran's mind, but everyone was wet and nothing would be gained from questioning them anymore.

"Go home. There is nothing you can do here. I'll speak with you all later. Harriet, you can stay."

Harriet hunched her shoulders and as the others walked away, she lowered her umbrella down as if it were a shield against his wrath, but he was too wet and dispirited to be angry.

"Harriet," he said. "If you knew where Mary Venning was last night, why the hell didn't you come to me?"

She sighed and looked away. "Because I made a promise and God knows, I have already broken one promise too many in the course of this investigation." She swung her gaze back to him. "I am not a police officer, Curran. I'm not bound by your rules, and, for what it's worth, I don't believe she killed Sir Henry."

Curran paused before admitting, "For what it's worth, neither do I, but I needed to be able to ask her those questions, Harriet. Her running did not help her cause."

"She was frightened, Curran and what did it matter if you believed her or not? As you have often pointed out to me, the evidence doesn't lie. She had a motive to want Sir Henry dead—"

"And she had the opportunity, and the means were found in her baggage."

"I was here because we made a pact. After she spoke to Sarah, I was to take her to you."

"So, what is this evidence she said she had?"

Harriet shrugged. "I assume it was letters and statements proving Sir Henry's calumny, but I wasn't shown it. Is there nothing on her body?"

"Not that I could see."

"I'm sorry, Curran. I know I should have come to you last night, but she promised me she would hand herself in as soon as she had met with Sarah Bowman. That's the only reason I am here... to take her straight to you."

"And you believed her?"

She swung her gaze to the other side of the lake where mortuary attendants were loading her body onto the cart.

"I did," she said in a small, low voice.

He sighed. "Very well. What is done is done. Now I have to explain to Wallace that our missing main suspect has turned up dead." He paused. "I won't mention your involvement."

He just prayed Wallace would not ask too many questions.

Harriet's mouth turned down at the corners. "I don't think it matters, Curran. Wallace already has a bad enough opinion of me. I am proving a liability to the redemption of your career."

She looked so miserable that if it had not been so public a

place, he would have kissed her, but he had to content himself with touching her hand.

"Never that, Harriet. I do a fine job all by myself." He managed a smile. "Go home. We'll talk later."

She turned and walked away from him, her back straight and her head held high.

He sighed. No doubt her heavy-handed meddling had compromised the case, but there were many more times when her curiosity and observations of the people around them had given him an insight that he, a mere man, would never have seen. She had believed Mary Venning was innocent, and he trusted her instinct.

The mortuary cart trundled away, and Curran huffed out a heavy breath. He now had three deaths, including a high-ranking government official. The thought occurred to him that Mary's death could be seen as suicide and an admission of her guilt. After all, her brother had drowned himself. Weighed down by the guilt of murdering Sir Henry, had she taken her own life? It was not a possibility that he could dismiss, except for one thing. Where were the important papers she was supposedly delivering to Sarah Bowman?

While he waited for his men, he walked down to the water's edge, looking for the envelope with Mary's papers. Mercifully, the rain had let up, and he stood beside the lake, taking a moment to gather his thoughts.

She had died in a beautiful spot, a still lake on which a pair of white swans, imported no doubt, from England, glided by, unruffled by the commotion on the bank. Behind him was the heavily wooded tree line between the lake and the road. Would anyone passing by on the road have noticed anything? He dismissed that thought. The bush was too dense.

The mud at the water's edge had been too badly disturbed by the actions of Barker and his helpers in bringing Mary out of the water to provide any useful evidence, so he wandered along the path a little further on. Several yards away from where Mary had been pulled ashore, he stopped, hardly able to credit his good fortune. Clearly visible in the mud was the impression of a man's boot print.

Curran crouched down, hoping the print might tell him something about its wearer. The boot was a couple of sizes smaller than his boot and, from the depth of the impression, he could assume that it had been made by a slight man of middle height.

Had Mary's murderer stood here, watching his handiwork drift into the reeds? The thought brought a cold shiver to Curran's heart.

Or was it just a coincidence?

Curran ordered Greaves to take a plaster cast of the boot print and joined Singh, who was ordering a close search of the area. Curran added the instruction to look for a beige envelope.

"Let's get back to South Bridge Road," Curran said. "I need to get into a dry uniform."

As they walked back to the place Curran had parked the motor vehicle, Singh said, "So, Curran. You have lost your main suspect. What is the Chief Inspector going to say?"

"I shudder to think," Curran said.

He voiced the doubt that was rattling around in his mind. "Is it possible she took her own life?"

"Why do you think that?" Singh asked.

"Her brother died that way. He jumped from Waterloo Bridge into the Thames."

Singh regarded him. "I think, Curran, there is more to this case than you have told me."

Curran nodded. "I think some, if not all, of these recent deaths are related to an old case of mine, Singh."

"And I think you should tell me what you know, Curran."

Too weary to obfuscate any longer, as they drove back to headquarters, Curran related the story of James Venning and Sir

Henry Cunningham's vices and the cover-up that had led to his self-imposed exile to Singapore.

He didn't often see his sergeant display emotion, but the look of utter disgust on Singh's face told him everything he needed to know.

"Three deaths that have been clumsily made to look like possible suicides is too much of a coincidence, Curran. Do you think that the child, Amelia, was lured away for Sir Henry's pleasure and something occurred that caused him to kill her?"

"That was my first thought, but I don't think it was possible within the time frame and given the man's state of health. But then again Mary Venning may have witnessed something that night and that is why she had to die." He paused. "But Sir Henry was dead before Mary died. There is someone else involved and it can only be someone with access to Sir Henry." He shook his head. "I am casting chaff into the wind, Singh. Do you have any thoughts?"

"With the Venning woman dead, if one rules out the governor and his staff, that leaves Lady Cunningham, his private secretary, or his valet," Singh said. "It is not many suspects."

Curran grunted in agreement. It was a very small pool of suspects and whatever his thoughts on Lady Cunningham's culpability in her husband's death, he couldn't imagine her stalking her maid to the lake in the Botanic Gardens and drowning her.

"I need to speak to them, but Wallace has made it quite clear I am to stay away. He will deal with them."

"Hasn't stopped you before," Singh remarked.

Curran gave his insubordinate sergeant a scathing glance.

"Before I do anything, I need to report to Wallace," he said.

An interview he did not look forward to.

# FORTY-TWO

Wallace had not reported for duty, but the unpleasant interview could not be delayed. Curran left Singh and drove up the Wallace's house. Sadie Wallace greeted him at the door with a tirade about the unhealthy atmosphere, the uncooperative servants, and her general unhappiness. Curran had neither the time nor the patience to deal with Sadie. He made appropriate, sympathetic noises and asked to speak to Sadie's husband in private.

With obvious bad grace, Sadie showed him into the bedroom where Wallace reclined on a pile of pillows, his face gray and drawn. Curran inquired about his health and was told that the doctor had ordered him to stay put. But Wallace was no fool. He narrowed his eyes and asked why Curran had come seeking him out.

Curran took a breath. "We found the Venning woman. She's dead."

"What do you mean, our chief suspect is dead?"

If he had been well, Wallace's fury would have been incandescent, but he could barely raise his voice above a croak.

"Found in the lake at the Botanic Gardens about seven thirty this morning," Curran said.

"Did she kill herself?"

"We won't know until Dr. Mackenzie has seen her," Curran said.

Wallace ran a hand across his eyes. "Dear God, Curran. Fix this unholy mess before I get back to work, or you will find yourself doing duty in the Sudan."

Curran took Wallace's words to mean he now had *carte blanche* to conduct the investigation as he saw fit, without restrictions on access to witnesses, and beat a hasty retreat.

He would have liked to go straight to Thomas Barker's studio on Pulau Saigon but first, he needed to check on progress at South Bridge Road.

As he entered the Detective Branch, Nabeel stopped him.

"This morning, very early, a lady delivered this to the front desk."

Curran took the sealed envelope the clerk held out for him. On the front, someone had written in a neat, educated hand. *For Inspector Curran's eyes only.*

Curran took the envelope over to his desk and carefully slit it open. A small object fell onto his blotter. A single, small purple glass bead. His breath stopped in his throat.

He left it where it had fallen and opened the enclosed note.

*Dear Mr. Curran. Excuse my haste, I don't have much time. I found this bead on the night of the ball when I was assisting Lady Cunningham to undress. It had been caught in a fold of her skirt. I don't know why I kept it, but I have carried it with me since that night. Now I know where the bead came from, and I know how the girl obtained the dress. I promise you I will hand myself in after I have met with the journalist this morning. Mary Venning*

Curran swore. He leaned his hands on his desk and looked down at the small, glass bead that suddenly meant so much. If only Harriet had told him where Mary Venning was hiding. He could have brought her safely into custody and she would be alive now to share the information she now carried to her death.

He picked up the envelope, note, and bead and carried them over to the evidence table. When he compared the bead to those on the dress, there could be no doubt that it had come from the same dress. This corroborated the evidence of Heather Mackenzie. At some stage, Amelia had encountered Lady Cunningham. The dress had been torn and the beads he had found in the private dining room at Government House, and this one that had caught in Lady Cunningham's clothing, had become dislodged.

He told Greaves to log the note and bead as evidence and shared the development with Singh.

Singh stroked his beard and frowned. "Lady Cunningham is seen going up to the gallery and now this," he pointed to Mary Venning's note, "links her to Amelia Hardcastle's death. She has also the best access to her husband, but why would she want him dead?"

That was a good question. She was ambitious for her husband. There would have been nothing she wanted more than to be the wife of the Prime Minister of Great Britain. From that perspective, she would be the last person to want him dead. But she was no fool. She knew about his secret life and the ramifications if it came to public knowledge. Disgrace would be a worse fate than death.

"And what about Miss Venning? I can't see Lady Cunningham ambushing her maid in the Botanic Gardens this morning. There is more than one person involved here," Singh continued.

Curran nodded. "I agree. Who knew she would be at the Botanic Garden? Sarah Bowman, Thomas Barker, and Harriet.

Unless she made contact with anyone else, only those people. I shall start with Mr. Thomas Barker. I want to know exactly how and why Mary Venning came to his door yesterday, and then I will face Lady Cunningham."

# FORTY-THREE

"Another death? Who?"

Julian Edwards handed his sister a glass of whisky and sat down beside her. He had come home for lunch and had been surprised to find Harriet at home. She had sent a note to Esme, excusing herself from attendance at the school. She needed some time alone if only to castigate herself for her lack of judgment and foolish missteps. In short, she was wallowing in self-pity.

Harriet nodded. "Mary Brown, or should I say, Mary Venning."

Julian frowned. "Who's Mary Venning?"

Harriet stared at the amber liquid in her glass. She was tired of keeping secrets, tired of lies, and tired of impossible promises. Taking a deep breath, she told him the Venning story, concluding, "It's all my fault. I should have gone to Curran last night."

For a moment she thought Julian would agree, but he shook his head. "Harriet, you did what you thought best."

"But if I'd told Curran where he could find Mary, she would still be alive."

"You made a promise."

"A foolish one in the circumstances," she said.

They sat in silence for several minutes before Julian spoke.

"Is it possible Lady Cunningham knew that her maid was really Mary Venning?"

Harriet shrugged. "I don't know what to think anymore, Julian. Three people are dead. Amelia died at the ball. And then Sir Henry dies. Mary says a tin containing poison was left in her luggage and now Mary is drowned and the evidence she claims to have had about Sir Henry's activities is missing."

"And what does Curran think?"

Harriet shrugged. "Whatever his thoughts, he's not sharing them with me. After today, I'll be surprised if he ever talks to me again."

Julian continued, "It all seems to be connected to the original Venning case, doesn't it? What if Henry Cunningham tried to seduce young Amelia but when she rejects him, he throws her out of the window? An appalled Mary Venning then poisons Sir Henry... but who drowns her?"

"Oh, good heavens, Julian, it's not that simple."

"Isn't it? If you ask me, it comes down to something Sir Henry Cunningham was involved in on the night of the ball."

"No. He was unwell. He went to bed early. We both saw him leave."

Julian visibly deflated. "Hmm... how does anyone know he was actually unwell? He could have sneaked back in. No one would have seen him go up the back stairs."

Harriet glanced at her brother. "You were there. He certainly looked unwell, and he still had to get from the house to the ballroom without being seen and servants were going backwards and forwards to the kitchens."

The bell across the hedge at the school tolled and Julian grimaced. "I suppose I should get back to it." He heaved himself to his feet. "I won't be in for dinner tonight."

"Meeting?"

Julian flushed. "No, I'm taking Esme to the cinematograph at the Alhambra."

Harriet smiled. "After the week she has had, Esme will be glad of a night out."

"I thought so too. Do you want to come?"

Harriet shook her head. "No. I'll be glad of an early night. Right now, I just want to curl up under my bed and keep the world at bay."

"It's probably dusty under your bed. Stop feeling sorry for yourself, Harri. It does no one any good."

Julian left her to her dark thoughts, and she put her feet up on the daybed with Shashti, once again going over all her actions and not liking the conclusion she reached.

A car turned into the driveway and for a moment Harriet's heart skipped, hoping it might be Curran, but it was Griff Maddocks, and she knew why he had come.

"Is it true?" Maddocks was all business. "Another person connected with Government House is dead?"

Harriet regarded her friend. "What have you heard?"

Maddocks rolled his eyes. "We have been told that Sir Henry Cunningham died peacefully in his sleep yesterday and this morning one of the Cunninghams' staff was found drowned in the swan lake at the Botanic Gardens. Has this got anything to do with our late-night message delivery service?"

No point in prevaricating. Harriet nodded. "Yes. The note we delivered last night was to arrange a meeting between a woman called Mary Venning and Sarah Bowman. She died before she got to us."

Maddocks frowned. "What is Sarah Bowman up to?"

"She's your colleague, Griff. Hasn't she told you?"

Maddocks shook his head. "I would like to help her, but she has the barricades up. One of your lot, Harriet."

"My lot?"

"A suffragette with something to prove."

It was said with a smile, and Harriet looked at him curiously. "Griff, do you like her?"

He shrugged one shoulder. "Maybe... or maybe I am just attracted to strong-minded females."

"You will have to ask her. I'm in enough trouble with Curran already. I should have told him where Mary Venning was hiding last night."

Maddocks patted her hand. "I'm always a shoulder if you need one."

She managed a smile. "Thank you, Griff, but I need to make this right somehow."

"What are you going to do?"

She shook her head. "I don't know. For now, I'll just sit here and feel sorry for myself."

Maddocks frowned. "I hate seeing you like this."

"It will be all right, Griff. One way or another."

But I have to do something to make amends with Curran, she thought.

# FORTY-FOUR

Barker's studio on Pulau Saigon took a little finding among the maze of mildewed and decaying buildings. The old shophouse had once sported a green painted door, but the paint had long since weathered and Curran risked splinters just knocking on the door.

Barker himself answered it. He had changed into dry clothes, but his hair still clung damply to his forehead. Curran was annoyed to find Samrita, sitting on a battered daybed, her feet tucked under her, apparently perfectly at home in the large open space that served as Barker's home and studio. He would have preferred to interview both of them alone.

"Inspector, welcome to my humble abode," Barker said, waving a hand around a space cluttered with canvases and easels. "I wish it was in happier circumstances."

"Tea, Robert? The kettle has just boiled," Samrita said.

"What are you doing here?" Curran demanded of his sister.

She caught Barker's hand, her face troubled. "I was waiting for Tom and Mary to return. Tom told me what happened. Such a terrible thing."

"So, you also knew about the meeting Mary Venning arranged for this morning?"

"Yes. I intended to come too, but Thomas felt I wouldn't be needed." Her mouth drooped. "I'm sorry we involved Harriet, but she knew the reporter and we didn't."

Curran's head spun with questions ranging from the nature of the relationship between his sister and the artist, through to their involvement with Mary Venning.

"Tea," he said. "Thank you."

While Samrita busied herself in an area behind a curtain at the rear of the studio, Curran's gaze swept the room, taking in the stacked canvases including a few early studies for the portrait of Sir John Anderson he had seen at Government House on the night of the ball. There was no doubt the young man had talent.

Samrita emerged with a tray bearing three chipped cups without saucers, an old, chipped, brown earthenware teapot, and a plate of Indian *Jalebi* and Malayan *Kuih Sari Muka*, a reminder of the blend of cultures that could be found in the streets.

She poured three cups of a light, spiced tea and sat down beside Barker, once again taking his hand in hers. Barker glanced at her and smiled.

"I am sorry, they are not fresh," Samrita said as Curran picked up a *Kuih Sari Muka*. "We purchased them yesterday."

Conscious he had not had so much as a cup of tea that morning, Curran bit into the coconut and pandan-flavoured glutinous rice slice. He declined the offer of a second cup of tea and dusted off his fingers.

"I have questions for you, Barker. Let's start with how you knew Mary Venning?"

"As I told Mrs. Gordon—" He stopped. "Did she not tell you?"

"No, I haven't spoken to her yet."

"I was at school with James Venning's brother—"

"I don't recall a brother?"

"Yes. Marcus... He died in South Africa. James was quite a few years younger than me. My parents died when I was young, so I was brought up by an elderly uncle. James's mother had been a friend of my mother, so she kept an eye on me. I'd dine frequently at the Venning's home and Alice Venning would feed me up. She was a marvelous cook." He smiled, but there was sadness in his eyes.

"And?"

"James was very excited about getting the patronage of Sir Henry Cunningham and at first it was everything he wanted. He finally had the opportunity and the allowance to pursue his music, but a few months before his death, he changed. He became quiet, withdrawn, and nervous. If anyone touched him, he would physically recoil. I thought it was just a phase he was going through." He smiled without humor. "We artistic types go through phases, Inspector."

Curran glanced at his sister. So much he didn't know about her. Would he class her as an 'artistic type'?

"After he died, Mary told me the whole ghastly story, and then, of course, it all got swept under the rug. Two years ago, I received a note from Cunningham inviting me to do a portrait of his wife. Imagine my shock when I found Mary Venning working in the house as Lady Cunningham's maid. She swore me to secrecy and asked if I might be able to discover some sort of damning evidence of Sir Henry's activities."

"Did Lady Cunningham know Mary's real identity?"

Barker shrugged. "I don't believe so. I asked Mary, and she said she had never revealed her real name."

"And you painted Lady Cunningham's portrait?"

"Yes. She was very pleased with it." His mouth quirked. "It's not hard to paint a beautiful woman."

Evangeline Cunningham was probably in her forties, but she had retained a certain haughty handsomeness that had improved, rather than diminished with age. As far as beauty went, Curran considered true beauty came from within and he had seen the ugly side of her.

"Why didn't you mention that you knew Lady Cunningham when I spoke to you last time?"

Barker shrugged. "I didn't think it had any bearing on the matter. It was a professional arrangement, Inspector. I can't say we were close confidantes. I turned up at their home at the appointed hour and left. We might have exchanged some chat about the weather and that was it."

"So you found nothing to assist Mary Venning?"

Barker shook his head. "No. I only encountered Sir Henry on one occasion and then only in passing. Cynically, I suppose, I was too old and not to the taste of Sir Henry and his friends."

Curran shook his head to rid himself of the memory of James Venning's last letter with its detailed descriptions of Cunningham's soirees and the sordid activities conducted behind supposedly respectable walls.

"How did Mary Venning make contact with you here in Singapore?"

"I met up with Mary at Government House when I took the portrait in for the unveiling. She managed to take me to one side and said she had the evidence she had been looking for, but just needed some way to get it to the authorities. She gave me a sealed envelope and told me to keep it safe until she came to collect it."

"Where did you hide it?"

Barker swung his gaze to the curtained-off area. "There is a loose floorboard under the bed. I put it in there."

"Show me."

The area behind the curtain consisted of an unmade bed covered in colorful fabrics and a table on which a small, portable paraffin stove topped with a kettle stood. A chair and a rickety wardrobe completed the furnishings.

Barker knelt and lifted the floorboard beneath his bed, revealing the gap between the floor and the ceiling below.

"I found it empty this morning. She must have taken the envelope with her."

"And you didn't hear her leave?"

"No. I was asleep on the daybed. She must have passed me on her way out, but I didn't hear a thing. I'm a heavy sleeper."

Curran could have groaned aloud. He had been so close. If only she hadn't run. Whatever evidence she had discovered was lost now, taken by her murderer. Who would be most damaged by the papers Mary had accumulated? Once again, it came back to Lady Cunningham.

"Did you meet Charles Gilmore or Finley Ellis when you were working for the Cunninghams?"

Barker frowned. "I saw them once or twice, but not to speak to." He spread his hands. "I'm sorry I can't be of any more help, Inspector."

Curran rose to his feet, circling his helmet in his hands. His gaze strayed around the room. "You mentioned you were painting the Hardcastle girls. Do you have the portrait here?"

Barker nodded. He stood up and flicked back the sheet that covered one of the easels. He had depicted the two young girls, dressed in white dresses, their hair loose, seated together with a small, white fluffy dog. Curran could not recall ever seeing Amelia Hardcastle in life, but the portrait confirmed everyone's description of her as a budding beauty. The simple innocence of the portrait, captured so well by Barker, saddened him beyond belief.

"I intend to give it to the parents," Barker said. "No charge."

Samrita gathered up the cups and replaced them on the tray, carrying them through to the living quarters.

Curran looked around the room and his gaze fell on an open trunk from which spilled a cornucopia of brightly colored silks and satins. Curran wandered across to the box and pulled out a crumpled paisley shawl of exceptional quality.

"My dressing-up box." Barker smiled. "I like to play with

different textures, see how they fall on the body, how the light changes them."

"Did you bring this with you from London?"

"The box? Yes. I used to buy cast-offs from the flea markets off Smithfield. Ladies who don't know value will just throw out their outmoded ball dresses and you can pick them up for a song."

Curran turned to face him. "Dresses like the one Amelia Hardcastle was wearing?"

Barker glanced at the curtained-off area, from which the splashing of water and clink of cups indicated Samrita was washing the cups they had used.

"I never saw what she was wearing," he said.

"A sort of purple color with beads on the bodice," Curran said, ruing the fact he didn't have an image of the dress with him.

Barker shook his head. "Not one of mine. As I said, those sorts of garments are easily obtained."

Curran folded the shawl and laid it back in the box. He wandered among the canvases and easels, stopping at the largest easel. A good-sized canvas had been placed on it and covered with a cloth.

"It's just rough," Barker said, too quickly. "Not worth looking at."

Behind him Samrita gave a startled squeak and he lifted the cloth away. If the subject had not been his sister, he may have considered it a very fine painting, but some hitherto unknown paternalism rose in him and he turned to look at his sister. She looked down at the floor. Curran let the cloth drop and let his gaze drift from one guilty face to the other. He fixed Barker with a hard stare, lost for words.

"That's my sister. I paid you to give her lessons, not—"

"Samrita is a joy to paint, Curran," Barker interrupted. "You might as well know. She's agreed to come with me to Australia. They have a lively art community in Melbourne, I believe."

But Curran's gaze was on his sister. "Where did this idea of going to Australia come from? Is this what you want, Samrita?" he asked.

"I belong with Thomas." She held out her hand to Barker. Her chin lifted and she met his gaze with an oddly familiar defiance. He had seen it in his cousin Eloise. "We are lovers."

The blunt summary of their relationship rendered Curran speechless. He had been absent from Singapore for months, but surely after everything Samrita had been through with the Topaz Club and the murder of Ashton Blake, she wouldn't willingly throw herself into a relationship?

"I see," was all he could find to say.

Samrita stood up and crossed to him, taking both his hands in her own. "Robert, I owe you my life and I do not mean to hurt you, but a life with Thomas offers me a chance to be truly free and pursue my art."

"Do you plan marriage?" Curran enquired.

Samrita shrugged. "No, and don't look like that. I don't belong in your world, Robert. It is just fortunate I have found somewhere I do belong. For now, it is enough just to be together."

Barker stood up and joined them. He laid his hands on Samrita's shoulders. "I love your sister, Curran. I would never do anything to hurt her."

"Besides," Samrita said. "You are hardly one to complain of a lack of propriety. Did you not live with Khoo Li An?"

Curran nodded. "I did, and you are right. It would be hypocritical of me to accuse you of impropriety, but it is different for a man."

"I think you would need to tell Khoo Li An that, Curran. Living as your mistress does not seem to have affected her future. Is she not married now and in charge of her brother's trading companies?"

"She is."

"Then give us your blessing. That is all I am asking."

Curran thought of Li An. Theirs had been a grand, desperate

passion born of adversity. They had clung to each other while the world around them seethed and roiled, but Li An had recognized that it was a passion that could never last and she had let him go. He had found another deep, long-lasting, and abiding love, one he could build a life on.

Yes, he understood that love did not have boundaries and if Samrita had truly found someone who nurtured her soul, then far be it for him to stand in her way or make hypocritical moral judgments, but he couldn't help but worry for his sister. He acknowledged his own double standard, but any number of unpleasant scenarios started to play through his mind, all ending with his unmarried sister pregnant and abandoned in a country she knew nothing about. Even if Lavinia thought he had no right to play the overbearing older brother, he could not let her go without saying something.

He placed his pith helmet on his head and straightened.

"We will talk later, but right now, I have three deaths on my hands."

# FORTY-FIVE

The flag over Government House flew at half-mast and a gloomy air hung over the building, accentuated by the stormy skies.

Claud Severn showed Curran through to the magnificent office on the ground floor. Sir John stood up behind his enormous desk, which was covered in reports and papers.

"I am returning to London," Sir John said, waving a hand over the papers. "Trying to write a brief for my successor."

"We will be sorry to see you go," Curran said with genuine warmth. The affable Scot had been popular with everyone.

"Thank you, but I'm sure that's not why you're here. What can I do for you now, Curran?"

"We found Lady Cunningham's maid this morning."

Sir John raised an eyebrow. "That is good news. Has she confessed to her part in his death?"

"No. She's dead. We found her body in the lake in the Botanic Gardens."

Sir John blinked and sat down with an audible thump. He shook his head. "Good God, another death. Poor girl. Did she take her own life?"

*What was this obsession with suicide?* Curran was about to say no, but thought better of it.

"We don't know yet."

"So, what are we required to do?"

"I need to speak with Lady Cunningham."

Sir John appraised him with a knowing eye. "I am not sure the lady will wish to speak with you. What is the source of her antipathy to you, Curran?"

"An old case," Curran replied.

Sir John rose to his feet again, indicating the interview with him was done.

"Unfortunately, Lady Cunningham is not in residence. My daughter has taken her to lunch to distract her for a few hours. She will be back later this afternoon and I will break the news to her about her maid."

Curran heard the finality in the man's tone and let it rest. He would face Lady Cunningham later in the day.

Curran pointed to the morning's edition of the *Straits Times*. "I am curious as to why the press is reporting Sir Henry died peacefully in his sleep."

Sir John's lips tightened. "We thought it best to minimize gossip and now his killer is also dead, we will try keep his cause of death quiet."

"No autopsy, no inquest, and no truth?" Curran said.

"Curran, I understand your zeal, but there are other forces at play here. Whitehall—"

Curran swallowed his thoughts about Whitehall. "So Sir Henry will be buried with all the pomp due to a minister of State and the truth about him will go to the grave with him? Like the business in KL, filed away quietly never to see the light of day?"

Sir John's eyes flickered. "Precisely. Now, is there anything else I can do for you?" Sir John asked.

"I need to speak with Sir Henry's valet and his private secretary."

The governor nodded and almost looked relieved. "In that case, I'll leave you in Severn's hands for those interviews."

Severn, in turn, waved at the staircase. "You know the way. You don't need me to guide you."

Curran found Finley Ellis in Sir Henry's bedroom. Mercifully, the room had been thoroughly cleaned, the bed stripped of all bedding and the floor scrubbed. However, a residual smell of death still lingered over the carbolic.

Curran stood at the door watching as Ellis laid each item of the late Sir Henry's clothing out on the table and folded it with precision before laying it in the traveling trunk.

"Good morning, Ellis," he said at last.

The man started dropping a silver-backed hairbrush he had been holding.

"Inspector."

"A sad task," Curran said, waving a hand at the trunk.

Ellis sniffed. "Tragic... tragic. Have you found the evil girl who did this?"

"Yes."

"And did she confess?"

"No." Curran paused on the brink of telling Ellis of Mary's death, but thought better of it. "How well did you know Miss Brown?"

"She came to work for Lady Cunningham about two years ago. It is hard not to get to know someone when you live in the same house and serve the same people, but she kept her own counsel, and I wouldn't say I knew her well."

"Were you friends?"

"Good God, no. Colleagues no more. She was considerably younger than me, Mr. Curran. We shared no interests in common. I really have nothing to tell you that will be of any help."

Curran paused long enough for Ellis to become fidgety.

"Do you recall James Venning?" he asked at last.

"Of course I do. A most unfortunate affair and your part in it is not forgotten, Curran."

Curran ignored the jibe. "Did you know Mary Brown was his sister?"

Ellis clutched the shirt he had just picked up to his chest. "Good God. I had no idea."

Either Ellis was a very good actor, or the news genuinely took him by surprise.

"Did she ever speak to you about him?"

"No." Ellis laid the shirt down and tried, unsuccessfully, to smooth the rumples. "If she was James Venning's sister, then I can understand why she might have held something of a grudge. As you well know, the Venning family held Sir Henry responsible for the boy's death. I recall the mother coming to the house on more than one occasion."

"As Sir Henry's valet, he could have had few secrets from you. Sir Henry is dead. You can't hurt him now. Tell me, were you privy to his entertainments?"

Ellis stiffened. "I will speak no ill of the dead. Sir Henry was always good to me—"

"He paid you well to keep your mouth shut?"

Fire blazed in Ellis' eyes. "Sir Henry's private life was his business. If he had certain needs, that makes him no different to you or me, Inspector."

"It does when the needs involve young boys and girls. You don't need to protect him anymore, Ellis."

Ellis straightened. "You will hear nothing against Sir Henry from me, Mr. Curran."

"Did you know Mary Brown—Mary Venning—was gathering evidence to bring Sir Henry's proclivities to public attention?"

Something flickered in Ellis's eyes, but he replied, "No, I did not. If she did so, she was very discrete in her probing."

"When did you last see her?"

"I told you, she delivered Sir Henry's tisane to his room as I was assisting him to bed. If I had known it was poisoned—"

"What makes you think the tisane was poisoned?"

"What else could it have been? I might only be a valet, Mr. Curran, but I know enough to see for myself that Sir Henry did not die peacefully in his sleep. That evil girl did for him."

"Then who killed her?"

Ellis stared at him. "She's dead?"

"Yes, we found her body this morning."

Ellis stared at him. "How?"

"Drowned."

"That is terrible news, Curran, but how should I know who killed her?"

"If Mary Brown had wanted help from a friend, would she have come to you?"

"Me?" Ellis' surprise seemed genuine. "I would have been the last person she would have asked for help."

"Why?"

Ellis affected a shrug. "I told you, we were not friends. Now I think about it, she tried asking me questions along the lines of what you have just intimated, but I am loyal to Sir Henry. I told her nothing."

"Thank you, Ellis. Do you know where I will find Gilmore?"

"You've just missed him. He's gone out to organize our transport back to England. He'll be back later this afternoon."

Curran glanced at his watch. It was already one o'clock, and he needed to see if Mac had any news for him before he went any further.

---

"What have you found?" Curran demanded, without preamble as he entered the hospital morgue.

Mac, seated at the desk writing notes, looked up.

"And a good afternoon to you, Curran." Mac glanced at the shrouded body on the table. "Let me show you something."

He stood up and pulled the sheet back, revealing Mary's cold, dead face, mottled now, her eyes mercifully closed. He turned her head to one side and Curran saw what he had missed at the lakeside, a nasty wound to the back of her head.

"Could that have happened postmortem?"

Mac cast him a scathing glance.

"She drowned," he confirmed. "But only after someone struck her over the head and held her down in the water. There are bruises on the back of her neck and her arm where he held her."

Curran stared at the doctor. "It's a frightening similar situation to how Amelia died—a blow to the head and then finished off in another way."

"Subdue them first and then it would have been the work of a minute to finish them off. You didn't happen to find a rock with blood and hair on it?"

Curran shook his head. "If the murderer had any sense, he would have thrown it into the lake."

*He would have stood by the side of the lake and thrown it...*

Was that the reason for the boot print some yards from where Mary had died?

The flag over Government House flew at half-mast and a gloomy air hung over the building, accentuated by the stormy skies.

Claud Severn showed Curran through to the magnificent office on the ground floor. Sir John stood up behind his enormous desk, which was covered in reports and papers.

"I am returning to London," Sir John said, waving a hand over the papers. "Trying to write a brief for my successor."

"We will be sorry to see you go," Curran said with genuine warmth. The affable Scot had been popular with everyone.

"Thank you, but I'm sure that's not why you're here. What can I do for you now, Curran?"

"We found Lady Cunningham's maid this morning."

Sir John raised an eyebrow. "That is good news. Has she confessed to her part in his death?"

"No. She's dead. We found her body in the lake in the Botanic Gardens."

Sir John blinked and sat down with an audible thump. He shook his head. "Good God, another death. Poor girl. Did she take her own life?"

*What was this obsession with suicide?* Curran was about to say no but thought better of it.

"We don't know yet."

"So, what are we required to do?"

"I need to speak with Lady Cunningham."

Sir John appraised him with a knowing eye. "I am not sure the lady will wish to speak with you. What is the source of her antipathy to you, Curran?"

"An old case," Curran replied.

Sir John rose to his feet again, indicating the interview with him was done.

"Unfortunately, Lady Cunningham is not in residence. My daughter has taken her to lunch to distract her for a few hours. She will be back later this afternoon and I will break the news to her about her maid."

Curran heard the finality in the man's tone and let it rest. He would face Lady Cunningham later in the day.

Curran pointed to the morning's edition of the *Straits Times*. "I am curious as to why the press is reporting Sir Henry died peacefully in his sleep."

Sir John's lips tightened. "We thought it best to minimize gossip and now his killer is also dead, we can keep his cause of death quiet."

"No autopsy, no inquest, and no truth?" Curran said.

"Curran, I understand your zeal but there are other forces at play here. Whitehall—"

Curran swallowed his thoughts about Whitehall. "So Sir Henry will be buried with all the pomp due to a minister of State and the truth about him will go to the grave with him? Like the business in KL, filed away quietly never to see the light of day?"

Sir John's eyes flickered. "Precisely. Now, is there anything else I can do for you?" Sir John asked.

"I need to speak with Sir Henry's valet and his private secretary."

The governor nodded and almost looked relieved. "In that case, I'll leave you in Severn's hands for those interviews."

Severn, in turn, waved at the staircase. "You know the way. You don't need me to guide you."

Curran found Finley Ellis in Sir Henry's bedroom. Mercifully the room had been thoroughly cleaned, the bed stripped of all bedding and the floor scrubbed. However, a residual smell of death still lingered over the carbolic.

Curran stood at the door watching as Ellis, laid each item of the late Sir Henry's clothing out on the table and folded it with precision before laying it in the traveling trunk.

"Good morning, Ellis," he said at last.

The man started dropping a silver-backed hairbrush he had been holding.

"Inspector."

"A sad task," Curran said, waving a hand at the trunk.

Ellis sniffed. "Tragic... tragic. Have you found the evil girl who did this?"

"Yes."

"And did she confess?"

"No." Curran paused on the brink of telling Ellis of Mary's death but thought better of it. "How well did you know Miss Brown?"

"She came to work for Lady Cunningham, about two years

ago. It is hard not to get to know someone when you live in the same house and serve the same people, but she kept her own counsel, and I wouldn't say I knew her well."

"Were you friends?"

"Good God, no. Colleagues no more. She was considerably younger than me, Mr. Curran. We shared no interests in common. I really have nothing to tell you that will be of any help."

Curran paused long enough for Ellis to become fidgety.

"Do you recall James Venning?" he asked at last.

"Of course I do. A most unfortunate affair and your part in it is not forgotten, Curran."

Curran ignored the jibe. "Did you know Mary Brown was his sister?"

Ellis clutched the shirt, he had just picked up, to his chest. "Good God. I had no idea."

Either Ellis was a very good actor or the news genuinely took him by surprise.

"Did she ever speak to you about him?"

"No." Ellis laid the shirt down and tried, unsuccessfully, to smooth the rumples. "If she was James Venning's sister then I can understand why she might have held something of a grudge. As you well know, the Venning family held Sir Henry responsible for the boy's death. I recall the mother coming to the house on more than one occasion."

"As Sir Henry's valet, he could have had few secrets from you. Sir Henry is dead, you can't hurt him now. Tell me, were you privy to his entertainments?"

Ellis stiffened. "I will speak no ill of the dead. Sir Henry was always good to me—"

"He paid you well to keep your mouth shut?"

Fire blazed in Ellis' eyes. "Sir Henry's private life was his business. If he had certain needs, that makes him no different to you or me, Inspector."

"It does when the needs involve young boys and girls. You don't need to protect him anymore, Ellis."

Ellis straightened. "You will hear nothing against Sir Henry from me, Mr. Curran."

"Did you know Mary Brown—Mary Venning—was gathering evidence to bring Sir Henry's proclivities to public attention?"

Something flickered in Ellis's eyes, but he replied, "No, I did not. If she did so, she was very discrete in her probing."

"When did you last see her?"

"I told you, she delivered Sir Henry's tisane to his room as I was assisting him to bed. If I had known it was poisoned—"

"What makes you think the tisane was poisoned?"

"What else could it have been? I might only be a valet, Mr. Curran, but I know enough to see for myself that Sir Henry did not die peacefully in his sleep. That evil girl did for him."

"Then who killed her?"

Ellis stared at him. "She's dead?"

"Yes, we found her body this morning."

Ellis stared at him. "How?"

"Drowned."

"That is terrible news, Curran, but how should I know who killed her?"

"If Mary Brown had wanted help from a friend, would she have come to you?"

"Me?" Ellis' surprise seemed genuine. "I would have been the last person she would have asked for help."

"Why?"

Ellis affected a shrug. "I told you, we were not friends. Now I think about it, she did try asking me questions along the lines of what you have just intimated, but I am loyal to Sir Henry. I told her nothing."

"Thank you, Ellis. Do you know where I will find Gilmore?"

"You've just missed him. He's gone out to organize our transport back to England. He'll be back later this afternoon."

Curran glanced at his watch. It was already one o'clock and he needed to see if Mac had any news for him before he went any further.

———

"What have you found?" Curran demanded, without preamble as he entered the hospital morgue.

Mac, seated at the desk writing notes, looked up.

"And a good afternoon to you, Curran." Mac glanced at the shrouded body on the table. "Let me show you something."

He stood up and pulled the sheet back revealing Mary's cold, dead face, mottled now, her eyes mercifully closed. He turned her head to one side and Curran saw what he had missed at the lakeside, a nasty wound to the back of her head.

"Could that have happened postmortem?"

Mac cast him a scathing glance.

"She drowned," he confirmed. "But only after someone struck her over the head and held her down in the water. There are bruises on the back of her neck and her arm where he held her."

Curran stared at the doctor. "It's a frightening similar situation to how Amelia died—a blow to the head and then finished off in another way."

"Subdue them first and then it would have been the work of a minute to finish them off. You didn't happen to find a rock with blood and hair on it?"

Curran shook his head. "If the murderer had any sense he would have thrown it into the lake."

*He would have stood by the side of the lake and thrown it...*

Was that the reason for the boot print some yards from where Mary had died?

# FORTY-SIX

Shortly after Maddocks had left, Harriet received a note from Charles Gilmore requesting her assistance with some urgent typing. Harriet read it several times, wondering about making an excuse. In the end, she decided she would be a fool to turn down some paid work, and it gave her an opportunity to see Lady Cunningham. Maybe a suitably contrite apology for her intemperate words might go some way toward making amends with Curran.

At Government House, she asked to speak with Lady Cunningham and was advised that her ladyship had just returned from lunch with Mrs. Farrant and was resting. The staff member scuttled upstairs and returned with the news that Lady Cunningham would receive her.

Sir Henry Cunningham's widow sat at a small writing desk in the elegant and tastefully decorated withdrawing room where she had received Harriet and Lavinia.

As Harriet entered, Lady Cunningham rose in a single graceful movement. Even dressed in full mourning, she managed to make Harriet feel decidedly dowdy.

"Well, Mrs. Gordon?" she demanded without preamble.

"I came to express my condolences on the death of your husband and to apologize," Harriet said. "I spoke out of turn about matters that do not concern me."

Something that might have been a smile caught at the corner of Lady Cunningham's lips.

"That takes courage, Mrs. Gordon. Are you hoping that I might refrain from lodging a formal complaint with Inspector Curran's superior?"

"You are free to do what you wish, Lady Cunningham." Harriet paused. "I venture only to say that I am not sure lodging such a complaint will do much except ruin a good man's career and expose your late husband's proclivities to a wider range of people at a time when you would prefer he was remembered for his more positive traits."

Lady Cunningham's mouth became a thin slash.

"My husband was a highly respected man," she said.

"But an imperfect one."

"None of us are perfect, Mrs. Gordon. Will that be all?"

"I was there when they found your maid. I'm so sorry," Harriet said.

"Sir John tells me that the silly girl drowned herself," Lady Cunningham said.

Harriet kept her peace.

Lady Cunningham's shoulders relaxed. "Your apology is accepted, and I will not be reporting Curran for his indiscretion. As you say, what is the point? It doesn't bring Henry back and I shall be leaving Singapore the day after tomorrow to take my husband home for a proper burial."

The door opened, and both women turned to see Charles Gilmore.

Without looking up from the paper he held, he said, "Evie, I've made the booking. First class suite aboard the *Britannic*. We leave on the morning tide—"

"Mr. Gilmore," Lady Cunningham said, her voice tight.

He looked up and his eyes widened as he took in Harriet's presence. "My apologies, Lady Cunningham, I didn't know you had company."

"Mrs. Gordon just called in to express her condolences. She was just leaving," Lady Cunningham said.

"Mrs. Gordon is here to do some work for me. You'll find the documents I need typing beside the typewriter. The quicker you get started, the quicker we will be done."

Harriet cast Gilmore a quick smile as she walked past him and the door shut behind her. She paused in the hall and glanced back at the doors to the drawing room.

*Evie,* Charles Gilmore had called Lady Cunningham, not only by her first name but a diminutive. In no book of etiquette would that ever be permitted. It left only one conclusion... there was something more to the relationship. Although she was well into her forties, Lady Cunningham was still an attractive and compelling woman and one, Harriet suspected, who enjoyed her power over men, particularly younger men. She had met the type before—one of her mother's friends had scandalized the Wimbledon social circle by running away with a man ten years her junior.

Tempted though she was to look through the keyhole of the now firmly shut door, Harriet Gordon was better than that. Even if Gilmore and Lady Cunningham were in a relationship, what bearing did that have on Amelia's death... or Mary Venning's?

Sir Henry, on the other hand—

She couldn't wait to tell Curran.

# FORTY-SEVEN

I t was long past five when Harriet laid the last of the neatly typed letters on Charles Gilmore's desk. He flicked through them and nodded.

"Thank you. I could not have done any of this without your help, Mrs. Gordon. The amount of paperwork involved when a Minister of the Crown dies—"

Harriet cleared her throat. "There is the small matter of remuneration, Mr. Gilmore."

"Of course."

Gilmore pulled a tin from a drawer and unlocked it.

He quirked an eyebrow at her. "You are also owed for the work you did for Sir Henry."

Harriet named her fee and tucked the fresh, crisp pound notes into her purse.

"If there is nothing else, Mr. Gilmore?"

He shook his head. "No. We will be on a ship the day after tomorrow, thank God. I can't get home soon enough."

Harriet bade him good night and made her way out of Government House. It had been a long day, and she felt drained, longing for nothing more than a quiet evening with Julian and Will, and most of all, a gin and tonic.

"Harriet!"

She had been so lost in her thoughts as she crunched down the long driveway to hail a ricksha at the gate that she had taken no notice of the vehicle that had passed her. Now she turned to see Curran running down the graveled driveway to catch up with her.

"What are you doing here?" he asked.

"Mr. Gilmore asked me to help with some typing and I wasn't going to turn down the chance to earn a few pounds. The money will be useful. We have to sort out supplies for Will. He will be leaving soon." She remembered the conversation with Julian. "Curran, I've been meaning to tell you. Will wants to talk to you about his father."

She saw the hesitation in Curran's eyes. "What does he want to know?"

Harriet shook her head. "I'm not sure, but he looks up to you and I think he is looking for reassurance that his father loved him and was not an evil man."

"John Lawson was weak, but none of us are perfect. He loved Will and if that is what Will wants to hear, that is what I will tell him."

Harriet smiled. "Thank you. How has your day progressed?"

"Frustrating." He cast a glance at the magnificent residence. "This is my second visit for the day. According to Mac, Mary Venning was hit over the back of the head before she drowned. I have more questions that need answering."

"You need to hurry, Curran. Lady Cunningham and her party will be leaving the day after tomorrow."

He smiled. "I'm close, Harriet. If nothing else, before she died, Mary confirmed that at some point in the evening, Lady Cunningham was in contact with Amelia Hardcastle."

"How?"

"She found a bead from the dress caught in Lady Cunningham's dress."

Harriet gasped. "Do you think Lady Cunningham—"

"No, I don't think Lady Cunningham hauled the girl's body to the window and threw it out. Someone else was involved."

Harriet laid a hand on his arm.

"Someone like Charles Gilmore? I think Lady Cunningham and Gilmore are having an affair."

He stared at her. "What on earth makes you think that?"

"I was talking to Lady Cunningham, and Gilmore walked in. He addressed her as 'Evie'. Nobody uses that level of familiarity with someone like Lady Cunningham unless they were more than just polite acquaintances."

Curran frowned. "I'll need more than a feeling, but thank you, that is useful. Now stop trying to help, Harriet."

She looked down at the neatly graveled carriageway beneath her feet. "I suppose Wallace was not pleased about Mary's death?"

"No, he wasn't."

She looked up, willing him to believe her as she said, "Curran, Mary promised she would go to you. I would never have agreed to the plan otherwise."

"I know. She sent me a note. I just wish she had trusted me with what she knew about Sir Henry."

"Sir Henry Cunningham was a monster, and the world deserved to know that such monsters walk among us. Do you know what it is to be a woman, Curran? To live every day in fear, because we do! Every street we walk down, every hansom cab we climb into, we are wondering if we are safe and if our children are safe..."

She trailed off... *if our children are safe*. How many children did the Cunninghams have? Lady Cunningham had mentioned daughters. Had they reached the age of being potential prey for their father and his associates?

The thought sickened her, but remembering what James

Venning had written about the indiscriminate selection of their victims, it was not beyond the realms of possibility that the Cunningham girls were vulnerable.

She grasped Curran's sleeve. "Curran, if you speak with Lady Cunningham, ask about her children."

"Why? What has that got to do with these deaths?"

She explained her thoughts, and he nodded. "That is heinous, Harriet."

"But not impossible? A woman would do anything to protect her children."

He shook his head. "It's moments like this that I am glad I have you to give me a woman's perspective on the world."

"And there's a girl, one of the household staff. The girl who turned down Sir Henry's bed at night. She told Mary that on the night he died, Sir Henry had tried to have his way with her."

Curran stared at her. "Mary told you this?"

Harriet nodded. "As unwell as he was, he hadn't changed."

"Did Mary tell anyone about this girl?"

"Yes, Lady Cunningham."

Curran exhaled. "Thank you, Harriet. I need to find this girl. You don't have a name?"

Harriet shook her head. "I'm so sorry for betraying your trust in me."

He smiled and brushed her cheek with his fingers.

"Harriet, you are forgiven but I have three murders on my hands. I promise I will make things right between us when these cases are closed."

He turned to leave her and looked back. "What exactly were you doing talking to Lady Cunningham?"

She looked down at the ground. "I apologized to her. If it's any consolation, she told me she will be taking no further action on my indiscretion."

Curran said nothing for a long moment.

"Thank you, Harriet," he said. "Now excuse me."
And he turned and walked away from her.

# FORTY-EIGHT

As he walked back to the house, Curran mulled over what Harriet had just told him.

He asked to speak with the *majordomo*, who obligingly produced the girl who was responsible for Sir Henry's room. The girl crossed her arms and refused to say anything. Curran looked her up and down. She wore the black-and-white uniform of the Government House staff, but her hair had been fastened with a gold comb, studded with what looked like precious stones.

"Where did you get that?" he asked her.

The girl's eyes widened. "It was a gift." Her voice shook.

"An expensive gift," Curran noted. "Who gave it to you?"

"Mr. Ellis," she said. "Can I go now?"

"Why?"

But the girl shook her head and would say no more. He let her go. He would speak with Ellis, but he suspected that the comb had been given to the girl to keep her silence.

He asked after Gilmore and was told he had returned, so he made his way to the room Gilmore had been using as an office.

Charles Gilmore had pushed the typewriter to one side and was working at the table. He looked like a man who had spent a long day sorting paperwork. A damp lock of hair had fallen over his eyes, and he was working in shirtsleeves, his collar loosened and his tie hanging loose.

He looked up as Curran entered the room.

"Not now, Curran. Can't you see I am swamped! Sir Henry's death requires a great deal of paperwork!"

"I'm sure it does, and now you have another death to add to your workload."

Gilmore's eyes widened. "Who?"

"Lady Cunningham's maid."

"Oh yes, Lady Cunningham told me she had been found in a lake in the Botanic Gardens early this morning."

"When did you last see her?"

Gilmore frowned. "The night Sir Henry died. She brought Lady Cunningham a wrap while we were at dinner. It was a little breezy I recall. The rumor is she poisoned Sir Henry. Is that true?"

Curran ignored the question. "Where were you this morning about seven thirty?"

Gilmore laughed. "I was in here, in my pajamas, dealing with this..." He swept a hand across the papers that littered the table. "If you doubt my word, ask the staff. At least one of them brought me a cup of tea. Now, if there's nothing else, I need to get on with my work, Curran."

Uninvited, Curran took the remaining chair.

"What exactly is keeping you so busy?"

"When an important Government official dies overseas, there are the onward arrangements to cancel, transportation of the body back to England—"

"And you are telling the world he died in his sleep?"

"Yes... a heart attack. Bromidia is known to weaken the heart, and he wasn't strong—"

"Did you see his body, Gilmore?"

Gilmore gave a small cough. "I did."

"A man doesn't die like that of a heart attack. He died from a large dose of arsenic."

Gilmore's mouth dropped open. If he was acting, it was convincing.

"But there was no autopsy. How can you possibly know that?"

"We're not fools, Gilmore. There are other ways of testing for these things without the need for an autopsy. Furthermore, we believe he had been systematically poisoned with arsenic over quite a period before the final, fatal dose."

Gilmore sat back in his chair and mopped his face with a crumpled handkerchief. "I knew he'd been unwell for a while, but the doctors put it down to gastrointestinal issues caused by this stressful job. Who would want to poison him?"

Curran crossed his legs and steepled his fingers. "Plenty of people. Let's start with you. You and Lady Cunningham are having an affair. There's a motive right there. It would suit Lady Cunningham to be rid of her husband—"

Gilmore jumped to his feet. "That's outrageous, Curran. Evie would never—"

He realized what he'd said, but it was too late. He sank back in his chair and buried his face in his hands. Curran let the silence pass between them before he said, "Well? Are you having an affair?"

Gilmore raised his head. "I deny that there is anything improper between me and Lady Cunningham. How dare you make such a suggestion." His denial lacked conviction.

"Of course, you always call your employer's wife by a diminutive?"

Gilmore cleared his throat. "We have become close friends by dint of nothing more than our proximity, Inspector, and I resent your implication. I should lodge a complaint—"

Curran let that pass. "There is a queue, Mr. Gilmore. If Lady Cunningham did not poison her husband... who else would have a motive or an opportunity to do so, particularly over a consider-able length of time?"

"How long?" Gilmore asked

Curran shrugged. "Hard to tell without an autopsy, but from all accounts he has been unwell for some time."

Gilmore shook his head. "I can't believe this was going on right under my nose."

Curran said nothing. *Watch, wait, gauge the reaction...*

Whatever his relationship with Lady Cunningham and Curran was now certain Harriet had been right, he didn't see Gilmore as an administrator of poison. That required proximity and a subtlety that the private secretary did not possess.

"Did his health improve when Lady Cunningham was away from London?"

Gilmore licked his lips. "I suppose it did, but I can't believe Lady Cunningham would do such a thing. What about the girl... Brown?"

"Who is now, conveniently, dead? What was your relationship with Lady Cunningham's maid?"

"Relationship? None. She kept herself to herself, as she should. She was a lady's maid. I had no reason to talk to her."

"Are you aware of the case of James Venning?"

A muscle twitched in Gilmore's cheek, belying his next words. "Remind me."

"James Venning was a young man who committed suicide. He implicated your employer in his death. Mary Brown, as she was calling herself, was his sister. I've asked you this before, but as his personal secretary, you must have been aware of Sir Henry's proclivities, the private soirees with his friends involving underage youngsters."

Gilmore said nothing and the two men held each other's gaze for a long, long time before Gilmore flicked his eyes away. "I turned a blind eye. Whatever Sir Henry chose to do in his personal life was none of my business."

"But what if it ever became public and risked ruining his rise to power and, by association, yours... and risked disgracing his wife?"

Gilmore stared at him. "It would have been unfortunate."

"Did you ever attend one of his soirees?"

"No!" Gilmore snapped. "No. I was appalled and ashamed to be even remotely connected to them. It was a part of Sir Henry's life I had nothing to do with and I certainly did not condone or participate in it."

"And what about his wife? Did she initiate the affair with you, or did you offer to provide her solace?"

Gilmore stood up and made a show of straightening his tie. "I am a gentleman, Curran. I won't hear or say a bad word about Lady Cunningham."

Curran rose to face him. "And you had nothing to do with Mary Venning?"

"Nothing, I assure you, but if, as you say, she was this James Venning's sister, then she had the perfect motive for slowly poisoning Sir Henry. If it were my brother..."

His revulsion was written on his face.

"Then why is she dead?"

"Remorse? I don't know. I was told she drowned herself, didn't she?"

"No. She was hit over the head and drowned," Curran said. "There is a murderer among you, Mr. Gilmore, and none of you are leaving the island until he or she is caught."

"We have passage booked on a ship the day after tomorrow. We will be leaving then regardless of your wishes, Inspector."

"Then you better hope we have the murderer in custody by then or you will be traveling with a killer."

Gilmore licked his lips. "What makes you think it is one of us?"

"No one else has the proximity to Sir Henry that his wife and personal staff have. One of you is responsible for the death of Sir Henry and Mary Venning and, quite possibly, Amelia Harcourt."

"I utterly refute that suggestion," Gilmore said.

Curran recognized he would get no further with Gilmore, so he bid the man good evening and went in search of Claud Severn. He needed to speak to Lady Cunningham, and time was running out.

A weary and harassed Claud Severn directed him to the undertaker.

"Mrs. Farrant has taken her to finalize the arrangements for the transport of Sir Henry's body."

Curran thanked the man and turned on his heel. Severn called out after him.

"This is a very distressing time for her, Curran. Watch yourself."

# FORTY-NINE

Ravensway & Co. in Orchard Road was the best-known undertaker in Singapore catering to the European population. No expense had been spared in wooing the bereaved, from the wood paneling and deep carpeting in the reception rooms to the most ornate and expensive coffins that could be procured. The firm also boasted a magnificent hearse drawn by four matching black horses. Death in the harsh tropical climate was not uncommon and Ravensway did do a good funeral.

Adolphus Proctor, principal of the firm, greeted Curran in the reception room.

"Inspector, what can I do for you on this fine day?"

"Is Lady Cunningham on the premises?" Curran asked.

Proctor frowned, "She is, but—"

"I would like to speak with her."

Proctor ducked his head and excused himself. He reappeared in a short time and advised Curran that Lady Cunningham had no wish to see him and asked he respect her privacy at this moment.

Curran had run out of patience with Lady Cunningham.

Despite Proctor's protests, he pushed past the little man and entered the private viewing room.

The room was decorated in dark burgundy velvet and lined with yet more wood paneling and was oppressively warm despite an electric fan, which whirred and clacked above his head. The elegant surroundings could not quite disguise the miasma of death and formaldehyde emanating from the coffin that stood on a draped plinth in the middle of the room.

Lady Cunningham stood by the open coffin. Sir John's eldest daughter, Mrs Farrant, sat on a chair in the corner clutching her handbag and looking a little pale. Both women wore unrelieved black. Curran inclined his head to Mrs. Farrant, who returned the gesture.

"Curran, how dare you—" Lady Cunningham began.

"I came to pay my respects," Curran said and came to stand beside Lady Cunningham.

Sir Henry reposed on the white satin, dressed in a black morning coat with a cravat and diamond tie pin. His hands were neatly folded over his chest, but he wore fine black leather kid gloves and if the marks Mac had mentioned were still there, they were not visible.

Curran had to admit Ravensway had done a fine job with the embalming. Sir Henry certainly looked better than he had when Curran had last seen him alive, let alone as a contorted corpse on the floor of his bedroom. He might have done service at Madame Tussaud's.

"I am sorry to intrude, Lady Cunningham—"

"No, you're not, Curran." Lady Cunningham's gaze did not move from a study of her husband's face. "They have done a very good job with him. He looks better than he has in months."

She held a lace-edged handkerchief to her nose but her eyes were dry.

"How long had he been unwell?" Curran asked.

"Months. His doctor in London said it was stress... probably an ulcer. He counseled against making this journey, but Sir Henry was adamant."

"Let us cease the pretense. We both know he was poisoned, Lady Cunningham, and had been for months before he even set foot on the ship. All the symptoms you just described are consistent with arsenic poisoning and it was arsenic, not Bromidia, that finished him off."

Behind him, he heard a stifled gasp from Mrs. Farrant.

Lady Cunningham didn't move, her gaze remaining fixed on her husband's carefully painted face.

"They told me you had found arsenic in Mary's room. There is your culprit, Inspector."

"Who told you?"

The pause was infinitesimal. "Sir John," she replied.

Curran had no recollection of mentioning the finding of the tin of arsenic to Sir John Anderson, but he moved on.

"Did you know Mary Brown's real name?"

Her shoulders shifted beneath the black silk dress as if she were bracing herself and this time, she cast him a sideways glance from beneath her lashes.

"I could lie, Curran, but yes, I knew she was James Venning's sister. I took her on in the belief that her family was owed something by mine. She needed work, and I needed a maid. She proved an excellent lady's maid. I never for a moment believed her capable of..." She lifted the handkerchief to a dry eye again. "Of this."

"She told me that she hadn't revealed her real identity to you."

"That is quite true, but it doesn't take a detective to do a little digging. I knew quite well who she was, but if she chose to hide her name, then so be it."

"If she were indeed guilty of your husband's murder, why did someone kill her?" Curran ventured.

Lady Cunningham's gaze swung to Curran, genuine bemusement on her face. "Who said she was killed? I was told she drowned herself in the pond in the gardens. Death by own hand ran in that family, as well you know."

"She was murdered," Curran said. "It may come as a surprise, but we can tell the difference between suicide and murder. She was hit over the head and drowned, just as Amelia Hardcastle received a wound to the head before being thrown to her death."

"Inspector!" Mrs. Farrant jumped to her feet.

"It's all right, Georgina," Lady Cunningham gestured for the woman to sit again. "The Inspector and I are old sparring partners, but Mrs. Farrant is correct. There is no need to take that tone with me, Curran. If she did meet her fate that way, at least you can't blame my husband. He had been dead twenty-four hours." Her eyes flashed. "I am not going through this with you again, Curran. Enough. Leave me now."

"Have you informed your children of their father's death?"

The question seemed to take her by surprise. She blinked. "My children?"

"You do have children?"

"Yes, two daughters and a son."

"How old are they?"

"The eldest girl is fourteen. I don't see what they have to do with his—"

She met Curran's eyes and for the first time, he saw genuine fear and remembered Harriet's words. *A mother will do anything to protect her children.*

"On the night he died, did Sir Henry assault one of the household staff?"

"I have no idea."

"And did you buy her silence with a gift?"

"Enough, Curran! I resent the implication."

"You knew a journalist had the Venning letter and now you knew that Sir Henry was still capable of assault. It was all unraveling for you, Lady Cunningham. Was it easier just to finish him off and blame it on a weak heart?"

"Curran—" The color blazed in Evangeline Cunningham's cheeks. "Be careful what you say—"

"I have one last question," he said. "Who were you meeting in the gallery in the ballroom, the night of the first murder?"

Her eyes widened. "I have no idea what you mean, Inspector. I never went up to the gallery."

"You were seen and a bead from the dress the girl was wearing was found in your clothing. Was it Charles Gilmore?"

"Who told you that? Mary Venning? I wouldn't believe her... she was probably trying to deflect blame onto me for her own purposes."

She staggered and would have fallen if Georgina Farrant hadn't leaped to her feet and caught her arm, guiding her to a chair.

"Inspector Curran, please... Lady Cunningham has been through enough," Mrs. Farrant said.

He had pushed her far enough, but he was running out of time. If she left on Saturday, she would be out of his jurisdiction, taking with her the answers to his questions.

# FIFTY

Curran returned to South Bridge Road after his confrontation with Lady Cunningham. Singh and Greaves stood beside the evidence table, both deep in thought. Singh looked up as Curran entered, and he joined the two men at the table.

He leaned both hands on the table and ran his gaze across the evidence they had accumulated, covering the three deaths... all such innocuous objects, but each one had contributed to the deaths of three people.

"We have been waiting for you, Curran," Singh said. "Greaves?"

Greaves blinked behind his glasses. "There was arsenic mixed in with the Bromidia," he said. "Not a huge dose. If Sir Henry administered his usual dose, it would account for his symptoms over the last few months."

"So what killed him?"

"There was a massive amount in the tisane. I found traces of arsenic in the teapot and cup as well," Greaves said. "Someone really wanted him dead."

"Someone who didn't know much about poisons," Curran

said. "Is it possible they thought he would simply die peacefully in his sleep, death attributable to a weak heart and an excess of Bromidia? The perpetrator poisoned the tisane and tipped out the Bromidia to cover up the ongoing poisoning."

"Without thinking to rinse the bottle or the teapot," Singh said. "It must have come as something of a shock to see exactly how he died." Singh paused. "A death not attributable to a peaceful death in his sleep. I do not believe it was your girl, Mary Venning. Everything points to Lady Cunningham."

"And she was the one who planted the arsenic in Mary's luggage?" Greaves suggested.

"Lady Cunningham knew exactly who Mary was. She had the perfect puppet to blame the poisoning on," Curran said.

"But why was she poisoning him and why kill him off now?" Greaves voiced the questions in Curran's mind. "There were no fingerprints, by the way. But if it was Lady Cunningham, why was she systematically poisoning her husband?"

"I suspect it was to keep her husband on the verge of ill health and discourage his unsavory activities," Curran said.

Singh shrugged. "But why kill him now?"

"For that, I think we have to thank the reporter, Sarah Bowman. Lady Cunningham might have been afraid that the story of her husband's proclivities and the death of James Venning might come out at a time when he was reaching his full potential politically." Curran shrugged and glanced at his watch. "We can make all the suppositions we like but we're running out of time. Lady Cunningham leaves on Saturday." He turned to the blackboard. "Let's look at Amelia Hardcastle. The key time is nine-thirty when the choir finished singing and supper was served. Amelia slips away to the gallery to meet up with Oliver Strong, followed, I presume unknowingly, by Lady Cunningham."

"Lady Cunningham again," Singh put in.

"We have the bead Mary Venning found caught in Lady Cunningham's dress. It would certainly imply Lady Cunningham had some contact with the girl, but she was not the one who threw her from the window. She could not have lifted her over the sill without difficulty and by the time we think Amelia was thrown, Lady Cunningham was back in the ballroom," Curran said. "Amelia went up to the gallery to meet the young man. I think we can presume she didn't go to meet Lady Cunningham."

"Who was Lady Cunningham meeting? Sir Henry had said his farewells to his hosts and retired to his bed chamber accompanied by Charles Gilmore," Singh pointed to the timeline. "Can we exclude Ellis?"

Curran frowned. "Yes, I think we can exclude Ellis, but Gilmore... I have good grounds to believe Gilmore and Lady Cunningham are involved in a relationship."

"How did you find that out?" Greaves asked.

Curran cleared his throat. "Just something that was said."

"But Gilmore was with Sir Henry," Greaves pointed out.

"Are we sure he was with Sir Henry the entire time?" Curran said.

Singh shrugged. "We can check the witness statements again." He tilted his head and examined the blackboard. "So, are we working on the assumption Amelia Hardcastle interrupted Lady Cunningham and a man?"

"What other man?" Greaves said. "If it wasn't Gilmore. Who else did she know in Singapore?"

Curran's blood ran cold. He didn't want to do it, but he took the chalk and wrote up: *Thomas Barker.*

"The artist? How does he fit in?" Singh asked.

"He knows Evangeline Cunningham. He painted her portrait in London."

Singh glanced at Curran. "Isn't he the one involved with Samrita?"

Curran clenched his jaw and nodded.

"It is getting late," Singh said. "We will do better to come back to this in the morning. Curran, come home with me for dinner."

Curran glanced at his watch. He had missed lunch, and it was now eight o'clock and he was hungry.

"But Sumeet Kaur will not be expecting guests," he protested half-heartedly.

"My Sumeet cooks enough to feed an army. You are always welcome."

If it came to a choice between one of Sumeet Kaur's fragrant curries or overcooked meat of dubious origin in the police lines, Curran did not have to think twice. He clapped his friend on the shoulder.

"Thank you. A meal with your family is always a tonic."

He needed a chance to think how best to tackle Thomas Barker, and how to do it in such a way as to not alienate his sister.

# FIFTY-ONE

Sumeet Kaur greeted Curran warmly and without surprise. She and the children had already eaten, but she produced a hearty meal for the two men without apparent effort.

"Have you solved the terrible murders?" Sumeet Kaur asked as they ate.

Curran glanced at Singh before replying with a careless shrug. "It is a matter of proof."

"You mean you know who did it?" Sumeet's eyes gleamed with curiosity.

"I think we are getting closer," Curran said carefully.

"There was another death this morning," Singh remarked calmly. "But as the Inspector will tell you, we have little evidence. They have been clever."

"Or lucky," Curran added.

He pushed his empty plate away. "That was a wonderful meal, Sumeet Kaur, but we must get going. There is someone we have to see."

"Barker?" Singh asked and Curran nodded.

"The lonely life of a policeman's wife," Sumeet Kaur said.

A.M. STUART

Curran smiled. "I promise we will try not to be too late. Even policemen need to sleep."

Sumeet Kaur shooed them out of the door. As the two men stepped out onto the five-foot way outside the shophouse, Singh's brother greeted them and they stopped to pass a few minutes with him as he sat cross-legged stitching a pair of western-style trousers. Serangoon Road throbbed with the usual crowd of workers returning home from their jobs. They cast the two policemen sidelong looks and scurried past.

"How is Hardit?" Curran asked as they walked back to the vehicle.

Singh sighed. "I have listened to what he has to say, and it seems that he is set on going to India and joining the Army. I must let him go with my blessing or be forever cursed. Parenthood is a hard thing, Curran."

Curran thought about Samrita and thought he didn't need to be a parent to feel the weight of that responsibility.

From behind them, further down the road, past the temple, a shout went up, followed by the crack of a weapon being fired. A woman screamed, and the crowd dispersed as if a stone had been dropped into a pond, running in all directions.

With a policeman's instinct, Curran fumbled for the silver whistle, which hung on a cord around his neck and blew hard. Singh did the same and the two men turned and ran toward the center of the commotion, a jeweler's shop just beyond the temple.

Curran had the Webley in his right hand as two men ran from the doorway, one carrying a sack of some weight in both arms, the other a revolver.

"Stop! Police!" Curran yelled as behind him Singh blew hard on his whistle again.

What happened next seemed to take on the odd sensation of both happening too fast to comprehend and too slow to react. The armed robber raised his weapon. Curran flung himself to one side as the weapon cracked.

The Webley dropped from his hand and he stumbled backward, landing on the five-foot way with a thump that knocked the breath from him. He lay on the dusty paving as the commotion continued to whirl about him, wondering why he had dropped his weapon.

Only when he put his right hand down to stand did pain hit him with the force of a blow. He looked down at his arm. Bright arterial blood spurted from his wrist and the pain now radiated up his arm. He clapped his hand over the wound, but it oozed between his fingers.

Singh was by his side, and curious onlookers were crowding in. Above him, a sea of faces wavered in the hazy street light.

"Stand back, stand back. You, Curran, lie still. Do not move," Singh said. "I need... cloth. Something to bind this wound."

The world began to swim, and dark edges were closing in on Curran's vision.

"Those men, Singh... your priority..." he managed.

"They are long gone, Curran. That looks like it hit an artery."

Curran found he was in no mood for general conversation about the nature of bullet wounds.

Singh fired off rapid orders in a mixture of Punjabi and Hindu as Curran tried to make sense of where the bullet had found its mark. Was it serious? Stupid question. All gunshot wounds were serious, without exception.

"Gursharan! Is he going to die?" Sumeet Kaur's voice.

"No," Singh replied. "But we must get him to hospital. I will fetch the motor vehicle. Sumeet, press on the wound," Singh said, and Sumeet knelt beside Curran with cloths in her hand.

She *tsked* as if he were a small child who had grazed his knee, and he found her presence strangely calming as she pressed the cloths hard against the wound.

"Can you get a message to Harriet?" he asked, surprised at how weak his voice sounded.

"Of course. Here is Gursharan with the motor vehicle. He

will get you to the hospital. Let me just tie a bandage. I think the bleeding has slowed, but I will come with you."

Her attempt to secure a bandage around his wrist produced words he would not normally say in front of a lady, but Sumeet Kaur remained unruffled.

Curran heard the roar of a motor vehicle engine, his motor vehicle.

"Singh. Terrible driver..."

"Don't speak, old friend," Singh said. "You men, help me here..."

Curran swore from pain and frustration as Singh hauled him to his feet, his arm around his waist. Just as the investigation had taken a turn, he did not need this.

Other hands were assisting him on the short walk to the motor vehicle as dark clouds gathered in the corners of his mind.

*Must stay conscious.*

By the time he had been bustled into the back seat of the motor vehicle with Sumeet Kaur still holding his wrist in an iron grip, he surrendered and let the dark clouds wash over him.

# FIFTY-TWO

The General Hospital buzzed with activity even at this late hour, the warm air tinged with the smell of antiseptic and unwashed humanity. Harriet and Julian stood in the main entrance casting around for a friendly face.

"Harriet, what are you doing here?"

Harriet fell into her friend Doreen Wilson's arms.

"It's Curran. Hardit Singh told us he had been shot. Where is he, Doreen? Can I see him?"

Doreen extricated herself and held Harriet by the forearms.

"Now, now, don't take on. Come with me."

Julian put his arm around Harriet's shoulders, and they followed Doreen to a small office where the capable nursing sister sat Harriet down in a chair. Even when dealing with the most difficult patient, Doreen cultivated a calming demeanor and Harriet found herself relaxing.

Doreen put her hands on her hips and surveyed Harriet. "Look at you, lass. You're shaking like a leaf. You sit there and I'll fetch us all a nice cup of tea," Doreen said, the warm vowels of her Lancastrian childhood washing over Harriet.

"Harri, I've never seen you like this." Julian took her hand.

"If I lose him, Ju—"

She wanted to cry, but there were no tears. She had already wept for one man—and a child—and it seemed she had no tears left for another overwhelming grief.

"I know," Julian said and gave her hand an understanding squeeze.

For a brief instant, he let his heart write its own pain on his face. He understood that some grief went too deep for tears. He had lost his long love, Jane, just before their wedding.

They sat in silence until Doreen returned with a tray on which three cups and saucers were balanced, along with a pile of biscuits. She handed Harriet a cup.

"What news?" Harriet could have shaken her friend out of her calm composure.

"Doctor Mackenzie is seeing to him. He's in good hands and it is not as serious as first thought. Now take a deep breath and drink your tea and I'll see what's what."

Doreen left them, and Harriet did as she was told, allowing the initial shock to fade. Of course, Curran would be fine, she told herself. He'd been in scrapes before and come through. But the minutes ticked on and by the time Doreen returned, the panic had begun to rise again.

She jumped to her feet, and Doreen laid a hand on her shoulder.

"He's resting. You should go home," Doreen said. "There is nothing you can do here except get in the way."

Harriet shook her head. "Not until I know... one way or another."

Mac appeared in the doorway, engaged in the act of rolling his shirtsleeves down.

"All's well," Mac said. "The bullet went in through his wrist and lodged near his elbow. It appears to have bounced off the bone so no breakage. It mustn't have had much momentum when it hit, probably a ricochet. The main worry is the loss of blood. It nicked the artery, but you can thank Sumeet Kaur. She kept the pressure on all the way to the hospital. He'll be sore and sorry for a while, but he was damned lucky."

Harriet hadn't been aware that she was holding her breath, but now she let it out in a whoosh and the room began to spin. Julian caught her and sat her back on the chair.

"That's a relief," Julian said.

Harriet glared at her brother. "Julian, I've been a doctor's wife. A bullet wound of any kind is serious."

"As you have cause to know," Mac remarked, referring to the bullet wound to her leg that Harriet had sustained in the Batu Caves in December. "He needs to be sensible and rest."

Harriet went through the possible risks: sepsis; the blood loss... so many things that could still kill him. Harriet also knew Curran and the chances of sensible rest and recuperation while he was in the middle of a case were unlikely.

"Can I see him?" she asked.

"Harriet, it's late—"

"Please."

Mac hefted a sigh. "I've given him a pretty strong dose of morphine, so he'll hardly be conversational." He turned to Doreen Wilson. "Sister, please conduct Mrs. Gordon to the patient. She is not to stay longer than five minutes."

Doreen put an arm around Harriet's shoulders and led her down the quiet corridor, their heels echoing on the linoleum. Curran had been put in a small private room, lit only by a single lamp in a corner. A nursing sister sat on the one chair in the room.

"Take a break, Elsie," Doreen said, and the nurse left the room.

Harriet thought it could hardly be possible for someone to lie so still and not be dead. Curran's eyes were closed, the eyelids gray, and his lips bloodless. Heavy bandaging on his right hand and arm told its own story, and Harriet's heart swooped.

"I'll be outside," Doreen said and slipped out of the room, leaving Harriet alone.

Harriet picked up Curran's left hand that lay outside the single sheet that covered him and kissed it.

"Curran, if you die, I'll be left with nothing," she said and because she had nothing left, she closed her eyes and prayed.

# FIFTY-THREE

Curran looked up at the ceiling and struggled to remember how he had come to be in hospital. He knew it was the hospital. It smelled like a hospital, that odd combination of carbolic, floor polish, and boiled cabbage. Only when he tried to lift his hand did he remember exactly why he was here. He had been shot. He looked down at his right arm, heavily swathed in bandages, and wondered exactly what the damage was, followed by the odd thought that it might mean he couldn't play cricket again.

He turned his head to look at the glassed double doors leading out onto the broad veranda. A woman sat hunched in a chair close to the door intent on some sort of needlework. He allowed himself a smile. He had never seen Harriet Gordon engaged in such a womanly occupation. To judge by the frown on her forehead, it was not, perhaps, her favorite pastime.

"Harriet?"

She looked up with a start, pricking her finger with the needle and swearing aloud in a most unladylike manner.

He held out his good hand, and she dropped her needlework to the floor, almost falling in her haste to be at his side. She grasped his hand in an iron grip, as if she feared he might drift away from her.

"Curran! How dare you do this to me! What were you thinking rushing after an armed robber?"

That was fair. Memories of that brief moment of recklessness began seeping back into his consciousness.

"It's what I do," he said. "Run toward trouble when everyone else is running away."

She closed her eyes, but tears leaked from beneath her lids.

"I know," she mumbled.

"Harriet, I'm sorry."

He frowned, turning his head to look up at the ceiling as he struggled to find the words, grappling with realizing how much this woman meant to him. His fingers tightened on hers and her tears now flowed unchecked.

He managed a smile. "Harriet Gordon, I love you. Please stop crying."

"I can't," Harriet said, releasing her grip on him and dashing at her eyes with her hand. "I've lost too much in my life already. I couldn't bear to lose you too."

"I'm not dying," he protested. "And I have no intention of doing so in the line of duty."

"Am I interrupting?" Euan Mackenzie's dry Scottish accent came from the doorway.

"You are," Curran said. "I was just telling Harriet that I am not dying."

Mac's mustache twitched. "Not today," he said. "You'll excuse us, Harriet. I need to talk with my patient. I suggest you go home and get some rest. Leave this one with us."

Harriet nodded. She stooped to pick up her fallen needlework, stuffed it into her bag, and bent over Curran. Her lips brushed his forehead.

"I'll see you later."

As the door closed behind her, Mac said, "She's been here since daybreak. No convincing her there are proper visiting hours."

Curran gingerly raised his right arm. "Verdict?"

Mac stood over him, his hands in his pockets, his face grave.

"You know something, Curran, I am getting mighty tired of patching you up. I think you need to find a more sedentary occupation."

Curran managed a smile.

"Singh thought a ricochet caught your outstretched arm. Sheer bad luck. The projectile went in through your wrist, clipped the artery, and lodged near your elbow." He handed Curran a jar with a flattened piece of metal. "Souvenir."

"Permanent damage?"

Mac shrugged. "Catapulting shrapnel is going to leave some damage that I can't fix. The biggest risk was blood loss, and you can thank Sumeet Kaur for keeping you alive long enough to get to the hospital. Can you move your fingers?"

Curran obliged, relieved to be able to comply with the order, but the effort sent waves of pain shooting up his arm. He groaned aloud.

"I can give you more morphine," Mac said, the words dragging with reluctance.

Curran shook his head. "No. No more. You know what happened last time"

They both recalled the days following the near-fatal stabbing in Penang. He had come perilously close to developing an addiction to the painkiller.

Mac nodded. "As you wish."

"Mac, seriously, how soon can I get out of here?"

Mac shook his head. "I am not letting you go for at least a week if not longer. You lost a lot of blood, Curran. Just for once, be sensible and do as you're told."

Curran swallowed. "I have a murder investigation—"

"No, you do not. Your Chief Inspector can see to it now that he's back on his feet. If you let me have a look at my handiwork, I'll let you rest."

But rest did not come easily, and when the bell rang for visiting hours to commence after lunch, his first visitor flew through the door, almost throwing herself on top of him.

Samrita grasped his good hand and held it against her cheek. "They said you were dying," she said. "Are you dying?"

"No," Curran replied.

She nodded. "Good. I would be very cross if you died." Her face sobered, and she laced her fingers in his. "You and Thomas are all I have."

The mention of Barker reminded Curran of his suspicions.

"Sam, about Thomas. Do you love him?"

Samrita frowned. "Is this the time to be talking about this?"

"It is if you are planning on absconding to Australia with him. For my piece of mind, I need to be certain that it is the right decision."

That was the wrong word. Her shoulders stiffened.

"It is not for you to make decisions about me," she said.

He held up his good hand. "I didn't mean it like that. It's just that I care about you. God damn it, sister of mine, I might even love you enough to want to see you are safe."

She blinked. "Love is a strong word, Robert."

He cleared his throat. "I mean it. Just tell me you are certain of Thomas Barker."

"Why would I not be?"

He paused. "The night of the ball," he said. "Were you with Barker the whole time?"

"The ball?" She frowned. "Why are you asking me about this now? There are others to do your work. You could have died last night."

"Were you?"

"Yes... no... when the choir started singing, he said he had someone who wanted to talk to him about a commission."

"When did you see him again?"

"I think it was just before the fireworks finished." She patted his arm. "Enough talk. It is time for me to leave, and Sergeant Singh is waiting in the corridor. Don't let him bother you. You must rest."

"Everyone keeps telling me that."

Curran closed his eyes, suddenly very tired. Rest did not seem to be possible with a queue of visitors.

"Are you awake?"

He opened his eyes. Gursharan Singh stood in the doorway, like a *jagar* guard.

"Yes, I'm awake. I am told I have your wife to thank for saving my life last night."

Singh nodded. "You do. She is a stubborn woman, my Sumeet. If she decides you are not going to die, then she will ensure that you do not."

"Thank her for me." Curran drew a breath. "What news?"

"We caught the jewel thieves," Singh said. "A *dhoby* saw one throw the weapon into the Stamford Canal and recognized him as a regular at a cafe nearby. You have many friends, Curran, and many who would want to see such men punished. As they will be."

Curran had a suspicion that the jewel thieves were already sore and sorry for themselves but felt no pity for them.

"Good work," Curran said. "We need to follow up on Barker and Lady Cunningham."

Singh drew in a breath. "The Chief Inspector is back at his desk, Curran. The matter is out of your hands."

Curran swore.

"Then please present my compliments to the Chief Inspector and tell him that I need to speak with him urgently."

Singh rolled his eyes. "The doctor said—"

"I know the doctor's thoughts. We are too close to resolving these murders, Singh. I need to speak with Wallace." As Singh turned to go, Curran added. "Can you send my batman in with a clean uniform and do you have my Webley?"

"I do and, before you ask, I have left your motor vehicle outside the hospital. What do you wish me to do with it?"

"Leave it there for the time being."

Singh narrowed his eyes. "Curran, what are you thinking?"

Curran managed an innocent smile. "What is it the Boy Scouts say? Be prepared?"

# FIFTY-FOUR

It was late in the day before Chief Inspector Wallace stomped into his room accompanied by Singh, by which time Curran was chafing with impatience.

"You took your time," he said.

"I am not at your beck and call," Wallace retorted. "How are you? You look terrible."

"Thank you. I was lucky... or unlucky, depending on which way you look at it."

"It is one way to solve crime that I would prefer you don't use again. At least we caught the bastards who pulled a gun on you."

"And at least they didn't kill me," Curran added drily.

"There is that," Wallace conceded. "You are officially on sick leave. Why did you want to see me?"

"The Government House deaths," Curran said.

Wallace stiffened. "Not your concern anymore."

"We are running out of time, Wallace. When does Lady Cunningham leave Singapore?"

"Tomorrow morning—"

Curran straightened in bed. "You have to stop her."

Wallace frowned. "Why?"

"Because I believe she is responsible for the death of Sir Henry Cunningham and possibly also Amelia Hardcastle."

Wallace stared at him. "Have you gone mad? Lady Cunningham?" He turned as if to walk out of the room, pausing at the door and looking back at him. "You better have a damn good reason for suspecting her."

"Have you got the time to listen to my thoughts?" Curran said.

Wallace glanced at the door, sighed, and sat in the visitor's chair. "Go on."

"First Amelia Hardcastle. We can be reasonably certain she died between nine thirty and ten in the private dining room off the gallery. As to who was responsible... it was not Sir Henry Cunningham or Oliver Strong." He held Wallace's gaze as he said, "I believe Lady Cunningham took the opportunity for a brief rendezvous in the private dining room with a man, only to be disturbed by Amelia Hardcastle."

Wallace's mouth dropped open. "Curran, be careful about making those sorts of allegations. What man?"

"Amelia had gone up to the gallery for a tryst with her young man in the private room. I believe that is where she changed into a dress she had brought with her, the one she was wearing when she died. A witness saw Lady Cunningham slip away from the supper and take the back stairs to the gallery meaning she would have been in the gallery or the private room at the same time as Amelia Hardcastle. I think Amelia surprised Lady Cunningham and her lover and one or other of them killed her to keep her silent."

Wallace blew out his cheeks. "And who do you think the man is?"

"It could have been Charles Gilmore..." Curran began, still reluctant to voice his suspicions of Thomas Barker. He wanted to speak to the young man himself before he brought in Wallace and his size ten boots. "I am reasonably certain Lady Cunningham and Gilmore are having an affair."

"Gilmore? But we have plenty of witnesses to see him leave with Sir Henry. Damn it, Curran! I saw him myself."

"But was he with Sir Henry for that entire critical time?"

"Ellis can confirm that... or not," Wallace said.

"I would be reluctant to rely on Ellis. He is loyal to a fault," Curran said.

Wallace glanced at Singh. "Get one of the chaps to have another look through the witness statements, Sergeant." He turned back to Curran and shook his head. "Between us, given Sir Henry's tastes, you can't blame Lady Cunningham for looking elsewhere but a rendezvous in such a public place? Anyone could have walked in. I can't believe it of her, Curran."

"Believe it or not. If you want corroboration, Mary Venning found a bead from Amelia's dress caught in Lady Cunningham's dress. She was there, Wallace. She may not have thrown Amelia from the window, but she was there."

"And we trust anything that Venning girl said?"

"I don't think she was lying about finding the bead and someone was scared of what she might say. That is why she is dead."

"And the girl's missing uniform?"

"It went into the dumb waiter and the killer collected it to dispose of at his leisure."

Wallace shook her head. "And what about Sir Henry? All the evidence points to the Venning girl and my recommendation to the coroner will be that Mary Venning was responsible for Sir Henry's death."

Curran rolled his eyes. "Everything was contrived to point to her. I know I'm right, Wallace. Lady Cunningham killed her husband and used Mary as the scapegoat. She planted the evidence on Mary."

Wallace snorted. "Why on earth would Lady Cunningham want to kill her husband?"

"A reporter was about to publish a story detailing Sir Henry's sordid past and Lady Cunningham could never have borne that sort of exposure, which, you may recall, is why she shut down our original investigation. What went on behind the closed doors of the Cunningham townhouse may have been unpleasant but not nearly as unpleasant as an arrest and trial would have been. Cunningham was tipped to be a future Prime Minister. She couldn't have a jumped-up reporter like Sarah Bowman, splashing the Venning story across the papers."

"And how does this reporter know about Venning?"

"She has a copy of the Venning letter. She wanted me to verify its authenticity."

Color rose to Wallace's cheekbones and Curran suspected if the Chief Inspector was not in a weakened condition from his recent illness, Wallace would have exploded. Instead, he said in a carefully modulated voice. "Why didn't you tell me about this before? How the hell did she get a copy of the letter? The original was destroyed."

Curran glared at his superior. "And you knew? You were complicit in the destruction of evidence?"

Wallace cleared his throat. "You have to understand—"

"Spare me," Curran said. "And you wonder why I have difficulty confiding in you. As far as Sarah Bowman is concerned, I made it quite clear I would not cooperate, but after Lady Cunningham discovered the journalist was poised to print, she may have panicked. We also have a witness at Government House who was assaulted by Sir Henry on the evening he died, so even incapacitated as he was, his base nature could not be contained. Lady Cunningham tried to buy her silence but the girl has, I hope, been persuaded to make a statement."

"Go on."

"I have strong reason to believe that Lady Cunningham had been systematically feeding arsenic to her husband over a long period and on the night he died, she chose to finish him off, probably hoping the world would think he died peacefully in his sleep.

Unfortunately arsenic is not so obliging. All she could do was stop us from conducting an autopsy. She didn't reckon on Dr. Mackenzie and Greaves finding a way around that inconvenience."

"How did she administer the poison?"

"I think she would add arsenic to Sir Henry's Bromidia. She tipped it out, which is why the bottle was empty when we found it. She wanted us to believe that Sir Henry had consumed the bromide in a bid to end his life. Murderers, as we both know, are not necessarily very clever, and I doubt Lady Cunningham knows anything about how poisons work and what we can do to trace them. I am guessing, but after she left the dinner table she went to her husband's room to bid him good night and added the fatal dose to the teapot that Mary had brought up to Sir Henry's room. She must have returned later that night to see if her plan had worked and seen the result of a fatal dose of arsenic poisoning. She emptied out the Bromidia, but failed to rinse the bottle or the teapot, which contained the fatal dose."

Wallace sat in silence for a long moment before shaking his head. "Curran, if this is true—"

"You know it makes sense, Wallace."

"Then who killed Mary Venning?"

"Mary Venning was on her way to give her evidence on Sir Henry to the journalist when she was killed. If she killed Sir Henry then who killed her? Did she hit herself over the head and then drown herself in the lake?"

Wallace shook his head. "Yes, well, that's not entirely explained. It is possible that the evidence from the girl's autopsy is not conclusive?"

"Mac is never wrong. She has a wound to the back of her head consistent with a rock."

"You are not suggesting Lady Cunnigham was lurking in the gardens on the off chance the girl happened past? Couldn't she have slipped on the wet path and hit her head?"

"And rolled herself into the water, and held herself under until she drowned. Don't forget the bruising, Wallace. It would have been in Lady Cunningham's interests to stop Mary from reaching the journalist. She could have sent someone to stop her."

"But who else knew of the meeting?"

Curran took a breath. "The artist Thomas Barker, my sister Samrita and Mrs. Gordon, and, of course, the journalist."

Wallace's eyebrows drew together. "Your Mrs. Gordon is an interfering busybody, Curran."

Curran took a deep breath and ignored the insult. "Did you know Thomas Barker was also acquainted with Lady Cunningham? He painted her portrait back in London, and his movements on the night of the ball are not completely accounted for."

Wallace sat in silence for a long moment. "Are you implying he was the man Lady Cunningham was consorting with?"

"I'm not saying anything. I was on my way to speak to him when this happened..." He tapped his bandaged arm.

"You can't prove any of this, Curran."

"No. But you're not arguing with me."

Wallace shook his head. "No. It's plausible, but it doesn't get us over the *prima facie* evidence still pointing to the Venning woman in relation to Sir Henry's death."

"And I will maintain it was planted. When do they sail?" Curran asked.

"Tomorrow morning."

"We need to interview Lady Cunningham, Gilmore, and Ellis again."

"WE don't need to do anything, Curran. Leave it with me. I'll go up to Government House now."

"What about Barker?"

"He can wait until the morning," Wallace said.

Curran took a deep breath, trying to draw the scattered thoughts together. There was a good reason he was going to see

Barker. Something did not ring true. Something the man had said...

As the door closed behind his superior, Curran threw his head back against the bedhead in frustration. At least Wallace had listened to him, but would he act in time to stop Lady Cunningham from leaving the country? He had a horrible feeling his superior would drag his feet, preferring the neat solution offered up to him of blaming Mary Venning.

# FIFTY-FIVE

On her way into the hospital, Harriet passed Chief Inspector Wallace, storming out. She ducked out of his way, not wishing for another confrontation with the man. A cold shiver ran down her spine and she hurried to Curran's room to find him sitting on the edge of the bed, mostly dressed but with his uniform jacket undone and a thin sheen of sweat on his forehead.

"What are you doing?" she said.

"I can't do the buttons," he replied.

"You shouldn't even be out of bed."

"I should. I'm running out of time. Wallace has gone to confront Lady Cunningham but he won't get anywhere with her. He only has supposition and no actual evidence. I have to speak to Thomas Barker."

"Barker? Why?"

Curran drew a breath. "Because he is mixed up in this somehow, Harriet. If I can get some sense from him, we might have the evidence we need to stop Lady Cunningham from leaving the jurisdiction. Help me with these bloody buttons and I'll fill you in."

As any further argument regarding the wisdom of his actions seemed pointless, Harriet obliged with the buttons and boots as Curran explained his theory of Amelia and Sir Henry's deaths.

She buckled on his Sam Browne and settled his injured arm into a blue sling.

"So you think Lady Cunningham encountered Amelia and may have had something to do with her death? Who was the mystery man she was meeting? Gilmore?" she asked.

"I don't think so. They are rechecking the statements, but I am fairly certain Gilmore was with Sir Henry during that critical half hour."

"Who else could it have been? Who did Lady Cunningham meet?" Harriet mused. "If not Gilmore or Ellis. She knew no one else." Realization dawned on her. "She knew Thomas Barker."

Curran nodded. "Barker," he repeated. "It comes back to Barker. His movements during that time are unaccounted for and I've remembered that there was something he said about the dress. When I went to his studio, I noticed he kept a chest of clothes, I started to ask him about the dress Amelia was wearing and he denied it was one of his but I never showed it to him so how would he have known?" He let out a breath. "I don't want to believe it, Harriet. I like the man and, more importantly, so does Samrita, but he is the only other possibility. He could hold the key to this whole business. That's why I have to see him tonight. I asked one of the nurses to send a message to Singh to meet me at Barker's studio, I just need to get there myself."

"I can drive you," Harriet said. "Your motor vehicle is outside."

Curran stared at her.

"I told you, Julian gave me lessons while we had the use of the vehicle."

He closed his eyes. "Thank you, Harriet. That would be helpful."

The shophouse in Pulau Saigon looked even more dilapidated in the daylight. As Harriet drew the motor vehicle to a gentle halt, Singh disengaged himself from the shadows and came over to meet them.

"Have you been waiting long?" Curran asked.

Singh shook his head. "About ten minutes. There is light in the room upstairs, but no one has been in or out."

Curran climbed out of the motor vehicle and leaned against the nearest wall momentarily before straightening.

"Harriet, wait here. Singh, can you knock on the door?"

Singh rapped on the faded and twisted door and the elderly servant, Min, opened it. Harriet did not understand what was said but from the shaking of Min's head, she assumed Barker was not at home.

Samrita appeared behind Min. She wore a paint-spattered smock over her clothes and was wiping her hands with a cloth.

"What is going on? Robert, you look terrible. You shouldn't be out of the hospital. Oh, Sergeant Singh... Harriet, is that you in Curran's vehicle? What are you all doing here?"

"I need to speak to Barker?" Curran said.

"He's out delivering a painting," Samrita said.

"Where will I find him?"

"At the Hardcastles' house. He wanted to give them the portrait of Amelia and her sister."

"When did he leave?"

"About an hour ago. Why do you want to speak to him?"

But Curran had turned to Singh. "If you drive, we can probably catch him." He glanced at Harriet. "Can you and Samrita make your way home from here?"

"Of course," Harriet ceded her place at the wheel of the motor vehicle to Singh and the two women watched the vehicle drive away.

"I don't understand," Samrita said as she led the way up the stairs to the studio. "Why does Robert need to speak to Tom so urgently?"

"He has some questions for him."

Samrita gave her an appraising glance from narrowed eyes. "Why?"

Harriet shrugged. It was better that Samrita didn't know of Curran's suspicions. "If you've finished here, we will hail a hansom and go to Lavinia's."

"I will just tidy up. It won't take a moment. I lost track of time and the light's too poor to do any more work."

Upstairs in the gloom of the studio, Samrita had lit a kerosene lamp, casting the room into dark shadows. She had been working on a botanical painting of an orchid. The flower lay on a table beside the easel, an exquisite purple orchid, now beautifully rendered in watercolors.

"That's lovely," Harriet said with genuine admiration.

"Thank you," Samrita replied. "I would like to finish Lavinia's commission before we leave."

"You are determined to go to Australia with Mr. Barker?"

Samrita nodded. "Yes."

"Do you love him?" Harriet asked.

Samrita's eyes widened. "What sort of question is that?"

"A perfectly straightforward question."

Samrita hitched a shoulder. "Love is a strange concept, Harriet. He is a wonderful artist and teacher and," she cast Harriet a glance from under her eyelashes, "and a good lover. Do I love him? I don't know. Do we ever know?"

Harriet thought of Curran and her heart-aching need for him. "Oh yes," she said. "We know."

Samrita smiled. "Then I am happy for you."

She picked up her paintbrushes and methodically wiped them with the cloth, leaving them to stand in a large jar of murky water. Harriet leaned over and picked up the cloth

Samrita had been using and her heart stopped. She looked up at Samrita.

"Where did you get this?"

"I found it among Tom's rag collection. I needed a clean cloth for my new paintbrushes."

Harriet spread the square of cloth on the table. Before it had been used to clean the brushes, it had been a pretty, lace-edged handkerchief with the letter A embroidered in the corner. She looked up at Samrita.

"You probably don't recognize this," she said, "but it is the handkerchief Amelia Hardcastle had pinned to her uniform on the night she died."

Samrita's mouth opened. "I just picked up the nearest cloth," she said. "I didn't look at it. Harriet, what does it mean?"

Harriet glanced around the room, her gaze falling on the box of second-hand clothing.

"Samrita, does Barker own an evening gown of amethyst satin with an embroidered silk organza overskirt and a beaded bodice?"

Samrita stared at her. "Yes. Thomas did a painting of me wearing it." Samrita pointed to the trunk. "It should be in there. He calls that his dressing-up box. You look in there and I'll look for the painting."

While Samrita went through the stacks of canvases propped against the wall, Harriet scrabbled through the array of silks and velvets. She found two old-fashioned evening dresses, one of deep burgundy velvet and the other of pink satin.

"I can see no amethyst evening dress," Harriet concluded, straightening.

Samrita stood holding an empty wooden frame. Harriet took it from her. Whatever had been tacked to the frame had been cut out, leaving ragged edges still adhering to the wood. There was sufficient paint on the raw edges to suggest that somewhere within the missing painting there had been something of an amethyst color.

"I feel ill." Samrita clutched her hands to her heart as if the ragged edges were slashes to her own body. "Why did he do that?" she said aloud.

"Why did I do what?"

Both women swung around, neither having heard Thomas Barker's soft footfall on the stairs.

# FIFTY-SIX

"Thomas. You're back." Samrita took the frame from Harriet and looked down at it. "This was the painting of me in the amethyst dress, wasn't it? I loved that painting. I was going to give it to my brother as a gift before I left."

"Were you?" Barker's eyes narrowed and the temperature in the room seemed to dip.

He took the frame off Samrita and tossed it in a corner. "It wasn't good enough, Sam. I burned it." He smiled and straightened his shoulders. "Perhaps he would like that one?" He pointed at the half-finished painting of Samrita reclining on the daybed.

"That would not be appropriate," Samrita said.

"I suppose not," Barker responded, tilting his head and regarding the reclining nude with a frown.

"Were the Hardcastles pleased to have the painting?" Samrita asked.

"Very pleased," Barker said. He looked around the studio. "I shall be sorry to go. I've grown quite attached to this place."

"When are you planning to leave?" Harriet asked.

Barker glanced at Samrita and reached into his pocket. "I have tickets on the next ship to Melbourne the day after tomorrow."

"So soon?" Samrita said. "That's impossible. I can't leave my brother. Did you know he has been injured?"

Barker's eyes widened in genuine surprise. "I hadn't. Badly injured?"

"He was shot trying to stop the Serangoon Road jewel thieves. He's in hospital, Tom. He nearly died."

"I'm sorry to hear that," the man said, but his tone oozed insincerity.

He crossed to Samrita and took her by the chin, lifting her face to meet his gaze. "The tickets are bought and paid for. You will be coming with me." It was a statement, not a question.

"Tom, you're hurting me." Samrita pushed his hand away.

"Sorry," he said.

"Did you say sorry to Amelia Hardcastle when you threw her out of that window?" Harriet said.

Barker dropped his hand and backed away from Samrita. He swung his gaze onto Harriet. The color had drained from the artist's face and his fingers clenched and unclenched.

"What do you mean?"

Harriet swallowed. Her mouth had gone dry. What had possessed her to speak up like that?

"There's no one else Lady Cunningham could have been meeting with," she said.

"Harriet?" Samrita's gaze went from Barker to Harriet. "What are you saying?"

"Your friend here had a rendezvous with Lady Cunningham on the night of the ball," Harriet said. "Curran was right."

"You were upstairs with another woman?"

Samrita slapped Barker across the cheek. Barker swallowed and his mouth worked as he rubbed the reddening spot on his cheekbone.

"Samrita, she meant nothing to me. I only met her to tell her that I had found you. That—"

"Spare me!" Samrita said. "I don't care that you were lovers back in England, but I do care that a young girl died to keep your secret."

"It wasn't like that," Barker turned from one woman to the other. "It wasn't. It was an accident."

"Then you should tell the police," Samrita said.

"I can't. You have to see that. My career... our future together..."

"There is no future together, Tom," Samrita said. "Do you think I can pack up my life and follow a murderer to Australia as if nothing happened?"

"I am not a murderer." Barker enunciated each word.

Harriet held up a hand. "Please Mr. Barker, there is nothing to be gained now. If it was indeed an accident, then that is what you need to tell the police."

He shook his head, and in one swift movement picked up the knife he used to cut canvases from the table. The blade glinted in the light.

Harriet's stomach swooped. Barker stood between the women and the stairs and there was no other way out. There were tears in his eyes as he swung from one to the other.

"Damn it. Why did you have to spoil everything?"

Harriet had no idea who he was addressing. He could have been talking to himself.

"Both of you. Sit down on the daybed where I can see you," he said. "Samrita, I love you. But you see I can't let you go, not now that you know."

"Oh, Tom," Samrita said with what sounded like genuine sadness in her voice. "I really could have loved you... I did love you."

He took a step toward her, but she backed away. The distraction was all that Harriet needed. She picked up the stool beside her and flung it at the artist. He ducked out of the way, but the action put him off balance and he stumbled, falling to one knee.

Neither woman wasted a second, dashing toward the stairs as Barker let out a roar and stumbled after them. They reached the front door to find it locked. Samrita grabbed Harriet's hand, and they turned for the back of the house.

In the kitchen, the elderly servant, Min, was dozing on a stool by the fire.

"Run, Min," Samrita shrieked, but the warning came too late.

As the women reached a back door leading out onto a lane, Barker caught the old woman by the arm and held the knife to her throat.

"Stop where you are, ladies," he said.

In those few minutes, he had gone from a broken, desperate man to a wild-eyed monster Harriet no longer recognized. She did not doubt that this Thomas Barker was quite capable of slitting the old woman's throat without compunction. Samrita found Harriet's hand.

"Back up to my studio," Barker said, "And I suggest you do as I tell you and no one will get hurt."

They trudged up the stairs to the studio, and he gestured to them to sit on the daybed.

Still holding Min, who was white-faced and gabbling in Chinese, he snatched up a bundle of silk cords and threw them at Samrita.

"Tie up your friend," he said.

When Samrita hesitated, he pressed the point of the knife harder against Min's throat, provoking a squawk from his victim.

"I'm so sorry," Samrita whispered as she bound Harriet's hands in front of her.

"And her feet," Barker ordered.

Once Harriet had been immobilized, he flung Min toward Samrita.

"And her."

Samrita complied. The old lady sobbed and muttered but obediently held out her hands for Samrita to bind.

"Tell her to shut up!" Barker yelled.

Samrita murmured a few words in Chinese and Min fell silent.

With two of the three women immobilized Barker seemed to relax. He pulled Samrita toward him.

"I'm so sorry," he said again as if saying the words expunged the crime he had committed. He stroked her hair with the hand holding the knife. "You have to understand. Amelia... it really was an accident. She fell backward and hit her head on the statue."

*What would Curran do? Keep the man talking...*

"She wasn't dead when you threw her out of the window," Harriet said, tired of his maundering.

Barker swung his gaze on her. "What do you mean?"

"Amelia Hardcastle was still alive when she went out of the window. Whatever happened to her before that may not have been intended, but that act was murder." She paused. "And what about Mary Venning?"

Barker ran a tongue over his lips. "What about her?"

"Are you going to tell me that was an accident?"

Barker's mouth trembled. "She was my friend."

"But you still killed her? Why?"

Barker shook his head. "She knew... she guessed. I took her down the path beside the lake. It was too narrow for two people so she went ahead. All I had to do was pick up a rock—"

Whatever else he had been about to say was interrupted by a fierce pounding on the front door and the piercing shriek of a police whistle.

"Police!"

Harriet knew that voice and relief swept through her.

Gursharan Singh.

Barker pulled Samrita into him, pressing his knife against her throat. Min began to whimper again.

"Not a sound. Any of you." He kicked Min's leg. "Shut up, you."

Min fell silent.

Something hard crashed against the door. The old, dry wood cracked. Another crash and this time the door gave with a bang and crash of splintered wood. From where she sat, Harriet had a good view of the stairs and her heart lurched as the formidable figure of Gursharan Singh burst through the broken door.

Barker moved to the top of the rickety staircase, still holding Samrita. She clutched the arm in which he held the knife as if she hoped to hold it away from her throat, but a trickle of blood ran down to her collar.

Her view of the stairs now obscured, Harriet ground her teeth in frustration. She looked down at the cord binding her wrists and realized Samrita had tied the knot in such a way that she could, with little difficulty, reach it and undo it with her teeth.

With Barker's attention on the man below him, she worked quickly. The cord was slippery, and the knot gave easily. She untied her legs and was free. Min opened her mouth, but Harriet put her fingers to her lips as she rose to her feet. She looked around the studio for something she could use to distract Barker and decided on the large glass jar filled with Samrita's paint-brushes.

She removed the paintbrushes and took a few steps toward Barker.

"Barker!" she yelled.

He turned, and at that moment, she flung the contents of the jar in his face. It might only have been water, but it was enough. He roared and let go of Samrita, the knife falling to the floor, skittering away across the floorboard as he dashed paint-stained water from his face.

Samrita screamed and Harriet realised that when he had pushed her away it had been in the direction of the stairs, and she was tumbling downwards.

Barker, still wiping his face, lunged at Harriet, but she skipped out of his way, thrusting the easel with Samrita's portrait in front of him. He tripped on it and fell as Gursharan Singh, holding Samrita with one hand and his service revolver in the other hand, came charging up the stairs. Behind him, Curran took the stairs more gingerly, his Webley in his left hand.

Singh dumped Samrita unceremoniously on the floor, where she lay gasping for breath. Singh produced a pair of handcuffs and, with a knee in Barker's back, secured his hands behind him. Barker lay still, all the fight driven out of him. He emitted a sound that could have been a sob or a laugh. It was hard to tell.

Harriet untied Min. All the woman's distress had passed, to be replaced with a fury that she directed at her now former employer, even aiming a kick to his ribs.

Curran walked over to the fallen artist and stood looking down at him as Singh rolled the man onto his back.

"Thomas Barker," Curran said. "I am arresting you for the murder of Amelia Hardcastle—"

"And Mary Venning," Harriet gasped. "You have to ask him about Mary Venning."

Curran nodded. "In due course."

The clump of heavy boots on the rickety stairs announced the arrival of two breathless police constables. Singh gestured at the man on the floor.

"We need to get this man to South Bridge Road." As he spoke, he hauled Barker to his feet by his collar. Barker stumbled down the stairs in the grip of the two constables, followed by Singh, leaving Curran alone with the three women. He holstered the weapon and crossed to Samrita and helped her to stand. She fell against him and he wrapped his good arm around her.

"You have poor taste in men," he said, provoking something between a laugh and a sob from his sister.

"Can you walk?" he asked.

Samrita straightened, wincing as she tried to put weight on

her left foot. He helped her across to the daybed and knelt to inspect her ankle.

"I think it is just sprained," he said, "but you need to go to the hospital."

"And so do you," Harriet said.

Curran subsided onto the daybed beside his sister. "I'm fine," he said. "I have to get to South Bridge Road and interview Barker."

Harriet knew better than to argue. She picked up the broken wooden frame with the traces of the purple dress. "You were right. The dress Amelia was wearing came from Barker," she said. "He painted Samrita wearing it."

Curran closed his eyes and nodded.

"Harriet, can you take me to South Bridge Road and then take Samrita to the hospital to have her ankle checked?"

Harriet opened her mouth to protest, but he shot her a look that silenced her.

"You can lecture me later."

# FIFTY-SEVEN

## SATURDAY, 15 JULY

In the interview room at South Bridge Road, Thomas Barker sat hunched on an uncomfortable steel chair, his manacled hands on the table in front of him, his hair and face still damp and liberally streaked with diluted paint and to judge from the tracks in the paint, it looked as if he had been crying.

What a damnable waste, Curran thought, as he surveyed the artist. His arm ached abominably and his head swam. He knew he should be anywhere except in this hot, stinking cell.

"When did your affair with Lady Cunningham start?" he asked, without preamble.

"I'm not saying anything." Barker looked up at him with defiance in his eyes.

Curran sat back and considered his next move. If Barker had decided to be uncooperative, the opportunity to glean the much needed information to prevent Lady Cunningham from leaving Singapore, would be lost.

He leaned forward. "Look, Tom," he said. "I don't see you as a cold-blooded killer. What happened at the ball? Was it an accident?"

Barker looked up and for a moment, Curran thought he would speak, but his gaze slid sideways. "I want to see a lawyer."

"That is your right, of course," Curran said, trying to keep his tone even and friendly. "It will go better for you if you tell me exactly what happened with Amelia Hardcastle and Mary Venning."

Tears filled the artist's eyes again. "I want to see a lawyer," he repeated.

Curran looked up at Singh. "Put him in a cell and we will talk again tomorrow. See if Clive Strong is available first thing tomorrow."

Singh led the artist away, and Curran sat back in the chair. The door opened and Wallace walked in.

"No luck with your man?"

Curran shook his head. "He wants a lawyer."

"What do you have?"

"Shall we start with kidnapping? He held my sister, Mrs. Gordon and his servant hostage. According to Harriet, he claims Amelia Hardcastle's death was an accident. She fell and hit her head, but we know she was alive when he threw her out of the window. That was not an accident. He's not saying anything about Mary Venning." Curran ran his good hand over his eyes. "I'm done for the night, Wallace. He can stew. How did you go at Government House?"

"What do you expect? The lady is admitting nothing. Her boat sails on the morning tide, Curran, and there is nothing we can do to stop her."

Curran closed his eyes. "So Mary Venning and Thomas Barker have to bear the guilt?"

"I've ordered a thorough search of Barker's studio," he said. "Maybe we'll find something new."

Curran pushed back the chair and stood up. The world swooped around him and he had to catch the corner of the table to stop himself from falling.

Wallace caught his arm. "Tan is outside with the motor vehicle. Go back to hospital and leave Barker to me, Curran."

Curran shook his head. "No. I'll be back in the morning, Wallace. I have to see this through."

Wallace harrumphed but didn't argue. "See you at seven sharp," he said.

———

A night in the cells had knocked the last of the fight out of Barker. He sat with his head down, filthy and stinking, his face sheened with sweat. Oliver Strong, who was not pleased to be dragged out so early in the morning, put a handkerchief to his nose.

Curran still felt muzzy headed, but better than he had the previous evening and refused Wallace's offer to do the questioning. Greaves hunched over a small table in one corner with pencil and paper poised to take notes. Singh had accompanied the prisoner and Wallace had placed a chair in the far corner to watch the interview. With so many people in the small space it was going to get uncomfortable very quickly.

"I've spoken to my client," Strong said. "He is aware of the consequences of his actions."

"I'm going to hang," Barker said and started to cry.

"That is for a judge to decide. Not us. However, a confession and genuine contrition may lead to some leniency," Curran said.

Barker shook his head. "No. Not for what I did." He looked up. "Mrs. Gordon said the girl was still alive when I did what I did. Is that true?"

Curran nodded. "Not dead, but certainly dying. Whatever led to the injury to her head, she died from a broken neck sustained in the fall and that is on you, Barker," he said. "What about Mary Venning?"

Barker looked away. "She was my friend."

"Very well. Let's start back in London with Lady Cunningham. Were you having an affair with her?"

Barker gave a snort of humorless laughter. "It wasn't really an affair," he said. "That implies emotions were involved. It was just a physical attraction. Her husband had his peccadilloes and so did she. Cunningham commissioned me to paint her portrait. It meant we were alone together, and one thing led to another. The secrecy was exciting and when I saw her at the ball, I knew I had to have her again."

"Did anyone know about your previous entanglement?"

"Mary did. There are few secrets from a lady's maid, but I had no contact with Evie after I finished her portrait. I thought it was all over, but then I saw her again at Government House and the attraction was still there."

"You were there with Samrita," Curran said.

"That was different. Believe me when I say that I love Samrita deeply and I always will. She is my muse, my soulmate—"

"Spare me." Curran could not keep the disgust out of his voice. "Let's start with the dress. It was yours, wasn't it? We searched your studio and we found the portrait you did of Samrita hidden under floorboards," he paused. "Along with Amelia Hardcastle's school uniform."

Barker glanced at Strong, who said nothing.

Curran laid the portrait out on the table between them. It was so good, he could almost imagine Samrita coming to life in the amethyst dress. What had looked like a rag on Amelia shone on Samrita.

"I spent a little time with Amelia when I was doing the preliminary sketches for the portrait. We got talking, and she told me she wanted to impress a young man and she would never do it wearing school uniform, so I stupidly loaned her the dress. I thought nothing more of it."

"So on the night of the ball, you contrived to meet Lady Cunningham in the private room off the gallery?"

"Yes. She slipped me a note when we shook hands. We... umm... We had so little time and we were not going to waste it. Then Evie heard something, and we found her—Amelia."

"Where was she?"

"Hiding behind the curtain. She looked like an idiot in the dress I had loaned her—a little girl wearing her mother's dress. I think she had seen everything, and she was shocked. She started to cry. Evie held her by the arms and shook her but that only made her cry harder. She started fighting Evie and Evie hit her across the face to shut her up. She lost her grip and Amelia fell backward." He screwed his eyes shut. "It was awful. I can still see it... still hear it. She hit her head on the damn statue and went quite still. I... we... thought she was dead and I panicked."

"And the dress, was that damaged in the struggle?"

Barker nodded. "Beads went everywhere."

"What did the two of you do?"

"Evie told me to pull myself together. She would return to the ball and I had to tidy up. She told me not to leave any evidence. Evie was superb, Curran. She swept from the room as if nothing had happened, leaving me with the girl. I honestly thought Amelia was dead."

"So, you decided to muddy the waters?"

"I thought maybe people would think she jumped from the window." He spread his hands. "I don't know what I was thinking, Curran, I just needed to divert attention from the room we were in."

"What happened next?"

"The fireworks had started. I was sitting in the dark, wondering what to do when someone opened the door and called the girl's name."

"Her mother," Curran said.

Barker had the grace to look away. "I waited for a few minutes and checked the gallery was empty and I picked her up and," he swallowed, "threw her out of the window. She may have only been little, but she was heavy. It only took me a few minutes to clean up. It took some time to find all the beads from the dress but there wasn't a lot of blood. I used her school uniform to wipe down the statue and floor and put everything in the dumb waiter to collect later."

Curran laid the blood-smeared school blouse on the table. Barker grimaced and nodded.

"And then...?"

"I rejoined Samrita and her friends. No one knew... Evie was wonderful. You'd never have thought anything amiss. After the body was found, in the commotion, I took the opportunity to retrieve the girl's clothes from the dumb waiter. I'd brought a satchel with me, just in case the portrait needed any touching up, so I just stuffed them in there and brought them back to my studio." His voice cracked. "I wanted to believe it was all a bad dream, but it wasn't. I haven't slept a night since then."

"Did Lady Cunningham say anything to you about her husband's illness?"

Barker shook his head. "There wasn't much talking, Curran."

"And you have had no further contact with her since that night?"

"No. On my honor. I never saw or heard from her again. It was like nothing happened." His voice rose. "She just went on being Lady Cunningham, and my life has been destroyed."

"Curran..." Clive Strong growled.

"Let's talk about Mary Venning."

Barker buried his head in his hands, sobbing uncontrollably.

Curran nodded at Singh. "Some water for Mr. Barker."

Curran took a breath and waited for Barker to settle. Barker set the tin mug down with a shaking hand and looked up.

"You thought yourself clear of suspicion until Mary Venning turned up."

A muscle twitched in Barker's cheek. "Everything I told you about Mary was true. She was an old friend, and we were genuinely pleased to see each other. She trusted me with the papers she intended to use to expose Sir Henry. Damning stuff," he said. "I read them."

"Where are they?" Curran asked.

Barker shook his head. "I burned them on the kitchen fire when I got back from the Gardens."

Curran suppressed a flash of annoyance. If he had searched Barker at the time... but then again, he had no reason to do so.

"What happened on Thursday?"

"I was working in my studio alone when Mary came to the door. I don't know how she found her way, but there she was... disheveled and hysterical. She said she was going to be blamed for Sir Henry's death. She said she had nothing to do with it, but the poison had been found in her suitcase and she knew exactly what had happened. Evie Cunningham had set her up."

"Good God." The normally phlegmatic lawyer, Strong, stared at his client.

Barker looked at him. "It's true. Mary had believed Lady Cunningham didn't know her real identity but then she realized Evie had known all along. The nightly ritual of the tisane provided the perfect means and the final blow was leaving the poison in her suitcase." Barker turned back to look at Curran. "That's right, isn't it? Motive, opportunity, and means. Mary had all three."

"You are quite right," Wallace put in.

"Why did you kill her?" Curran asked before anyone else interrupted.

Barker closed his eyes, and his mouth trembled.

"You have to understand. Mary knew I had once had an affair with Evie Cunningham. All she had to do was tell you and you would have guessed it was probably me Evie met at the ball."

"That's hardly a reason to kill her."

"I wasn't worried until Mrs. Gordon made her promise to hand herself in to you after she met with the journalist. That night, after everyone had left, she woke up and said she couldn't get back to sleep, so I poured us both a drink, and we sat talking about the old life... about Marcus and James and her mother. She asked to see some of my work so I showed her... I didn't stop to think about the dress. When I showed her that portrait," Barker stabbed a finger at the painting of Samrita, "I saw in her eyes she recognized something about it. She made an excuse and returned to bed. I lay awake worrying about what she had seen and what she would say."

"I had showed her the dress," Curran said.

"Before light, I heard her moving around, so I pretended to be asleep. She crept past me and went down the stairs, and I heard her talking to Min. I thought that was it. She would leave for the meeting with the journalist without me, except I had her papers, so she had to come back. I pretended nothing had happened and retrieved the papers for her. I told her I would escort her to the Botanic Gardens as I knew my way around them."

"And she trusted you?"

Barker gave a shuddering sob. "Stupid, stupid—" He sniffed, wiping his nose on the soiled sleeve of his shirt. "She was different with me and I knew that she knew it had been me with Evie that night. My whole life would be destroyed... I would lose Samrita." His voice had risen to a hysterical note. "It was going around and around in my head and I had to stop her meeting up with you."

"So you killed her."

Barker's breath was coming in short, sharp gasps, his eyes wide and unfocused. He was fixed on something over Curran's shoulder, a memory... a nightmare, a moment's bad decision.

"It was a simple matter to take her to a quiet part of the

gardens by the lake. I pretended to see someone and when she turned away from me, I picked up a rock from the garden bed and hit her over the head and..."

"And drowned her."

Barker blinked and nodded. "I killed her." He looked at Strong. "They will hang me, won't they?"

Strong sighed and hitched a shoulder. "We will do our best."

Barker lowered his head. "I deserve to hang. I saw the Hardcastles last night. We destroyed their lives, Evie and I... and Mary... she had already suffered enough. I panicked, that's all. Panicked over nothing. Now I will lose everything."

"And the world will lose a talented artist," Curran said and Barker buried his face in his hands and began to sob.

Curran pushed back his chair. "Lock him up," he said to Singh.

Alone with Wallace, Curran leaned back in the chair and closed his eyes. The world was starting to spin.

"Three crimes of stupidity," he said to Wallace. "All committed for one reason only... to protect reputations. Have we let Lady Cunningham slip away?"

Wallace shook his head. "Her ship sailed this morning. I hate to say this, Curran, but we still only have circumstantial evidence to link her to her husband's death."

"But we have Barker's testimony that she had the altercation with Amelia Hardcastle that resulted in the girl's death."

"And, even on Barker's word, that was more of an accident. I will telegraph Scotland Yard and have her arrested as soon as she arrives back in England but with a good lawyer..." He spread his hands. "As we both know Amelia Hardcastle died from a broken neck and the only person responsible for that is Barker. He is the one who will have to look the Hardcastles in the eyes at his trial. Sometimes, Curran, we can't always bring the wrongdoers to justice. You know that." He rose to his feet. "I would like to say you did a good job, Curran, but as usual you were insubordinate, disobeyed orders, and failed to follow proper process. When you are back on your feet, I will have no choice but to formally deal with you."

"Of course you will," Curran mumbled. He was looking down at his right wrist where a star of bright blood had seeped through the heavy bandaging. "If you will excuse me, Wallace, I think I am going to—"

The roaring in his ears grew louder, and the world went black.

# FIFTY-EIGHT

SUNDAY, 30 JULY

J ulian drew Curran's motor vehicle to a halt in front of the Mackenzie's beach house, pushed the driving goggles to the top of his head, and stepped out to assist Harriet from the back seat.

"How long do you want?" Julian asked.

The rest of my life, Harriet thought, but she smiled at her brother and Esme sitting beside him in the front seat.

"Take as long as you like," she said. "I'll be here. Are you ready, Will?"

Will scrambled out after her.

The front door opened, and Samrita came out to meet them. She wore a painting smock over a simple, white sprigged muslin dress with her dark hair coiled in the nape of her neck. There was paint on her cheek, and she looked cool, fresh, and lovely, and not at all heartbroken.

She greeted Harriet with a warm hug and a kiss on both cheeks.

"This is a surprise," she said.

Harriet held up the basket she carried. "We come bearing lunch. How is your patient?"

Samrita laughed. "Grumpy. A typical convalescing male."

Curran had paid the price for his 'gallivanting' as Euan Mackenzie had put it and had only been allowed to escape the confines of the hospital in the last couple of days. Euan Mackenzie had let him go on condition that he stayed at the Mackenzie's beach house with someone to look after him. Those someones were Samrita, aided and abetted by Curran's batman Ahmed, who proved he had more talents than just polishing boots, and Huo Jin had sent her niece, Rosie, to look after them all.

Samrita looped her arm into Harriet's and led her into the house.

"He will be pleased to see you," she said. "You will find him down by the beach. I'm in the middle of a painting so I will leave you in peace."

Harriet left the basket with Rosie and crossed the sparse, sandy lawn to the fringe of palm trees. A low, weathered teak daybed with bright, Indian cushions had been set up in the shade and Curran had stretched out on this, his Panama hat pulled over his eyes, a book spreadeagled across his chest. He wore a linen shirt, and a pair of loose linen trousers rolled up almost to his knees. His feet were bare, and a half-empty bottle of Tiger Beer was buried in the sand beside him. His right arm was still lightly bandaged.

"Are you asleep?" Harriet said rather too loudly.

He visibly started, swore, and subsided back in the daybed, pushing the hat back from his eyes and squinting up at her.

"Harriet Gordon, you really should not sneak up on people like that, particularly those in a weakened state."

She smiled, sensing no real annoyance in his tone.

"You look very relaxed," she said.

"How could I not be? I have everything a man could need... a pile of good books, a gramophone, regular meals, and a decent beer... servants at my beck and call and all my well-meaning friends and colleagues have heeded my wishes to be left alone." He paused. "I am bored senseless. How did you get here?"

"Julian has taken Esme for a picnic. They will be back to collect me... us. I have brought Will with me. Are you up to talking to him about his father?"

Curran nodded. "Of course."

Harriet smiled. "I will go and chat to Samrita and leave you to talk to Will."

---

This had not been a conversation Curran had been looking forward to. It had been his decision to keep John Lawson's involvement in the death of Sir Oswald Newbold out of the official record and he had done it in the full knowledge that secrets are notoriously hard to keep. It was unfortunate that rumors had reached the boy.

Will slid onto the bench beside him. The boy was barefoot and wearing a woolen bathing costume. He carried a threadbare towel.

"Good morning, Will," Curran said. "Nice morning for a swim."

"Good morning, sir," Will replied, his voice high and tight.

"When are you off to school?"

"End of August," Will said. "Uncle Julian is going to take me over."

"Are you looking forward to it?"

Will shrugged one shoulder and looked away. "I'll miss everyone here."

"You'll be home for Christmas?"

Will nodded and they sat in a protracted and increasingly awkward silence.

"Will, you wanted to ask me about your father?"

Will raised his eyes and looked Curran in the eye as he nodded.

"A boy at school said Papa had killed someone and got what he deserved. Was he a bad man?"

*In the murky gray shadows between good and bad, where did John Lawson fit?*

"He was a weak man, Will. He let himself be dragged into an enterprise he should never have been a part of and once that happens it is almost impossible to climb out."

Will fixed him with an unblinking gaze. "Did he kill that man?"

Curran sighed, recalling the dark stillness of that hospital room and the dying man who had been this boy's father.

"Yes, he did. I think, if it helps, your father had been pushed to his limit, and he didn't mean to kill him."

Will still fixed him with a hard, narrow-eyed look. "But you didn't tell anyone."

John Lawson's son had his whole life in front of him. Will had suffered enough. At the time, it seemed unfair to burden him with the public knowledge that he was the son of a murderer, but Curran did not know how to begin to explain that to the boy.

"No. What purpose would that have served? Your father was dead. Newbold was dead and had no one to mourn him."

"But you're a policeman. You should have told. When I'm a policeman—"

"When you're a policeman you will learn that there is a difference between justice and doing what is right. Your father had paid the price for what he did. The only person who could be punished for what he did, was you. Sometimes there are no simple answers, Will."

Will was silent for a long moment.

"You did it for me?" he said in a very small voice.

Curran nodded.

"I miss him," he said at long last.

Curran nodded. "My mother died when I was born, and my father disappeared from my life when I was a little younger than you. No matter how many kind, loving people fill the void, you will never stop feeling that absence. You just have to learn to live with it."

Will nodded. "I keep remembering that last time I saw him in the hospital. I keep hoping it was all a dream and he is really alive and will come back."

Curran thought about his own father, who he had thought dead but had been alive. He had never come back, never contacted his son... That was a pain that would never go away.

"try to remember the happy times, Will. Tell me one happy memory you have of time with your father."

Will tilted his head to one side. "He took me fishing once. Up in the mountains behind the mine in Burma. Mama packed us lunch and we spent all day and didn't catch anything."

"That's a good memory to hold on to."

Curran took a deep breath. He had no such memories of his own. His father had been banished from his life almost before he was old enough to recognize him, but he often thought of his grandfather and the long hours spent in the stables. Those were good memories.

"Was there anything else you wanted to ask me?"

Will looked up at him and grinned. "Yes. When are you and Aunt Harriet getting married?"

Curran laughed. "That is none of your business. Why don't you go for a swim before lunch and give me a chance to talk to your Aunt Harriet."

# FIFTY-NINE

Harriet stood on the veranda watching the progress of the conversation between Curran and the boy, wishing she could listen in.

"Will worships the ground he walks on, doesn't he?" Samrita joined her, wiping her paintbrushes with a rag.

"He says he is going to become a policeman when he finishes school. Julian, of course, has other plans. I hope Curran can set his mind to rest. Will may only be eleven, but he's had a great deal of unhappiness in his life." Harriet turned to the young woman beside her. "What about you, Samrita? I know you thought highly of Thomas Barker."

"Curran is right. I have an appalling taste in men, don't I?" Samrita said, but her smile belied the sadness in her eyes. "Thomas Barker gave me far more than I could have wished for, but to answer a question you once asked me, I don't think I was in love with him. I was in love with the idea of him... and as you said, the prospect of living a life outside the constraints of society." She straightened. "And now I am going to plunge straight into the middle of that very society I wanted to avoid. I had a letter this morning from Mr. Ridley at the Gardens. He showed some of my work to a visiting professor from London and they are going to offer me a scholarship to go to London and study botanical painting at the Kew Gardens."

"Samrita, that is wonderful news," Harriet exclaimed.

"It is rather," Samrita said. "Imagine if I had got on a boat and gone to Australia with Thomas, the opportunity would have been lost."

"Promise me one thing."

"Anything."

"Before he leaves for school, can you do a little portrait of Will? I want to remember him as he is now."

Will had left Curran's company and was running toward the crystal clear waters lapping on the beach with a whoop of sheer boyish delight.

"Of course." She cast Harriet a sideways glance. "I shall return to my painting. It is your turn to talk to Curran."

Harriet pulled off her shoes and stockings and walked barefoot across the scraggly grass to Curran's bench. He glanced up at her.

"How did it go?" she asked.

He shrugged. "Hard to tell. He keeps a lot to himself."

"I would rather have waited till he was older, but we promised ourselves that when he asked, we would tell him the truth. I'm not one for secrets."

Curran patted the bench beside him. "Come and sit beside me, Harriet Gordon, and tell me the gossip."

She took Will's place beside him, and he slid his uninjured arm around her, drawing her into him so her head rested on his shoulder. It seemed to her that she fitted as if they had been made for each other.

She looked up at him. "How are you really?"

"Mending," he said, and she understood that the word carried with it a much deeper meaning than the pure physical. Even before she had arrived in Singapore, Curran's life had been a headlong plunge into places that would have broken a lesser man.

"So... you want gossip," she said. "I think Julian is finally going to propose to Esme today."

"That is excellent news. I'm pleased," Curran said.

"If Julian hasn't asked her to marry him on this nice little romantic picnic he has been planning all week, I shall personally crown him with his cricket bat."

Curran smiled. He had some color back in his face. When she'd last seen him in the hospital, pale and feverish, she had been desperately worried, but his eyes held life again, even if there were still dark circles under his eyes and lines of pain around his mouth.

He shifted slightly, wincing.

"When will you go back to work?" she asked.

He shook his head. "When Mac permits me. Wallace can manage without me. What other news?"

"Maddocks has taken Sarah Bowman out for dinner on a couple of occasions."

"Has he indeed? What about Doreen Wilson?"

"She has left for Hong Kong."

"Pity. She is an excellent nurse."

"She is going to a matron's position—"

"Robert!" Samrita's voice came from the veranda. "Another visitor."

Sidney Wallace was striding across the grass toward them. Harriet sat up and tried to compose herself.

"Sorry to interrupt. Won't keep you," Wallace said. He took off his hat and scanned the pleasant surroundings. "Nice place this."

"Singapore does have its pleasant spots," Harriet said.

"Yes, well, I'll be sorry to leave," Wallace said.

Harriet straightened. "You're leaving?"

"I've told Cuscaden I'll wait until you're fit enough for duty,"

Wallace said, "but Mrs. Wallace is adamant she's not staying any longer than she has to."

"She's hardly given it a chance," Curran said.

"Final straw was when some bloody great snake ate the kitchen boy's dog in front of the children."

"Were they very fond of the dog?" Harriet asked.

"It was one of those nasty little yappy things, but yes, the children had got quite attached to the flea-ridden beast. Hope it gave that snake indigestion. That was enough for Mrs. Wallace and to be honest, Curran, I don't think I'm made for this climate. I've got a nice little garden back in London and I miss my roses."

"And a job?"

Wallace smiled. "The Yard'll have me back. Bit of a feather in my cap solving the Government House murders."

Harriet opened her mouth and shut it again.

"So you get the credit for my hard work?" Curran scowled. "You spent the entire time lying around in bed, yelling at everyone."

Wallace looked affronted. "You should be bloody grateful you still hold your commission, Curran. As it is, the job's yours, Curran. Should have been yours in the first place."

"What about Lady Cunningham?"

"Her ship docks in the next couple of days and she'll be arrested for Amelia Hardcastle's death," Wallace scowled. "Mary Venning will go down in the record as Sir Henry's murderer."

"No!" Harriet protested. "That's not fair."

"That, Mrs. Gordon, is the power of evidence and the power of knowing how to manipulate it. One thing that puzzles me is why she was keeping him unwell?"

"I can answer that," Harriet said. "To protect her own children. Her daughters had reached an age where they would be of interest to Sir Henry's circle of perverts."

"Not just his circle," Curran said. "Their own father."

Harriet shivered. "How awful."

"Sadly, it happens, even in the best of families," Curran said.

Wallace shook his head. "I don't often say this, Mrs. Gordon, and I'll deny it if you ever say anything to anyone else, but he deserved the death he got. Poisoning was too good for him."

"I think she hoped that by keeping him unwell, he would lose interest, but the night he died, he proved himself still capable of taking what he wanted and she panicked," Curran said. "A potential assault allegation coupled with the threatened publication of the Venning letter and her whole future crumbled. Better to be the widow of an important man than the wife of a disgraced and convicted man. He should have come to justice six years ago. How many other innocent lives has he destroyed in that time?"

Wallace cleared his throat, and he looked away. "I tell you what, regardless of what others might think, I'm not going to let this rest when I get back to London. It's a pity Barker burned the other papers the Venning girl had collected, but we can start again. A proper investigation this time without interference from her ladyship."

"Nothing I would wish for more," Curran said, "but we both know that nothing will come of it."

Wallace shrugged. "Maybe not, but I can but try." He stood up. "I've taken up enough of your time. I'll leave you to it. Take your time, Curran. I want you fully fit for duty before you come back."

"Sir," Curran replied.

They waited until they heard the roar of the motor vehicle departing.

"All those lives she destroyed... Amelia, Mary, and Thomas Barker. In a way they were all her victims. Just as she covered up the crimes being committed by her husband," Harriet said. "I hope my father gets the prosecution brief."

"That is the aristocracy for you," Curran said. "As I just told Will, sometimes justice does not come into it. On a brighter note, did Samrita tell you her news?" Curran said.

"Yes. It's a wonderful opportunity for her." Harriet paused. "Can you afford to send her to London?"

Curran shrugged. "I hope the scholarship will cover most of it but otherwise, I'll find the money."

Harriet sighed and curled up in the circle of his arm again, listening to the gentle lap of the water and the rustle of the palm leaves above them. Samrita had joined Will and stood on the seashore, her skirt kilted up, watching the boy sporting in the water like a porpoise.

"It's all changing," Harriet said. "Will's going to school, Samrita's going to London, Julian and Esme—"

His lips brushed the top of her head. "And us?"

She twisted to look up at him. "What about us?"

"I've had a lot of time to think, Harriet," Curran said after a while. "If you can bear to take me as I am, then I would very much like to have you in my life ..."

She laughed.

"I thought you would never ask," she said. "Of course, Robert Curran. If that was indeed a proposal, then I accept."

"It was, and thank you." He cleared his throat. "In my pocket... I've been carrying it around on the off chance."

Harriet laughed at the acrobatics required for Curran to produce the small, silken bag from his pocket.

"I should go down on one knee, but even if I could, I suspect you would just laugh at me." He fumbled with the strings of the bag and pulled out a gold ring, set with a single sapphire surrounded by small diamonds.

"Have you been raiding the evidence cupboard?" Harriet said.

He laughed. "Tempting, but no. This is a Burmese sapphire but obtained completely legally. I thought you might appreciate the reference to our first meeting. Singh's cousin in KL made this for me. I hope it fits."

She touched the lovely, clear blue stone, a reminder of the case that had brought them together. So much had happened since the day she had found Sir Oswald Newbold dead on the floor of his study.

She had never imagined that it would bring this mercurial and honorable man into her life, and the thought that he would be by her side for the rest of her life brought tears to her eyes.

He brushed the hair from her forehead. "Why are you crying?"

"Happy," she managed with a twisted smile. "Very happy. I love you so much, Robert Curran."

"Harriet Gordon, I love you." He smiled. "I love your fatal curiosity, your refusal to do as you are told, and above all your integrity."

He took the ring from her and slid it onto her finger.

"Marry me..."

Harriet smiled at him, her heart bursting as she whispered, "Yes."

Curran glanced at the water from which Will had emerged dripping and laughing to take the towel Samrita held out for him.

"How long do these things take to arrange? I would like to do it before Will and Samrita leave," Curran said.

Harriet nodded. "That is a lovely thought. Now, Robert Curran, I would very much like it if you would kiss me."

They took their time in that kiss and then they kissed again, their bodies melding into each other, until Curran forgot about his injured arm and made an unwise move. It caught him, extracting a yelp of pain from him.

He swore, and Harriet laughed.

# SIXTY

SATURDAY, 27 AUGUST

"This is not my first wedding day," Harriet protested as Louisa Mackenzie insisted on readjusting the hat Harriet had chosen to match her gray silk dress. "It doesn't have to be perfect, and you are just making me feel even worse."

"Where is Samrita? She was supposed to be here with the orchids half an hour ago," Louisa fussed.

Esme Prynne, keeping watch on the front veranda hurried in. "She's here."

Julian, who was officiating, had taken Will and departed for the cathedral a good hour earlier. It was only Harriet, Louisa, Esme and now Samrita clutching an artfully arranged bouquet of Lavinia's finest orchids.

Harriet took the flowers and stood quite still in the middle of the living room, surrounded by the three women. She had no full-length mirror in which to admire her reflection and now the moment had come, she could not ignore the rabble of butterflies in her stomach.

"How do I look?" Harriet asked at last.

"Mem looks very fine. Like a woman should look on her wedding day."

All the women turned to look at Huo Jin, who stood in the doorway to the corridor leading back through the house to the back door. Behind her, lurking in the shadows, Lokman and Aziz, and Harriet realized with a pang that from today, this would no longer be her home. These dear, good people, who were as much a part of the headmaster's house as Julian and Will, would no longer be there for her. She would have a new home and a new household.

Huo Jin advanced into the room and held out a small packet wrapped in red and gold paper.

"Very auspicious," she said. "We wish you to have this as a memory of us."

Harriet took the packet and unwrapped it. Inside a small, green, jade frog with a coin in its mouth nestled in tissue paper.

"Place him in the wealth corner of your home and he will bring you good fortune," Huo Jin said.

Harriet had no idea where the wealth corner of anyone's house could be found, but she would treasure the little ornament. Impulsively, she threw her arms around Huo Jin's neck and hugged her. It was a little like hugging a broomstick, but she could do nothing else. She also hugged Aziz and took both of Lokman's hands in her own, tears gathering in the corner of her eyes.

"Where will Mem be living?" Aziz asked.

"We are renting a nice little bungalow not far from here," Harriet said.

She had found the bungalow by sheer chance. One of the parents at the school had to make a hurried return to England and was anxious to offload the tenancy. Well set back from the road, in a treed neighborhood, it came fully furnished, had three good sized bedrooms, a large living room, and, most important to

Harriet, a wide, accommodating veranda. Huo Jin's niece, Rosie Chen, had agreed to join the household as a housekeeper and the beleaguered cook from the Wallace's house had happily joined them. It also had enough land and a stable to allow Curran to retrieve his beloved Leopold from the stables and return him to the care of his former syce, Mahmud.

In short, it was perfect.

"What have you agreed about Will?" Louisa asked the question that Harriet and Julian had spent long hours discussing.

"Will leaves for school in Colombo in a few days," Harriet said, her heart wrenching a little at that thought. "When he is home, he is free to come and go between us but," she glanced at Esme, "Julian is his principal guardian so officially he will be resident here but Shashti," she stooped to pick up the little cat that was both hers and Will's, "comes with me."

Esme, who was to marry Julian at Christmas, smiled. "I think it will work out perfectly."

Outside, a motor vehicle came to a screeching halt.

Louisa, all business, straightened. "Ladies, it is time to go."

Harriet turned to Huo Jin. "You are coming?"

"I have the pony trap all ready for us, Mem," Aziz said. "We will see you at the church."

"Are you ladies ready?"

Dr. Euan Mackenzie, resplendent in a morning suit appeared at the door.

"Harriet, my dear, you look splendid." Euan Mackenzie was not given to paying compliments and Harriet bobbed a curtsy.

"Why, thank you."

It had been a matter of some discussion as to whether Harriet should have someone to 'give her away'. She had been married before and had already been 'given away' by her father but in the end, it seemed fitting to ask Euan. He had been one of James Gordon's oldest friends and it seemed to Harriet that Euan served the symbolic task of finally letting James and her old life go.

An enormous Bentley, arranged by Euan Mackenzie, waited outside the house and it fitted all four women with Euan in the front seat.

Harriet glanced out of the window at the little house that had been her home for the past eighteen months and felt a pang of nostalgia at the life she was leaving behind. It would be Esme's home now... Esme and Julian would be married at Christmas when the school term finished. As a married woman, Esme would have to relinquish her position and she needed to give the governors of the Ladies Academy time to find a replacement.

In the meantime, a new home and a new life waited for Harriet.

———

Inspector Robert Curran of the Straits Settlements Police Force was described by those who knew him, as a courageous police officer. He had faced danger and death and overcome them, now he stood in the vestry of St. Andrews Cathedral, fighting back a strong desire to throw up.

He tugged at the high, stiff collar of his ceremonial uniform, sure that it was melting in the heat. His batman, Ahmed, had outdone himself with the starch, the brass polish, and the boot polish. Everything gleamed, from the buttons on his jacket, the Sam Browne, the sword and frog to his boots.... And, he was fairly certain, his face.

"Relax," Griff Maddocks said. "You look as if you are about to face the Spanish Inquisition. It's only Harriet."

*But what if...?*

*What if I'm not good enough for her? What if I let her down? What if...?*

Julian laid a hand on his shoulder.

"You are making me nervous," he said. "Stop twitching, take ten deep breaths, and enjoy the day."

Will poked his head around the vestry door. "The car's here."

No more time for nerves. Julian led the way out into the cathedral. Curran cast a glance down the nave, surprised and overwhelmed by the number of people who crowded the pews, all smiling broadly.

Julian took his place and Curran turned to face him. He didn't dare look around again. Maddocks stood beside him, appallingly relaxed.

Behind him the congregation rustled, and he swallowed, forcing his breath to steady as he turned slowly. Harriet stood at the door of the church, her arm tucked into Euan Mackenzie's elbow, Louisa a few steps behind. She held a magnificent bouquet of orchids in her left hand and her face was shadowed by a fashionably wide-brimmed gray hat trimmed with ostrich feathers.

The aisle seemed to go on for miles, but even with the distance between them, he could sense her gaze meeting his, her lips parting in a smile and he smiled in response as the organ struck up the Bridal Chorus by Wagner. She began the agonizingly slow progress down the aisle until, relinquishing Mac's arm, she came to stand beside him.

Her fingers found his, and she looked up at him from under the brim of the ridiculous hat.

Harriet, wise, clever, Harriet Gordon had, for some reason decided she wanted to spend the rest of her life with him.

In that moment he prayed that life would be a long and happy one.

# SIXTY-ONE

## THE STRAITS TIMES 29 AUGUST 1911 WEDDING AT ST. ANDREWS

*The marriage took place at St Andrews Cathedral this last Saturday between Inspector R. Curran of the Straits Settlement Police and Mrs. H. Gordon, widow of the late Dr. James Gordon of Bombay. The wedding was attended by close friends and presided over by the bride's brother, the Reverend Edwards, principal of St Thomas Preparatory School.*

*Mrs. Gordon was attended by Mrs. Mackenzie and Dr. Mackenzie performed the duty of the bride's father. The bride wore a fetching gown of gray silk, trimmed with lace, and carried a bouquet of orchids provided by Mrs. L. Pemberthey-Smythe from her extensive collection. The groom wore full ceremonial police uniform and was attended by Mr. G. Maddocks of this paper. The couple left the church to an honor guard of officers of the Straits Settlements Police Force.*

*A wedding breakfast was held at Raffles Hotel. The bride's bouquet was caught by Miss Prynne, principal of the Singapore*

*Ladies Academy who is to be joined in matrimony to the bride's brother in December.*

*The happy couple have left for a short honeymoon at an undisclosed location.*

*S. Bowman Straits Times*

———

*A note from the author:*
*If you are craving a little more of an 'aah' moment, remember that I am still at heart a romance writer.*
*If you would like some exclusive 'director's cut' material, I have put together a few short scenes of newly married life...*
*you can download AFTER THE SPEECHES HERE*

# AFTERWORD

*A note from the author:*
*If you are craving a little more of an 'aah' moment, I am still at*
*heart a romance writer.*
*If you would like some exclusive 'director's cut' material, I have put*
*together a few short scenes of newly married life...*
*you can download using this QR CODE*

# AFTERWORD

# AUTHOR NOTES

Thank you for reading AGONY IN AMETHYST. I am not going to say that this is the last you will see of Harriet and Curran but I do feel that this series arc has concluded. I am not sure what their future adventures will look like together as a couple, but please feel free to subscribe to my newsletter for news!

King George VI was crowned on 22 June 1911 with great pomp and ceremony. Reports filled the Straits Times and other newspapers, and a party was held at Government House with fireworks – resulting in the unfortunate incineration of one of the residences on the grounds. Unfortunately, I couldn't work that into the story!

I have based this story around the beautiful building off Orchard Road, built as Government House, but which is now known as the Istana, or the residence of Singapore's elected President and Head of State. Those familiar with the Istana will know it does not have a ballroom such as that described in the story. However, in my research, I found the detailed plans, drawn up for the construction of just such a building, and with a liberal dash of writer's discretion, I added the ballroom to Government House (you will find the plans on the Agony in Amethyst Pinterest board).

The governor of the time, Sir John Anderson, was a widower who relied heavily on his daughters Catherine Perkins and Georgina Farrant to act as first ladies. Both ladies married in Singapore. In 1911, Sir John was recalled to London before his final posting to Ceylon (Sri Lanka).

His private secretary, Claud Severn was indeed an Australian who went on to become the Colonial Secretary for Hong Kong. He married late in life and died in England. There was a whole cast of characters that I could have included but, according to my editor, they added little to the story and I was probably just showing off!

Now to the serious stuff. You may wonder where a writer's ideas come from and sometimes it is a case of truth being stranger than fiction. I was casually browsing the internet looking for information on the contemporary Secretary of State for the Colonies, Sir Lewis Harcourt. As I read through the entries online, my eyes widened. It was an open secret in polite society at the time that Harcourt was a sexual predator of the worst kind. Indeed, part of a ring of such predators. He came undone when the mother of one of his victims made a noise about the man's conduct. Harcourt died in his sleep from an overdose of Bromidia. It was ruled misadventure but was more likely to have been suicide.

Finally, as I have mentioned before, these stories are set in the colonial past and the attitudes and society of the time are not reflective of our modern society. They do not reflect the views of the author but are based on historical facts.

I hope you have enjoyed the HARRIET GORDON MYSTERIES and do keep following me for news on further adventures of our beloved characters.

Alison Stuart 2024

# ACKNOWLEDGMENTS

There are always two acknowledgments that take pride of place in my books. Firstly my ever-patient husband who is happy to brainstorm, take me traveling for research and has been known to provide occasional cups of tea and glasses of wine as required.

And, of course, my amazing writing group, The Saturday Ladies Bridge Club, for being there with virtual cups of tea and sympathy, necessary brainstorming, and tissues as required. I also wish to note that this book started life in Tasmania at a crime writer's retreat (Terror Australis Festival 2023) and I am grateful to the friends I made on that retreat who were happy to help to tease it out with a special note to my friend Adrienne M., who can take full credit for the title.

Finally, there is the team required to get a book to publication. Starting with my fabulous cover designer, Fiona Jayde of Fiona Jayde Media Services who totally understood the brief for this book (and the last book), my structural editor, Jennifer Toney Quinlan, my copy editor, Cathleen Ross and of course the aforementioned husband for his critical beta reading!

I couldn't do it without any of you!

# ABOUT THE AUTHOR

Australian author, A.M Stuart, creator of the popular Harriet Gordon Mystery series, lives in Melbourne, Australia but over her life she has travelled extensively and lived in Africa and Singapore, experiences which she brings to her writing. Before becoming a full-time writer, she worked as a lawyer across a variety of disciplines including the military and emergency services.

As well as the Harriet Gordon series, writing as Alison Stuart, she is multi published in historical romance and short stories with settings in England and Australia and spanning different periods of history.

If you enjoyed this story, please leave a review or a rating on your favourite review site or bookstore.
**AND YOU ARE INVITED TO SIGN UP TO ALISON'S NEWSLETTER.**

# BOOKS
## by A.M. Stuart/ Alison Stuart

FEATHERS IN THE WIND (BOX SET)

**Regency/World War One**

GATHER THE BONES

LORD SOMERTON'S HEIR

A CHRISTMAS LOVE REDEEMED (Novella)